THE CURSE OF THE BLESSED

R.C. Huye

Dedication

To my mother for planting the love
of reading and writing within me.

To my father for being my unceasing cheerleader.

To the person who believed in me
when nobody else did, even me.

The Months and Days of Zorda

Translated From the Ancient Language of Okara into the Modern Tongue

January: Mactire
February: Sneach
March: Pisht
April: Bándar
May: Bláthe
June: Sútalune
July: Búiche
August: Iasch
September: Arbhore
October: Sealga
November: Bebha
December: Fúior

Monday: Ayone
Tuesday: Dhá
Wednesday: Trie
Thursday: Ceath
Friday: Súvig
Saturday: Beis
Sunday: Seach

The Moons of Okaran years

The Days of Okaran Weeks

Trigger Warning

This text has been faithfully collected and transcribed by the historians of the Writers Guild of Sutoran. It contains violent language, violent physical interactions, mentions of sexual assault, suicidal ideation, and mentions of suicide. Take care of yourselves, and please seek help if needed. And, if you continue, then voyagers, I pray you enjoy your journey into ancient Zorda.

Pronunciations

Mispronunciations will not be tolerated.

- o Camari: *Kuh-marr-eee*

- o Morris: *More-isss*

- o Eben: *Eee-bin*

- o Aldred: *Al-drid*

- o Krakent: *Kruh-kent*

- o Sutoran: *Suh-tore-in*

- o Onaydo: *Oh-nigh-doe*

- o Spas Folámh: *Spa-z-Foe-la-mm*

Excerpts from The Writings of the Exiled

It started with a whisper. A murmur across space that had been dark and empty for centuries. Then, it became louder and louder, intensifying and growing.

An echo.

A shout.

A declaration.

The gods of the heavens grew bored in their cerulean palace. They wanted something new with which they could distract themselves. So they created it.

They created the creatures and the plants, taking ideas and breathing them into existence. They created water and stone, wind and rain, dark and light. They created sound and silence, beauty and pain. But it wasn't enough. They wanted something else, something more. So they created man.

They created man in the image of themselves, giving him the abilities they had but giving him limitations they didn't have as to separate him from them. They put a limit on man's life, unwilling to share their immortality with another creature. They gave him weaknesses that they themselves feared. And then they created many more men and women, separating them around the land that they'd created. They then settled down and watched the creatures they'd made, finding them entertaining and amusing.

There were a few gods, however, that were kinder and more compassionate than the others. They loved their creations and felt a responsibility for them. They wanted to see them grow and learn. They wanted to see mankind thrive. So they helped the man.

The Compassionate Ones revealed themselves to mankind and told man what they were and how they had created everything, the earth and plants, the animals, and all forms of life. And they gave man other things that they had yet to have. They gave them the gift of fire, showing how to make light and warmth out of nothing so that they need never fear what they couldn't see. They gave mankind wisdom so that they might learn from their mistakes and better themselves; so that they might create just as the gods had.

In return for these gifts, mankind built monasteries and temples to worship the gods, erecting statues and monuments to pay homage to their creators. All of the gods were pleased by all of this and continued to watch mankind grow, sometimes interfering in both positive and negative ways. But the Compassionate Ones felt they hadn't given all that they could give yet. A murmur started in their minds that they could do more, turning into a shout, and finally a declaration that they could and would do more for their creations.

So they gave some of mankind one more gift. The Compassionate Ones decided to give some of mankind the one thing that the gods valued more than anything else. They gave the gift of sight.

Choosing a number of goodhearted, intelligent people, they gave them the gift of sight, so that they could see things that no one else could. They could anticipate occurrences, interact in ways others couldn't, and help the world.

The other gods, the Disruptors, had seen the Compassionate Ones give the humans the gift of sight, and they were angered. They did not think mankind deserved to own one of the talents that separated the divine from the human. So, on the darkest night of the year, when the moon and sun were concealed and the Compassionate Ones were asleep, the Disruptors approached the humans and told them what the Compassionate Ones had done. They told them of the blessed, calling them seers and using the name as an insult. They told them of their gifts and how only specific people had them. They took all of this information and planted it into the heads of the humans as if they had possessed it all along. They then cursed the blessed furthermore. They gave them blemishes so that any human could see them and know what they were and do what they wished.

When the sun and moon returned and the Compassionate Ones woke, they were horrified with what they found. The seers were being hunted and slaughtered, killed gruesomely by those who hadn't received the gift. The Compassionate Ones tried to undo what the Disruptors had done, but they weren't strong enough, and the Compassionate Ones couldn't erase the dark blemishes or the bright adages that made the seers into targets, nor could they take away the memories and knowledge from the other humans.

Unable to simply erase the blemishes, the Compassionate Ones had a different idea. They made the ugly dark spots beautiful, turning them into swirls of patterns that told stories of life. The colorful adages were made simpler so that the seers could hide them, turning them into something naturally occurring, something that could easily be concealed.

Having done this, the seers were protected, and the Compassionate Ones were happy. The Disruptors were outraged at being outsmarted once again and told mankind of the adages and markings that revealed a seer. They decided to only tell the strongest and the most bloodthirsty, the most capable killers. Then they sat back and watched as the seers were hunted by a group of men that banded together and dedicated their lives to ridding the world of what they'd come to believe as evil.

The Compassionate Ones watched alongside the Disruptors, helping the seers and the fair people of mankind wherever they could, while the Disruptors encouraged the seer hunters and watched with manic glee as each day seers became more and more reviled and hated, until one day they hid themselves away completely, afraid to show their faces and their gods-given talent. The hunters inherited the land and built seats of power, and the seers remained hidden, waiting for a day when they would be delivered.

One does not overcome death.
They are consumed by it, or they embrace it.
You lose yourself to it either way.

—Field Journal of Aiden Lorian

Chapter One

Aiden

The screams still affect me. It's strange that the blood, the feeling of my sword slicing through flesh, even when they hold my gaze as they die; it all hurts me, but not as much as the screams do. The screaming makes me hesitate. The screaming fills me with self-loathing and disgust, fills me with heartbreak for what I'm doing and who I've become.

Maybe it's because I know that human beings are by nature proud and fierce. Maybe it's because I know that something has to be completely and utterly terrifying to make someone scream and beg me for mercy; *beg*. Or maybe it's because I screamed like that once when I was still a child, so I know exactly what it takes to instill that level of fear. And now I am that terrifying thing.

I always push past the hesitation, the knowledge that I'm not doing the right thing. Seers are demons, witches, and *evil*. They are privy to knowledge that no one should have, and they use it against humans, against King Aldred. Seers are uncontrollable creatures of magic. They need to be stopped, and as the king's royal assassin, it is my duty to do so. Or so we've been forced to believe.

My men and I found two hidden seer villages, just where the scouts said they would be. We killed them, wiping them out, men and women alike. Their houses we burned, their livestock and feed we pillaged, and their children we sent to the facility the king of three generations prior built specifically for seers. There, they will be raised to use their powers for the good of the kingdom. Again, so we've been forced to believe.

But at the second village, not only did nine men escape, but a woman fell to her knees and begged me for mercy, her colorful trait shimmering in the light of the fire that ate away at her home. I still can't get her screams out of my head. They're lodged in my mind like a knife, sharp and painful til the very end. I want to pull it out. I want to twist it in deeper.

I refuse to think about what happened after she begged.

"Aiden, get your head out of your ass and pay attention to where you're leading your horse," Eben grunts, pulling me out of my thoughts. The majority of the platoon has ridden ahead with the prisoners and the ransacked goods, but the five of us stayed behind for a few days so that Eben, who was wounded in the battle, could have a brief period of rest to gather his strength. The three other men who stayed with us were Miller, Grant, and my half-brother, Morris. Together, we five are a squad that others fear; we are the men who inspire so many nightmares. They are my brothers, and we are a family.

A family of murderers.

"Aiden, pay attention!"

I jump as Eben says my name again, sounding annoyed at my unfocused state of mind. My horse has slowed to a crawl without my noticing, and I am falling behind. I nudge him with my heels and regain the lead with Eben on my right and the other three riding behind me, Miller taking the back and keeping watch.

"Where is your brain today?" Eben grumbles, shifting in his saddle and rubbing his thigh just above where he has stitches. I'm sure the days of riding have done nothing to ease his pain from where a sword clipped his leg.

"Just thinking," I reply, running my hand through my sweaty hair and ruffling it further.

"Always a dangerous thing for you," Grant teases as his horse pulls closer to mine, earning a chuckle.

"Yes, well, sometimes it can't be helped," I joke, turning on my saddle and surveying the woods to my left, looking for anything out of the ordinary. We are a few hours out from a village called Krakent, where we will restock our supplies before continuing on our way to Sutoran, the capital city of Zorda.

"What is it that has your breeches in such a bind?" Morris calls from behind.

I hesitate, opening and closing my mouth before I sigh, settling with my usual, unproblematic response. "I was just thinking about home-"

"*Stop.*"

Miller's voice echoes from behind us, and we all immediately pull up on our horses 'reins, drawing to a halt, our hands resting on our weapons. Miller has the eyes of a hawk and is always our scout, his calm and quiet disposition perfect for that of a spy. Several seers escaped the last village, and we were unable to catch them. We're all on edge, unsure if they are following to attack us or not. If Miller has seen something, it's bound to be them.

Miller rides up to my side, followed by Grant and Morris, his eyes narrowed. "Nine men left side. Five possibly with weapons, four definitely armed."

"What kind of weapons?" Do I need my sword, my daggers, or my bow?

"I saw a bow, two swords, and a spear," he replies curtly, all business. I nod before turning to face the others.

"Form a defensive circle. Morris, you go for the one with the spear, Miller-" I'm cut off mid-order by a whistling noise followed by excruciating pain. An arrow strikes my right shoulder and lodges there, sending rivers of pain down my arm. "Bleeding hell!" I swear as I try and fail to move my arm, finding it useless.

My men draw their weapons, Miller with a bow, Eben with an ax, Grant and Morris with swords. More arrows fly, one of them luckily deflecting off of Morris 'sword. Even he looks surprised, his brown eyes widening as the wood splinters against his blade, his hand moving from the force. Two more arrows a split-second later, another miss, and another hit. The arrow strikes my shoulder just below the first, putting me in agony and making my vision dance as blood oozes down my arm onto my horse's fur coat. They must remember me from the village; remember I am the leader, the king's assassin. They are trying to take me out first.

Smart. It's exactly what I would do.

Men charge from the forest towards us, shouting a battle cry, thirsty for revenge. Miller drops the two archers with his bow before they can shoot again while Grant, Eben, and Morris charge. I try and fail to draw my sword, slumping against my horse with a groan of frustration as blood pours from my wounds and the pain turns white-hot. Miller turns to me, his bow primed for another shot.

"You're no good to us like this; you'll only get killed. Go, hide in the woods until this is over; we'll find you."

"And leave like a bloody coward while my men fight two to one? I don't think so!" I object even as I start to lose feeling in my hand, and my vision goes spotty. Miller's usual calm façade cracks with impatience.

"I don't have time for this, and this isn't up for discussion. You'd give one of us the same order; now go."

"Skies above, Miller, I will not-"

Miller rolls his eyes in impatience before he turns and releases his arrow. It grazes my mare's flank without drawing blood, sending her galloping into the forest with a squeal of fright. I'm in too much pain to do anything but hold on for dear life as she gallops away from the fight. The last thing I see of my men is Eben separating someone's arm from their torso with a mighty swing of his ax before the trees and shadows swallow me up.

Seizures are not something that I or anyone here is well-versed in. I would advise treatment and discovery of the causes, and if that is not possible, then restriction of the patient's freedoms and stimulants.

–Correspondence from the

Royal Hospital of Sutoran

Chapter Two

Camari

I hate summer. It is hot, it is humid, and I *hate* it. The gods must have created it just as a punishment, giving us five moons of unbearable heat.

"Camari, quite dallying and come out here!"

I jump at Adeline's voice as she hollers at me from the front room, my hair drifting into my face from the abrupt movement. I'm in the back storage room where we keep all of our medicines and dried herbs, as it is cool and shady during all seasons. As tempted as I am to ignore her call, I know it most likely means we have another patient. So, with a heavy sigh, I walk out to see what she needs and leave the cool room behind with the silent promise of my return.

Adeline is standing at the patient bed in the corner of the front room where a young man named Walter sits, holding his arm out to her and wincing as he moves it in the motions she demonstrates. She looks up when I enter and smiles briefly at me before turning back to Walter, gingerly taking his arm and feeling the elbow joint before humming at what she finds.

"Not broken or dislocated, just jammed. Cam, put together a tea with white willow bark, boswellia, and some ginger for flavor. It will help with the pain and inflammation."

I nod, retreating willingly to the storeroom to grab the proper bag before returning to Walter and Adeline, handing him the bag with a smile.

"Be generous with the honey," I advise as he takes the bag, holding it up to his nose and sniffing it. He wrinkles his nose at the scent as Adeline fastens a sling around his shoulder to keep his arm close to his chest.

"I'll be sure to do that," he assures me, tucking the tea bag into his pocket before looking back up at me with a smile. Living in such a small village for so long, everybody knows everybody. Walter and I have grown up together, playing games with the other children and eating at each other's homes. He is a copy of his father, with tousled chestnut hair, brown eyes, and tan skin that is riddled with small white scars. His father is a carpenter, and Walter is following in his footsteps. His craft gives him muscular arms and good money, but he is also always getting injured as he learns.

THE CURSE OF THE BLESSED

"You need to be more careful, Walter; you're in here all the time," Adeline reprimands, seemingly reading my mind. Walter just smiles at me over her bent head, his eyes sparking with light humor.

"Ah, but what if I'm doing that on purpose?" he asks lightly. I flush even more and look away, pointedly ignoring his implication.

"Then there's cause for concern, and we should check you for a head injury." I tease, doing my best to defuse any possible tension. It seems to work because Walter laughs gently as Adeline ties the last knot on Walter's sling and stands up, her hands on her hips.

"There! You should be good to go; just drink a cup of tea before bed and come back if the pain gets worse. Try to take it easy for the next few days as well, won't you?"

Walter stands from the bed, smiling at both of us. "Thank you, Ms. Dorsar; I'll be sure to do that. Good to see you again, Camari."

"Good to see you, Walter."

He tips his head to me before he turns and walks out of the door, whistling a merry tune. I sigh in relief once he's gone, wiping my brow once again. Gods above, I can't wait for summer to end.

"Don't complain; I know it's hot. Two more weeks of summer and then you'll be complaining of the cold." Adeline grumbles as she turns and walks over to where the table sits pushed against the wall. She plops down into her chair and begins to sort dried herbs into piles. I sit down across from her and begin to help, my hands quickly becoming stained from the fragrant plant dust.

"Me, complain? Never."

Adeline cracks a smile, her dark eyes gleaming with humor

"Honestly, though, I feel as if I'm an oven."

"I know you do, but you-"

"I know, I know." I sigh, cutting her off before she repeats the same excuse I've been told every day of my nineteen and a half years. It gets repetitious, and I get the gist.

As I sort the different leaves and herbs, my eyes grow slightly foggy, and I blink against the milky spots, swallowing a yawn of boredom.

"Watch what you're doing!" Adeline snaps, swatting my hand and making me jump as I lurch back into reality. "We want them whole, not pulverized!"

"Sorry," I mutter, blinking several times more as my efforts to separate the leaves grow gentler. A buzzing develops in my ears like a bothersome bee is in my head, and slowly, I zone out again, allowing my imagination to fly away.

Crack, a stick snaps underfoot.

Light shines down on me blindingly.

Run.

"Camari, are you listening to me?" Adeline's voice pierces my daydream and I bite my tongue as I flinch, my hands lifting in front of me without thought. Adeline scrutinizes me, her eyes narrowed in suspicion.

"Were you-"

"Just daydreaming, sorry," I say quickly, resisting the urge to pinch the bridge of my nose as a headache forms. "The heat is affecting me, that is all."

Adeline hums, holding my dark eyes with her own before nodding. "Very well. We're finished here. We need a new bar of soap if we are both to bathe at the end of the week, as you won't let me trim your hair."

"Yours is barely any shorter," I mutter under my breath, not that she hears. Adeline only hears me when she chooses to.

"Run to Seller's for some more and get some fresh air," she says without looking up. I tamper down my eager smile and rise quickly, fetching my coin purse from our shared room. I sit back down to tie the laces on my boots, and Adeline grasps my chin gently, lifting my eyes to her once more. "Back before dark, and don't dawdle too long. See if you can find some more wild garlic flowers while you're out."

I nod once more and she releases me. The door thuds shut behind me, and I smile, my shoulders relaxing as I take in the outdoors. The sun is bright outside, but a pleasant breeze blows, shoving my long red hair out of my face, the stands sticky with sweat. I lift my face to the wind for a moment and enjoy being outside and alone, even if just for a few moments, before I begin walking. The moments of freedom are always fleeting.

I wipe another bead of sweat off of my forehead as I walk the dusty street, nodding and smiling at people as I pass. I know everyone in Krakent, or I know them without really *knowing* them. They have always been distant with both my mother and I, talking to us politely when they see us but going on their way as soon as they can. My mother moved into the village when I was just a week old, a twenty-one-year-old woman by herself with a heavily scarred right arm, next to no money or belongings, and a newborn daughter but no husband, just to top it all off. We were bound to draw attention, and this village never forgets anything. Gossip is what fuels the hearth fires that cook their meals. It has become one of the gods that they worship at the monastery, and I feel no desire to genuflect to it as they do. Especially when I grew up often being the center of it. I remember growing up, hearing whispered conversations that the sight of me would trigger about my father's whereabouts and my 'wild 'inclinations. The words 'volatile 'and 'ill-mannered 'were being thrown about like a blown-up pig's bladder by the butcher's children when I had done nothing to earn such titles. I learned to tune them out, but not before I memorized all of the words and their meanings. Only when the children heard their parents and brought it to me would I defend myself and Adeline as I saw fit. When I was six, a child asked me why mother's arm was so ugly and who had burned her, and I had no answer, but that child meant no harm. Another time, a boy taunted me about my mother being a freak, drawing charcoal streaks on his right arm to imitate her burn scar as he danced around me in the shade of a crepe myrtle. Both of our parents conveniently had their backs turned, so I broke his nose and was pulled off of him as he cried, still kicking the air. After that, I was branded the wild child publicly instead of just privately, though at least then, I had earned the title. From then on, only a few children were allowed near me, one of them being Walter. Walter's Da always treated me like family and did the same for Adeline, fixing our door in the winter to keep out chills and making me a hairbrush for my twelfth birthday. I've learned that men like him are a rare breed, too few and far between.

Turning the corner, I come onto what is known as the Seller's Street. Both sides of the street are lined with stores and taverns, wooden booths erected outside of storefronts and people bragging about their goods. It is their livelihood, one Adeline and I always try to support. I walk slowly, my gaze dragging along the wooden stands for anything that might catch my eye as the shade of the booths and the crepe myrtle trees envelop me and offer relief from the sun. Strangely, most of the stands are empty or sparsely stocked, even the stand that sells animal-shaped rocks that never sell. I stop at a stand selling scented soaps, knowing the woman who runs it. Her name is Greta, and she is a cheerful woman with pale ginger hair and a freckled face that is almost always smiling.

"Good morning, Greta; how are you faring to-day?" I ask politely, looking at the soaps with little interest. Greta smiles at me, being one of the few people in Krakent who actually likes me due to the fact that a few winters ago, her son was suffering from a horrible fever; Adeline was without hope, but I refused to give up. I sat beside him all night, wiping his brow with cool clothes and trickling broth down his throat. His fever broke the next morning and I'd never been so proud of myself.

"Hello, Camari, it's good to see you! How's your mama, still saving lives?" she asks in a singsong voice. I smile, picking up a purple-scented soap and smelling it. The scent of lavender reaches my nose, and I quickly put it down as nausea rises in my throat, my smile wavering.

"She's doing well; we fixed Walter's arm just this morning."

"That boy is injured more often than he's well."

I hum my agreement, picking up a green soap and sniffing its piney fragrance before changing the subject. "It looks like half of the stalls have been wiped completely clean of their product. Did I miss some sort of sale?" I ask, setting down the soap I was looking at.

"Oh, I forget; y'all are always so busy up in that cottage that you never know the happenings!" Greta exclaims, her hands fluttering wildly at the realization that she now has someone to gossip to. I lean forward, waiting for her to talk while suddenly filled with the dull acknowledgment that I'm being an ena-bler.

"You see, three mornings ago, a large group of the king's soldiers came through here with caravans of loot and a wagon full of prisoners. They restocked all of their supplies, and a few bought some trinkets to bring home to their wives and children. I say, my soaps were bought by quite a few gentlemen saying they were for their wives, but I think they probably needed them more."

I smile at her joke so that she won't be offended, but struggle against a frown. "You said a wagon full of prisoners? Prisoners from where?"

"Oh, they said they'd just returned from raiding two hidden seer villages a ways from here. Can you imagine, seers? And so close to us! Horrible thought." Greta shudders, but I strive to keep her on track, my interest piqued with the opportunity to learn more without Adeline here to censor my knowledge of the world.

"So the wagon was full of seer prisoners?"

"Oh no, dear, they kill the seers. They're too cor-rupted by their magic by the time they reach the age of a young man or woman like yourself, and they're killed. The kids are the prisoners. Yes, the king has a special rehabilitation estate for the children. It really helps them see their true potential and learn to do what's best for the kingdom! Use their gifts for good and all that." Greta says cheerily as she stacks her soaps into becoming piles.

Corrupted by what? Power?

I frown as I think, absentmindedly agreeing to buy the pine-scented soap. Seers are a menace on the continent, using their powers to gain unlawful wealth. There have been rumors of seer uprisings, the creatures forming a rebellion against the king. I know the story of how they were created but were immediately corrupted and changed the future to harm and kill people, how whole kingdoms were destroyed at their hands. I've never seen any proof of their crimes, but those wars were centuries ago. The descendants of the first seers will forever pay the price, as their forefathers proved nothing good can come of something that cannot be had by all. They are still hunted by the king for the good of our kingdom and slaughtered. I've simply never heard of a rehabilitation estate before or of corruption still happening to this day.

Maybe the corruption never stopped.

"Thank you for the soap, Greta. Please tell Mikael I say hi," I say, quickly withdrawing myself from the conversation and continuing on my way, tucking the bar of soap into my pocket. She spoke the truth; Adeline and I are never aware of the happenings in town. Three mornings ago, we had a patient who accidentally caught their leg in their own hunting trap, pulling it out of the socket and ripping something on the inside. We were too busy to check what was going on outside, and I had forgotten about it. But now I know.

Leaving Seller's Street, I walk for a while longer, and after twenty minutes or so I enter the forest. I walk slowly, jumping a thin stream and wandering beneath branches dripping with curtains of moss and crusted with green algae. Arriving at a familiar tree stump, I sit down with a sigh, pulling my hair over my shoulder and running my fingers through it to rid it of some of its tangles as I think. How horrible to have your parents slaughtered and your homes destroyed, only to be taken away to a rehabilitation estate where you know no one and can trust nothing. It might be for their own good, but it still sounds frightening, especially for a young child. But if they're truly as dangerous as people say, then maybe it's for the best. Manipulation of the future could be a devastating ability in the wrong hands, so why risk anyone having it at all? What were the Compassionate Ones thinking?

I stand, pushing away those dangerously blasphemous thoughts with a toss of my head. I'm about to start walking back to the cottage, planning to take the long route to prolong my freedom as well as hopefully happen upon more wild garlic, when I hear a voice.

"Bleeding hell!"

I jump, my hand immediately going to the hilt of the four-inch dagger Adeline ensures I always have by my side, my heart racing.

Who is there?

"Dammit!" It's more of a groan now, the voice heavy. I flinch again but then relax slowly. The voice sounds like that of a man, and he sounds injured. I know it could be dangerous, but my instincts from growing up as a healer's daughter beg me to go and see if he needs help. I relent.

Pulling my dagger out of the leather sheath that I keep concealed in my skirts, I step forward cautiously, a stick snapping under my foot. "Hello?" I call out, taking another step. A bird flies away at my voice, startling me, and I shield my eyes from the overtly bright sun as I take another step that brings me into the shade of a beech copse. There is a rustling sound, and then a voice calls out to me.

"Who's there?" The voice rings out clearly, a deep, masculine voice filled with suspicion and unease.

I round a clump of birch trees and come upon the man to whom the voice belongs. He appears young in age, maybe a few years older than myself, with sandy brown hair that is streaked with mud, light hazel eyes, and tan skin. He is dressed in simple trousers and a loose shirt, but he has a leather sword belt with a high-quality sword attached to it, as well as several equally nice daggers. He also has on a black leather baldrick with a dagger slid into it, and he unsheathes it when I come into view, his hazel eyes scrutinizingly narrow.

I pause where I stand with my dagger in hand, taking in his features and size, before my gaze goes to the two arrows sticking out of his right shoulder at an awkward angle, causing wounds that drip a steady flow of blood onto the forest floor. I inhale sharply and walk forward, re-sheathing my knife as I drop to his side. "I can help; hold on!"

He leans away from me distrustfully, his grip on his dagger tightening, and he focuses oddly on my hair for several moments. He proceeds to scan me up and down, and I wait for him to be done before I speak, unable to completely mask my annoyance at his behavior as caution still screams in my mind.

"Well, now that you're done with that, I'm going to need to cut these arrows to pull them out, and it will hurt quite a bit," I say clearly, holding my hands up in front of me but not touching him yet.

"I've had this done before," he tells me slowly; his deep voice is no longer filled with suspicion but rather curiosity.

Trying not to guess why he's been shot more than once, I pull out my knife again. He stiffens slightly at the sight of the blade, but this time, I ignore him, grabbing hold of the shaft of one of the arrows and holding it steady. He inhales deeply as I begin to saw against the wood, emitting a small grunting noise when I snap it in half. I do the same thing to the second arrow before gesturing wordlessly for him to roll onto his left side so that I can see the two arrowheads on the other side of his wounds. Only when his back is turned do I let out my woosh of air and shake my hands out, adrenaline still filling my body. Spotting the two arrowheads easily, I stick my thumb, pointer, and middle finger into the first wound slowly, bracing his shoulder with my left hand. Wrapping my fingers around one of the sharp, blood-covered heads, I tug it out swiftly. He curses again at the pain and then takes a deep breath, making me jump as he speaks suddenly.

"I'm sorry, my lady, my words are not appropriate for your ears," he groans, surprising me with his manners.

"Seeing the entire situation, I think an allowance can be made," I reply, smiling slightly. No one has ever called me a lady before.

He returns my smile, only to grimace and curse once more as I pull out the second arrowhead. Blood begins to trickle from the wounds faster than it was before.

"Do you have a cloth or rag, even a blanket, I can use to stop the bleeding? An extra shirt?" I ask him, looking around us for something I can use. He shakes his head, his eyes widening slightly with a panic that will only make him bleed faster. Thinking quickly, I stand up and bend over, grabbing hold of my skirt.

Of all of the days to wear my good skirt, it had to be today.

Pushing the snobbish thought away; I cut a long strip from the fabric before dropping back down beside him. Lifting his arm to the proper angle, I begin to wrap his shoulder, pulling it tightly to stop the bleeding. His breath catches in his throat occasionally, but otherwise, he remains stoic and silent. Impressive for a man with multiple holes through his shoulder.

I'm tying the last knot, preparing to tell him what to do next, when I feel something cold and hard press against the back of my neck, and I hear a new voice. "Don't. Move."

I freeze, my hands stilling on the man's bandage, and release a shaky breath that ends up being a whimper as I realize there's a sword point at my neck. The injured man's eyes widen and flit between me and whoever is standing behind me.

"No, Eben, don't! She found me and removed the arrows; she's helping. For the gods 'sake, put your damn sword away." His voice still has a level of pain, but he speaks strongly and with an air of confidence and anger, a leader.

The blade at the base of my neck disappears, and I release another breath that comes out more like a sob, blinking as my eyes burn with tears of fear. Without letting myself think, I drop quickly to the ground and roll to the side, coming up on my feet with my dagger drawn as I take in my new surroundings. The second man is huge, a verifiable bear of a human. He has black hair, ruddy, light brown skin, and a scruffy beard that makes him look older than he probably is, and there's a large, black, equally scary horse behind him that I assume is his. Besides the sword he holds, he has an ax strapped onto his belt and a dagger in his leather boot, the hilt barely visible. He eyes me with distrust and annoyance as if I'm an obstacle he can easily discard and wants to.

Not a good man, then.

"Put your weapon away," he growls, raising his sword again.

"You first!" I challenge despite the fear shooting through my body, raising my dagger. I'm both shocked and proud that I stand my ground, even prouder that my hand doesn't shake and reveal my terror.

"Eben, put your sword away *now!*" The injured man snaps, looking at the second man with barely concealed rage. At that moment, three more men walk through the brush, each of them armed equally and leading horses. They stop and stare at the scene in front of them until, one by one, their eyes end up on me. They don't look nearly as rude as the second man, more curious and almost comically surprised.

"Eben." The injured man barks again at the second man, and reluctantly, Eben sheaths his sword with a scowl. I keep my dagger out, still unsure of what the hell is going on, unsure if I'll be able to keep the terror from my voice.

"So," one of the new men says in an accented but merry-sounding voice, grinning at me in such a friendly way it is almost off-putting, "what did we miss?"

"This is-" the injured man cuts off and looks over at me apologetically, still acting the gentleman, "I'm sorry, I didn't get your name."

"Camari." I force out, my heart still pounding in my throat. *What should I do?*

"This is Mistress Camari." The injured man continues. "She was helping me when Eben arrived and overreacted *stupidly*, causing all of this confusion."

"No surprise there," one of the men says with an eye roll. He looks a bit like the injured man, with different coloring but similar jaw and facial structures.

"Don't mind him, lass; he's just an eejit," the man with the Northern accent says, smiling over at me.

Eben scowls at him, and my fear slowly begins to ebb. Trusting my gut, I sheath my dagger, keeping my hand on the hilt just in case.

"Who are you all, and what do you want?" I demand, eyeing the first man's wound. The healer part of me is begging me to finish bandaging it, to get him back to the cottage where I can stitch him up. But I need answers first.

"I'm Grant," the cheery man says before gesturing to each man in turn. "The eejit is Eben, the bleeding one is Aiden, this is Morris, and this is Miller."

"What are you doing here, and why do you have so many weapons?" I ask. This time Morris, the one that looks like the bleeding man-Aiden, speaks.

"We are on our way to Sutoran. We're-"

"Tradesmen." Aiden cuts him off, grimacing as he tries to sit up. Morris looks at him for a second but remains quiet so that Aiden can continue. "We are on our way to the capital with a load, but we were robbed by bandits. They stole everything else we had, injured Eben and myself, and left. The only goods we have left are the weapons we managed to strap to ourselves for safe-keeping."

I roll his tale around in my mind, but other than a few remaining questions, I can find no outstanding flaw in it. Glancing at Eben, I see that he is indeed standing rather stiffly, his right trouser pant leg stained with blood.

That checks out as well.

"I know the village healer." I begin slowly, watching Aiden for any sign that he's lying. "You're going to need stitches and several days of bed rest. You can't ride a horse with those injuries. I can-I can take you all to her."

"We don't have anywhere to stay; we don't know anyone in the village-" Morris begins, but I interrupt.

"We have a tavern with rooms for rent; you can stay there." They all seem hesitant to accept, looking at each other silently. I scowl, crossing my arms over my chest. "If my village's hospitality isn't good enough for you, please, go bleed out on the road and let the vultures get free-"

"No, there's nothing wrong with your village." Aiden interrupts quickly, the corner of his mouth turning up slightly. "Thank you for your offer, my lady; we're happy to accept."

Lies are a form of darkness. They conceal reality, and if they exist for too long, then once they finally recede, the darkness may have killed everything it hid.

—The Religious Text; The Book of Wisdoms

Chapter Three

Aiden

"What the hell is going on, Aiden?"

After asking the woman-Camari, to give us a moment to speak, my men waited for her to get out of earshot before barraging me with questions.

"We need help," I say, cutting them all off. "I'm still bleeding, and Eben obviously reopened his leg wound. We need actual medical attention-no offense, Morris-and supplies. This is the best offer we're going to get until we reach Bareilles."

"The platoon is waiting for us in the Spás Folamh!" Eben argues, appearing annoyed by the whole situation.

"And they can wait for another week or two; they have plenty of supplies and we're not on any time constraint. Besides, we'll only slow them down if we arrive half-dead."

"What was that story? Tradesmen? Why not tell her the truth?" Miller asks quietly, speaking for the first time since he arrived.

"I doubt anyone in the village will be very trusting if we tell them we're soldiers in the king's army who also happen to be exceedingly wounded. They might make some wild assumptions and rob us, or worse, think they're in danger and panic. Tradesmen just seemed a better alternative," I explain. Slowly, my men nod in understanding. With that settled, I turn on Miller with a glare. "You disobeyed my orders and acted rashly."

"You were injured, behaving like an imbecile, and they were targeting you." he counters, crossing his arms and narrowing his gray eyes.

"It wasn't your decision to make!" I snap, my voice hard. My patience left when Eben showed up and held a sword to an innocent woman's neck, all because he made an assumption based on her hair. It makes me feel ill that I've hardly acted any differently.

Miller nods curtly. "I still think I did the right thing, but I won't disobey your orders again."

It isn't quite repentance, but it is good enough for me, and as good as I will ever get from Miller. I nod and turn to Eben, who still looks mutinous. "What the hell was that back there? She's an innocent village girl, and you almost *beheaded* her!"

"I thought she was a seer out to finish her father's job! Did you see her; you must have thought it as well," Eben says defensively, squeezing the hilt of his sword.

"But I ordered you to stand down, and you did not!" I argue, ignoring the kernel of truth in his words. "Do you no longer accept orders from your commander?"

"You know I do," he grumbles, scowling, while Grant watches on the entire time with a huge grin, nodding at me encouragingly.

"Then next time I ask you to stand down and to stop threatening an innocent girl, fucking listen!" I snap, my tone scathing. Eben nods, turning away from me with a disgruntled look. He's never handled criticism well, especially not when it comes to our jobs. A job I fear he might enjoy.

I turn to the others and address them all in a clear order. "Think of it this way: we get a week off in a small, unproblematic village. Enjoy your time, make the most of it, and don't *threaten anyone's life*. We are tradesmen until we leave, got it?"

"Yes sir. "

Honey is truly a healer's secret weapon and lover when it comes to most if not all injuries or ailments.

—Excerpt from the Natural Remedies Guidebook

Chapter Four

Camari

The sun is just a sliver in the sky by the time I return home, now shivering from the cold; the weather in Zorda never makes much sense. I was alone when I left this afternoon, but now I have five men trailing behind me on horses so big they could carry three people with ease. Aiden offered to let me ride with him, as did Grant, but I declined. I don't trust them enough to get on a horse with them yet, and Aiden obviously needs his own.

I glance back at him, finding his horse. He's slumped against its neck, his skin pale and sweaty. He's awake, but barely, and I can tell by looking at him that in another half hour, he'll pass out if he doesn't get treated. The sight of my cottage growing closer both relieves my anxiety and rekindles it, and I pick up my pace, barely restraining myself from running. Adeline would have my hide if I ran through the village, especially with my skirt as ripped up as it is.

I stop outside my cottage door and turn back to the men behind me, watching as the healthy three dismount and await my instructions. It is incredibly strange to be in charge of such…capable men.

"Eben and Aiden can come in here with me to meet the healer. I'll need help getting them inside, and then the rest of you should go find the tavern down the way and rent some rooms. You can come check on them in the morning," I say, my voice filled with a confidence that I definitely do not feel.

"Are you sure she can help both of them?" Morris asks, glancing back at Aiden with concern. I'm saved from having to answer as the door to my cottage opens, and Adeline walks out, her eyes fastened on me.

"Camari, what-" she cuts off when she sees the other men, her eyes lingering on all of their weapons. "What is going on here?" she asks in a voice that is deathly quiet.

"Adeline, two of these men have injuries that need immediate treatment," I explain immediately, the look in her eyes causing goosebumps to appear on my arms. "Can we treat them?"

Adeline studies the men in silence for several seconds before finally, her attention comes back to me. "You have a lot to explain, Camari," she says quietly so that only I can hear.

"I know, but they need help now. Please." I hold my breath, waiting for her decision. Adeline holds my gaze for several seconds, seeming to be at war with herself.

"Bring them in," she says finally, breaking the silence. I sigh in relief, smiling at my small victory. Morris and Miller nod politely to her before each of them does as ordered. Miller and Grant help Eben's considerable weight from his horse, ignoring his assurance that he can dismount by himself, while Morris goes to Aiden. I go to assist Morris instinctively, not liking Aiden's skin color at all.

"-Ready?" Morris is asking Aiden, his forehead creased with concern.

"I could take on a whole band of attackers; I'm much better than I look," Aiden assures his friend, his voice weak and his words slurring together. I smile at his attempt to comfort his friend and walk up, offering my arm. Working together, Morris and I get Aiden off of his horse and share his weight, each of us taking one of his arms over our shoulders. Aiden groans quietly at the movement but otherwise says nothing, which worries me. Silence is rarely better than noise when one is wounded.

Entering the cottage, I lead Morris and Aiden over to the patient bed and help lay Aiden down while Eben takes a chair. Morris, Miller, and Grant stand back hesitantly, looking from Aiden and Eben to the horses outside.

"Go," I reassure them. "They'll be okay here, and you can come first thing tomorrow."

Morris hesitantly nods, and then they're gone, leading the horses down the road to the tavern.

Adeline enters the cottage, shuts the door behind her, and surveys the scene in front of her before snapping into action. "Camari, get two bowls of hot water, bandages, towels, needles and thread, and the salve of honey, marshmallow, aloe, and calendula. Their wounds need to be cleansed before we sew."

"Yes ma'am." I obey her orders and move into action, accustomed to her brisk pace by now. Thankfully, there is a kettle of water heating on the stove, and I quickly pour that into two bowls, setting one beside both men before fetching the salve, an abundance of bandages and towels, and the sewing kit. When I get back, Adeline is kneeling beside Eben with her sleeves rolled up and her hair pulled back.

"Get started on the other one; be sure to scrub your hands first." She gives instructions without looking up from where she's scrubbing out Eben's leg wound, ignoring his grunts and groans.

I wash my hands and arms in the remainder of the water in the kettle before walking over to Aiden, taking several deep breaths to slow my racing heart. This will be my first time healing someone unassisted. Now is not the time for mistakes.

Pushing him onto his left side, I take out a pair of shears and cut away both my makeshift bandage and Aiden's shirt, wincing as I peel the wet fabric away from his flesh. Tossing it to the ground where it lands in a pile, I dip a towel into the steaming bowl of water and begin to wipe the blood away from his shoulder and chest so that I can get a better look at the wounds.

"Why are you doing this and not her?" Aiden asks drowsily, blinking his eyes several times to help them focus, his head tilted to the side so that he can see me.

"I'm her daughter. I've been trained for this my entire life. Don't worry, I won't let it scar too badly," I say lightly as I finish wiping away the blood and reach for the salve.

"I didn't know she was your mother. You didn't say-" Aiden says, hissing as I begin to apply the salve, making sure to get it into the wound itself, front and back, the sticky paste fusing my fingers together partially.

"It didn't seem important." I put the lid back onto the salve and wipe my hands on a fresh towel before I reach for the sewing kit, swallowing the fear in my throat.

"So, how does it look?"

"I think you'll survive."

"Thank the gods; I was worried there for a moment," he says, managing sarcasm despite his weak state. That inspires confidence in me, and I manage to thread the needle on my first try, getting the pinchers ready.

"Bite down on this," I instruct, placing a rolled-up towel in his mouth. "The salve should numb the wounds somewhat, but this is still going to hurt."

"Wonderful," Aiden mumbles around the towel. I stare down at his shoulder for a moment, take a deep breath, and then I begin. The needle goes in, the pinchers grasp it and pull it through, I tie a knot and cut the cord, and then I repeat again and again. Aiden stiffens like a plank, grunting around the towel in his mouth, but otherwise remains still. Amazed by his self-control, I keep going, and soon, I'm no longer worried or doubtful; I'm in the mindset. Before I know it, all four entrance and exit wounds are sewn shut and I'm tying the bandages in place, making sure not to wrap them too tightly. Looking up at Aiden's face, I see that he finally passed out as I'd expected, his face peaceful. I gingerly remove the towel from his mouth before I sit back on my heels, feeling exhausted. My gaze trails from his bandaged shoulder, and I examine his bare torso. There are several upraised patches of skin that are paler than the rest, marking past injuries that have healed and scarred over. He has an awful lot of scars for a tradesman.

An awful lot of muscle as well. Is he truly just a tradesman?

"Camari."

I look up, my cheeks burning as I realize I've been staring for several seconds. Adeline stands over the bed, thankfully looking at the bandages and not at my flaming face. She nods her approval before gesturing for me to join her in our bedroom. I rise silently and tiptoe past a sleeping Eben, his head resting at an odd angle in his chair with his mouth agape. Entering our bedroom, I've barely shut the door before Adeline snaps.

"What in the gods 'names is going on? How do you know these men; where are they from?"

"They are tradesmen that got attacked and robbed by…well, *robbers*, on their way to Sutoran. Eben and Aiden were injured in the fight. I found Aiden in the woods, and then the others found us, and I- I couldn't just leave them there! They needed medical attention!" I say defensively, shrinking under the anger in her eyes.

"Camari, your compassion is a wonderful thing, but if you don't check it, it will become your downfall. You don't know these people, yet you brought them to our home!"

"We receive visits from strangers all the time; we're *healers!*"

"I knew I should never have let you go out today; I knew you couldn't be trusted!" Adeline snaps, her eyes flashing angrily. I shrink back, swallowing as her words hit their mark.

"I can't be trusted? Is that what you think?" Guilt appears in my mother's eyes as she hears the hurt in my voice, and she opens her mouth to apologize, but I cut her off, unwilling to listen. "Excuse me, Adeline, but our patients should probably be observed overnight. I'm going to go do my job, as *they* trust me to do it."

With that, I leave the bedroom and return to my seat at Aiden's bedside, leaning against the wall behind me as exhaustion slams down. He's still unconscious, but already his color has improved. Triumph pumps through my veins for a moment before the anger and hurt return, pushing it away.

After laying a blanket over Aiden and Eben's unconscious forms, I wrap one around myself, not wanting to return to the room I share with Adeline and lean back against the wall, falling asleep.

I wake the next morning to the sound of people speaking quietly, their low voices unmistakably masculine, and I remember with a rush everything that happened yesterday. I struggle to crack my eyes open, exhaustion weighing heavily on my eyelids. The front room is awash with sunlight, illuminating Aiden and Eben as they speak quietly. Eben has pulled his chair over to Aiden's bedside and they appear to be arguing, Eben appearing angry. I sit up slowly and stretch with a purposeful groan, reminding them of my presence. They cut off immediately, both of them turning to face me.

"Good morning. How are you both feeling?" I greet them, standing up and rubbing my eyes.

"Better. Thank you, my lady," Aiden says, smiling slightly at me.

"Just Camari, please, I'm no lady." I correct him, smoothing my torn and wrinkled skirt.

"Camari," Aiden says slowly with a slight frown as if he's testing out how it feels to say. I examine him, comparing his appearance to a mental checklist. His skin color has improved dramatically, returning from the pale white it was to the deep tan I assume it naturally is. His voice is strong, if not a little hoarse, and he is stiffly sitting propped up in the bed, not appearing to be in too much pain.

"You need tea," I declare, turning and walking over to the empty kettle.

"Tea?" Aiden calls after me in confusion as I refill the kettle from our bucket of well water, set it on the stove, and poke at the dying embers inside the stove with an iron rod.

"Medicinal tea." I clarify, tossing several pieces of wood into the oven before I shut the door. "For your aching muscles. It will help with the stiffness."

"How do you know they're stiff?"

I set out two clay mugs and begin to put in the proper leaves and herbs, answering him over my shoulder. "I can tell by how both of you are sitting. And it's basic inductive reasoning. You fell off your horse, both of you were attacked and injured, and you're both sitting as stiff as logs. The solution: tea."

The kettle comes to a near boil quickly, and I lift it from the stove, filling the mugs to the brim and watching as the leaves begin to float up. After putting a liberal amount of honey into each mug, I bring them over to the patients, careful not to spill. Aiden accepts his with a thank you while Eben simply grunts. He seems to be in a constant foul mood, which is annoying, to say the least.

Aiden takes a sip of the cooling tea and jerks back from the mug, his face screwing up in disgust. "What the hell is in this?"

"Willow bark, boswellia, ginger, and honey," I recite, flashing back to the day before when I gave the same tea to Walter. "It's disgusting, I know, but it helps relax muscles and promotes healing."

"And you're sure it'll *help* our health?" Aiden asks doubtfully, looking down at the murky contents of his mug. I can't help but smile over the rim of my mug at his obvious disgust, knowing from experience just how truly vile Adeline's teas are.

"Yes, I'm sure. Down it quickly and keep it down."

After a moment's hesitation, Aiden obeys, throwing back the contents of the mug with a pained grimace, Eben following suit. I collect their mugs and watch as Aiden screws up his face, obviously fighting to keep the tea down.

"Don't worry, you begin to get used to the taste," I assure him, sipping from my own mug of plain water.

"You mean we have to take more of that stuff?" Aiden asks, his eyes momentarily widening in dismay. This time, I can't help a small laugh, his face appearing almost comedic in its dread.

These patients should be interesting.

The grandest castle and the widest ocean could seem like the smallest prison cell to one who is not capable of experiencing anything else.

—The Journal of Maren Landry

Chapter Five

Aiden

Three days after I was shot, I am finally allowed to get out of bed. Camari and Mistress Dorsar were adamant about me not getting up, insisting that my body needed time to recover and restore all the blood I lost, but enough is enough. Eben and I are still far from healed, but I need to move around, or I'll go mad.

"Okay, just be sure to sit back down if you start to feel light-headed or weak," Camari instructs from where she stands at my bedside, watching on with an eager smile on her face. We've formed a friendship of sorts over the past few days, one that her mother obviously despises. I have no idea why, but the woman hates me. I can't imagine how she'd react if she knew who or what I really am, and I don't want to ever find out.

"Any other tips, or can I stand now?" I inquire, grinning at Camari's hovering. "It might be surprising for you to learn, but I have been standing and walking for just over two decades now. I'm actually rather good at it."

She scowls crossly at me, crossing her arms. "You're the first patient I've tended to all by myself; I have the right to be cautious. Now, stand up."

Bracing my hands on the side of the bed, I obey, pushing myself to my feet. I sway for a second, my legs weak after so many days without use, and my head slightly light, but then I'm up and standing. I grin, shifting my weight from one foot to the other and stretching out my aching muscles. "Look at that, I'm fine. No need to squawk like a mother hen."

"Are you light-headed? Shaky?" Camari presses, taking my wrist and checking my pulse before examining my face for any sign of discomfort.

"A little crowded, but otherwise, fine," I assure her, earning another one of the glares that I'm beginning to grow accustomed to. Camari takes a step back and observes me, obviously still wary of any lingering weakness.

"I didn't realize you were so tall," she murmurs as if to herself, a small frown creasing her forehead. She flushes immediately, but I just chuckle lightly, running my hand through my hair.

"It feels good to be standing."

"I'm sure it does," Eben grumbles from where he sits in the second bed, scowling at me. Unlike me, he isn't allowed up for at least another week, having apparently torn his leg muscles.

"You'll be up soon enough," I assure him, looking around the cottage. Now that I'm on my feet, it appears a lot…smaller than before. More confined, with just two rooms off of the main room that I'm in.

"You better live for me until they let me up again," he says, shooting a scowl at Camari. She glares right back, raising a copper eyebrow.

"Each time you try to stand up, you prolong your bed rest. Try to stand up again, and I'll have you in bed for a *moon*."

Eben mutters something under his breath, but Camari isn't perturbed. "How about a 'yes, Camari, thank you for your help'? Unless, of course, you'd like two moons. Three?"

"Thank you for your help," Eben grinds out, his face practically red with anger.

"Aw, you're welcome, Eben, it's my pleasure!" Camari oozes in an overly sweet voice, smiling brightly. Eben makes a rude gesture, but she has already turned her back to him, ignoring the surprise that I'm sure is visible on my face. I've never met a woman quite as…cold cut as Camari. If she has something to say, she says it, never dancing around a subject. It's both fascinating and strange, especially when she interacts with Eben, who is in a rare state due to his injury.

"Why don't you try walking a bit and see how that goes?" Camari suggests, glancing around the room before backing up to stand by the wooden table that sits alongside the far wall. I obey, walking towards her easily, my leg muscles aching with the need to walk farther. My whole self aching with the need to *move*.

"Can I go on a walk outside?" Camari hesitates at my request, glancing at the door. "Please?" I add, desperate for fresh air.

At that moment, the door opens and Mistress Dorsar walks in, pulling a heather gray shawl from her shoulders as she takes in the scene before her. "You're up," she comments, standing beside Camari.

"He wants to go for a walk outside," Camari informs her without looking away from me, still frowning in thought.

"As long as he takes it slow, he should be fine. Maybe just down the road and back for today," Mistress Dorsar says before walking away, setting her shawl down on the table.

"Alright then, let's go," Camari says, fishing a strip of leather from her pocket and tying her long hair back with it, the copper waves gleaming in the sun that streams in through the window. It's a beautiful, if not unusual shade, the color of fire and gold mixed together.

Mistress Dorsar looks up, frowning slightly at us. "You're going with him?"

"He can't go alone; what if he passes out or gets lost?" Camari points out, shooting me a glare as I open my mouth to protest. Apparently, she wants to get out as much as I do.

"I suppose. Just be careful, and-"

"I know." Camari cuts her mother off abruptly, annoyance flashing through her eyes. "We'll be fine."

She turns and walks to the door, pulling it open and walking out without another word. I glance from the door to Mistress Dorsar, who is staring after her daughter with eyes aflame, before rushing after Camari. She's waiting for me at the edge of the cottage, scowling down at the dirt road.

"Everything okay?" I ask cautiously, unsure what I've gotten myself into. Gods above, please don't let me be involved in some mother-daughter spat.

"Fine, I'm just excited to get out," Camari replies with a forced lightness to her words. "Come, let me show you my village."

I fall into step beside her as we begin to walk down the street, adjusting my sling so that it isn't cutting into my good shoulder as much. We walk in an amicable silence, both of us enjoying the warmth of the sun's rays and the coolness of the breeze.

"How long have you lived here?" I ask, peering into the window of a shop as we pass.

"Always. I've never been anywhere else."

"Nowhere? Not even to Norwatag?" I ask in surprise, naming the nearby village that is built on the seashore.

"No. I've heard it's beautiful," Camari says, her eyes misting wistfully. "I'd love to see the ocean one day. I heard that it's not really blue but that it just reflects the sky."

"That's true, but the water is so clean, it's like glass. And there are fish of all different colors that will come up to you if you stand still enough."

"That's what Walter told me; he went to the ocean last summer with his Da."

"Who's Walter?"

"Oh, he's my friend in the village," Camari explains, a slight blush tinting her cheeks. I nod, unsure of how to receive her reaction. Thankfully she changes the subject as we turn onto a new street, the plan of sticking to her street apparently forgotten.

"We're almost to Seller's Street; I'll introduce you to my other friend, Greta."

"What is Seller's Street?"

"It's a street in the village comprised completely of shops, taverns, and people selling things in booths, like a market. They were completely wiped clean a few days ago, but they should have had time to fill up again."

"Oh? Why were they 'wiped clean'?" I ask, fidgeting with the strap of my sling again. I can't wait until I can take this blasted thing off. I despise feeling confined in any way.

"A caravan of the king's soldiers came through here and restocked on supplies before heading to Sutoran," she explains, glancing away from me as a bird flies in front of us, chirping loudly. I'm grateful for the distraction, quickly masking my surprised expression. That means we're only a few days behind my platoon. But slowly, they'll get farther and farther ahead while my men and I are stuck here. I can only hope they don't get so far ahead that we can't catch up with them.

We turn another corner and come onto a bustling street filled with people, voices ringing out and mixing together.

"Sugar dates! Sugar dates and beans! Sugar dates and pistachios!"

"Sheep's wool blankets, the softest in Zorda!"

"Amulets of protection, no seer will be able to read your future!"

Camari frowns at the man selling amulets, leading me past him to the stall of a cheery ginger woman selling bars of soap. "Good morning, Greta, how fares the soap business?"

Greta looks up and beams at Camari, her round face becoming the picture of kindness. "Hello, love! I've sold more these past few days than I can handle; I'll be out soon!"

"Make sure to save a bar to use on Mikael; the gods know that boy needs it."

Greta laughs, stacking a few cerulean blue bars on top of each other. "I caught him trying to bathe the cat the other day. I don't reckon he'll ever try that again. The entire floor was soaked with water."

Camari grins, her smile lighting up her whole face. "I'm glad he's so rambunctious."

Greta's attention turns to me and her eyes widen slightly, roaming up and down in a way that makes me feel like a prime rib or a horse at auction. "Camari, who's your friend?"

"Oh, I'm sorry, this is Aiden. Aiden, this is Greta," Camari says, gesturing between the two of us.

"It's a pleasure to meet you." I smile, bowing lightly to Greta. She flushes, giggling slightly.

"Aren't you a charmer? Oh, Camari, where'd you find him?"

"In the woods," Camari says distractedly as she surveys the colorful soap bars. I quickly turn a laugh into a cough, looking away as I school my smile into obedience.

"Is that where young people meet nowadays?" Greta chortles. Camari looks up with a frown, the implication obviously lost on her, and I truly laugh this time at the expression of pure confusion on her face.

"We should probably be getting back before your mother begins to worry," I tell Camari, preventing her from telling Greta how we truly met. The story would end up all over the entire village, and that's the last thing I need.

Camari scowls at the mention of her mother, sighing heavily. "Oh, you have no idea," she mutters before turning to Greta, a smile once again pasted on her face. "I'll see you later, Greta?"

"Of course! Have a good day, my dear; give my love to your mother," the woman replies, still staring at me out of the corner of her eye. I nod at her once more before Camari and I turn and head back the way we came, Camari still scowling.

"I take it you and your mother don't get along," I say cautiously, unsure of what exactly to say. Camari laughs bitterly, twisting a loose strand of hair around her finger.

"If she had her way, I'd be locked up in a jar for safe-keeping, never allowed out."

"Maybe she just wants to keep you safe?"

"Safe from what?" Camari exclaims, spreading her arms. "Safe from the safest, smallest village in Zorda? We haven't had anyone dangerous here in… in a very long time." She cuts off, seeming to disappear deep into her thoughts.

"Even small villages can have hidden dangers," I comment quietly, annoyed with myself for getting into the middle of their argument. I can't seem to help it though. Camari's emotions and thoughts are all so powerful, almost explosive. It's hard not to get drawn in by their strength.

Camari emerges from her thoughts with a frown as we turn onto her street, picking up her pace. "And yet I wouldn't know because I've never left."

"Is there any reason for her to still be so protective, any past trauma that could be an influence perhaps?"

"Not anymore." Camari's eyes go distant, and I'm struck suddenly by the darkness of her irises. "Just a crippling fear that she seems to wish I inherited. I just…didn't."

"Maybe something will change soon, you never know," I say optimistically as we pause outside her cottage door, trying to get rid of her glum expression.

THE CURSE OF THE BLESSED

Dear gods, when did I become the optimistic one?

"Krakent repeats the same cycle every week; it never changes. It will be the same when I'm ninety, and I'll still be here, dreaming of living a life that has already passed me by," Camari says with an air of finality before stepping into the cottage, ending our conversation with that sad remark.

Running keeps me sane, keeps the ghosts from catching up for longer than the length of a night-mare. The longer I stand stagnant, the greater the chance of being dragged down. If it weren't for Morris, the gods know I may not mind being dragged completely under.

—Field Journal of Aiden Lorian

Chapter Six

Camari

I *really* don't like Eben. I know he's injured; I know he's stuck in Krakent while he has places to be, but does he have to be so *miserable?* He snaps at the other men when they come to visit, he is rude to Aiden whenever Aiden goes out for a short walk or simply moves about the cottage for a bit, and every time I walk into the room, he scowls. It's almost as if he's angry I *saved his life.*

It's been five days, and already I'm looking forward to the day that Eben leaves. Aiden, however, I'll miss. He's become a friend, and I enjoy his company. We go on walks together every day as he regains his strength, and he doesn't judge or reprimand me for being myself and speaking my mind, for asking questions I've been told are unbecoming to ask. It's refreshing, and I find myself spending more and more time with him if only to escape Adeline. It's strange, a man I found in the woods becoming my escape, and yet that day seems like so long ago now; it's rather unsettling.

Adeline and I haven't truly spoken since our argument, setting a new record for how long I've managed to hold a grudge against her. All I want is an apology, but it's starting to look like I won't be receiving one. That shouldn't be of any surprise; my mother has never given me a genuine apology in my nineteen years of life. Beginning to expect one now would be the same as giving into the height of delusion.

I shift the basket I have in the crook of my elbow, wiping beads of sweat from my forehead with my free hand. I'm on my way to the woods, sent by Adeline to gather some of the wild-growing rosemary I spotted a few days ago. She seems to have no problem talking to me if it is to order me to do something.

The sun beats down on me cruelly, making my hair stick to the back of my neck and my bodice feel unusually tight. I tug at the collar of my cover uncomfortably, feeling miserable in all of my layers. I cannot wait for the cooler weather to arrive.

Stepping off of the road and entering the forest, I walk for a few minutes before locating the rosemary plant. I unsheathe my dagger and use it to cut a handful of sprigs, the plant's crisp scent filling the air. I've always loved the smell of rosemary; it reminds me of calm evenings spent baking or lying in a patch of clover in utter peace. I raise a sprig to my nose and inhale deeply, letting the scent wash over me and calm the small bit of anxiety I get whenever I enter the woods alone.

I stand and begin to make my way back to the road, the basket swinging from my hand as I walk through the shady woods. I pass the place where I found Aiden and I pause, looking around. I can see the trampled grass and the broken branches of a bush, evidence of what happened. I'll admit a small, paranoid part of me is worried that Aiden and the other men are lying about something. But I have no proof, and most of them have been nothing but kind. It's probably just Adeline's paranoia becoming my own, so I push it away.

But as I turn to leave, my eye catches on something on the ground. Walking slowly towards the glimmer I see in the leaves, I kneel down and set aside my basket. I push aside leaves and pine needles, sure I saw something. My hand touches something hard and I pick it up, wiping away the dirt and mud that covers it so that I can see the details. It is a pendant, about the size of a vitike, a form of coin in Zorda. It is silver and gleams in the light once I've wiped it clean. Etched onto its surface is an image, the silhouette of a flying rukh against a large horizontal almond shape with a circle inside of it. Something about it seems familiar, and I'm sure I've seen it before, but I can't place where. No one in Krakent can afford something as nice as real silver, let alone a pendant. And even if they could, it would be so precious there is no way they would simply leave it here in the woods.

Who's is it? Where did it come from?

Unsure of what I should do, I pull my leather hair tie free and slip the pendant onto it, tying it around my neck. Tucking the pendant under my shift, I decide to ask Aiden about it later and pick up my basket once more, continuing back to the road and putting it out of my mind for now.

After returning to the village, I'm walking slowly back to the cottage in an attempt to prolong my free time, when Walter jogs to catch up to me. "Hello, Camari, how are you today?"

I turn and smile at him, pushing my hair out of my face. "Hi, Walter, how's your arm?"

"Perfect." Walter demonstrates, moving his arm in a wide circle. "Your mother is a miracle worker."

"And yet, I see a bandage on your hand!" I grab his right wrist and lift his arm so that his hand is in the air, revealing a white bandage wrapped around his palm. "What did you do now?"

"Oh, that's nothing. The chisel slipped a little yesterday morning, is all," Walter says with a nonchalant shrug.

"Did you visit Adeline to see if you need stitches?"

"Yes, and I don't. She's the one that bandaged me," Walter says. He looks at where my hand is on his wrist and smiles softly, his eyes crinkling. I let go quickly, looking down at the road as we walk. I hate it when he does that, when he sees something that just isn't there. I don't want to hurt him, but I don't feel the way he does. I don't feel a spark. And yet, he's the only person who has ever shown any interest in me, be it friendly or more than friendly. Shouldn't that be enough?

"You need to be more careful; pretty soon, you'll just be one big scar," I comment lightly, trying to break the tension.

"Ah, but only when I'm injured do you show that you care," Walter says, smiling crookedly. I sigh, despising where our conversation has gone.

"Look, Walter -"

"Camari!"

I cut off, turning around to find Aiden walking quickly towards us with a smile on his face. Walter stiffens beside me, his back ramrod straight.

"Hello, Aiden, how are-did you go *running?*" I take in the sweat-soaked shirt sticking to his torso like a second skin and leaving nothing up to the imagination, the sling holding his arm in place appearing equally sweaty.

"Yeah, with Miller, but he couldn't keep up." Aiden chuckles, running his hand through his hair, only succeeding in making it stick up more. He seems to notice Walter for the first time, looking him up and down quickly before offering him a friendly smile. "Hi, I'm Aiden."

"So I gathered. I'm Walter." Walter offers his hand for Aiden to shake and Aiden accepts, shaking it firmly. "How do you know Camari?"

"She helped me out when I was hurt, and my friend and I are staying with them while we recover," Aiden explains, gesturing to his sling. Walter nods, tucking his hands into his pockets.

"She's great that way; she helps anyone that's injured." Something in Walter's voice is off, but I don't get a chance to dwell on it because at that moment, Miller appears, jogging half-heartedly to Aiden.

"Ah, you finally caught up." Aiden grins at his friend as he reaches us, his darker skin glistening with sweat.

"Have fun trying to beat me back to the tavern," Miller pants as he runs right past us, smacking Aiden hard on the back of the head as he runs past him. Aiden seems unperturbed, nodding a farewell to us before continuing on after his friend. I watch as they run off, smiling slightly.

"Fools, both of them. Who on earth runs on a day as hot as this? They'll pass out," Walter scoffs. I shake my head, shifting the basket on my arm.

"I think it will take more than heat to make Aiden pass out," I laugh, continuing towards the cottage. Walter frowns for a moment before taking a step back the way we came.

"I just remembered, Camari, I have to go. I'll see you later?"

"Okay?" I reply, confused, but he doesn't even stay long enough to hear my answer. He's already walking back the way we came. I continue on my way home alone.

I'm helping Adeline clean the dinner dishes that evening when she starts a conversation, not looking up from the plate she's scrubbing.

"You did a good job sewing up Aiden's wounds; they're healing nicely."

I look up in surprise, my hand stilling on the plate it was drying. "Thank you."

"We should be able to remove his stitches in a few days, and then he'll be able to go stay at the tavern with the others while Eben heals." she continues, starting on a new plate. I ignore the small part of me that is sad at his looming departure, forcing a smile.

"That's good. I'm glad he's healing so fast."

"I've noticed how well the two of you have been getting along." Adeline meets my eyes for the first time, pushing a strand of silvery-blonde hair behind her ear. "I hope you've been careful."

"Skies above, Adeline, he hasn't seen my arms! No one has! Will you trust me for once? Maybe give me a little credit?" I hiss, anger surging through me. "I've never done anything to encourage such doubt!"

"That's not what I was talking about. I mean, I hope you've been careful about getting too attached to him," Adeline explains, setting down the plate she was cleaning and meeting my gaze straight on.

"What do you mean, *attached*?"

Adeline sighs softly as if I've said something ignorant. "It's obvious you've developed a relationship with the man, Cam; I just don't want you getting too attached, is all."

"What do you mean, relationship? We don't have a relationship; he's just a patient," I say hotly, even as I sense the falsehood in my words.

"You've developed a friendship, which is a form of a relationship," Adeline lectures. "And all I'm saying is I hope you realize he's leaving in a few days. I don't want you getting hurt, Cam."

"I'm not some love-sick schoolgirl that is going to throw herself at a man she's known for less than a week. Thank you for your concern, but I'll be fine," I snap in a low voice, dropping my towel on the counter and turning away from her. Aiden and Eben are sitting in silence, watching us openly. While they couldn't hear any of what was said, they undoubtedly watched our entire argument. With my face burning with embarrassment, I stalk into the bedroom and slam the door behind me, dropping down onto the blanket I've been sleeping on while Eben occupies my bed. How dare Adeline insinuate...it's not true anyway. It's as if she's been searching for things to make me stay away from Aiden ever since he showed up. Well, jokes on her; I'm not manipulated that easily.

Rolling onto my side, I don't open my eyes when Adeline comes in and prepares for bed, refusing to be the first person to seek forgiveness for our argument.

Danger, wrongness; death; it lurks behind every rock.

Run.

The light is blindingly bright and burns the ground beneath our feet.

We shouldn't have trusted him.

They're going to kill me.

What do they want?

Turn back. Run. RUN.

I jolt awake, slapping my hand over my mouth to muffle a yelp of fright. My heart races, and I can feel it pounding in my chest like a drum, my ears ringing. I press my shaking hands to my face and exhale slowly and shakily, my shivering fingers feeling soothingly cold against my skin as a headache blooms beneath my skull. The ringing in my ears slowly begins to fade but I remain in the same position, holding my head and taking deep, controlled breaths. Control. As if that is something I have ever had.

THE CURSE OF THE BLESSED

Ever since childhood, I've had episodes. They're basically where I have nightmares, but occasionally I am awake. They almost never make sense, but Adeline always makes me talk about them, telling me that talking about them will help me put them out of my mind. Then she gives me a special brew of tea made for other people who have 'episodes', and she makes me rest for the remainder of the day. I usually hide my episodes from her or pass them off as daydreams, but sometimes they ambush me, and I'm left defenseless, and they seem to only be growing stronger and more frequent. I'm convinced they are from overheating and have told her that several times in the vain attempt to get out of wearing so many layers. It never works. This is the first full-on episode I've experienced in over a moon, and my head screams at me that it disliked the experience as much as I did.

I lie back down slowly and pull my blanket over my chest, still shivering as my heart rate slows.

It was just a dream. A figment of my imagination.

I repeat that mantra until sleep claims me.

One can run as far and for as long as they like. They can manipulate, lie, and kill to get where they want to be. But nothing can prevent the will of the gods.

–The Religious Texts; The Book of Wisdom

Chapter Seven

Aiden

Eben and I are not deemed healed enough to ride a horse at the one-week marker, and we are forced to push our departure off for another week. The news doesn't bother me nearly as much as it should, and I go about life like normal. Or whatever my new normal seems to have become.

A week after my injuries occurred, my arm is out of the sling, and my stitches have been removed, though I'm under strict orders to restrain myself from using it for anything strenuous.

While my men are ready to get going again, I can tell they're also enjoying their stay in this charming village. We've been overdue for a vacation for a long time, and this is just the short break we need. Besides Eben, everyone's moods have improved over their days of rest, but Eben's always in a sour mood, so there's not much that can be done there.

Camari and Mistress Dorsar are still avoiding each other after the quiet fight they had a few days ago, though I have no idea what that was about. I just know Camari looked angry and hurt, and some strange part of me wanted to stand up and defend her from whatever her mother was saying. Not that it's my place at all. I blame that strange urge on exhaustion and too much sun and push it forcefully from my mind.

Meanwhile, any time that I'm not with my men, I'm with Camari. We can be doing anything, walking, gathering supplies for her mother, even cleaning out the storage closet they have, and yet doing it with Camari makes it fun. Her free spirit and confidence are contagious, and I find myself more comfortable around her than I am around almost anyone else, save for my men. She seems to enjoy my company just as much, a fact that makes me smile and regales me with stories of her childhood. I learn that she and her mother moved to Krakent when she was just a newborn baby, and the village has never fully accepted them. I learn that she has a scar on her right knee from when she tried to climb to the top of a magnolia tree but overestimated the tree's height. I learn that she's been friends with Walter since childhood, and doesn't really spend time with many other people. The entire time I learn about her, my guilt grows bigger and bigger. I can tell her nothing about me in return, no past anecdotes or tales, no childhood adventures or discoveries. My life is a locked chest, and I can't give anyone the key. And it pains me to keep so much from her. Even if it isn't technically lying, it feels like it is. And still, even as the guilt eats away at me, I am happier than I've ever been. A week of Krakent has me sleeping through the night and waking up without a weight on my shoulders. My head is clear and untroubled by thoughts of what I have done, who I have become, and ones that are too scary to truly pronounce. I feel more free than I ever have, and I know that so much of that is due to Camari. I find myself waking up every morning eager to see her. And while I know that soon it all will end, I find myself dreading the day that it does because that is when I will no longer be able to escape reality.

I'm returning from an afternoon walk with Camari on day eight when I find all of my men gathered in the cottage, obviously waiting for me. I stop in the doorway, finding Miller. He meets my eyes calmly before looking over at Camari, his message clear.

"Camari, would it be too much to ask you to give us a minute alone?" I say slowly, quickly figuring out just what this is about.

Camari nods, glancing around quickly before stepping back towards the open door. "I'll just go see how Greta is faring."

The door clicks shut and we all wait in silence for a minute, making sure no one else is listening in.

"What's going on?" I ask finally, breaking the fragile silence.

"Well, we've decided we need to talk about just what our plans are," Morris explains, shifting slightly on the bed. "Or rather, lack thereof."

"We had a plan last time I checked."

"And what was that plan? Stay here for who knows how long until I'm well enough to ride? We need to decide what day we're leaving," Eben says, crossing his arms. "We can't just stay here forever."

"And we're not going to. The healers said that you aren't healed enough to ride a horse without your leg splitting wide open. If we leave now, you'll be dead before we reach the Spás Folamh!" I argue, gesturing to where his bandaged leg rests propped up on the bed.

"But if we wait too long, we won't catch up with the platoon in time. We can't make it across the Spás Folamh without their supplies; we just don't have enough, and we don't have enough money to buy all that we'll need either," Miller says calmly.

"We need to perfect our timing so that Eben has as much time as he can to heal while still being sure we catch up to the platoon in time," I agree, running my hand through my hair as I think. "What if we leave in two weeks? That will give Eben another fortnight to recover, and we'll still have plenty of time to catch the platoon."

"Are you sure we'll still be able to catch the platoon?" Grant inquires, sounding worried. "I don't fancy dying of dehydration in the desert."

"We'll have plenty of time," I assure him, stifling my own worries at the same time. This is for what is best for Eben. This is not me being selfish.

So why don't I believe that?

"Then it's settled," Miller declares with an air of finality. "We leave in a fortnight."

The strange thing about living in a small village, even for a short period of time, is discovering that everyone knows *everyone.* And that's not at all an exaggeration; there's not a person here that everyone doesn't know, and that makes being a visitor *very* interesting. Everywhere I go, whispers and stares follow me as people gossip about who I could be without ever getting the courage to ask. It's all really annoying honestly, especially when I'm with Camari. I've noticed that when we're on walks together, the whispers seem to amplify. People stare openly, not even bothering to hide their judgment. Camari seems indifferent to it all, but I notice the slight stiffening of her shoulders when she hears a rude rumor or the way she grits her teeth when people stare. She's not immune.

"Why do they stare like that? It's driving me crazy?" I mutter under my breath one day, scowling at the couple on the road that is watching us judgmentally. Camari's face flashes with surprise before she schools her expression into nonchalance, but I saw it. The hurt in her eyes.

"Just ignore them; don't give them the satisfaction of knowing we notice," Camari replies grumpily, shifting a little away from me. *Now, what's that about?*

"Okay, but *why* are they staring? Have I done something to draw their attention? Did I offend them in some way?" I don't like the stares all of the time. While I don't have to worry about anyone recognizing me since the identity of the royal assassin is always kept secret, it still makes me uneasy.

"You're new here, and they live their lives gossiping; that's plenty of reason alone," Camari explains, playing with the pendant that she wears around her neck. "And you've been spending a substantial amount of your time with me; that's bound to draw some extra attention."

"I don't understand. You've lived here your whole life; why would they gossip about you?" I frown, no less confused than I was before. This is why I abhor small towns.

"Ah, that's where you're wrong." Camari raises a finger and smiles bitterly. "I've lived here since I was a few weeks old; that's not my whole life. Everyone here was born here, as were their parents and their parents before them. People move here, and they never leave. But Adeline showed up here with a newborn baby in her arms and declared herself a healer. People have never really gotten over that. Walter is the only one who willingly associates with me besides Greta, and I think even she partially believes the rumors and just doesn't care. That or it makes her feel like she's involved in some sort of scandal. Either way, since it is well known that Walter is the only man to ever show any interest in me, they are bound to gossip about the newcomer who also spends time with me."

"So they're gossiping about my association with you, not me particularly?" I clarify, frowning at the idiocy of this whole situation.

"Yup. If you don't want to be gossiped about, don't walk with the witch." Camari smiles, though it's obviously forced.

"That's bullshit!" Camari jumps slightly at my exclamation, her eyes widening in surprise. I lower my voice, aware that I probably spoke louder than intended, but keep going. "Why would I stop associating with the only person in this village that I like, the only person in this village that seems genuine and kind, just because of some stupid rumors?"

"Because…that's what everyone does," Camari says slowly, her cheeks turning slightly pink.

"And that's completely insane," I repeat, glaring at someone that we pass as he stares at us. "I'm afraid you're stuck with me for the time being."

"Okay, just know they're going to talk even more." Camari shrugs, tucking a strand of hair behind her hair.

"Then let's give them something to talk about." I reach for her hand and place it in the crook of my arm without giving it a second thought. Her eyes widen and she flushes bright red, even the tips of her ears going pink. A small, masculine part of me is filled with satisfaction at her reaction, while another part of me is surprised at how much I enjoy the feeling of her hand on my arm.

You are in dangerous territory, Aiden.

We walk down the street just as before, only now it's exceedingly obvious we're walking together. I actually laugh at one point at the surprised look we get, and then Camari joins in. Soon, we're both bent over, laughing so hard we're gasping.

It's not until late that night, while I'm lying in my bed in the cottage, that it hits me. There are many things I enjoy about spending time with Camari, her dark eyes, the way her smile lights up her face, and the questions she asks that she doesn't even realize are funny. The best thing is that when I'm with her, I can completely forget my past. When I'm with her, I'm me.

I'm in so much trouble.

We are healers, not magicians, mistress. Whatever scars you suffer with, we cannot erase. Blemishes of the skin often heal on their own, and if they don't after everything that you have described, then they most likely never will.

–Correspondence from the Royal Hospital of Su-toran

Chapter Eight

Aiden

I move to the tavern to join my men, discovering that I've been keeping Camari's bed from her without realizing it. She never said a thing, but I suspect she's happy to have it back, and I'm more than comfortable staying in the tavern.

Eben stays in the cottage for two more days before he too joins us at the tavern, though he's put under strict instructions to take it slow as he gets back to his feet.

Just like that, things begin to go back to the way they were before. Our scheduled departure grows steadily closer, and we buy what supplies we can to prepare. I still go on daily walks with Camari, trying to spend as much time with her as possible before I have to leave. Suddenly, it's two days until I leave, and I find myself dreading it, though I can't for the life of me say why. I refuse to acknowledge it.

Camari and I are on another walk together, and I listen as Camari tells me one of her childhood stories. It's late afternoon, and the only other person out is a man saddling his stallion outside the tavern at the end of the street. I personally like the solitude, enjoying Camari's company without all of the other people around. I'm going to miss her more than I want to admit.

"Do you have everything you need for your journey?" Camari asks, seemingly reading my mind.

"Yes. We're all packed and ready for an early departure. Eben can't wait to depart."

"And I can't wait for him to depart either," Camari says, crinkling her nose at the mention of my second in command. "Though, I'll be sad to see you go."

"Oh? My company proved to be worthy of your time?" I ask sarcastically, smiling despite my efforts to remain serious.

"I know; it surprised me as well. You'll have to come back and visit before I forget all of your good qualities and group you in with Eben." Camari continues on with the sarcasm, not noticing how my smile weakens slightly. She won't ever see me again, and I won't ever see her again. That's how these things go; no one knows who I am or what we are. We'll leave, and she'll move on; I'll leave her to find someone else. Someone else will hold her hand, make her laugh, and bring joy into her life, a joy that I could never supply. I'll leave her to live her beautiful, promising life. And I'll move on to continue destroying my desire for mine.

The thought sobers me up, and my smile instantly disappears as nausea rises up my throat. Camari notices and frowns, tilting her head to the right the way she does when she's focusing. "What's wrong?"

A shout saves me from having to answer, and we both spin towards the man outside the tavern. His horse has spooked at something and it bucks, its back leg clipping him in the shoulder. The man flies back and lands on the ground with a thud, not stirring.

"Gods above!" Camari gasps. She runs towards the man, and I follow, my stomach turning when I spot blood on his shirt. Camari drops down beside the man and examines his wound with expert precision, ignoring his groans as he turns his head from side to side, not opening his eyes. Blood soaks through the shoulder of his shirt and begins to seep into the ground, staining the dirt a muddy crimson.

"I need something to use as a bandage, a blanket or a towel," Camari says quickly, a hint of panic in her voice.

"Here, take this," I say, taking off my tunic and handing it to her. She takes it and quickly wraps it around the man's shoulder, pushing it down with her hands. Blood continues to gush, though, and soon my shirt is similarly soaked, the blood coating Camari's hands.

"It's not enough!" she exclaims, looking around frantically." Do you have a jacket or something?"

"No. Let me go ask at the tavern; surely they'll find something?"

"There isn't time." Camari closes her eyes, her face paling excessively until each of her freckles stands out like a mark on a map. She curses under her breath and then sits back, lifting her hands to the buttons of the cover she perpetually wears. She unbuttons it quickly, her hands shaking, and pulls it off, trembling. She immediately begins to wrap it around the man's shoulder, her back turned to me, but all I can do is stand and stare. Stare at the brown marks trailing from the tops of her shoulders to her wrists, the ones visible through the fabric of her shift. Stare at the scalsen that seem to encase both of her arms.

Gods have mercy. *Camari is a seer.*

I hear someone inhale sharply behind me and turn around, spotting Morris staring at Camari with similar shock. His eyes meet mine, and I shake my head, answering his silent question. I wave my hand swiftly in his direction before turning back to Camari and he nods, slinking away quickly.

Camari has finished wrapping the man's shoulder and is pushing down on it. She stays that way for several minutes, not speaking or even acknowledging my presence, and I stand there silently, a weight settling heavily in my heart.

Finally, she slowly sits back on her heels and lifts her hands, studying the wound. "Okay, we can move him slowly. We need to get him back to Adeline's."

She stands, wiping her hands on her skirt to no avail, and gestures towards the man without looking at me. "You'll need to carry him, and we need to move quickly. I-I need to get back to the cottage."

To get another cover. I fill in her sentence mentally, carefully picking up the unconscious man. My shoulder twinges slightly at his weight, but otherwise is fine, and I begin to quickly walk back to the cottage. Camari says nothing to me the entire walk and moves quickly in front of me, crossing her arms over her chest and jumping at every noise. It pains me to see the confident young woman I know reduced to a jumpy, fearful girl, desperate to hide her arms again. I realize she's probably hidden them her whole life, that no one's seen her marks before. So who told her what they are, and that she should hide them?

When we reach the cottage, the front room is empty and Camari sighs in relief, pointing towards the patient bed before running into her bedroom. She returns moments later with a new cover on, her hands still shaking. She ignores my gaze as she goes about taking care of the man, cleaning and sewing up his wound before wrapping it in a thick layer of bandages. Mistress Dorsar returns when Camari is halfway done and helps her finish up, not paying me any attention.

I sneak away and return to the tavern to wash the blood off of me and get a new shirt before I walk back to Camari's, suspecting she's going to want to talk to me. Sure enough, she's sitting on the ground outside her door when I walk up, wringing her hands in front of her nervously. When she spots me she shoots up, her eyes widening slightly. I wait several seconds in silence, watching her as she thinks over what she's going to say. Some stupid part of me wants her to tell me the truth, wants her to trust me with it. But she's too smart for that.

"I was born with excessive birthmarks, caused by complications from my mothers' pregnancy." She begins quietly, still wringing her hands. "They're nothing contagious or anything like that; I just have always had them. I hide them because people might get the wrong ideas if they see them, and no one has *ever* seen them."

Her dark eyes are wide as she speaks, and when she finally meets my gaze, I can't look away. They're dark pools of fear, hurt, longing, and regret, and they call to my own pain-filled past like a siren.

I swallow hard, resisting the urge to reach for her, to comfort her. I have to remind myself that this is all a lie, that she's been lying to me for the past three weeks. And I had no idea she could lie so well.

"Please, I know they're weird and ugly and such," she swallows hard, and it sounds as if she's repeating something she's been told before. "But I'm begging you, don't tell anyone. They already hate me; they already think I'm strange. If you tell people, I don't know-"

"Camari, it's okay." I interrupt, surprising even myself when I take one of her hands in mine. Gods, why did I do that? It's so small compared to mine, her skin as soft as a flower's petal.

She cuts off, surprise evident on every inch of her face, and stares at our joined hands before looking up at me.

"I-I won't tell anyone," I promise, my heart breaking. Even if I could keep that promise, Morris has already seen her, too. By now, all of my men know. And it shouldn't matter; this entire scared look is most likely just a façade. And yet, it makes me feel violently ill to know I'm stuck.

There's nothing I can do.

"You won't? Oh, thank you!" Camari gasps in relief, her eyes pooling with water. Before I know it, she's thrown her arms around my neck and is hugging me, her shoulders shaking in relief. I can't stop myself from hugging her back, my arms enveloping her tiny waist. Her scent of rosemary and honey envelops me, and I close my eyes, hating myself more and more with each second. How dare I hug her? How dare I *touch* her at all? She deserves so much better than this.

And yet, I can't get myself to let her go.

All of my men are waiting for me in my room when I get back, their faces solemn.

"So, what's the plan?" Grant asks, looking pained, as I'm sure I do. I swallow, nausea burning in my throat and stomach at what I'm about to say. But I have no choice. My freewill was stolen from me the moment I signed the contract. I know the consequences of breaking it.

"The morning we depart. We'll take her then and bring her with us to the caravan. She'll go to the facility with all of the other seers."

R.C. Huye

The highest order of the law is obedience to your sovereign and king. Failure to uphold this law will result in death or a punishment akin to it.

–Excerpt from Zordan Laws and Commandments

Chapter Nine

Camari

I move my spoon around my bowl of stew idly, lost in thought. I've been reliving the previous day's events since I woke up, my brain seemingly unable to process what occurred.

I've never shown anyone my birthmarks. Adeline made sure I knew not to from a very young age. *People won't like them. They'll see them and they'll hate you. People don't like ugly things,* she would tell me over and over as she helped me button up my cover when I was little. Those words have always stuck. *People don't like ugly things.* But Aiden didn't seem to think they were ugly. I thought he did; the shocked look on his face made me feel ashamed and disgusted with myself all over again. But then he came back, and he didn't think I was ugly; he didn't hate me.

He came back.

THE CURSE OF THE BLESSED

I look down at my left hand where it is resting on the table. When he took my hand, I almost stopped breathing. My skin tingled wherever he touched it, almost as if it was on fire. I had no idea I could feel like that. Greta told me once that when her husband kissed her for the first time, it was like fire, and that's when she knew she was in love. I never believed her; I always thought she was just storytelling, but now I'm not so sure. When Aiden took my hand, when he wrapped his arms around my waist -

"Cam, are you alright?" I startle from my thoughts with a physical jolt, looking up to find Adeline watching me in concern. "You've been staring at the table for the past five minutes."

"I'm alright, only tired," I assure her, sitting up straighter in my chair and forcing a spoonful of cold stew down my throat.

"I take it the tradesmen are leaving tomorrow?" Adeline asks, looking at me over the top of her bowl, a strange look in her eyes. "Have you said goodbye to Aiden?"

"Yes. They leave too early tomorrow morning for me to wake up and see them off," I lie, looking down at my stew and avoiding my mother's eyes. I went the entire day without seeing Aiden, and I was beginning to wonder if he was going to leave without saying goodbye, but he stopped by just before sunset and asked me to meet him on the outskirts of the village in the morning so that he could say goodbye. When I saw him coming, my heart raced, and I agreed without thinking. Maybe Adeline was right when she called me a fool. But it's Aiden, *my* Aiden, though I don't know when I started thinking of him as such. And after tomorrow morning, I won't see him again for a long time, if ever. I want every second I can get.

"I know you'll miss your friend, but it will be nice for things to go back to normal," Adeline says, smiling softly to herself. I hum my agreement, unwilling to admit that I dread the return of normality. It will be straight back to being lonely with only Walter for company, whom I now know for certain I have no romantic feelings for. Adeline may like normal life, but I do not. I want *more*.

"Are you sure you're alright, Cam? You're not having another episode, are you?" Adeline asks me, raising an eyebrow expectantly. I quickly shake my head, defusing her suspicions.

"I really am just tired. I think I'll go to bed early if it's alright with you," I say, rising from the table. Adeline nods wordlessly, and I can feel her gaze on my back as I walk into our bedroom, shutting the door behind me. Kicking off my boots, I take off my cover, bodice, and skirt and climb into bed, wearing only my shift, eager for the next morning to arrive. I hold the pendant I wear around my neck, the one I found in the woods. I wasn't sure why, but when I finally remembered it, I couldn't bring myself to return it. And now I simply desire to keep it because it's his.

Oh gods. I am in so much trouble.

THE CURSE OF THE BLESSED

I lay awake early the next morning, staring at the roof as the sun slowly rises, bringing with it a faint golden light. I've been awake for several hours, kept awake by nightmares of sticks cracking under my feet and the shouting of men that made no sense.

Being careful not to make the bed creak, I slip out from under my blanket and begin to dress, pulling on a fresh shift, my clothes and boots, and finally, the dagger that I tuck into the waistband of my skirt. I briefly contemplate wearing my only dress instead of the skirt and bodice I wear almost daily, but decide against it. That would be too much, and I'm nervous enough as it is without feeling the need to justify what I'm wearing should Aiden not feel…should things go differently than I hope. Running a brush through my hair, I loosely braid it back, the long braid hanging down to my lower back. I pause by the door as I pull on my cover, adjusting the sleeves as I glance over my shoulder. If Adeline wakes while I'm gone, she might worry. Grabbing a scrap of parchment and a charcoal pencil, I quickly leave a note on the table.

Adeline,

I agreed to help Greta set up her stand today; I'll be back before lunch. I remembered my cover; don't worry.

Love,

Cam.

I make sure my cover is secure before I step quietly out of the door, slowly lowering the latch behind me. Krakent is silent this early in the morning, mist still hovering in the air as the sun has yet to burn it away. I enjoy the cool morning air as I walk, tilting my face back to greet the sun's rays.

I walk quickly and leave Krakent twenty minutes later, stopping to wait for Aiden. I don't have to wait long before Aiden appears, riding towards me on his horse, the mist curling around his horse's feet. My heart skips once again at the sight of him, and I can't help the smile that breaks across my face. He looks so handsome, sitting tall on his saddle. If I didn't know better I would think he was a soldier, not a mere tradesman.

Aiden dismounts and approaches me, his horse's reins in one hand while the other rests in his trouser pocket.

"Well, look at you back on your horse," I say, glancing at his mare with admiration. Aiden smiles weakly, his hazel eyes shimmering with something akin to regret. A pang of unease shoots through me, and my smile fades. Something isn't right; I can feel it in my bones. This isn't the way I thought I'd feel saying goodbye to him, not sad, but…afraid. "Aiden, are you okay?"

"I'm so sorry, Camari, more sorry than you'll ever know," he says softly, his voice filled with resignation. In fact, everything about him has changed from the vibrant young man I know to a dark, shadowed man who appears miserable in his own skin. This isn't my Aiden.

"Sorry for what?" I ask as unease steals into my gut. I've never seen Aiden like this; he's so…sad.

"I can't let you go," he says quietly, holding my gaze. Anyone listening in might think that was a romantic confession, but I know him; I can read him. He's not speaking metaphorically right now. My hand goes to the hilt of my dagger, and I take a step back, filled with cold unease.

"What do you mean?" I ask, fighting to keep my voice even as every bone in my body begins to scream at me that this is not right.

"NOW!" Aiden shouts suddenly, his voice cracking just barely, and I don't give it a second thought, dropping my hand as I turn around and bolt back the way I came, picking up my skirts as I run. I hear footsteps that are then replaced by the sounds of a horse's hooves. Suddenly two horses shoot out of the mist, pulling up in front of me and rearing, caging me in. I shriek in terror and narrowly turn to the right, pushing myself off the ground as my feet skid in mud, and continue to run. I hear more horses coming, and I run into the forest, panting and thinking desperately as fear pumps through my veins. What do they want? What are they going to do to me? Why Aiden? Why would he do this?

It doesn't matter; none of them know the forest like I do; I'll be able to escape.

Jumping a log, I round the group of birches only to fall backward as two more horses appear, circling me so that I'm trapped against the trees. I refuse to give up and clamber to my feet, beginning to climb the nearest tree with shaking hands. My breath comes out of me in pants due to exertion and terror. I'm pulling my foot onto a higher branch when a hand catches my ankle, pulling on my leg.

"NO!" I shriek, holding on to the branch above me with all of my strength as panic shoots through me. Another hand clamps onto the same leg and I am pulled on again, my hands slipping on their hold. Tightening my grip on the branch, I lift my free leg from its step so that I am hanging from just my hands, and I twist, striking behind me with my free foot. The heel of my boot connects with someone's face and I hear a muffled curse as my leg is released. I pull it up quickly and go to climb onto the next branch, only for it to snap under my weight. I fall down to the forest floor, the air leaving my lungs as I hit the leaves. I cough, dazed, and roll over, gasping for air and struggling to get to my feet. Hands grip my upper arms and haul me up, Eben's voice by my ear, cursing.

"Bloody bitch, up and broke my nose!"

"Be gentle, she's just defending herself," Aiden orders as he appears on his mare, followed by Miller and Morris.

"Let me go, you bastards!" I scream, twisting around. I manage to get Eben to lose his grip and immediately drop to the forest floor, rolling so that I rise to my feet with my dagger out.

Aiden takes a step closer and I turn, pointing my dagger at him. "Don't come any closer! None of you move."

Aiden stops, raising his hands, and I take a deep breath, shoving my hair out of my face. "Turn around, walk away, and leave me alone," I say with forced calm, my hands shaking.

"We can't, Camari," Aiden says, risking another step forward.

"Yes, you can! I don't know what you want, but I have no money, nothing but a knowledge of herbs. You know that! You know *me*. Let me go!" I beg, my breathing choppy. Aiden's eyes glint again, and he tilts his head.

"You truly have no idea what you are, do you?" He sounds genuinely surprised, his hands lowering.

"I'm pissed, that's what I am," I counter, my chest heaving against my bodice as I fight to calm my breathing. Grant snorts, receiving a glare from Aiden.

"No, Camari, you're not normal, you are a-"

Morris takes a step forward, his hand resting on the hilt of his sword and pulling it out halfway. I throw my dagger at him without hesitation and Aiden cuts off, shouting, "NO!"

Miller dives in front of the other man, knocking him down. The knife scratches his shoulder, and he hisses in pain, practically spitting in rage. My weapon gone, I turn to run but am tackled to the ground by Aiden, my face pushed down into the mulch and mud.

"NO! Let me go! Adeline needs me; let me go!" I scream, trying and failing to throw him off, succeeding only in getting mud in my mouth.

"I can't, Camari, I can't let you go!" Aiden yells at me before grabbing my wrists and hauling me up, holding my arms behind my back. I struggle for a few seconds before seeing that it is pointless. I will be better off saving my strength.

Eben comes forward and ties my hands in front of me, pulling the rope painfully tight with a vengeful grin. Morris begins to tend to Miller, and Grant walks forward with an extra horse that I deduce is for me.

"I save your life; I welcome you into my home, into my *life,* and you repay me by kidnapping me?" I ask Aiden as he leads me over to where everyone else is, all of them giving me either wary or guilty looks.

"Yes," he replies, pushing on my shoulders so that I sit down on the ground with a thump. I stare at his face, studying the man that I thought I knew, the man that I grew to care for over the past three weeks. But I see none of him. It's like I'm looking at an entirely new person, a man who hides his emotions so well I almost think he doesn't have any. That dark, sad man from the road just minutes ago has been replaced. Aiden is still shadowed, his eyes empty and his face blank, but that sorrow and depression are gone, replaced by a stern, focused look. The man I thought I knew, the man I let myself care for...he's not there at all. I never knew Aiden; I just wanted to think I did.

I am a fool.

"It took five men to catch one nineteen year old girl; pathetic," I spit, turning my anger on them rather than myself as my eyes burn with tears that I refuse to shed. Not in front of them.

Eben's nostrils flare and he stalks over. "No, it took five men to catch a demon-possessed bitch!"

"Eben, enough!" Aiden snaps. Eben huffs but nods, wiping blood off of his face with the back of his hand.

"I'll get out of here, and I'll report you to the king!" I threaten, looking into Aiden's eyes. The corner of his mouth tweaks up coldly and he speaks in a calm voice despite my threats.

"Go for it, tell the king."

"You don't care that you'll be executed?" I ask incredulously.

"Morris, what will happen when the king finds out what we've done?" Aiden calls, never looking away from my eyes. Morris looks up from where he is bandaging Miller's shoulder, his face also colder. Though I did just throw a blade at his head.

"We'll get a bloody award and a raise, that's what."

My blood chills and I take a shaky breath. "You work for the king."

"No shit, we work for the king," Eben grumbles, earning another look from Aiden. My mind races as I think everything through.

"I thought you were *tradesmen!* What does the king want with me? Are you bounty hunters? I'm just a healer's daughter; I'm no one!" I'm so confused; none of this makes sense.

Am I a prisoner of the king?

Aiden crouches in front of me and pulls out his dagger. I shrink away from him, clutching my arms to my chest. For a moment, I think I see a glimmer of regret in his eyes, but then it's gone. He grabs my arm and pulls it to his chest forcefully, slicing my cover away so that my arm is revealed to everyone. My heart aches at his betrayal as he shows my birthmarks to everyone, as he breaks his promise. I can't help the tear that makes its way down my cheek as my heart breaks, all of the trust I had in him dissipating.

"Do you know what these are?" Aiden asks, putting away his dagger. He then gently grabs a strand of my hair, his fingers brushing my neck and eliciting goosebumps, and holds it up in front of me so that I can see it. "Do you know what this is?"

"Yes, it's my hair and my arm." I shoot back, turning my head so that my hair slips from his grasp. He just ignores my attitude, gesturing to my forearm.

"These marks are called scalsen, and your hair is unnaturally bright and vibrant because it is your colorful trait," he explains, gesturing to that which he speaks of.

"No, they are called birthmarks, and my hair is just bright; it's not unnatural. Skies above, you are picky about your women," I say in a forced, angry tone, even as uncertainty echoes through my core. His words pluck some string in me that has been silent my whole life, and now it's starting to sing.

"Every one of your kind has an unnaturally colorful feature; hair, eyes, skin, nails, anything. And each one of you has scalsen somewhere. You have a lot of them, which just shows how powerful you'll be."

"What do you mean, *my kind*?" I ask despite myself, forcing bravado into my voice. Something tells me I don't want his answer. "Have healers been segregated into their own species?"

"You are a seer, Camari."

I inhale sharply, pulling away from him. "No, I'm not. I'm… different, but I'm not a seer!"

"Have you ever had such a strong feeling where it doesn't make sense, but you know what's about to happen?"

I stare at him, remembering my last episode, remembering the nightmares that kept me awake last night, remembering every moment when I knew what was going to happen before it did. This doesn't make sense. And yet…

Something on my face must answer his question because he stands and turns, walking over to the horses. But I still have questions, even as so many pieces fall into place.

"If you think I'm a seer, why don't you kill me? That's your job, isn't it? You're with the group of soldiers that went through town a moon ago after pillaging two seer villages; you're one of the kings seer hunters. So why don't you kill me?"

Aiden turns back, his eyes burning with something that I can't decipher, and crouches down in front of me once more, speaking in a low tone so that only I can hear. "Contrary to what you believe, I don't like killing seers. I don't want to kill you, Camari; that's the last thing I want. So don't give me a reason to.

To be a seer is to be a fruit that has rotted beyond salvation. The rot spreads from one to the next, and in the end it is necessary to eliminate the fruit before the rot consumes everyone and everything.

–King Aldred

Chapter Ten

Camari

I sit on the forest floor, staring at my feet as I force myself to breathe calmly. Am I a *seer?*

So many questions I've always had about myself are immediately answered and replaced with so many more. But no, I can't be a seer! I'm not. I'm not a seer; they're wrong. This is all just a bunch of co-incidences. How could I possibly be a seer? Seers are corrupted by power, insane and evil. They manipulate the future and have visions at will. I am none of those things and can do none of those things. Aiden is wrong. He has to be.

My captors are conferring a ways away from me, talking in hushed tones that I can't hear despite how hard I try. At one point, Aiden smacks Eben on the side of the head out of nowhere, making me jump, and Eben growls out something that has Aiden reluctantly nodding. When they finally turn back to where I'm sitting on the ground, I don't bother hiding that I've been trying to listen, watching them closely. Aiden walks towards me while the other four go about getting their horses ready, including the extra palomino that I assume will be for me. He stops in front of me, crouching down to meet my gaze.

"We are on our way to Sutoran, as I've no doubt you've already deduced. We will save a day of travel by going through Krakent instead of around it, and you will stay quiet, hidden beneath a cloak and hood. You will say nothing, you will not act out, and you will obey every order we give."

I scoff, tossing my head. "You honestly believe I'll be willingly kidnapped away and escorted from my home? Oh yes, that is logical."

Aiden grabs onto the rope around my wrists, tugging me closer and narrowing his eyes. They're cold, lacking any emotion. Lacking any part of the man I've come to care about over the past three weeks. "No, I don't expect you to listen. That is why I will make you a promise right here, right now. If you try to escape, if you disobey a single order and make yourself known to anyone you know, we will kill your mother."

I freeze, my heart stuttering. His eyes are serious, stone cold and firm. "You wouldn't," I whisper in horror, thinking of Adeline alone in the cottage, waiting for me to get home. She'll be getting worried by now, pacing across the floor or tugging at her hair.

"Yes, we would; if it's our only option, we will."

"You're evil," I whisper, unable to speak louder than that. His eyes flash with emotion but it is snuffed out almost immediately, replaced by a wall that I am already becoming familiar with.

"Maybe, but if your mother dies, it won't be on my hands. It will be on yours."

My heart squeezes as I realize he is right; if I disobey him before we leave Krakent, they'll go after her, and it will be my fault. I now know the consequences.

"Do we have a deal?" Aiden asks, standing up and crossing his arms. I stare up at him, my heart aching in my chest. When I first saw him I thought him handsome, I thought him kind, I let myself trust him. He is truly a monster.

"Yes, we have a deal." I force the words out, my voice rasping in my throat. He nods, turning and walking back to his men. I stare numbly at the ground, my lungs constricting with fear. This is real; this is actually happening. I am being kidnapped, taken away to probably be executed, and I can't try to get help in Krakent because then they will kill Adeline.

Oh gods, how can you let this be? I look up, peering at the slivers of sky visible through the leafy canopy. A surprising amount of time has passed; it is past lunchtime. They took far longer to plan than I thought. Adeline will be worried, possibly even out looking for me in the village. Whatever happens, I can't let her see me. It will seal her fate.

Aiden approaches again, holding a heavy black cloak with a large hood. He grabs my bound wrists and pulls me up effortlessly before wrapping the cloak around my shoulders, tying it at my neck and pulling the folds forward to conceal my clothes and bound hands. He refuses to meet my gaze as he fusses with the folds for far longer than is necessary, and I come to an abrupt conclusion. "You don't want to do this."

Aiden looks up at me sharply, his hands pausing on the rough fabric. "What are you talking about?"

"I can see it on your face. You don't want to do this; you don't want to kidnap me."

"You don't know what you're talking about," he says roughly, finishing with the ties on the cloak and pulling the hood up to conceal my face, hiding my hair from view and casting my entire face in shadows.

"Maybe, but I know at least some of who you are. You can't have lied about every second of the past three weeks I've known you; some of that had to have at least a glimmer of truth. You don't want this job; you don't like it; you might even hate it," I say as he adjusts my hood so that it conceals the most it can. His eyes bore into mine like cold steel when he meets my gaze, cold and angry. But I see the flicker of doubt in their depths.

"And how do you know that?" he snaps.

"Because otherwise, I would already be dead." My heart racing, I take it one step further and reach up, resting my bound hands on his where they hold the fabric of my cloak. He stares down at them for a moment before he looks back up at me, and before my eyes, I see him again, the man I know. I see the truth he is trying to hide from everyone, and the absolute torment on his face knocks the wind out of me.

Why is he doing this? What do they have on him?

"Can you truly tell me that these past three weeks meant nothing?" I ask quietly, my voice shaking slightly. "That two nights ago meant nothing? Can you honestly tell me that it was all an act?"

Aiden swallows hard, his grip on my cloak tightening. His eyes seem to practically burn with unspoken words, and hope races through me. And then his eyes flicker away from mine towards a movement behind me and he's gone, if he was ever truly there at all.

"I suppose you were far more naive than you thought," he says flatly, his hands dropping away. He turns around and walks to his horse, and Grant walks by from behind me a moment later, skirting me with a wide berth. I exhale slowly, my hands dropping as my lips tremble. There is nothing I can do. I cannot stand here and try to redeem a man who has done nothing but prove he never existed, that he was all a lie. I hate how much it hurts, and I hate the fear that is now taking over my thoughts.

Taking his mare's reins, Aiden leads her over to me and swings up into the saddle in one smooth motion. He holds his hand down to me and I frown at it, taking half a step back.

"What are you doing?"

"I'm not a fool, Camari. I know I can't give you your own horse, not until we've passed Krakent. You'll be riding with me until we are through the village; it will stop you from doing anything rash."

I clench my jaw, looking around. The other men are mounting their own horses, and the extra palomino is tied to the back of Grant's saddle. This appears to be my first order.

Gritting my teeth, I give him my bound wrists, grasping his forearm awkwardly with my hand. He helps pull me up, and I land in the saddle behind him with a plop, my skirt riding up to my knees. I quickly adjust my skirt and my new cloak so that I am completely covered. Unable to wrap my hands around his waist, I settle for holding on to the leather strap of his baldrick, squeezing it between my hands so that I won't fall off when the horse begins to move.

"Everyone ready?" Aiden calls to Eben, his torso vibrating beneath my hands where my knuckles are touching his back. His men reply that they are ready, Grant casting me an oddly pitying smile despite my situation. Though maybe that too was a figment of my naive imagination. Aiden nudges his mare into movement, leading the way back to the main road and leaving me to hold on tightly to the leather strap of his baldrick so that I don't go tumbling onto the forest floor, for the second time that day.

THE CURSE OF THE BLESSED

My heart beats at an unsteady pace as Krakent comes into sight, and I dig my fingernails into the leather strap, taking shaky breaths. My hands shake, and I feel hot all over, not just from the heat and the extra layers but also from the anxiety that pulses through me.

What if someone recognizes me? What if Adeline sees me? I believe firmly that even with this cloak on and with my hair and face concealed, she will recognize me if she sees me. I can't risk letting that happen. I squeeze the baldrick's strap tighter, my breath wheezing in and out.

"Slow, deep exhales, Camari, you're in a panic. Stay calm and loosen your grip. You're choking me." Aiden's voice startles me slightly, but I do as he instructs, though I yank slightly on the baldrick before loosening my grip. He adjusts it over his chest before glancing over his shoulder at me.

"Just do as I say, and everything will be fine."

"Easier said than done. I am easily recognized in this village; everyone knows me," I say, my voice still coming out shaky. "And after the three weeks that you were staying here, all of you are easily recognized as well."

"We'll deal with that if and when the time comes," Aiden responds, his voice losing the warmer tone that I hadn't noticed he'd added until it was gone again. Its absence is a stark contrast to how he used to speak. Now, he is all orders and commands, no emotions.

We enter the edge of town and I tilt my head down, my hood concealing me completely. Twenty minutes at the most, and I'll be okay; Adeline will be okay. Twenty minutes.

A few people look up at us as we ride by. Then more people look. And more, until I can feel their stares boring into my shoulder blades. "Aiden, this isn't working. They're all staring."

"Maybe it's just because they're not used to seeing us on our horses," Aiden mutters, his back vibrating as he speaks.

"No, it's because you're riding your horses through town accompanied by a stranger in a cloak in the peak of summer."

"You're overthinking this."

"And *you're* missing the point. I'm drawing attention to myself, and that's not good. You're getting plenty of attention already, and the cloak is just amplifying it. If I'm recognized, it's because the bloody cloak is drawing stares, not banishing them, and if you kill my mother because of your failed plan, I will-"

"Just give me a minute; let me think!" Aiden snaps, his shoulders tensing. A second later he lifts his hand and makes a gesture to the riders behind us before he turns his horse down an empty street, pulling over in the shadows before dismounting and helping me down. His four men ride up and dismount.'

"What's going on; is she causing problems?" Eben asks, sending a glare at me. I glare right back.

"Do you think I'm here out of choice?"

Aiden steps between us before Eben has a chance to reply, giving me a warning look over his shoulder. "Enough. Look, the cloak is drawing too much attention; it's doing the opposite of what we'd hoped. We need a new plan."

"We can't just let her walk down the street with us; everyone will recognize her and know she left with us!" Morris objects, crossing his arms. Grant and Eben nod their agreement while Miller simply stands quietly, watching us.

"First of all, it's not like I'm going to do something; I know what you'll do!" I snap, shooting a glare at Aiden. "Second, I have an idea, but it involves you trusting that I love Adeline enough not to risk her life for mine."

Aiden nods for me to continue, while Eben just looks disgruntled that I am being allowed to speak at all.

"Everyone here who knows me knows that I go on lots of walks out of the village. I will walk ahead calmly, and you will ride a good distance behind me until I'm out of town."

"Hell no!" Eben exclaims at the same time that Morris objects, "Yeah, right, I should give you my sword while I'm at it."

Aiden holds up his hand for silence, his face un-moving as he holds my gaze. "How can we know we can trust you?"

"You'd be a fool to trust me; I'll slit your throats given the chance."

Eben grunts, crossing his arms again and scowling at me. Aiden's lip twitches, and I spot it again, that glimmer of the man I thought I knew.

But he isn't real.

"But I won't risk Adeline's life, as I've made clear. Besides, you'll only be a meter or two behind me the entire time, and I can't outrun five horses." I point out bitterly.

Aiden glances at the men and they seem to have a silent conversation between them, consisting of facial gestures and chin jerks. I stand silently, watching them.

Finally, Aiden turns to me, his arms crossed. "If you break your word, I won't just kill your mother; I'll kill you. Miller can shoot you from fifteen yards."

I glare at him, narrowing my eyes as disgust pounds through me. "I already knew that, but thank you for the reminder."

Aiden holds my gaze for several seconds, his eyes scrutinizing me. Finally, he nods. "Okay, let's do it."

THE CURSE OF THE BLESSED

My shoulders feel remarkably lighter as I walk down the street, relieved of the heavy cloak. My wrists are unbound as well, and I pull my sleeves down to cover the red, raw skin. I now blend in with the people who walk down the sides of the street, ignoring the five stares boring into my back. I force a faint smile and make myself walk normally, with my chin up and my shoulders back, despite the turmoil my life has become.

Turning the corner, I come onto Seller's Street, the merchants fast at work. The sun burning down from above makes sweat trickle down my back. At least, I blame it on the sun.

No one gives me a second glance. As soon as they see me, they turn and continue on their way, just like always. For once, I am grateful for how unpopular I am among the village; none of them will stop to talk to me.

"Camari!"

Almost none of them.

I stop, spinning on my heel and pasting a smile onto my face as I see Greta waving at me excitedly from her stall, the soaps piled high in towers of different pastel colors.

"Hello Greta, how are you today?" I ask, walking up to her with a smile. Out of the corner of my eye, I see my captors slow their horses at the end of the street, watching me.

"I am well; I just wanted to ask you how your mother liked the soap!"

I remember the soap I bought, still sitting in my pocket. "I forgot to give it to her; it's still in my pocket." I hesitate, struck by an idea. "Actually, she might drop by today. If I leave it with you and write a note, could you give it to her?"

Greta frowns, tilting her head to the side. "Why can't you just give it to her yourself?"

"Oh, I'm going out of town for a few days, and I already said goodbye this morning."

"Okay, well I should be able to do that then."

"Wonderful, thank you!" I say with a cheery smile. Greta retrieves a scrap of paper and a charcoal pencil while I take the bar of soap out of my pocket, placing it on the counter. I write quickly, knowing I am still being watched.

Dear Mama,

I'm sorry. I disobeyed you, I made a foolish mistake, and now I'm paying for it. I know that you've lied, but I just wanted to let you know that you are forgiven. I love you, and I'm sorry.

Love, Camari.

I fold it up and hand it back to Greta with a smile, bidding her a cheery farewell before continuing down the street, my hands shaking.

"What was that?"

I jump as a hand wraps around my waist gently, and Aiden falls into step beside me, his shadow enveloping me. Glancing over my shoulder, I see that his horse is tied to the back of Miller's saddle, plodding along without its rider.

"I ordered a piece of soap to be sent to my uncle in Fallisae a few days ago and she asked me to give her the address again, that's all," I mutter, making a lie up on the spot as I try and fail to subtly shove Aiden's arm away. I hate that I still know his scent, that a minuscule part of me is still urging me to lean in closer. That part will have to learn the consequences of betrayal.

I must have been convincing with my lie because Aiden buys it, walking along beside me like a man spending time with his lover. "Well, now I'll be walking with you, just to make sure you don't have any more *uncles.*"

Maybe he didn't buy it.

I force myself to keep walking, force myself to let Aiden keep his arm around my waist as we walk down the street, the picture of amicable beaus. Several people glance at me, recognize Aiden and I, and go on their way again. A few weeks ago they would have stared incredulously and gossiped about it, but they're used to the sight of Aiden and I together now. Maybe if they weren't, they would be able to see that something is wrong. But they don't.

Aiden is quiet for a few moments, and when he speaks, it's in a low, quiet voice that rumbles up his throat. "I'm sorry."

I jolt slightly, turning to look at him. "Excuse me?"

"I'm sorry about all of this, Camari. I would maybe have…I don't know, but Morris saw you when you took your cover off, and he told the others. By then, it was too late," he says, his voice heavy. I stare at his face, my heart beginning to race as I recognize him again, as the mask of darkness falls away. The man I care for is still there…but is he real?

"Why?" I ask, my heart pounding. "Why does it have to be too late? I trusted you, Aiden. I don't trust many people, but I trusted *you*. I let you into my life."

"And I should never have let you," he responds, suddenly sounding angry. But not with me. "I should have walked away as soon as I was able; I just…I couldn't…I couldn't let you go."

His sentence fades off with those words, now filled with an entirely different meaning than before, and he falls silent, staring at me. I swallow, his eyes like flames to me, the moth. A silence falls around us where everything else fades, and for a moment it's just us in the universe. Then his eyes flicker to my mouth, and I jolt back into the present, my face burning. It takes several moments for me to realize we've stopped walking as well as talking and are just staring at each other. Standing very close.

I successfully shove his arm away as I jump back, digging my fingernails into my palms. That can't happen again. He *isn't* the Aiden I know. The Aiden I knew was virtuous and good. He would never play these mind games. "You're right; you *should* have walked away. Don't forget why I'm here, Aiden. I'm here because you are abducting me, forcefully taking me away from my home and my mother so that your king can kill me. Your apology will *never* be enough."

"He won't kill you," Aiden growls, a dark presence in his voice giving his words more meaning than he probably intended. "I'll make sure of it, he won't."

"Yes, because thus far your intentions have been so trustworthy," I spit, pulling away from him even further. He lets me walk alone, though he makes sure to stay within arm's reach in case I try to run.

We walk the rest of the way in silence, and we are almost to the edge of the village; we are almost out, walking down the last street that leads to the main road. Then I see Adeline.

She is walking down the street, her brow furrowed, her dark eyes worried. She doesn't see me, but I see her.

"No!" I gasp, panic flaring through my chest. I turn and duck behind a large beech tree, pressing my chest to it and peering around to watch her as she walks. She is rubbing the scars on her arm, something she only ever does when she worries. A pang of guilt shoots through me as I realize that I am the cause of that worry. She'll see Greta in just a few minutes; she'll receive my note and know that I am gone. I watch her walk away down the street, her blonde braid swishing against her back. I step out from behind the tree, watching as she rounds the corner and disappears from my view. And from my life.

When I turn to Aiden, he is studying me, frowning slightly at my expression. "What?" I ask crossly, crossing my arms over my chest and shifting my weight from one foot to the other.

"Nothing," is his reply. I ignore him, walking down the street with a heavy sigh. A few minutes later, we leave the village and are waiting on the side of the main road. Aiden leans against a tree while I pace, his hands tucked in his pockets. I can feel his gaze on me the entire time I pace, and I struggle to ignore it, to forget about what happened between us fifteen minutes ago. Because nothing happened, and nothing will happen.

His men ride up a few minutes later, and Eben immediately dismounts, pulling out another coil of rope and approaching me with a grin. I scowl as my wrists are bound, the knots pulled far tighter than necessary.

"I think that's sufficient," I growl through gritted teeth as Eben yanks it even tighter. He smiles at me, a smile completely lacking warmth, and turns back to his horse. I walk over to where the palomino stands, now tied to the back of Aiden's saddle so that I can't run off. Aiden helps me up, and I grip the reins as best I can with my bound hands, scowling again.

"You did well in Krakent, Camari; thank you for listening," Aiden tells me, his hands resting on my horse's neck.

"I didn't do it for you!" I snap, tossing my ragged braid back over my shoulder as best I can with tied wrists. He nods curtly, his hands slipping away from my horse. He turns and mounts his mare before nodding to his men and nudging his horse with his heels so that we start moving.

Aiden and I ride in the lead, my horse maybe half a foot behind his, while Miller rides in the back, scanning the area. Eben catches my gaze several times, always smiling viscously at me, a smile that holds a promise. I make a mental reminder to never be left alone with him.

I glance back once and find that Krakent is no longer in sight. With each step of my horse, I ride farther and farther away from the only home I've ever known.

R.C. Huye

King Rian reigned for 52 years and under him, Okara was born. Civilization flourished, different towns and villages were established, and the city of Sutoran was built, Sutoran in the ancient language translating to 'eternal grace.'

–Retractions from the Royal Historical Documents

Chapter Eleven

Aiden

I can feel her stare burning into my back as we ride, the swaying of our horses doing nothing to prevent her from boring a hole with her gaze. I thought I was living in hell before I met her, before I went to Krakent. I was a fool; I now know what hell is. Hell is developing feelings for someone you've lied to and betrayed. Hell is being around them every minute of every day while they hate you. While at the same time, you hate yourself for what you've done. But you're too weak to try to fix it.

"Stop it," I say without turning around.

"Stop what?" she asks, her voice bored and angry. She has so much anger, so much fight. It's admirable.

"Staring at me, stop staring at me."

"Oh, is something I'm doing making my kidnapper slightly uncomfortable? Well, by all means, I will stop! My only dream in life is to please you." Her voice drips with sarcasm and disdain. I sigh, knowing I deserve it but despising it all the same. I hate that I have to do this; I hate that this is who I've become. I should never have gotten close to her. I was walking a thin line, and at some point, I strayed. And I strayed far.

"Are you going to be like this for our entire journey?" I ask after a few moments. Gods, I know this is a horrible situation for her, but that doesn't make me crave her company any less. It doesn't make me want her any less.

I'm so weak.

"Do you honestly expect me to be happy to be snatched away from my home? What do you want from me, Aiden?" she snaps, sounding as lost as I feel.

If only you knew.

"I didn't want to take you, Camari, but-"

"But what?" she interrupts, her horse coming up beside me so that I can see her face. Her eyes burn with anger and grief, both caused by me, a thought that makes my chest hurt. Their dark depths catch my gaze, and refuse to let go. "If you truly didn't want to, then you wouldn't have done it. No one can force you to do something. The king isn't here; you could let me go, and no one would be the wiser, but you won't."

"I can't! I signed a contract, enlisting my services to the king! I cannot stray from it." I snap in a hushed tone, my grip tightening on the reins. It's the truth. The contract is binding. If I break it…

"And if you broke it, if you let me go, he'd never know. Do you honestly think what you're doing is right? Murdering hundreds just because they were born different?"

"We aren't going to murder you," I growl, trying desperately to change the subject as she voices the thoughts that I always struggle to push away. But I can't risk it, risk him finding out; the consequences are too great.

Camari faces forward once more, her face a mask once more. "You might disagree, but I see absolutely no reason that the king will give me special treatment."

I open my mouth to reply but stop, unable to think of something to say. She's right. There is absolutely no reason for King Aldred to let her live; she's just another seer to him.

But she isn't just another seer.

I close my mouth and face forward as well, choosing to remain silent for the rest of the day. It's better than speaking of things that are better left unspoken.

The sun is almost completely set by the time I call for us to set up camp. We ride a short distance into the woods before finding a place we deem will be a good campsite for the night. I dismount and give my horse's reins to Morris before walking over to Camari to help her down. She glares at me, gripping the reins tightly.

"Do you plan on coming down?" I ask, raising a hand to help her.

"You can either untie me and let me climb down myself, or I will sit up here all night," she replies coldly, brandishing her wrists.

"I'll have to tie you up again before we go to bed, you know that, don't you?" I ask wearily. I can't fight with her anymore; it is far too mentally taxing.

"At least I'll have the dignity of getting off of my own horse," she says hotly, holding her wrists out to me again. I sigh heavily before I unsheathe my dagger and cut away her ropes. She rubs her raw wrists with a muffled sigh of relief before dismounting smoothly, landing beside me on the forest floor with a small thud.

"Happy?" I ask, taking her upper arm and leading her over to where Eben is assembling a fire.

"Far from it," she replies darkly, sitting against a tree as far from Eben as she can. She crosses her arms and looks away, staring into the fire stonily. Knowing Eben is watching her, I leave and go to take her horse over to where the others are, stripping off its saddle and saddle pad before giving it a pat on the back and walking back to the fire.

Miller caught a rabbit and is roasting it on a spit, watching it carefully as juice runs out of the carcass, sizzling when it meets the flames. He gives me a nod as I sit down beside him, talking in a low tone.

"Long day?"

"You could say that." I sigh, rubbing my eyes wearily before slumping against the log behind us.

"I don't know her nearly as well as you, but I can tell you this: I've been watching her all day, and she's observant. She watches everything, and I'm willing to bet she memorized every turn we took on that road," he comments quietly, never looking away from the rabbit.

"Well, I don't plan on giving her a chance to escape, so it should be fine," I rasp, my mind only partially on our conversation. I can't get her accusations out of my head, and I desperately need to. Hell, I just need to get her out of my head altogether.

"How are you holding up? Dealing with her. I know the two of you were good friends." He glances over at me, his gray eyes scrutinizing.

"We were more than that, Miller," I say quietly, staring into the flames. "Or we could have been. I don't know. All I know is whatever we were, I've ruined it."

"Then why don't you do something about it?"

"She won't even talk to me, not that I can blame her. Thanks for the advice, but our friendship is gone."

"That's not what I'm saying, and you know it."

"Then what are you saying, Miller? I'm too tired for riddles." I snap impatiently, turning to face him. He meets my gaze, his face calm and unmoved like always.

"If you don't like the way things are, then do something to change it. Or just do *something*."

"You know better than most why I *can't*," I growl, resting my head in my hands.

"Well, if you're set on this path, then at least do it right!"

"Translate."

"I'm saying that she's smart, and she'll do whatever it takes to get free."

"You think I don't already know that?"

"Aiden, wake up! You just untied her and left her alone."

"With Eben! She's not alone, and we can all see her."

"Yes, because Eben can be trusted with her completely."

"What's that supposed to mean?" I ask, glancing over at Camari. Eben is standing above her, leaning against the tree she sits against. He says something to her, a sneer on his face, and Camari looks away, her face flushing with anger.

"That's what I mean. I don't know why, but he hates her," Miller says, giving the rabbit a turn over the fire. I look back at Camari, a pang of concern going through me. Eben is still talking to her, still smiling. She's staring down at her skirt, trying to ignore him, but I see her fists clench in her skirt, her jaw clench. I stand slowly, ready to walk over and stop whatever Eben is starting. The urge to protect her hits me like a rock, frustrating and strong, and I give into it. As I said, I am weak.

Everyone is acting strange today. I keep catching whispers and glances that make no sense. No one will meet my eyes. It's like they know something that I don't.

—Journal of Aiden Lorian

Chapter Twelve

Camari

"So, how long do you think you'll be left to live before the king ends your miserable life?" Eben asks me with a grin, leaning against my tree. I ignore him, watching the fire flicker and dance. Adeline always said my hair looked like flames. *Think about Adeline, not about Eben. Block him out. Or simply take pleasure in the raccoon mask of bruises he now wears.*

"Probably won't be long, though if you decide to make yourself useful, you might be given more time."

I take a long, slow breath but keep staring into the fire.

"See, I've heard the king is fond of female company; maybe he'll like yours."

I clench my jaw, my hands folding into fists in my skirt. Knowing I need to control my anger, I take several slow, deep breaths.

Just block him out.

"If he can get past those disgusting marks on your arms, that is. Those things would put any man off. No wonder you weren't married back in Krakent."

"If all men are like you, I'd say I was spared a living hell," I whisper to myself, trying and failing to ignore him. My temper is going to be my downfall.

"Your hair isn't half bad, though it's a strange color. Who knows, maybe he'll take you in as another whore; he is known to be merciful."

I fly up from the ground, advancing towards Eben. He stands up straighter and dwarfs me by several inches, obviously pleased I've reacted as he'd hoped.

"I will *never* sell myself to your king; I'd sooner rot to death in a ditch, abandoned and alone," I growl.

"Ah, you never know; that might be just what Aiden decides to do with you. And you don't have a father, do you? You never know, your mother could have-"

"DON'T TALK ABOUT MY FATHER!" I fly at him, swinging my fists, desperate to cause him pain. I land a blow on the side of his face, but he catches my arm and twists it, grinning as pain shows on my face. One arm caught, I swing with my other hand awkwardly. He steps back and catches me, holding my back against his chest with his arm around my neck.

"Pathetic, just like all of the seers," he growls into my ear. "You know why I do this job? Because it's *easy.* All your people do is *cower* when they see us coming. Probably because they've seen their death, they know they won't survive. Just like you won't."

I see Aiden, Grant, and Morris start towards us from the corner of my eye and grit my teeth. I will not allow them to stop this before I cause Eben some pain.

I lift my feet completely off the ground without warning. Eben staggers under my unexpected weight, bending down slightly, and I punch his healing shin with all of my strength with my free arm. He straightens up, cursing in pain, but I'm not done. Lifting my right foot, I step back, stomping on the arch of his foot as hard as I can. His grip loosens as he curses and bellows, and I twist out from under his arm so that I'm facing him, punching him in the nose before he can grab me again. He grabs his nose, the one I kicked earlier this morning, letting out yet another stream of curses that could curdle milk. I finish him off with a swift kick to the groin just before arms wrap around my waist, and I'm lifted off the ground completely, Aiden clamping my arms down by my sides. Morris and Grant grab Eben as he stands up, lunging at me.

"Enough! Eben, stand down!" Aiden shouts, his voice loud in my ear. Eben lunges one more time, Grant and Morris straining to hold him back.

"Bloody bitch!" he roars, his nose streaming blood.

"*Right back at you!*" I snarl, pulling against Aiden's arms, ready for another round. Eben growls at the insult, going to attack me again.

"Walk it off, Eben, walk it off," Miller says as he comes over. Aiden drags me away before I can hear what is said next, not stopping until we are out of both sight and earshot from the others. He releases me, and I stumble forwards but catch my balance, spinning around to face him with clenched fists.

"What is wrong with you?" he shouts, his breath heaving, his own hands clenched into fists.

"What's wrong with me? How about what's wrong with your goon back there!"

"You attacked him first! He could have killed you, Camari!"

"He goaded me; you should have heard what he said!"

"You shouldn't have taken the bait then!" Aiden shouts, taking a step towards me. I stare at him incredulously, breathing just as heavily as he is.

"How is this all my fault? I didn't ask for any of this! I didn't ask for you to come and uproot my life! I didn't ask to fall for a liar and a murderer!" I shout, throwing my hands into the air as my eyes burn with tears. "I didn't ask for *any* of this! How dare you try to pin the blame for *any of this* on me? *Fuck you,* Aiden!"

Aiden stares at me for a few seconds before he finally sighs, the fight going out of him. "I'm done with this. I get it; you didn't ask for any of this, but neither did I. You didn't ask to fall for a murderer, and I didn't ask to fall for a seer. It happened despite what either of us wanted, so you'll have to learn to deal with it."

"I should never have helped you in the woods; I should have let you bleed out," I spit at him, sweeping my hair out of my face with shaking hands as his words cut like knives. "I should never have welcomed you into my home; I should never have-"

He meets my gaze and holds it as I cut myself off. I start crying, tears pouring down my face and humiliating me further.

"I wish you had, too. But you didn't leave me there," he says finally. "And I didn't leave you alone as soon as I could. We both have to live with our mistakes now."

My shoulders sag, the fight leaving me as well. He's right. I didn't leave him.

But I should have.

When I wake the next morning, everything comes back in a huge wave. Being kidnapped, finding out I might be a seer, leaving Krakent, seeing Adeline, punching Eben in the face. Crying myself to sleep.

I go to push myself up only to fall back down, my bound hands twisting beneath me painfully. That part hadn't come back yet. After returning back to the campsite, Aiden tied my hands with a rope, tying the other end of it to the tree behind me so that I only have about a foot and a half of slack. Not enough to do anything.

At least he isn't underestimating me.

Gritting my teeth, I try again, this time succeeding in sitting up. Looking around, I see that everyone is still asleep. Everyone, that is, except for Miller. He sits against a pine tree directly across from me, watching me with three meters of space between us. Of all of Aiden's men, Miller was the one that I almost never saw, and when I did, his face was so blank that I couldn't get a reading off of him at all. I know him the least, so he is the most dangerous.

I ignore Miller, instead doing my best to stick to my routine of getting ready in the morning. I straighten my skirt and my cover, smoothing out the wrinkles and picking off leaves and pollen. I slept with my cover on; the thing I used to beg to be free of is now something I refuse to take off. I managed to smooth the edges of the sleeve together where Aiden cut it, tying it together at the edge of the sleeve so that my arm is still covered.

I run my fingers through my hair, pulling out leaf scraps and getting out tangles and knots before I braid it loosely over my shoulder. Holding the end of my braid, I look around for something to tie it with. Finding nothing, I let go with a sigh and my hair unravels down my back once more, falling around my face like a waterfall.

Looking back at Miller, he hasn't moved an inch and is still watching me, his eyes scrutinizing.

"So, you're Aiden's second in command?" I ask, leaning back against the tree behind me while I discreetly fiddle with the rope around my wrists, seeing if I can get them loose enough to free my hands.

"No, that would be Eben," Miller replies coolly, tossing a pinecone from hand to hand.

"That buffoon?" I scoff, "Not likely. Let me guess, Eben is his number two as far as muscle goes, but you're the brain. He goes to you for advice, and he leaves you in charge when he's gone."

Miller says nothing, but his eyes flicker briefly, giving me my answer.

"Thought so. No one in their right mind would actually trust Eben with a contingent of soldiers."

"You barely know Eben; how can you judge him so quickly and be sure it's fair?" Miller asks, lowering the pinecone to the ground. I lean forward against my knees, tilting my head as I think, my copper hair falling to the side.

"I'm a pretty good judge of character. I can judge him on what I know of him now. That's not saying my opinion of him cannot change, but for now, I'd say it's pretty accurate, as is my opinion of all of you."

"And what is your opinion of Eben?"

"Rash, angry, ambitious. He acts without thinking and likes to fight to make other people angry. It makes him feel like he's in control, like he is better than others. He's friendly enough with the people he cares about, such as you and Aiden, but he'll stab others in the back to get what he wants. And he's scared of seers. He won't admit it, but that's why he hates me so much. Accurate enough?"

Miller is silent for a moment before nodding slowly. "Yes, that's accurate. But, now that I know what you think of Eben, how have you judged Aiden?" Miller asks, his eyes gleaming with interest. And something else, something like a scheme. I frown, thinking for a moment before I speak slowly.

"He's careful; he likes to think everything through before acting. He cares for all of you; you're his family. He's smart, gentle, and caring to those who care for him." I look up to meet Miller's gaze and then realize what he's doing and close myself off. "And he's a coward, afraid to take a stand for what he believes in. He shoves all of his doubts down despite them being right. He's a manipulator, a liar, and most importantly, he is the murderer of hundreds, maybe thousands of innocent people. Just as all of you are."

Miller nods slowly, leaning back against the tree as he begins to toss his pinecone back and forth again. "Nothing in the world is that black and white, especially Aiden. Do you want to know how I have judged you?"

"I'll humor you," I reply. It's not like I have anything better to do. He nods, smiling thinly as he leans forward again.

"You are nineteen and still unmarried, hiding your arms and living with your mother, whom you don't call mother. You made the mistake of showing Aiden your arms, and all of this happened, so you have decided to keep them hidden from everyone else. You're smart, observant, and you know how to handle yourself. You overthink things and hide your fear under anger. You are also scared of attachment, not wanting to risk loving something only to lose it or be betrayed by it, which makes me think you lost a loved one as a child. A father maybe." Miller finishes, meeting my eyes with his black ones, void of any emotion except for curiosity. "Am I right?"

I meet his gaze, taking steady breaths to calm myself and the burning feeling in my gut. The scent of lavender rises up my nostrils like a phantom breeze, making my stomach churn with nausea. My hands are clenched in my lap, the rope forgotten.

"Couldn't be further from the truth," I say quietly, turning away and ending our conversation. The others stir and begin to rise, my second day of captivity beginning.

Later that day, as we ride, Aiden confers with Miller quietly, and I listen, straining my ears to hear their hushed tones. I don't catch everything, but I learn that we will have to cross a stretch of land called the Spás Folamh. Apparently, we will be following streams, but the way they were talking about them and some of the things they said make me believe that those streams dry up after a certain point, and we won't have them to guide us. So, if I am going to escape, it will need to be in the next two weeks;

anytime after that and I'll be stuck. I'll have no streams to follow and no chance to get home.

I wiggle my wrists discreetly, straining against the ropes that bind them together as I have been all morning. I've loosened the ropes slightly, and I figure by the end of the day, maybe early tomorrow, they'll be loose enough for me to slip my hands free. The ropes are chafing horribly and my wrists burn, the skin having broken an hour or two ago. The folds of my skirt now have dried blood on them, though it blends in with the brown fabric. Every turn of my wrists burns and draws forth more blood, but if it takes a little pain for me to escape all of this, then let it come.

I glance over at Aiden, finding him rubbing his shoulder absentmindedly. "How's your shoulder?" I ask, wincing as the ropes rub against a particularly sore spot on my wrists. He looks at me, his eyebrows raised in surprise at my question. I figure if I start making them trust me now, they'll be less suspecting later, perfect for me to escape more easily. At least, that's what I tell myself when the words come out of my mouth on their own accord.

"A little sore; hauling you off of Eben last night didn't help anything," he says, tilting his head side to side and popping his neck.

"I will not apologize for that," I tell him with an air of indifference. A smile tugs at the corner of his mouth, his eyes sparking with humor.

"I hadn't expected you to."

At least he has that much right about me. I don't apologize unless I believe I am in the wrong, and I am not in the wrong for attacking Eben. He is a murderer of hundreds of seers. Hundreds of my people.

I huff out a breath, facing forward again at the sobering thought. I still don't believe that I am a seer. My hair can be explained away easily; the scalsen, however, that is a harder thing to figure out. I glance down at my arm, pushing my sleeve up a few inches so that they are visible. Tan skin swirling in vines and patterns, odd, but I always thought they were slightly pretty, if only to myself. Now I'm not so sure.

I pull my sleeve back down, tucking my hands back into my skirts, and continue to strain against the ropes. I think back to whenever I had my first 'episode'. I was eight years old; it was seventh day, and I was walking to the monastery. I was by myself because Adeline was busy with a sick patient but still wanted me to go, teasing that if I didn't, the gods would smite me. The weather was cold, and not many people were out. I was alone as I walked, my hands shoved deep into the folds of my skirt. Suddenly, a wave of cold went through my bones, and I stopped. It wasn't like the cold outside; it was different, deeper. I had this gut feeling that I needed to run, to get to the monastery as fast as I could. I wasn't safe, and I knew it. Then I heard the voice, like my thoughts, but not.

Run; run or die.

I broke into a sprint without a second thought, my feet slipping and crunching on ice and slush. My hair was streaming behind me, and the wind bit at my face as I ran. A few seconds into running, I heard foot-steps behind me. I glanced over my shoulder and I saw a man chasing me, tall and dressed in a heavy black cloak. My heart raced as I ran, and I was pant-ing, emitting panicked noises as I ran. Tumbling around the corner, I hurtled down the street, the mon-astery in sight. The man was still behind me, and I could hear him gaining as I reached the steps of the monastery and began to run up the steps, taking them two at a time. I was almost to the top of the stairs when he grabbed me, throwing me down. I landed hard on the stone steps, my chin crashing against one and busting open. I screamed as his hands gripped my shoulders and turned me over, hauling me up. Panicked and not knowing what to do, I did the only thing I could think of. Bringing my foot up, I kicked him as hard as I could between his legs. He howled in pain, spewing curses as he struggled to his feet. While he was still trying to stand, I scrambled to my feet and ran into the monastery, getting help. I later found out he was a slave trader, kidnapping children and selling them as slaves to anyone with a good enough price. I almost became his next victim, and I still have a faint scar on my chin. That was my first 'episode', my first vision, and it saved my life.

Maybe I am a seer; would that be such a bad thing?

I look down at my wrists, raw and bleeding. I look over at my captor, riding his horse alongside mine and frowning as he thinks about something. I look back over my shoulder at Eben, finding him already looking at me. He sneers at me, and I face forward, my heart heavy as other people's words float through my mind.

I didn't ask to fall for a seer

People hate ugly things.

Yes, it would be a very bad thing.

It is late afternoon, the sun low in the sky, when I stiffen on my horse. No one notices me sit up straighter; all of them are focused on whatever conversation they're having between them. I look around, the hairs on my arms and the back of my neck standing straight up. There is nothing here; just trees, bushes, and shadows; nothing out of the ordinary.

A wave of cold sweeps down my spine, and I look around again, my eyes wide. Again, I see nothing. But I know something is coming.

I continue looking around as we ride onward, on edge. We reach a fork in the road, and Aiden goes to turn his horse left, my horse tethered to his, when I feel it again, this time even stronger. I blink, and an image flashes before my eyes of a man lying dead on the ground, bleeding out, surrounded by bodies. I yank on my reins without thinking, terror rushing through me in a wave at the sight, and my horse stops with a snort of annoyance. Aiden's horse stops with mine, and everyone else stops behind me, complaining loudly. Aiden looks back at me, frowning when he sees that I've stopped.

"What's wrong?" he demands, bringing his horse over to stand by mine.

"We shouldn't go this way," I say, clenching my horse's reins with a white-knuckled grip, my voice shaking as the image of the dead bodies replays in my mind, over and over again. Aiden frowns, looking back at the road he tried to take.

"It's the fastest way; it saves us days-"

"Aiden, we shouldn't go this way."

Aiden narrows his eyes when I speak his name without contempt, shifting on his saddle. "Did you see something?"

I hesitate, unsure of what I should tell him. My hesitation seems to answer his question. "What did you see?"

"What's going on?" Eben rides up, talking loudly. I ignore him, holding Aiden's gaze with mine.

"Aiden please," I ask softly, holding his gaze. Aiden's eyes soften and I think maybe he'll listen to me. Then Eben speaks, rolling his eyes.

"Oh, shut up. Aiden, don't fall for her act. She pretends she's had a vision, bats her pretty eyes at you, and gets exactly what she wants. It's probably a trap of her own."

I turn in my saddle and glare at Eben. "First of all, if you don't actually believe that I am a seer, why did you kidnap me? Second of all, how am I going to do anything with my hands bound like this?" I ask, lifting my arms so that they can all see my bloody wrists. Grant cringes behind Eben, looking guilty. I ignore him and turn back to Aiden, ready to beg. "Aiden, *please*; we cannot go this way. I'm asking you to trust me, just this once."

Aiden meets my gaze, but Eben's words have swayed him, and his eyes are firm once more. "I'm sorry, Camari, but you've given me no reason to trust you. We go this way."

"I've given you no reason to distrust me either; in fact, I believe it's you who proved to be untrustworthy!" I spit, yanking my horse's reins to make her stay. Aiden clenches his jaw, his mind obviously made up.

"We go this way."

He turns his horse and I'm dragged along, my horse stuck to him by the damned rope. The others fall in behind us, Eben giving me a smug look as I pass him. I ignore it, squeezing my reins as I ride and clenching my teeth, scanning both sides of the road. I turn my head side to side repeatedly, my hair flying over my shoulders and at my sudden movements. I catch Miller watching me once as I push a strand of hair behind my ears, his eyes uneasy. He can see that something isn't right; he can see I'm not lying. But he says nothing.

The rest of the afternoon goes by with me on edge, jumping at every noise. Aiden ignores me, facing straight ahead. Part of me is annoyed that Eben interrupted; I was so close to convincing Aiden of the danger. Another part of me is hurt that he listened to Eben over me, and that part doesn't make any sense.

Of course he listened to his supposed number two over me.

The sun is almost set, the day is almost gone, when another wave of cold sweeps down my spine, stronger than ever. I yank on my reins, stopping my horse and Aiden's. He turns to face me, his mouth open and ready to yell at me, when an arrow whizzes past his ear, lodging into a tree behind him. He spins to look in the direction it came from, and another one flies by, this time barely missing me.

We are under attack.

"Defensive formation! Miller, take them out!" Aiden shouts, drawing his sword with a metallic whine. At his orders, everyone maneuvers their horses into a formation in a matter of seconds. Miller lines up his sights with an arrow and lets it fly. It disappears from sight in the tree line and a moment later I hear the thud of someone falling. At the death of their comrade, our attackers charge from the trees, roaring a battle cry. I expect a small group of attackers, a group of roadside robbers and bandits. What comes out of the trees is a small army.

They're numbered at around fifteen people, all of them armed to the teeth with leather armor and weapons. They ride on horses and have swords drawn, axes held back and ready to be swung.

I look over at Aiden and see him calculating the numbers, seeing that we won't come out of this fight alive.

"Defensive positions," he repeats, his voice deathly calm. His men fall in, ready to fight. Except I am bound, weaponless, and practically being led to my death. Glancing around in a panic, the attackers getting closer with each second, I begin to strain desperately against the rope, ignoring the blood that begins to stream down my hands, dripping onto my horse's fur. I whimper as the rope fibers dig deep into my flesh, the knot getting looser with each tug. *I will not die like this.*

The attackers reach us and sword clashes against sword, horse ramming against horse. Everything is in a panic, so many different noises overcoming my senses. Aiden charges to meet the first attacker as another horse crashes into mine. She rears and squeals in fear, knocking me from her back. I fall to the ground, unable to hold on properly with my bound wrists. My back hits the ground with a thud, the air leaving my lungs, but I immediately struggle to my feet, rolling over and pushing myself up so that I can get clear of the fighting happening all around me. I stand at the side of the road, pulling desperately at the rope as people die in front of me. Aiden and his men are fighting incredibly well, all of them still on their horses and living, though Aiden has a cut above his eye that is dripping blood down his face. Miller is legendary with his bow, loosing arrow after arrow, knocking down one attacker after another. Eben roars as he swings his ax around like a giant with a club. Grant has thrown his javelin already and, to my surprise, is now fighting with a mace. He swings the spiked ball around, knocking a warrior in the jaw and sending him flying from his horse, leaving a trail of blood in his wake.

Looking around at the other fighters, my gaze catches on one of our attackers. She has blonde hair braided back out of her face and her right cheek has three blood-red streaks down its length, a warrior in woad. She wears leather armor on her chest and arms and has weapons strapped to every inch of her. What catches my attention is that she is staring straight at me. I catch her gaze by accident and hold it. She smiles at me and then raises her sword arm, calling something out. She kicks her horse towards me, and two other fighters fall in behind her.

They are coming to kill me.

I turn and run, stumbling slightly as I trip on my skirt. With a cry of pain, I manage to pull my right hand from the ropes, shaking them off of my left hand as I run. I pant for air, terror coursing through my veins. But I can't outrun a horse.

A hand strikes me on the back of my head and I fall forward, dirt getting into my mouth and eyes. I roll over and see that three attackers surround me: two men and the blonde-haired woman. They dismount and walk towards me, tightening the circle. I realize that the sound of the fighting has quieted down a good amount. Looking over my shoulder, I see Aiden and his men still fighting, an incredible amount of the attackers dead on the ground. Against all odds, they just might survive this.

I turn back to the current threat. The woman has her sword out and it hangs leisurely by her side, the sun gleaming against the steel. She smiles brightly at me, her trapped prey. "Well, now, what is a pretty lady like you doing with filthy men like them?" she asks, speaking in an overly sweet tone that is both extremely threatening and condescending at the same time. I know that if I beg, if I tell her I am their prisoner, she might let me go. But she might also kill Aiden and Miller, and I can't honestly say I want them dead.

Why don't I want my kidnappers dead?

She places the tip of her sword underneath my chin and makes me look up before moving it so that it catches a strand of my hair on the blade, bringing it up in front of my face before it drops back to my shoulder.

"What an interesting shade," she muses quietly, tilting her head to the side.

"I've been called many things; interesting has never been one of them," I say, watching the other two attackers as they shift, each of them with a drawn sword. One wrong move and I'm dead.

The woman smiles slightly at my response, shifting her feet again. "What's your name?"

"What do I get if I tell you? My life?" I ask, raising an eyebrow in skepticism. My attacker smiles again, and I try to look her in the eyes, but the sun shines directly onto her, veiling her eyes in shadows.

"No, but you'll have another person to remember you after I kill you," she replies, taking a step closer. I watch her, thinking. There's no way to get out of this; she is going to kill me whether I tell her or not.

"Camari; my name is Camari."

She nods, narrowing her eyes slightly. "Camari; an interesting name."

"Now that I've heard before."

She smiles yet again. "It's a pity I have to kill you, Camari; I could've sworn I've heard your name before."

"Well, do I at least get to know my murderer's name?"

"Cass," she says, tossing her braid over her shoulder. "And now, I *am* going to kill you."

I close my eyes and brace myself as I hear Aiden shout my name from somewhere behind me. But the pain never comes. I cautiously open my eyes, looking around. Cass is staring down at my arm, where my cover has split open again, revealing the swirls of vines and shapes. Now she knows I'm a seer; she might do something worse than kill me.

She crouches down and looks at my arm before meeting my gaze, her expression shocked. "You're a seer."

I look into her eyes, equally shocked at what I see. Her eyes are violet, an intense purple that is wholly unnatural.

Suddenly, there is a noise behind me. I twist my head around in time to see Aiden charging toward us, his weapon out. Morris is crouching next to where Grant is on the ground, his face waxy with pain. Eben is lying on the ground, clutching at his bloody leg as Miller stands over him, pressing down on the wound.

"Aiden, don't!" I shout, not wanting them to do something foolish for me. I am going to die either way.

Cass 'gaze snaps up to them before she nods to the two men beside me, who immediately start forward. The other surviving attackers follow their lead, and Cass looks back at me, her eyes unsure.

"Please, don't kill them," I beg her. Something flashes through her eyes, and then something hard connects with the side of my head and I see no more.

The king has his wife and children, his council members and advisors, and his aristocracy all to support him, help him serve the kingdom, and endorse his laws and commands. But there is one role that must be filled in another way.

—Zorda: Aristocracy, Geography, and History

Chapter Thirteen

Aiden

As the fight winds down, the threat slowly waning, I look around for Camari again, praying against all odds she got away after I cut the rope connecting our horses. Then I spot her, and terror shoots through me. She's lying on the ground, a sword held at her throat. She appears to be conversing with her attacker, a blond warrior with red woad striped down her face and neck. I yank on my horse's reins, trying to turn and get to her in time, even as my brain tells me it's hopeless, as despair starts to set in. I see Camari flinch as the sword presses against the hollow of her throat, her eyes closing in finality, and panic makes my heart race faster than it ever has before.

"Camari!" I scream, wishing I could do something to slow down time, to go back and take the other path. I need more time to fix what I've done, to take back the horrible things I've said.

Camari's head turns ever so slightly to me, though her eyes remain squeezed shut. Then, her attacker moves her sword away from Camari's throat, staring down at her arm where her scalsen are visible. Her attackers stiffen in surprise and I know right then that whatever is happening won't be good. What will they do now that they know she's a seer? Death may have been merciful.

Before I can reach her, the remaining four mercenaries surround me, all of them pointing their weapons at me from a different angle. I lower my weapon as I feel the cold point of a sword at the base of my neck, and I am unable to help Camari defend herself. Peering around one of my attackers as they surround me, I see Camari speak quickly, her eyes now open and flickering toward me. Her attacker slams the hilt of her sword into Camari's head out of nowhere. Camari crumples like a leaf, falling back onto the dirt road. I lunge forward on my horse with a shout, but the attackers around me close in. "No!" I shout, trying to maneuver between them. Something hits my head; pain reverberates through my skull, and my vision goes black.

When I wake up, I know immediately that something is off. The light beyond my closed eyelids is dim and patterned with shadows, like a tent. Just as I notice the pattern, the light brightens before darkening again, and I hear voices. I feel someone bump against my lower leg and open my eyes, forcing myself to lie still so that no one knows I am awake. Camari is pressed against me, putting as much space as she can between herself and the people in the tent. Her attacker is here, accompanied by four large men and a small woman with scalsen the color of the sky.

They're seers.

Camari is staring at them, her face shadowed by the canvas above.

"We aren't going to hurt you." I hear her attacker say. Camari gestures to her forehead for some reason. "I'm sorry, that was necessary," her attacker says, speaking in a surprisingly gentle voice. Why are they being so nice to Camari; is she not their prisoner? If not, why is she in the same tent as me? What do they have planned for us?

I am so deep in my thoughts that I miss out on what they say next. I catch my lapse and listen once more.

"A seer." Camari is saying, her voice filled with a mixture of wonder and curiosity. A new voice speaks, soft and feminine, also warm and friendly. I assume it is the second woman I saw, though I still know nothing about what is going on. It is time to wake up 'officially'.

I sit up with a groan as my muscles shriek in protest, sore from lying in the same position for who knows how long. My head swims at my movement, likely from where they hit me, and my forehead burns and itches oddly. I reach up to touch it but stop, looking down at my wrists. They are bound with rope, my fingers bright red from how tightly they are bound. My ankles are bound as well, the rope light against the dark, torn fabric of my trousers. I glance around and breathe a sigh of relief when I see my men, still passed out but breathing and looking well. Indeed, their wounds have been tended to and bandaged, which surprises me.

"Welcome to the party, assassin." The blonde woman who attacked Camari speaks in an overly cheerful voice, though her eyes are full of venom. I look at her violet eyes, knowing this is not going to go well, not if she just addressed me the way I believe she did. I'll be lucky if they don't execute me.

"What is this, another hidden seer village?" I ask, glancing around again. I can't see outside of the teepee, but the four warriors standing behind her give me a sense of what it is like outside. Dangerous.

The blonde snorts in laughter at my question, and the second woman, the brunette with blue scalsen, speaks, stepping closer and looking at me with contempt. "Like we'd tell you anything. We know who you are. Aiden Baltasar Lorian, the king's royal assassin. The only reason you and your friends aren't lying dead is because Camari here asked us to spare you."

I turn to Camari, surprised that she intervened for us. I wonder why what she asked matters to our captors, but one question at a time.

"I wonder why," I say, watching Camari. When she meets my gaze, however, her dark eyes are filled with rage. "Don't get all excited, *assassin*; I just didn't want some poor person to pass by and have to scrape your blood off of his boots," she spits, her voice dripping venom when she says assassin. No doubt she knows about the king's royal assassin; everybody does. Just very few know it's me.

I battle against a wave of guilt for not telling her my true title, for keeping another secret. Not that it should matter at this point; I've dug my hole.

"Camari, I was going-" I go to explain myself, but Camari cuts me off, still glaring at me in contempt.

"Don't, I don't care. You're a murderer and a kidnapper; what does it matter if I know your exact title or not? You were still stealing me away from my home," she says coldly, turning away from me. I shove away the guilt I feel and turn to watch our captors. The two women are surveying Camari, looking at her ruined clothes and bloody hair. The brunette crouches down and fingers a bloodstain on Camari's skirt before taking her hands gently and looking at her wrists. My eyes widen as I see what a mess they are, the flesh torn open and weeping in a way that is undoubtedly painful. I had no idea the ropes caused her that much pain.

Another way you've hurt her.

"We have a lot to do!" The brunette declares, standing up. Cass steps forward and takes Camari's upper arm gently, helping her to her feet before leading her towards the exit of the tent, the four guards stepping to the side to make way for them to pass.

"Where are we going?" Camari asks, her voice slightly panicked as she looks between the two women.

"We are going to clean you up; no seer in my care will be this filthy if I have anything to say about it," the blonde says. The last thing I see of Camari is when she glances over her shoulder at me, her eyes wide with panic. Then the teepee's flap falls back down, concealing the three women as they walk away and leave me with the four guards. One of them cracks the knuckles on his right hand, leering down at me, and I sigh, knowing what will come next.

This is not my first time being someone's prisoner.

Martha asks me why I insist on always wearing my head scarf and my long shift, even when I am on duty outdoors. She doesn't understand that once I wanted to be seen, but now that I have been, all I want to do is hide.

—The Journal of Maren Landry

Chapter Fourteen

Camari

I glance back at Aiden once more as I'm led from the tent. The light from the opened flap frames his face as concern flashes in his eyes. Then I'm out of the teepee, and it's all I can do to keep from gaping at what I see. We stand in a huge clearing in the woods, surrounded conveniently by cliffs on one half, the other half shielded by trees, thorns, and bushes. In the center of the clearing is a huge bonfire that lights up the entire space, casting flickering shadows. There are partial rings of teepees and tents around the fire, each teepee and tent with a different design and color scheme so that it is like a field of rainbows. They have a wooden penned-in area with four goats as well as a productive garden against the cliff face, vines dripping with large tomatoes and squash.

There are seers everywhere. They stand around the fire, cooking sizzling meats and bubbling stews; they stand in groups, talking and laughing together. A group of children play off to the side, laughing and chasing each other around in a game. I spot several seers positioned along the cliff face or in trees, keeping watch for threats and protecting their families.

I am left speechless as I take all of it in. Just a few days ago, I'd never seen a seer, and now I've seen hundreds. And I still know absolutely nothing.

Cass and Odette smile at my reaction, glancing around fondly at their home.

"What is this place?" I breathe, watching as a little girl with grass-green hair runs by, a small patch of scalsen visible on her throat.

"We call it 'Onaydo,' a word from the language of the ancients which translates roughly to 'Home of the Blessed,'" Cass says, looking around with a smile before taking my forearm again. "Come on; we have time to show you everything, but for now, you need to get cleaned up. You look like a wounded beggar."

I look down at my torn and stained clothes. "That's a bit of an exaggeration, don't you think?"

Odette makes a skeptical noise behind me, and Cass smiles. "See? I'm right."

They lead me through a maze of colorful teepees and tents, pointing out different homes and places as we walk.

"That red one is the smithy, oh, and that blue one over there, that's my tent. That green one is the armory, and the purple one is the granary, a massive food pantry of sorts."

We stop at a large burgundy tent with an elaborate design; Odette pushes the flap aside before stepping in, Cass leading me in after her. The inside of the tent has a carpeted bottom and is far larger than it appears from the outside. Beeswax candles light the space, showing me two new women inside, twins I decide, as I note their identical caramel-colored curls and freckled skin. They look up as we enter, smiling when they see Odette.

"We need hot water, towels, bandages, and clothes," Cass announces, leading me forward. The twins eye my bright hair before combing over me, taking in my appearance.

"I think you mean a miracle," one of them comments drily, though her voice is warm and her eyes spark with humor.

"Camari, these are our seamstresses of sorts; Theo and Liz. Girls, this is Camari. We saved her from some of the king's soldiers," Odette explains, smiling cheerfully. I cringe at the word *saved*, unsure if it's the most accurate word, but say nothing.

The twins smile at me, nodding in greeting. "Welcome to Onaydo, Camari," Theo says. At least, I think it's Theo; they look exactly the same, like a reversed reflection.

Before I know what is happening, we have two buckets of steaming water and a stack of towels, and the twins have begun bickering about what I should wear. They leave me behind a screen so that I can bathe without prying eyes; Cass and Odette leave after reassuring me they'll be back to fetch me.

I strip quickly, relieved to take off my bloody clothes. I use one bucket of water to wash, wiping away days' worth of dirt, grime, and a surprising amount of blood. I am amazed by the rings of dirt I find around my neck after just a few days of travel, though I did fall out of a tree and off a horse. My body is a mural of bruises, some purple and blue, some green and yellow. My upper right arm has the worst of it where Eben grabbed me, and dark bruises mingle with my markings. I can't wait until I see him again, awake. The most epic role reversal of all time, with me well dressed, clean, and untied while he is tied up on the ground. I smile wickedly at the thought, scrubbing my skin with a wet towel until it is pink and stinging.

I use the second bucket for my hair, washing out leaves and dried blood. The water feels amazing against my scalp, and I sigh in relief, massaging gently to get out anything tangled in my hair before gently wringing it out.

Leaving the two buckets of murky, rapidly cooling water behind the screen, I dry off with the large towel they gave me before wrapping it around myself, the cool evening air making my skin sprout goosebumps. I look down at where my clothes lay in a pile, torn and ruined. I don't want to put them back on, but I also can't bear to part with my cover. My mother gave it to me for my last birthday; she made it herself and signed her initials on the inside. I pick it up and shake it out, tucking it under my arm so that I can hold up the towel I'm wrapped in. The other clothes can be burned for all I care.

"Camari, are you done?" one of the twins calls, her shadow appearing on the far wall

"Yes!" I say, stepping out from around the screen. She smiles when she sees me clean, the blood washed off of my face.

"Oh, well isn't that better already! Now, Theo and I have put together a few clothing items I think will suit you. We thought we'd let you look at them and decide what you'd like to wear."

"That sounds wonderful," I reply with a smile, crossing my arms tighter around my chest as a wave of cold sweeps over me. Liz's gaze catches on the cover tucked under my arm, her eyes sweeping my markings briefly, making me rub my arms self-consciously.

"Would you like that cleaned?" she asks, gesturing to my cover. I hesitate, holding it out in front of me. Indeed, the tan cloth is covered in dirt and debris.

"Carefully please; it's special," I say finally, handing it over gingerly. Liz nods with a kind smile as she takes it from me, shaking it out and folding it into a neat square.

"I'll get it back to you in much better shape," she says cheerfully, tucking it under her arm before turning and gesturing to a stack of colorful clothes on the wooden table littered with scraps of fabric. "Those are for you to try; you're welcome to anything there. I'll just go get this to the washerwomen."

"Thank you!" I call to her as she walks out of the tent. I pick up the stack of clothes and step back behind the screen, looking through the given options. It is all beautifully made, the fabric of nice quality and the sewing and embroidery intricate. What makes me feel rather unnerved is the fact that every option is sleeveless. No covers to hide my markings. My *scalsen.*

Did Cass do this on purpose?

Having no other option, I begin to dress slowly, the fabric soft and cool against my skin. I chose a dress with a fitted top; the skirt split up the side for convenience. It's white and appears to be made of woven yarn so that it resembles lace, another layer of white fabric beneath it making it warm. It comes with a thin brown leather belt that ties around my middle, more for décor than convenience. I hesitate as I put on the dress, the straps in place of the sleeves, leaving my arms and shoulders visible to all. A dress like this, though incredibly beautiful, would never be deemed appropriate in Krakent. This much skin is only shown in Sutoran and by aristocrats. My scalsen are bright against my skin, there for all to see. I struggle to push away the urge to cover them up, to shrink away from everyone, pulling on my boots before I step out from behind the screen. Cass and Odette haven't returned yet, so I wait, my arms crossed, looking around the large tent. There's a comb on a small table as well as several leather strips, and I walk over, beginning to gently work the tangles out of my hair before I braid it, tossing it back over my shoulder.

Still rubbing my arms, I turn around when I hear voices. Cass and Odette walk in, talking cheerfully. They stop when they see me, smiling at my changed appearance.

"Well, Theo called for a miracle; she must have received it!" Odette exclaims teasingly. Her gaze lingers on my wrists, and she frowns, a dark look entering her eyes. "We'll need to bandage those."

I looked down at my wrists, still raw and painful. Cass rummages through a drawer on the table before coming back with a roll of bandages in her hand. She wraps my wounds gently, tying off the bandages before returning them to the drawer and smiling brightly at me.

"Ready?"

I take a deep breath, rubbing my arms again.

No.

"Yes."

I long to see you again. I know...but years have passed...I'll make you understand...I keep what I find. I am a patient man.

—Recovered Artifacts from Krakent

Chapter Fifteen

Aiden

My men and I sit at the edges of the circle that gathers around the large bonfire, ignoring those who stare at us. The guards have been very...friendly, and I now have a bruised face and split lip to prove it. It seems there are many in the camp who want some sort of revenge against me. Shocking, I know.

"This is literally the worst situation we could be in," Morris mutters, watching the seers gather around the fire, eating, laughing, and talking amongst themselves.

"How so?" Grant asks obliviously, watching the seers with interest rather than anger.

"We are in a camp of seers after having just slaughtered twelve of their comrades in a fight earlier today, and they have our prisoner who knows where doing who knows what to her. I still think she orchestrated this, by the way," Eben says, scowling at everyone.

"We've been over this; there's no way she could have; she was tied up with us the whole time. Besides, we were the ones who told her she was a seer, and the other seers almost killed her!" Grant argues impatiently, rolling his eyes at Eben. He's never had much patience for Eben's dark moods, preferring to look at the bright side of every situation.

"It doesn't matter; we need to focus on getting out of here alive," I snap, shifting uncomfortably on the hard ground. I still haven't seen Camari, though I saw the two women from earlier around the fire. They walked off a few minutes ago, laughing and talking together like nothing was wrong. There are other seers, though, that show signs of what happened earlier that day. A small group of seers huddle off to the side of the fire, staring at their food rather than eating it, their eyes red and puffy from crying. I know they are the family of those we killed, and I fight against guilt. For once, these killings were justified, explained away by self-defense. But even that doesn't take away all of the guilt.

I am startled from my thoughts by Grant as he whistles slowly, drawing our attention towards what he is looking at. Camari walks towards the bonfire, led by the two women from earlier. She has bathed and is clean, her skin shining with the lack of dirt. She wears a long, fitted white dress that looks to be made of lace. It hugs her form as she walks, a slit on the left side of her skirt going up to her knee for mobility. Her hair is clean and shining in the firelight, gleaming a fierce copper. She has it braided back, but a few strands have escaped, and they hang around her face fetchingly, accenting her cheekbones and defined jaw. But what really catches my attention are her arms. I've seen her scalsen in passing when she helped the injured man, but I hadn't paid much attention to them after the initial discovery. Now, with the straps of her dress letting them be seen by everyone, I notice them far better. They are… *beautiful*. They look like vines curling around her arms, surrounded by swirls, blooms, and spots. They trail from the tops of her shoulders to her wrists, ending like the cuffs of a sleeve. And they're beautiful. *Why didn't I ever notice that before?*

"She cleans up real nice." Grant whistles. Eben curls his lip, looking away from her with a scowl, and I am struck again by his hatred for her and the seers. The rest of my men and I do our jobs as we are required, but we don't detest the seers with every fiber of our being like he does, as King Aldred does. The king has reasons, but what are Eben's, and why does he hate Camari more than the others? I doubt he'd tell me if I asked.

Camari is led to the fire by the blonde, and all of the chatter ends abruptly, the seers looking up at the blonde and Camari with interest.

"This is Camari, and she is our newest seer!" The blonde announces, her voice filling the clearing. "We rescued her today from the hands of the royal assassin, who is now our prisoner!"

Camari cringes at the word 'rescued', and I smile slightly, knowing she wouldn't like being referred to as a rescue.

The seers cheer, walking up to Camari and welcoming her, taking her hands and smiling. I watch as she smiles at all of them, accepting the bowl of food they give her gratefully. But as soon as the chatter returns to normal and the blonde is busy talking to the brunette, she takes her food and slinks away. She sits down in the shadows of a teepee a few yards from me, her bowl of food sitting on the ground as she watches the seers. I note how she rubs her arms seemingly without realizing it, crossing them self-consciously. She still isn't comfortable with showing her arms.

Her mother sure did a number on her.

"What are you staring at?"

I look up at the blonde who now stands in front of me, her arms crossed. She glances over at where Camari sits, and her face shifts dangerously.

"What did you do to her?" she asks quietly, taking a step forward and resting a hand on the hilt of her dagger.

"What do you mean?" I say calmly, my men watching us silently.

"She's terrified to show her marks, and I want to know what you did to her to make her that scared. How long have you had her; where did she come from? I need answers."

"Then why don't you ask her?" I challenge with narrowed eyes, leaning forward. What is it she really wants to know?

"Because I don't want to make her talk about something she doesn't want to talk about," she replies, shifting her weight and jutting out her hip.

No, that's not the real reason. Why is she lying?

"I don't know what you want to know, alright? We've had her only for a few days. We took her from a village two days from here where she lived with her mother; we were on our way to Sutoran after clearing out two seer villages two weeks from here. That's all I know."

She narrows her eyes at me, tilting her head as she studies me. I stare right back, unfazed by her scrutinizing gaze. Her stare shifts from me to where Camari sits alone, leaning forwards against her bent knees and staring at the fire. She looks back at me and her eyes gleam with an understanding that *I* don't fully comprehend.

"No, it's not. But I need nothing else from you," she says, shifting her weight again before she turns and beckons some seers forward. They walk up and hand each of us a bowl of stew. I hold mine awkwardly with my bound wrists, trying not to drop it as I take a few sips of the broth. The blonde continues watching me for several more minutes, her thumb absentmindedly tapping the hilt of her sword.

"You're not what I thought the murderer of hundreds of innocent people would be like," she says finally, watching me.

"Things are never as they appear."

She nods slowly, taking a half-step back. "No, they aren't. Yet you are still the murderer of our people."

"Seers aren't human; they're vermin," Eben spits, scowling at her. In a blink, she has the point of her sword pressed against the hollow of his throat, making him tilt his head back to avoid impaling himself.

"And you aren't a human either; you're a monster," she growls, her voice deathly quiet. Eben swallows, for once silent, and she withdraws her sword, sheathing it before spinning on her heel and marching back to the fire.

"Do you ever just keep your damned mouth shut?" I snap at Eben, angry with him for his endless insults. For just a moment, progress was being made. He ignores me, hatred gleaming in his eyes as he watches Cass walk away.

I look away from him, turning back to Camari. She's standing up, her arms still crossed over her chest. She turns and catches my gaze, the fire illuminating her face. Then she turns and walks towards the fire. The brunette smiles at her, wrapping her arm around Camari's shoulders and drawing her into the circle.

I turn back to my bowl of stew; Camari's choice is clear. Not that I expected otherwise.

No one knows when a rukh will appear. All that is known is that when one is spotted, you best pray that it has appeared to aid you in your conquest. For if not, it will be the last thing that you see.

—The Mythical, Magical, and Mundane: Folklore of Zorda

Chapter Sixteen

Camari

I wake to pale, butter-colored sunlight streaming into my tent. I groan, rolling over with a sigh. Then I remember the past four days and sit up quickly. I am still in the spare teepee I was led to last night, sleeping on a low cot under a heavy wool blanket. I sigh, rubbing the sleep out of my eyes with the heels of my palms. I was at the bonfire late into the night, watching the other seers interact with each other. They were like a family, everyone knowing each other, laughing and talking together. I preferred sitting by myself, observing rather than joining in. And, if I must admit it, part of me felt guilty for being clean and taken care of while Aiden, Miller, Morris, and Grant were tied up and hurting. I know they've done the same thing to me, leaving me tied to a tree at night and pulling me out of a tree as well, but I still felt guilty. My feelings never make any sense.

I kick the blanket off, turning on the cot so that my feet touch the ground. I slept in the white dress, too tired to change and not having anything else to change into. Now, standing up and shoving my hair out of my face, I see that someone must have stopped by because there is a new stack of clothes by my bed, as well as a bowl of clean water to wash up with. I get ready quickly, splashing my face with water and swishing some in my mouth before I get dressed. They gave me a skirt similar to my old one, though this one has a reddish tint, accompanied by a white shift and a dark green bodice. They also gave me back my cover, now clean. I slip it on over my clothes, exhaling deeply and immediately feeling more secure. Pulling on my boots and running my fingers through my hair, I shove aside the flap of my teepee and step out into the morning light.

The camp appears to be just waking up, with a few people walking around. The sound of an ax hitting wood rings through the clearing, repeating again and again as someone chops firewood for the day. I walk slowly through the maze of tents and rainbow teepees, the dew collecting on my boots. The sun is rising steadily, bringing the summer's heat with it so that the top of my head burns, though not unpleasantly.

Reaching the middle of the clearing, I stop by the edge, watching as the seers go about their day. There is a small group of women cooking breakfast for the entire camp, stirring what looks to be a large pot of oats over a small flame while chatting.

I look over to where Aiden and the others are being held, the white and red teepee speckled with the shadows of the trees behind it. To my surprise, Aiden is already up, sitting awkwardly outside of his tent with his knees drawn up to his chest. He must have had to crawl out, I realize, again feeling guilt for how humiliating that must have been. But I'm not supposed to feel bad for him.

I walk over to where he sits, tossing my head to keep my hair out of my face. I don't know why I don't just turn and walk away after everything he's done. Or, actually, I do know why. Because he can give me the answers that I long for. And because despite being in an entire camp of seers, supposedly my own kind, I can't help but feel extremely lonely. And I don't feel lonely around Aiden.

Aiden looks up as I near, taking in my new clothing and the cover back where it belongs. I sit down beside him, bringing my knees up to my chest and wrapping my arms around my ankles.

"Rough night?" I ask him, watching a seer enter the clearing with a wheelbarrow of chopped wood and a familiar ax slung across his shoulders. I smile at the sight of Eben's weapon being used by his enemies.

"Not particularly, I'm just an early riser. You?" He speaks in a weary way, his voice heavy. I wonder how long he'll talk before his wall comes back down.

"Same. Anyone else up yet?"

"No," he says, knowing I mean his men. "They stayed up late, so I suppose they're making up for it."

"Plotting an escape?"

Aiden turns and looks at me, his hazel eyes open and honest. "Should I lie to you and say no?"

I look away again, thinking over his words. This is the man I know, the one from Krakent. This is the man I fell for. "No," I reply finally, surprising even myself. "But don't tell me anything more, otherwise I'll have to tell Cass and Odette what I know."

"The blond and the brunette?"

I nod, fiddling with the hem of my skirt.

"Are you just going to stay here forever then; is this what you want?" Aiden asks, surprising me again. I look up, meeting his eyes. I can't remember the last time someone asked me what I want, if anyone ever really has. It is refreshing, if not a little scary, that it is my kidnapper who asked me and not the seers who saved me.

Is this what I want? I look out at the camp; more seers are coming out and taking breakfast from the women, a group of armed seers leaving the clearing. Is this what I want?

"I don't know," I whisper finally, my head drooping. "It should be what I want, but everyone is so…strange. Not because they're seers, but the way they act. Twelve of their friends *died* yesterday, and they're still all smiles and laughter. It's…"

"Strange." Aiden finishes my sentence, his voice hinting that he thought the same thing. "Well, besides the strange, what *do* you know that you want?"

I study him for a second, knowing I might not get a chance to talk to him openly like this again. He has a few days of growth on his jaw, stubble shadowing the lower half of his face. His hair is unkempt, pushed out of his face in a half-hazardous way. He looks tired, confused, wanting.

I quickly look away, realizing I've been staring for several seconds. "I want to go back to my mother and ask her why she never told me, ask how it is that I'm a seer *if* what you say is true. I want a purpose; I want to feel like I belong somewhere."

"Do you feel that here?" he asks quietly, still gazing at me in a way that is increasingly distracting. I hesitate, closing my eyes briefly as the wind blows, kissing my face and tossing my hair about. I want to feel that here; I really do. But I don't, and shouldn't it be an instant thing to realize you're somewhere you want to be?

I open my eyes, sighing, and Aiden nods, receiving his answer. "No. I don't know! I doubt I can belong anywhere until I truly understand what I am. I know *nothing* about myself anymore." My voice cracks and I look away for a moment as I regain my composure, my lower lip trembling as my fears and sorrow are revealed through that one slip.

I have no idea who I am anymore. Or what I am capable of.

"What do you want to know, Camari?" Aiden asks me gently. I inhale sharply, the chance to learn the truth stimulating my heart rate.

"Everything."

Aiden smiles softly to himself and looks away, watching a bird struggle to unearth a worm a few meters away. "You are a seer. Seers have two defining features: scalsen and colorful traits. I have no idea why the colorful traits exist; only the gods know. But it is suspected that the scalsen are the source of your powers and that the more you have, the more powerful you will become. Being a seer is a trait that is passed down from a parent to a child directly. And as a seer, you have visions."

"I need more than that." I frown, locking all of his words away in my mind. "Tell me more about the visions, about all of the abilities of seers. I've heard so much; what is true and what isn't?"

Aiden scowls, his eyes darkening. "Almost everything you have heard isn't true, Camari. As a seer, the gods grant you the ability to have visions or glimpses of the future's possible outcome. You do not have the ability to have a vision on command. You do not have the ability to alter the future mystically or make things happen the way you desire. You cannot see people's thoughts or curse their future. Seers are not witches, vermin, or evil. You are people who have a gift that can cause harm, just as any other thing can cause harm. You are not a monster."

A large breath I didn't know I was holding gushes out of me and I hug my knees against my chest tightly, the anxious grip around my heart fading away.

I am not a monster.

"Then why the lies?" I ask him, still not completely satisfied. "Why all of the stories I hear from people in Krakent, from soldiers? Why do people claim that seers are evil? That they can do these things."

"Because it is easier for people to accept the slaughter of others if they think it is a death that is deserved," Aiden says darkly, his voice rasping in his throat. "And because when you know nothing of someone, your mind will fabricate lies about them so that you can claim to know something."

"Why do the people know nothing? Why are they kept in the dark about colorful traits, scalsen, and their abilities? Why can't they know?" I ask my final question.

"That is sadly above my pay grade. My answer is as good as yours." Aiden sighs heavily, scratching his chin.

"So, what now? You're no longer my kidnapper, though you did still kidnap me, and I'm no longer your prisoner. What do we do now?" I muse out loud. An idiotic part of me wants us to be friends again, wants us to go back to the way things were when he was just a man, and I was just a woman; before our lives got in the way.

Aiden sighs once more, stretching his legs out in front of him. "I couldn't tell you. I've never kidnapped someone before."

"No, you just kill them," I reply quietly. Aiden falls silent for several moments, and when he speaks again, I don't expect it.

"There are things you need to understand, Camari, things that are hard to explain without confusing even myself."

I turn my head and rest my cheek on my knees so that I am looking at him again, wanting to know more about the real him, the Aiden that is here, sitting in front of me. "Try."

Aiden shakes his head with a small smile, but the look in his eyes is far from humorous. After several more moments of silence, he speaks in a quiet voice, almost as if speaking to himself. "I grew up in a highly competitive family. Morris and I both did, and in an environment like that, you always feel like you need to fight to be seen. Everything I did. I wanted to be the best at it; otherwise, what was the point? So, when I joined the army at a young age as a page, I moved up remarkably fast, working hard so that nothing else mattered. By the time I was a commissioned soldier, I was the best of my year, probably the best there had been in many years. And it still wasn't enough.

"There was an…incident that happened a few years before I received my commission, and it made me viscerally *angry*. I decided that I would never be put in a vulnerable position like that again, and I trained even harder than before, dedicated to moving up as high as there was to go, to prove myself.

"When the king offered me the position of royal assassin, I accepted eagerly, thinking that I had finally shown just how strong I was. But he added a clause to the contract that I was entirely unaware of until it was far too late. I made a deal without knowing the consequences, and by the time I did, it was too late. I'm not saying I liked seers; that would be a lie, but the idea of killing someone unprovoked made me nauseous. But I was too afraid of the consequences to disobey my orders. I still am.

"I started the job, attacking every seer village the king ordered me to, killing any seer he wanted dead. I threw up after every village; I have for two years. I've been doing it for *two years,* and I hate it. I *hate* it, Camari; I hate the look in their eyes when they know that their time is up, that I'm the cause of that lost time. I hate the empty feeling I get after each village, like I'm only causing more problems, not solving them like a soldier is supposed to. I hate how many people I've hurt and how many horrible things I've done on his orders, all because I just grew up wanting to *prove* myself." Aiden spits the last words, his eyes flashing with anger, a complicated anger directed at both himself and someone else. I know that his story so far is incredibly vague and contains no details, but it's also the most he has ever told me about his life before we met, and for now, it's enough. And I can't help the pity I feel as I see the emotions in his eyes, the anger and despair. It doesn't take away all of the horrible things he has done. Those won't ever be forgotten, but the life he has described…I have a better understanding of what drove him now.

He turns and looks at me, his hazel eyes arresting mine in their gaze. "And I hate what I did to you, taking you after you healed me and treated me with kindness, threatening your mother, tying you up. You deserved none of that."

I swallow, surprised by this sudden apology just days after he snatched me away from all I've ever known. "You know I can't tell you it's okay because it's not. You still took me, you still killed hundreds of people and sent hundreds to some estate, and you still threatened my mother," I say honestly, toying with the end of a strand of my hair. Aiden looks away, pain clouding his eyes.

"But maybe one day I will be able to say that." I finish, meaning it. He looks up, meeting my eyes and smiling faintly. I return his smile, glad that I've helped him in some way with the burden he carries.

"I know you think you're a monster, Aiden, and I know a few days ago I would have wholeheartedly agreed, but you need to know you're not."

"How do you know that?" he asks, his voice quiet and filled with pain.

"Because you still worry about it. A monster wouldn't worry," I reply simply. He smiles at me again, this time his eyes warm and open, which still surprises me. But not in a bad way, not at all.

Reaching into my shift, I pull out the pendant I found in the woods all those weeks ago, the rukh against the almond shape in the background gleaming brightly despite the dents and scratches on the metal. "I found this in the woods near where I found you, and I believe it belongs to you."

Aiden takes it with a frown, stroking the surface, before recognition alights in his eyes, and he chuckles softly. "I was wondering where I lost this."

"What is it?"

"Honestly? I don't know. I found it in my father's house when I was little. I've always loved the rukh, a mystical bird that appears only in times of bloodshed and triumph and turns the tide. To me, it seems like a symbol of hope that, at the very end, we can still hope for a rukh to save us. I would keep it with me during the raids. It gave me a semblance of hope that something would happen to change…to change my life." Aiden trails off, his eyes burning into mine, and a complete silence encases us in which I am aware of nothing but him and the way our elbows are touching, the look in his eyes.

"Camari!"

I jump, my head shooting up from where it was resting on my knees. Cass is standing a few feet away, her hand resting on the hilt of her sword. She stares at Aiden and I for a few seconds and I immediately wonder how long she was standing there.

I stand, dusting off my skirt hastily. "Is everything okay?"

"Yes, I was just wondering if you wanted a more in-depth tour," she says slowly, still looking between Aiden and I.

"That sounds great!" I exclaim brightly, folding my hands behind my back as I force myself into the overly positive attitude that seems to be a requirement in Onaydo. Cass nods, brightening up. She leads me away, talking about which tents are which and who is who. I glance back over my shoulder once, but Aiden is gone, back inside his teepee.

There were some who were not happy to have Rian as their king and they left, traveling far, and populated the other lands and continents, eventually becoming the different cultures and kingdoms they are now.

—Retractions from the Historical Documents

Chapter Seventeen

Aiden

"What the fuck are you doing? Are you trying to bed the bleeding *seer*?" Eben roars, his hands clenched tightly into fists. I clench my own fists, my rage spiking.

"Shut the hell up, Eben!"

"What, you're bored here? Need something to do with your pent-up energy?"

"I said shut the hell up, Eben! If you ever stopped running your mouth, I'd explain to you."

"Explain what? That you-"

"I'm regaining her trust, dammit!"

Eben falls silent, and the others look more interested, shifting slightly. Morris looks up at me with a strange expression on his face after overhearing my conversation with Camari.

"We want to get out of here? Well, we're going to need help from someone who isn't tied up like a pig primed for roasting. Camari will be that someone!" I snap. Eben's shoulders relax slightly, his hands unfolding.

"You really think you can get her to help us escape just by pouring out some sob story?" Miller asks, leaning back against a tent pole.

"You heard our conversation; what do you think?" I respond, turning to look at all of them.

"I think I feel bad for using her, but you're a bloody genius," Grant says, popping his knuckles. The other men all nod, muttering something of the same sort. I turn to Eben, raising my eyebrows. "Satisfied?"

He nods, turning and dropping back down to the ground. I sigh, doing my best to push my hair out of my face with my hands tied together. At least Eben is silent, and yes, maybe I hope Camari will help us escape. But I wasn't lying to her. I did, however, just lie to my men. And somehow, compared to tricking Camari into helping us, that doesn't bother me quite as much.

Act as you would be mirrored, for mercy is a reflection of one truest self. How much mercy they will expend, or rather how little, shows one's character both to others, and to the gods. There is more than one form of mercy.

—The Religious Texts; The Book of Wisdom

Chapter Eighteen

Camari

Cass is a very enthusiastic tour guide. She shows me every tent and teepee in the hollow, introduces me to every seer we run into, and tells me everyone's histories and lives. By the time she feels I've seen enough, it is almost noon, and my head is spinning.

"Are you hungry? We can go get something to eat from the storage."

"Yes," I respond quickly, feeling ravenous from walking the entire hollow. Cass smiles, turning and leading me toward the storage tent, though I already know where it is from the tour. Shoving aside the flap, Cass steps in and holds the flap for me, letting it drop behind us and cut off the rays of sunlight. The inside of the tent is stocked full of food, all neatly organized. There are burlap sacks filled with oats, flour, salt, apples, and grains. They have cured and smoked meat, jerky and uncooked slabs of venison that have been rubbed in salt to cure. They also have eggs from the chickens Cass showed me during the tour and crates of fresh produce such as tomatoes, squash, cucumbers, and potatoes.

"Wow, this is excessive," I said, looking around. Cass shrugs, handing me a strip of jerky and an apple as she takes a bite out of her own apple.

"We have a lot of people, and we make sure that none of us ever go hungry," she says, leading me back out of the tent. "A lot of it we grow ourselves; some we get from travelers or convoys that get too close. Either way, we're provided for." I nod, taking a bite of my jerky. There are indeed many seers here. It makes sense to need this much food, but stealing…

Cass slows down, looking over her shoulder at me hesitantly. "Camari, the council will be meeting to discuss what we're going to do with the assassins, and they want you to have a say. Do you want to come? I understand completely if you don't, I just-"

"Yes, I want to come," I respond immediately, interrupting her. She blinks in surprise and nods.

"Okay, come with me then."

Oh, so this is happening right now.

I follow, eating my food as we walk. If they are going to decide Aiden's fate, I need to be there. Maybe I can prevent anything too drastic.

Cass leads me to a large tent, gesturing for me to step inside before her. I do so, looking around at my surroundings. There is a long wooden table in front of me with eight chairs behind it, facing the entrance of the tent. Seven people are already seated, and Cass walks past me, taking the final seat. She gestures for me to sit in the wooden chair in front of their table. I comply nervously, smoothing my skirt over my lap before I fold my hands and wait for someone to speak. The man at the center of the table speaks first, leaning forward on the table.

"Camari, welcome to Onaydo. As I'm sure you know, we are here to discuss the fate of your kidnappers. Could you please tell us their names?"

"Aiden, Grant, Eben, Morris, and Miller," I say clearly, my foot jiggling slightly with nerves. The man nods, writing something down on the piece of parchment in front of him before he looks up again.

"And this Aiden is Aiden Baltasar Lorian, the royal assassin?" he inquires, his green eyes pinning me to the spot. I nod, biting my lip. The man leans back again, his chair creaking at his movement.

"We don't get many prisoners here in Onaydo; our enemies either die or run. That being said, this is the man who has murdered thousands of our kind. This is the man who has sent hundreds of our children to prison, where their brains are wiped away. Does he truly deserve our mercy?"

I shift in my chair, listening uneasily. The woman to the man's right speaks, leaning forward so that her long brown braid falls over her shoulder. "But don't the gods require our mercy for all, sinners or innocent?" she asks, looking up and down the table, trying to prove her point.

"Yes, but since when do we follow every idea the gods have given us?" Another man counters, his hands threaded in front of him, showing off the scalsen on his knuckles. "And when have they ever done the same for us?"

"There's another thing we need to take into account," Cass says suddenly, leaning forward on the table and, to my surprise, looking at me. "This morning, I saw you talking with the assassin, smiling with him and being friendly. Do you have feelings for this man, and will they interfere with your vote on what we do with the prisoners?"

The entire council turns to look at me, some of them raising their eyebrows at me, the first man going so far as to glare judgmentally.

"Another girl, fallen to a pretty face." A council member sighs, shaking her head. I flush bright red, completely lost for words at the wildness of the accusation.

"I do not, I mean, I did"–

"Do you not realize who he is, what he has done to our kind?" The first man interrupts, looking at me in scorn. I stand so suddenly that my chair falls back, my hands fisted at my side. This is humiliating, and I will not simply sit and take it; I will be heard.

"Let me make this clear once and for all before all of your imaginations leave your sanity and sense of reality behind completely. I have no feelings for the assassin; I do not like him, I do not care for him. I've known those men for only a few days, and over that time, I've come to learn that they are not nearly as black-hearted as they lead you to believe. One of them is even kind, but I have no feelings remotely close to affection for any of them. But they still deserve mercy." I snap, fibbing slightly. They don't need to know that Aiden and I were friends for over a moon.

I right my chair and sit back down with a thump, tossing my head and crossing my arms. The council members all begin to share looks and talk quietly among themselves, annoying me further. If I am a part of this decision, like they said, I should be included in their conversation.

I glare at Cass, furious at her wild accusations, especially since she accused me of caring for Aiden in front of a room full of strangers. It was beyond humiliating. I was just talking to him, listening to him as he opened up for once. How did that come across as attraction? Any feelings I had for him died the moment he showed my scalsen to his men.

"I move we vote. Do we execute the prisoners, or do we show *mercy* and let them live, keeping in mind just how much mercy he has shown our kin," the first man says, sneering at the word mercy. My heart sinks at his tone, already knowing what everyone's votes will be.

"All for their execution; raise your hand," he says, raising his right hand. I watch, my breath coming fast, as one by one, each council member raises their hand. Cass meets my gaze, guilt still on her face as she hesitates. But she raises her hand, looking away from me again.

"Majority rules; it's settled. They will be executed tomorrow at dawn," the first man announces in a tone of finality. I jump up, capturing all of their attention.

"You say you will show them no mercy because of how little mercy he showed our kind, but don't the gods say act as you would be mirrored? Shouldn't we show them mercy in the hope that they will learn from us and do the same? Killing them will solve nothing; it is just another death in a war that has been going on for over a decade. Why don't you be the bigger person? Why don't we stop mirroring our enemies and act the way that we want them to so that they might mirror us instead?" I beg, gesturing with my hands and trying to make them see the error they are about to make. My hope skyrockets when the man meets my gaze and smiles.

"Because life is not a fairytale."

My hope plummets once more.

The council all stands and begins to walk out in single file, a few giving me sympathetic glances, but most of them ignoring me. Cass stops in front of me, her eyes apologetic. "I'm sorry, Camari; I tried-"

"Don't lie to me! You sat there and accused me of an insane infatuation, making me look like a lovesick idiot to the council. You didn't give them a chance."

"They didn't give our people a chance either! In the battle yesterday, they slaughtered twelve people!"

"And who attacked first? Who was hiding in the bush, armed to the teeth, waiting for us so that they could rob or kill us? It wasn't us!" I shout, my anger spiking. Her eyes flash and she takes a step back, looking me up and down.

"*Us?* Are you one of them now? I thought you wanted to be here; I thought you wanted to become one of us!"

"I don't want to become a murderer, and that's what you're about to be. Their blood will be on your hands, and you will be just as corrupt as them!" I say harshly.

"The decision is made, Camari; live with it. Now, I'm going to go about my day and hope that you come to your senses." Cass smiles coldly as if nothing just happened, brushing past me and walking out of the tent. I stand there in the now empty tent, taking deep breaths and trying to get my temper under control.

Aiden and his men will die, and Cass will do nothing about it, claiming she can't do anything. But maybe I can.

I spin on my heel and march out of the tent with my head held high, checking to make sure I'm not being watched before I duck into the teepee where the men are kept.

Punishments are assigned by royal officials, servants of the king such as commissioned soldiers or positioned officers, and the king himself when necessary. They range from a fine to execution. Execution is hated by some, but it is the favorite of others.

—Excerpt from Zordan Laws and Commandments

Chapter Nineteen

Aiden

"What do you mean, execute us?"

"They are going to execute all of you at dawn," Camari repeats, crossing her arms and peeking out the teepee's flap nervously. "I don't know how; I didn't inquire after the method. Suffice it to say, you are all dead men walking."

Morris curses colorfully while Eben pales, rubbing the back of his neck. This is all moving much faster than I expected. "When did they decide this?"

"Not five minutes ago. I was included in the decision as your abductee," she says dryly, still fidgeting anxiously. Eben sneers up at her from where he sits on the ground, his knee drawn up to his chest.

"And I bet you just sat there while they sentenced us to death."

Camari returns his stare with a cold glare, genuine hatred shining on her face as she looks at Eben. "Actually, I fought tooth and nail to save your miserable life despite being humiliated. Though, maybe I'll just help your friends and leave you; it wouldn't be much of a loss."

Eben snarls and goes to retort, but Miller holds up his hand, silencing him. "Enough, children. Eben, we don't have time for your filthy mouth; we need to find a way out of here."

I nod at him, grateful for his calm logic in the current situation. Turning back to Camari, I see that she is frowning, her head tilted to the side like it always does when she's thinking.

"What?" I ask. She jumps, looking back at me, but there is a small smile on her face.

"I have an idea!" she announces, combing her fingers through her hair. "They will execute you at dawn, so we need to leave before then. I have complete freedom, and I know where they keep their weapons. I can get all of us out of here."

I know her well enough not to be fooled by her language. "But?"

She meets my gaze, lifting her chin and squaring her shoulders. "But we need to make a deal first. If I save you, for the third time, might I add, you have to make me a promise. After I get you out, you will forget you ever knew me and never try to take me away against my will again. You will let my mother and I live in peace, and you will tell no one about me. Oh, and you will leave this seer village alone as well; you will not report it. Do we have a deal?"

"Hell no!" Eben roars at the same time Miller and I say, "Deal."

Eben turns to look at me in disbelief, his mouth open. "Are you serious? We can't let her go; she's a seer! And this village plans to kill us; we can't let them bloody get away with that!"

"Yes, we can, and we will. It's a small price to pay for our lives," I say impatiently, leveling him with a glare. I will not fight about this, and Camari is handing us an out. She is handing *me* an out from this terrible situation.

Eben scowls and sinks back down, looking at the ground. I turn back to Camari, who looks delighted at Eben's discomfort. "We have a deal; you get us out, and we will leave you and this village alone."

Camari nods, running her hands through her long hair again. "Good. Here's the plan."

The sun sets far too quickly, and we don't see Camari again, though I assume that is because she is getting things ready. It is a smart, well-thought-out, and dangerous plan. I don't trust it; things never go accordingly in situations like these.

Eben sat sullenly the entire time we came up with a solid plan, not contributing in the slightest. I am utterly sick of his attitude toward Camari, especially since she is now saving our lives for the second time and mine for the third. I'm on the verge of snapping every time he scowls at her. He was never like this before we went to Krakent.

Grant is the complete opposite of Eben and appears to be slightly infatuated with Camari, sighing as she walks out. "That's a woman after my own heart. Beautiful, smart, and not afraid to break some rules."

"And, let's not forget, a seer. Not to mention, she hates us." I point out, shifting my wrists carefully to scratch an itch under the ropes. I remember what I said to her two nights ago, '*I didn't mean to fall for a seer.*' I'm such an idiot for saying that to her, for being that cruel. Yes, I had feelings for her, and even though now I know she is a seer and those feelings are gone, I had no right to be that harsh. So if she hates me now, after everything I've done and all the lies I've told, it's understandable.

"She doesn't hate all of us, only Eben," Morris says, earning a glare from Eben and a grin from me. "And she definitely doesn't hate Miller."

Miller looks up with a frown, shifting in an attempt to get comfortable on the hard ground. "What do you mean?"

"I heard you two having a lengthy conversation the other morning while we were all still resting. She wouldn't talk to any of us, but she has a half-hour conversation with you? She likes you," Morris says simply, reverting back to his futile attempts to bite through the ropes around his wrists. Miller frowns slightly, shifting yet again.

"That's not how it was," he says immediately, looking at me.

"Then what *was* it like?" Grant asks with a grin, leaning forward.

"She was asking about everyone, just gleaning information off of me. That and insulting Eben."

Morris snorts in laughter, his teeth slipping off of the rope. Grant grins while Miller goes back to trying to get his feet out of the ropes around his ankles, gritting his teeth as the ropes chafe against his skin. He does glance at me once and nods slightly, and I shake my head. I don't care; Camari and I *were* friends, and we *did* have feelings for each other. I'm simply lucky that I've been able to get back to her being cordial with me. He owes me no loyalty on that topic.

I look out the flap of the teepee again, looking for anyone I recognize. My heart leaps with nerves when I spot Camari walking around, looking completely calm and composed despite what we are about to do. I let the flap fall closed again, leaning back against the side of the teepee with a sigh. One day of captivity, and my mind won't stop spinning; my bones ache from sitting still. I need to run, climb, fight, *do something*. The night cannot come soon enough.

THE CURSE OF THE BLESSED

The sun has long set when Camari returns to our tent, slightly out of breath and with her braid falling apart. She immediately pulls a small knife from her boot and begins to saw at the ropes around my wrists, talking quickly despite obviously being out of breath.

"At the edge of the clearing by the tree shaped like a heart, that's where the blind spot is in their watch. I've hidden what weapons and supplies I could snatch underneath the azalea bush directly next to it." The ropes on my wrists snap, and she hands me another dagger before she moves onto Grant's hands, leaving me to start on my ankles. "After all of you are free from your binds, wait for sixty seconds after I leave. When you hear the distraction, count to ten and then run, and I'll meet you behind the tree."

She finishes Grant's ankles while I free Morris and then moves on Miller while I start on Eben. "If anything goes wrong and after forty seconds I haven't reached you, then go without me. They keep their horses stabled in a cave at night; Cass showed me, and it's rather ingenious. It's hidden by vines and looks like a cliff face, but it's a large cave. You should be able to find it; it's directly uphill from the azalea bush." She finishes with Miller's ropes and stands, tucking the knife back into her boot. I grab her arm gently before she can turn and duck out, my heart in my throat.

"Are you sure this is going to work?" I ask, at a loss of better words. She opens her mouth and then closes it, hesitating, and I see the doubt in her eyes but also the commitment. "Be careful, Camari. Don't risk your life for ours; it's not worth it."

She nods once and then turns to go, and I release her arm, my heart pounding. We only have one shot at this.

Seconds inch by as we all wait on the balls of our feet. And then something explodes across the clearing, and we hear the boom as the ground beneath our feet vibrates.

"What the fuck?!" Grant's eyes widen as light flashes outside the tent flap briefly. I hold up my arm as I count to ten mentally, adrenaline racing through me. As soon as ten seconds pass, I fist my fingers, and we move as one, leaving the tent and running across the empty clearing. All the way across the clearing, a tent blazes with flames as smoke streaks into the sky. Shouts fill the clearing as people beat at the flames with blankets and throw buckets of water onto the tent. It's no use; there is no saving it.

We slip into the shadows by the tree that Camari mentioned and find the weapons, passing them out amongst ourselves. Morris kisses his sword while Grant hugs his mace. I ignore them both as I clip on my sword belt and turn, waiting for Camari to appear. Ten seconds bleed into thirty, and I hold my breath, waiting.

"We need to go!" Eben snaps, backhanding my shoulder. I don't look away from the clearing, my grip on my sword hilt tightening as my patience wavers.

"We will not leave without her."

"Aiden, she told us if she didn't make it after forty seconds…" Morris says slowly. I turn and level him a glare, and he trails off.

"We've done enough without abandoning her to try and escape alone," I order. "We do not leave without Camari."

At that moment there is a rustling in the underbrush, and Camari appears, gasping for air with smoke and charcoal streaking her face, her eyes somewhat dazed. "I just set that tent on fire, and it exploded. I didn't think that would work."

Grant shoves in front of me before I can speak, his eyes alight with excitement. "That was the best bloody thing I've ever seen! How did you do that?"

'There's no time," I say shortly, shoving past him and walking over to the bush. I pull out the two satchels with supplies that Camari stored there, handing one to Camari.

"Follow me. The horses are at the top of the rise; there's one for each of us. We need to be careful; as soon as they realize the fire was a distraction, they will be coming for us." Camari instructs quickly as she begins to lead us through the forest.

I step carefully, doing my best to stay in the shadows as we half walk, half run, bending over to avoid the moon's rays. We run for a few minutes before I hear someone scream.

"FIND THEM!"

"They're coming!" I shout, standing up straight. We run full-on, no longer trying to stay out of sight.

Getting to the horses is far more important than avoiding detection now. Holding the satchel to prevent it from swinging about, I run as fast as I can, glancing over to make sure the others are doing the same. I catch Camari's eye, and she looks away, but not before I can see the guilt in her eyes. She'll have to get over that guilt and come to terms with the fact that she chose to save an assassin over staying with the seers. It's too late to go back.

Blood gushes from wounds for a reason. Our bodies naturally flush out dirt and debris. The only problem is that we don't seem to know when to stop.

—Healer's Guide to Natural Remedies

Chapter Twenty

Aiden

We run like there is a stampede of horses behind us, pumping our arms for momentum. Sticks snap under my boots, and leaves crunch, slippery with early dew and moisture.

"This way!" Camari shouts, her copper hair streaming behind her as she leads us around a tree, turning to the right. Morris curses as a branch strikes him in the face, drawing blood on his cheek. I can hear people shouting behind us, footsteps thudding as the seers give chase. There's a whistling sound that I know all too well, and I veer to the side immediately. An arrow flies by, landing where I had just been a moment ago.

"Serpentine!" I shout, running as fast as I can while swerving back and forth so that the archers have a harder target. My men follow suit, and after Camari sees what we're doing, she picks it up fast, swerving back and forth between bushes and tree trunks. An arrow flies by so close it clips my ear, drawing blood.

"Shit!" I slap my hand over my ear, pulling it away and looking it over. My blood gleams in the moonlight, warm as it drips slowly down my neck. I ignore it and run faster, turning and following Camari as she runs up a steep hill. My breath burns in my throat, the cold night air making it ten times worse. The others aren't much better, breathing heavily and stumbling occasionally, but that means our pursuers are just as tired as we were.

We emerge from the tree line and find six horses, saddled and waiting. I don't know how Camari pulled it off, but I send up a prayer of thanks as I run to the gray and mount it quickly. Glancing around to make sure everyone else is on a horse, I kick mine in the flank, shouting at it to go. We burst into a gallop, riding west. Camari's horse rides on my left while Morris is on my right, Eben, Miller, and Grant speeding along in the lead. We swerve around tree trunks, our horses kicking up clods of dirt as they run through the mud, leaves sticking to the bottom of their hooves.

More arrows whistle by, and I look up into the trees, spotting archers stationed in branches, aiming down at us. I shout a warning to the others, letting them know about the archers in the trees. More arrows whistle by and my horse squeals in fear.

As we leave the last archer behind, I hear a scream of pain that makes my blood run cold and my heart stutter. Looking over, I spot an arrow lodged into Camari's shoulder, going all the way through. Another arrow strikes her lower back, and she cries out again in a wail, her voice full of agony.

"*CAMARI*!" I scream. Her horse rears as Camari falls against its neck, knocking her to the ground, and the shafts of the arrows break off beneath her weight, eliciting one more scream. I pull my horse to a stop and jump down, running over to her. The others stop, and Morris, Grant, and Miller dismount, rushing over. I fall to my knees beside her, trying to gently pick her up. She groans as my arm brushes her wound, and my sleeve immediately becomes soaked with her blood as it spills out.

"What do we do?" Morris asks, his eyes glinting with worry.

"Leave her!" Eben bellows, gesturing at us from his horse. We all ignore him.

I look up at my men, Camari still partially in my arms. "You need to keep going. I'll get her on my horse and catch up."

"Aiden, we can't just-" Miller protests, but I interrupt.

"Miller, you made me leave you when I was injured, and now I'm asking you to listen to me. You're in charge while I'm gone; take care of Morris. We'll catch up in a matter of minutes; now go."

Miller hesitates, uncertainty lingering on his face.

"Go!" I shout again. He nods, turning and mounting his horse. Morris gives me one last look.

"You better catch up; don't die trying to play hero."

I nod, and he turns, swinging up onto his horse. They kick their horses and ride off, leaving me with Camari on the forest floor.

I can hear the seers getting closer, their footsteps and thudding behind us. I shove my arm under Camari's knees, picking her up against my chest. She cries out at the movement, her eyes fluttering closed, and I run to my horse, placing her carefully on the saddle before swinging up behind her. I hold her against me with my right arm, grabbing the reins with my left hand and kicking my horse into a gallop. We take off through the forest, Camari's head leaning limply against my chest.

"Stay awake, Camari," I order, jostling her slightly. She whimpers, but her eyes don't open. I can feel her blood soaking my shirt, her hair matting with it.

"Stay awake, dammit!" I shout, jostling her again, this time much more roughly, as my heart races with panic.

"Shut up, or someone might think you care."

My breath stutters in relief as she speaks, her voice low and weak but there.

"And we wouldn't want that, would we?" I say, playing along. She smiles weakly, her eyes still closed against the rushing wind.

"No, we wouldn't." Her voice sounds weaker, and I know she is passing out again. I jostle her again, but this time she makes no noise.

THE CURSE OF THE BLESSED

My horse breaks through the trees, reaching the road and turning to run down it, away from the seers. I listen for their footsteps, but I can't hear them anymore. We lost them.

I sigh in relief but don't let my horse stop, knowing we still have a ways to go. When we do eventually stop, we've ridden for hours and the moon is directly overhead, its glow bright. My horse pants, frothing at the mouth, and I reluctantly let it pull over off of the road. Gathering Camari into my arms, I slide off of the horse's back, carrying her off the road before laying her down carefully on the ground. Tying my horse's reins to a tree branch, I unbuckle the saddle and let it fall to the ground, shaking out the saddlebag and treating it the same way before I return to Camari's side.

Her clothes are soaked with her blood, and more still leaks out slowly. I know what I need to do, and, with a sigh, I pull out the knife I used to cut the ropes we were bound with, my mind leaping back to the day we met. The arrowheads need to come out.

I believe he is tired of seeing me around, of having to justify my presence. Not just to myself, but also to his son and to the boys. They don't understand why I am different, and it breaks my heart to see them try.

—Journal of Maren Landry

Chapter Twenty-One

Camari

I am swimming in darkness like it is a lake, floating on top and not quite sinking, not yet. It is warm and soft, rippling underneath me, and I let it take me in. But there is this noise that stops me from sinking deeper, this voice calling to someone, saying someone's name. Saying my name.

Camari.

Wake up.

"Camari!"

My eyes open weakly, and the first thing I feel is pain. My back and shoulder burn like fire, lighting up my senses. I gasp in pain, whimpering and digging my fingernails into the soft ground beneath me. A warm, callused hand touches my cheek, so large it encases it almost completely.

"Camari, are you awake?"

"Yes," I groan, blinking again and trying to get my eyes to focus. Aiden's face comes into view, concern lighting his eyes.

"What happened?" I ask groggily, still trying to put together the pieces. Aiden swallows hard before replying, and that's when I notice the blood that has soaked his shirt and dried on his neck and his chin.

"You were shot, Camari, twice. I need to get the arrowheads out before I wrap you up."

"Just do it," I gasp quickly, not wanting to give myself time to be afraid. He nods and goes about his work. I turn my head so that I can still see him, watching as he pulls out the large dagger he keeps in his baldrick, his hands shaking slightly as he steps towards me.

"I'm going to have to cut your bodice open to reach the wounds; I'm sorry about that."

"I have layers on underneath; it's fine," I respond, flushing even in this dire situation. He nods, and after cutting the stays on my bodice, pulls it away and brings his dagger to my shift, bunching it up and cutting through it so that he can see my shoulder. He winces at what he sees, setting down his dagger, and I fight against a wave of irony that we met when I treated the exact same wound on him, location and all. Aiden sees my expression and smiles slightly, the irony not lost on him.

"Open your mouth," he instructs me. I obey, and he places the leather sheath of another one of his daggers in my mouth for me to bite down on.

"Ready?" he asks, meeting my gaze with raised brows. I nod, unable to reply with the sheath in my mouth.

Taking a deep breath, Aiden digs his fingers into my wound, trying to get a grip on the arrowhead. The pain is unbelievable, *indescribable*, like tendrils of flames shooting through every part of my body. I scream, digging my fingernails into the dirt hard enough that I fear they may snap. I bite down on the leather sheath until my teeth ache and tears pour out of my eyes; I breathe quickly and deeply, emitting animalistic noises of pain.

"Got it!" Aiden exclaims, his expression one of deep concentration. I feel a pull in my shoulder muscle, followed by another burst of searing pain that makes me scream louder than ever, and then the pain lessens by an amazing amount, though it still burns and itches terribly. Aiden holds up an arrowhead on a broken shaft, both his hands and the arrowhead coated in blood. He looks down at me, breathing hard around the leather sheath and shaking with the cold and blood loss.

"Can you do this?" he asks, his eyes full of worry. I nod, though in reality, I want to shake my head ferociously. He nods once and begins to gently roll me over so that he can reach my back. I whimper, turning my head to the side so that I am resting on my cheek and can still see him. His eyes meet mine, and he nods again at me before he pulls my shift loose from my skirt. His fingertips are cold and rough against my skin as he gently pushes up the edge of my shift so that he can reach my wound. I brace myself, clenching my fists and squeezing my eyes shut.

Gods, help me.

Agony; pure, white-hot agony shoots through me, echoing around and coming back in waves, again and again. I scream and sob, my voice cracking. Tears escape my shut eyes, mixing with the dirt beneath me and making mud that streaks my face.

"I'm so sorry, Camari. I'm trying. Just breathe." Aiden's voice is quiet and in the back of my mind. His voice cracks, filled with horror and pain as I scream and sob, wishing for it to be over.

"I've got it; I'm pulling it out. Breathe, Camari, just breathe." Aiden's voice grounds me as the pain intensifies, something I hadn't thought possible, and then retreats like a monster slinking back into its cave.

"It's out; I got it out. I'm going to bandage you up, and then we're done."

I spit the leather sheath out, shivering all over. I hear a ripping noise and then feel fabric being wrapped around my torso, tightening over the still-bleeding hole in my back. He then carefully helps me turn over, laying me down gently and wrapping my shoulder as well.

"Where'd you get the bandages?" I ask, my voice rasping against my wrecked throat.

"It's a blanket I found in the saddlebag. I didn't want to have to use your cover."

I smile weakly, touched that he thought of that. "Thank you."

"Think nothing of it." Aiden's hands are steady as he ties the strips of fabric and smooths my cut shift back over the wound. "You need to rest for a while to get your strength back, a day or so, and then we'll risk moving. Ideally, I'd give you far longer, but we can't afford that luxury."

"Just help me up; we'll go now," I order, trying to sit up, only to fall back down with a gasp of pain.

"Not a chance," Aiden says, putting his hand on my good shoulder to hold me down. "You've lost buckets of blood. It would be an act of insanity to move you."

"You were up and walking around just days after I healed you." I protest, glaring at him.

"I'm a fast healer. I have a high tolerance for pain and years of training, and my wounds weren't nearly as bad as yours, not even in comparison. The arrows in you broke off when you fell and ripped your flesh open."

"Skies above, I didn't need to know all that," I grumble, sinking deeper into the ground and giving in. He smiles victoriously, standing up and looking down at his bloodstained hands.

"I'm going to start a fire, get you comfortable, and wash the blood off of my hands. We'll rest, and maybe, depending on how you are in the morning, we'll move sometime tomorrow."

I nod, knowing I can't exactly fight him about the matter. Besides, I am exhausted, in extreme pain, and my head is swimming. I do my best to relax as Aiden goes about gathering wood, lighting it with his knife and a piece of flint stone. The warmth touches my skin from two yards away, the flames lighting up the darkness even more than the bright moon above me. Aiden walks over and bends down again.

"I'm going to gently pick you up and carry you over. Is that alright?"

"No, it isn't. Help me stand, and I will walk over," I say stubbornly, carefully lifting my good arm for him to grab. He frowns down at me, a doubtful expression on his face.

"I don't know if you can walk, Camari, it's probably not a good idea with-"

"Aiden, I've suffered numerous humiliations today that I don't care to repeat; help me stand or so help me, I'll get up by myself."

Aiden sighs, defeated, and bends down to help me. He carefully wraps my good arm around his shoulder, sliding his arm under me and wrapping it tightly around my waist to support me as I stand. I inhale sharply at the pain as I get to my feet, emitting a short whimper. Aiden looks over at me, his face uncomfortably close to mine, his hazel eyes concerned.

"Still walking?"

"Still walking," I say through gritted teeth, leaning heavily on him as I walk. His arm tightens around my waist and we slowly walk to where he laid out the other blanket for me, Aiden mostly carrying me after all. He lays me down gently on the blanket, and I groan, my head swimming and my whole body aching.

"You should have let me carry you," he grumbles, though he sports a small smile even as I scowl at him.

"Not another word, Lorian." For some reason, his smile slips away as he hears his last name, and his eyes turn somber.

"I'll get some more wood for the fire; you get some rest," he says, turning and walking off before I can say anything else. I frown at his retreating back but am too tired to wonder about his reaction. Shifting slightly on the blanket, I turn towards the fire's warmth, closing my heavy eyes. I drift off to sleep before Aiden returns, too tired and warm to stay awake.

*King Keegan renamed Okara, eradicating the flags
of the all-powerful, all-seeing rukh that was
Okara's insignia. Zorda was born, their flag depicting a sun over a three-colored sea and the dawn of
a new era.*

—Retractions from the Royal Historical Documents

Chapter Twenty-Two

Aiden

I walk carefully through the woods, stepping
over large sticks to avoid making noise as I search
for dry firewood. My hands are still coated with
Camari's blood, now dry and itchy against my skin. I
rub my palms together, trying to get it off in an attempt to ease the sick feeling in my stomach. It
doesn't work, though the blood mostly flakes off.
There is nothing that can be done for my clothes,
though, and I don't doubt I have blood all over me.
Camari bled so much; it's a wonder she's still awake
and able to talk, let alone be sarcastic. Her screams
ring in my ears, echoing and making my skin erupt
in goosebumps. The feeling of her flesh around my

fingers as I grope for the arrowhead, her blood rushing down my hand, makes my stomach flip over again.

Stumbling against a tree trunk, I bend over and heave, losing the contents of my stomach onto the pine straw below. Wiping my mouth with the back of my hand, I take a deep breath, trying to ease the nausea caused by Camari's wounds.

She's okay; everything's going to be fine.

I crouch, picking up a dry piece of wood before I turn around and walk back towards where I left Camari, running my hand through my hair with a sigh. It was a relief to have my hands free; the rope was irritating, and not being able to use my hands was obnoxious. Then I remember how I kept Camari tied up the entire time and how her wrists were torn open and raw. I shove aside the pang of guilt and frown, glancing down at my own wrists. They are red and raw, with a few spots where my skin has chafed and scraped off, but Camari's are far worse. One's wrists could get as bad as hers if kept tied up, but it would take far longer than the two days she was tied up. It would take maybe a week, probably more. So why were hers so bad?

I think back to when she was riding on the horse before she warned me not to take the left road. Had she been acting strangely? She was sitting still on her horse, her hands hidden in her skirts. The skirts were stained with blood. She must have been fighting against her ropes discreetly, trying to loosen them so that she could slip her hands out. The fact that she would continue to do that despite the pain impresses me. She must have been trying to escape, to get away, and I'm not honestly surprised. I think a small part of my mind knew from the moment she found me in the woods that she would be trouble, possibly more than she was worth. And I wasn't foolish enough to think she wouldn't try to escape. I just didn't notice her subtle attempts. Anyone in her situation would have tried to escape, to get away from me. I am a monster; what should I expect?

I look up at the sky, trying to gauge what time it is. The moon is slowly descending, making way for the sun's appearance. It will be morning in a matter of hours, and I have no doubt that Camari will make us travel, wounded or not. She is annoyingly stubborn that way.

I hope my men haven't gone too far ahead and that we'll catch up with them soon; I worry that they've been caught. I know Morris will be waiting for me; he is loyal, always letting me take the lead. He'll listen to Miller while I am gone. Miller truly is my number two; Eben is far too hot-headed for the job. But he is useful in other ways, and he has been part of our brotherhood for as long as myself. You put up with each other's flaws when you're a family.

I emerge from the woods, the fire bright and glowing still. Camari is asleep, her face relaxed and her hair billowing under her as she sleeps. I look down at her, smiling slightly. She looks so peaceful, which is funny considering what a fire-breathing devil she can be when she wants to, riddling Eben speechless with a few well-thought-out words.

I sit down next to her, throwing the piece of wood I grabbed into the fire. A burst of sparks fly up, floating into the sky and looking like orange stars before they blink out, one by one.

I look back down at Camari; her cheek smeared slightly with mud and dirt. I have no idea what will happen after she is well enough to travel on her own. She sure as hell won't come to Sutoran; that is the last place I want her. And she won't want to be around Eben more than she needs to be. But she can't be by herself yet; she is far too weak and injured, and I plan to continue on and find my men. So that leaves the problem of what we will do after we find them. Maybe she'll leave after that, returning to Krakent and her mother. I don't know, though; I have no idea what we will do after she is healed. I won't back out of our deal; she is free from us, and that is that. I just have to figure out what to do next.

I hesitate for a second but pull the rukh pendant from around my neck, gazing at it for a moment before I rest it in her hand. She is lost, unsure of who or what she is, where she should go or what she should do. She needs a rukh. And I already got mine.

This contains remedies for most physical ailments that commonly occur. Know that if a cure for an emotional ailment is what you seek, I regret to inform you that you will not find that in any herb.

—Healers' Guide to Natural Remedies

Chapter Twenty-Three

Camari

I wake to the sound of Aiden moving around, killing the fire and feeding the horse. I prop myself up, stifling a groan at the movement. I feel clear headed, which is definitely a good thing, and starving. But my shoulder and lower back throb with a deep, burning ache.

Aiden looks over at me, smiling when he sees me awake. "You look like shit."

"Thank you for the unneeded honesty," I reply dryly, wincing as I pull all of my hair over one shoulder, trying to pick out some of the mulch and dried blood.

"How are you feeling?" he asks, walking over and sitting down beside me. I eye his shirt, coated in dried, rusty brown stains.

"Surprisingly well, given I lost that much blood. Thirsty and hungry."

"That's good," he says with another smile. He pulls the satchel toward him and takes out the canteen, handing it to me with a warning to drink slowly. I obey, refraining from reminding him that I'm a healer and know exactly what to do. The water goes down well and I sigh in relief, my pain instantly lessening, and when I feel no nausea, I risk eating the apple he hands me, the juice making my hand sticky. My shoulder and back ache horribly, sending waves of pain through my body that are hard to ignore, but all in all, I am well off. I am alive.

"We're riding today," I announce, tossing my apple core with a wince and using more water to wash off my hand. Aiden sighs, rolling his eyes.

"I knew you'd say that."

"Well, it seems we're finally getting to know each other," I respond, wiping my hands on my skirt, though it is filthy too and doesn't do much good. Holding my hand out, I look up to Aiden with a raised brow. "Help please."

"Let me saddle the horse first so that you don't have to stand very long," he says, turning away and picking up the satchel. I watch as he shakes out the saddle pad and slowly begins to reassemble everything, taking time to stroke the horse's nose for a few moments. Now that we're alone and on even ground with no more secrets or responsibilities between us, our fight from a few nights ago comes rushing back into my mind.

THE CURSE OF THE BLESSED

I didn't ask to fall for a liar and a murderer.

I didn't ask to fall for a seer.

"We should probably talk," I say slowly, picking at a scab on my wrist, "you know, about the other night."

Aiden stills halfway through tightening the girth on the saddle and his face flushes, something I've never seen a man's face do before.

I should not find that funny.

"Yes, I suppose we should," he says slowly as he stands up, rubbing the back of his neck as he turns to face me. A silence falls between us as we stare at anything but each other, him staring at the ground while I continue to pick at scabs.

"Things were said," I blurt out finally, ready to crawl out of my skin, "and I think we should both just clarify what was meant."

Aiden nods, not being of any help, and I scowl. *I guess I'll start.* "I said that I…fell for you."

"I remember." Aiden coughs, sitting down a few feet away from me.

"Fell as in past tense," I say, staring up at the sky and praying to sink into the ground. "I had feelings for you back when we were in Krakent, but those feelings went away when you showed my scalsen to your men."

"I'm sorry," he says softly, surprising me. "Breaking your trust almost broke me."

"It doesn't matter, it happened. I've forgiven you, and maybe I can get back to trusting you but trusting *you.* The Aiden I fell for in Krakent doesn't exist; I didn't actually know anything about him. He was a fantasy." I trail off, a wave of sorrow going through me. I'm grieving for someone who never truly existed, but still, it hurts the same.

"I understand," Aiden says, picking up where I left off. "Neither of us truly knew each other. You didn't know who I am or what-what I've done," Aiden breaks off, clearing his throat, "and I didn't know that you are a seer."

I frown, hit by an illogical wave of hurt. "So it's not that I'm a different person or that I lied to you, because I didn't; it's purely because of the ugly markings on my skin?"

"No, that isn't-i didn't mean it like that!" Aiden assures me, standing up. He also looks like he'd like to sink into a hole, which makes me feel slightly better. "Your scalsen are beautiful, Camari; they truly are. I didn't mean it the way it sounded. I meant…You lost your feelings for me because I lied to you, because you never truly knew me. And I lost feelings for you because…"

I wait, watching him as his eyes flick back and forth, his brain obviously spinning, but no explanation comes out. A minute passes, and finally I exhale heavily, giving up. "It doesn't matter, Aiden. Whatever the reason, we've clarified that we don't have any of those feelings anymore, right?"

"Right." He echoes me, clearing his throat. "Are you ready to keep moving? We should put as much distance between us and Onaydo as possible."

I hold up my hand again, ready to leave this entire conversation behind, and he takes it, his large hand encasing mine. He pulls me up gently, but my legs buckle, and I start to fall back down. He catches me quickly, his hand circling my waist and steadying me, holding me against him as I get my balance. I blame the blood loss; it made me weak. I look up and find Aiden looking at me, his eyes soft.

"Are you okay?" he asks quietly, his face close to mine. Too close. I start, realizing how close we are standing, his hands on my hips and my hands on his chest. His face is mere inches away from mine; his hazel eyes the color of fallen leaves, his sandy brown hair hanging over his forehead. This close-up, I noticed he managed to shave, his jaw smooth except for a spot at the corner of his lip where he missed a few stray whiskers.

Then I realize we've been standing like this for several seconds, and I am far too close to him.

"Yes," I say, pulling away abruptly so that his hands slip from my waist and smoothing my skirt as an excuse to look away from him. Aiden clears his throat as he steps around me to take the horse's reins, leading it over to where I stand.

"I'll help you up before I get up," he tells me, gesturing to the horse. I nod, walking over to the horse. Grabbing onto the pommel of the saddle, I place my right foot in the stirrup, wanting to climb up by myself. Taking a deep breath, I push with my leg and pull with my arm at the same time. Pain stabs through my back and shoulder, my back having a muscle spasm. I hiss air out of my teeth and fall back to the ground, slumping against the saddle as I breathe heavily against the pain. Aiden stands to my left, his arms crossed over his chest as he watches me.

"I can help you," he says, lowering his arms and stepping forward. I raise a hand, stopping him as I shoot a glare at him.

"I can get up by myself." I hiss, turning back to the horse. I don't need him touching me again. Sweat breaks out on my forehead, but counting to three in my head, I pull and push at the same time, determined to get up by myself. My wounds tear and burn, but I get my leg over the horse's back, breathing heavily. Wiping sweat off of my forehead with the back of my hand, I feel warm liquid beginning to seep into the bandages around my shoulder and torso and know I've opened my wounds again. Still, I got up by myself, and that is all that matters.

Aiden grabs the pommel of the saddle and swings up behind me with annoyingly little effort, settling into the saddle and taking the reins. His chest is warm and hard against my back, and I resist the urge to lean against him, tired already from just getting onto the horse.

"Let's go," I say, holding on to the horse's mane. Aiden nudges the stallion on its side, and he starts forward. We travel at a steady pace, both of us silently acknowledging that I can't handle anything faster. The horse has a smooth, long gait, which is much preferable to a short, bumpy one. I try to keep my discomfort to myself, doing my best to keep my grunts and gasps quiet, but I know Aiden is well aware of my pain. We've been riding for a few hours, the sun shining down on us and making me miserably hot on top of achy, when Aiden speaks, breaking the long silence.

"Do you want us to stop? We can rest until to-morrow." He offers, his arm brushing mine as he turns the horse's reins slightly.

"No, I'm okay. We need to find the others." I in-sist, wincing as my wounds pulse again.

"Camari, I can see you bleeding through your shift," Aiden says in exasperation, pulling the horse to a stop. "We only have a few more days of road left before we're in Spás Folamh, and we won't be able to rest nearly as comfortably there. Take advantage of the woods while you have them, and heal."

"If your men go too far into Spás Falamh without you, you won't be able to catch up and might not be able to make it back to your home."

"That's not your concern." Aiden's voice is filled with frustration with me, but I am not relenting.

"Look, I'm sitting down, so I'm technically rest-ing. We need to carry on because despite how annoy-ing you are, I don't want you stranded here. We can catch up with your men, and by then, I'll probably be well enough to leave. That way, Eben won't get any ideas about taking me to Sutoran."

"We promised we won't; he'll keep his promise," Aiden says firmly; his faith in his men is unshakeable.

"Well, still, we need to find them, and to do that, we need to ride the bloody horse, so let's go. I promise that if the pain gets too bad, I'll tell you."

"No you won't," Aiden scoffs, but I hear the smile in his voice, and he kicks the horse into movement again.

We ride for several more hours, the heat horrible. At one point we stop only to take off any extra layers in an effort to cool off. Aiden douses his shirt with a small bit of water from the canteen, frowning when he looks at me.

"Your bandages are almost soaked through."

I twist to look, which is a mistake, and whimper at the wave of pain but wave him off feebly. "I'm fine; let's just keep going."

"You're going to fall down dead because of your stubbornness." he declares, helping me onto the horse before swinging up behind me.

"Well then, you'll be free of me at last."

I hear him chuckle slightly behind me as we ride and smile to myself, several degrees cooler and in a better mood. With the hot sun glaring down on me, probably giving me a very dark tan, not to mention many more freckles, I am warm as well as tired. That combines with the steady movement of the horse, and I begin to doze, my chin slumping against my chest. I finally fall asleep, falling back against Aiden as my exhaustion takes over.

I wake up as our horse stops moving, the change in motion jarring me from my sleep.

"Wha- How long was I asleep?" I ask, wincing as I sit up straighter and rub my eyes. The sun has set and the sky is purple with the colors of twilight.

"A few hours. You needed it." Aiden leads the horse off of the road and a few yards into the woods before stopping it again, swinging down from the saddle. He holds up his hand to help me down and I go to accept it, but he moves past my hands and grasps my waist, lifting me down. I let him, knowing I am too weak to get down myself. My wounds are worse than I want to admit, and it irritates me. I'm not good at being injured or sick. I heal people and help people; I do not like being healed or helped.

Aiden sets me gently on the ground before he steps back, leaving me feeling suddenly cold, and takes the horse over to a patch of grass. I walk over as he ties the reins to a low branch and begins to un-buckle the saddle, letting it fall to the ground, as I am too weak to pick it up. Aiden raises his eyebrows at me but lets me help, taking the saddle pad and shaking it out before he hangs it on a tree branch to dry out. He strokes the horse a few times on the back, murmuring appreciatively in its ear. "Thanks for carrying us so far, boy."

I smile at him but turn away, struggling to stay standing as my pain levels begin to rise. I do my best to shove it away and help gather firewood, but Aiden must see pain on my face, and he stops me. "I'll do this; sit down and rest."

I object despite the pain in my back, not wanting to be a burden. He gives me a firm look, and I know he won't change his mind, so I sit down with a sigh of relief, leaning back carefully against a tree trunk.

Aiden gets a fire going quickly, stacking wood in the flames before sitting down beside me with a sigh, looking just as tired as me.

"How far did we travel today?" I ask, stifling a sigh. Aiden stokes the fire as he speaks, making embers fly up.

"We got pretty far actually; we're about two days of travel from the Spás Folamh. We'll leave the road tomorrow and continue to travel west. There will be grass for the first day, and then after that, when it's barren, we'll be in the Spás Folamh."

"No sign of your men?" I ask, looking over at him. He sighs, running his hands through his hair in a weary way.

"No, not a sign."

"We'll find them, Aiden," I say gently, smiling at him. He looks over at me with his own smile, though it appears forced.

"I hope so."

An easy silence falls between us as we both prepare to sleep, the only sounds being those of the fire crackling and the horse snuffling around through the grass. I look over at him, watching as he lies with his arms tucked beneath his head, a light frown creasing his forehead. I know that face; he's worrying. I swallow, turning back to face the fire as I'm struck by a wave of grief, because I *don't* know that face. At least, I thought I did; I thought I knew him. I thought I'd met a man who finally made me feel what I've longed to feel, who made me long for more. I thought I'd met someone who wanted me the way I've always wanted to be *wanted,* who cared. But even though Aiden isn't simply this horrible, murderous monster, even though he's a mixture of the monster and the man I knew, he's still not the man I knew. That man was pure, funny, caring, and, most importantly, he wasn't dangerous. But that man is gone; he's dead. And now my heart is broken, yearning for him and constantly searching for him in the Aiden I have now. It's torture, feeling a pull to him when he's not *him.* To still have these feelings when I know that my Aiden disappeared the second he saw my marks…it's torture.

"Camari, are you okay?" I jolt as Aiden rests his hand on my elbow, realizing with a start that I'm sobbing, tears streaming down my face. "Are you in pain? What is it?"

I lean away from him and lay down with my back to him, blocking him out. "Nothing, I'm fine. Just go to sleep."

"Camari-"

"It's nothing!" I insist, tears still streaming down my face. He's silent for a moment, and then I see his shadow recede as he settles back down. I continue to cry, biting my fist to muffle the sound, my tears turning the ground beneath my cheek into mud. My mind continues to torture me, replaying the moment I told Aiden about my scalsen. I remember how he took my hand in his and the look on his face, of such compassion and tenderness, it still makes my heart ache. The way he hugged me, holding me as if he never wanted to let me go.

He isn't real. I need to let him go.

But the tears keep coming.

In its wrath, the rukh works with the gods and their power and manipulates the weather to fit its desires. Any storm, quake, or heat that occurs could be caused by a rukh as it manipulates to its advantage.

–The Mythical, Magical, and Mundane: Folklore of Zorda

Chapter Twenty-Four

Camari

We left Onaydo five days ago and have been riding for four. We left the *road* two days ago, now riding across grassy hills and plains, the woods on either side slowly thinning more and more until they are all but gone. The previous afternoon, I noticed the grass was getting yellower and scarcer, and now, after a few hours of riding, it is gone altogether. The greenery has been replaced by broken and cracked earth, sand, and rocks. I look around, not liking how open it is. There are rocky crags and red-tinted stones, a few brittle trees that lack any leaves and provide no shelter, and a wide open sky as far as one can see, stretching in every direction. The clouds are nonexistent, and the sun burns down on us.

Aiden is in charge, leading us alongside a thin stream that goes in the same direction we are trying to go. According to Aiden, it goes most of the way but will dry up in two weeks or so, and then we'll have to go without it. He is confident he knows the way, saying he's undergone this journey many times, but I am less sure. What if we get lost without water or a guide? I hoped we would catch up with his men by now, but they seem to have continued on without us, and we still haven't found them. What if we never do? I can't go all the way to Sutoran with Aiden; I need to turn around before the river dries up. I've only stayed with him this long because I'm still healing and haven't been able to take care of myself. I am healing quickly, though, and in a few days, I'll be able to fend for myself well enough. But what if we don't find his men by then; could I really leave him out here by himself?

I push the thoughts away, telling myself I'll deal with it when the time comes. And it is coming fast.

Aiden never brought up my sobbing fit the other night, and I'm grateful for it, desperate to put that pain behind me. I need to move on, to keep my focus ahead of me and not lament over the past. Most importantly, I need to forget any feelings I did or still do have because they are irrelevant now and need to go.

It occurs to me that I've now been gone from Krakent for nine days, soon to be two weeks. How has so much happened in a matter of days? I've been kidnapped, I've discovered I may be a seer and found a whole village of other seers, I've been shot, and now

I am riding farther and farther away from Krakent with my would-be kidnapper. Shouldn't that scare me more than it does? I am comfortable around Aiden; I might even trust him again. He hasn't been using his wall; he's just been Aiden with me, and it's so easy to forget everything when he's himself, to forget he's not the Aiden from Krakent. I can't explain it, but somehow, I just know that he won't double-cross me again, just like I know he didn't want to in the first place. Maybe it's foolish, but I don't suspect he'll turn me in. His feelings for me may be gone, but he still had them. I may be a seer, but that doesn't warrant complete hatred, not from him. And he has honor. Granted, he is an assassin, but he still seems to have more honor than anyone I've ever met.

I turn my head and glance at him out of the corner of my eye. He's staring straight ahead with a determined look on his face, his jaw set. He's darkened several shades from the sun, as have I. While he was a few shades darker than me to start with, making me think he has some ancestors from the foreign kingdom Bheofraige that lies across the sea, I now have skin almost as dark as his.

"Do you see that?"

Aiden's voice pulls me from my thoughts, and I face forward once more, looking at where he points. There appears to be a dark cloud building up in the distance, blocking out the sun in that area.

"A rainstorm, right?" I guess, glancing back at him. His eyes are dark, and he shakes his head, looking grim.

"No, it's a sandstorm."

"What's a sandstorm?" I ask, confused. "And don't tell me it can rain sand because I'm not *that* naive."

"It's a strong wind that carries sand with it. I've seen one bury a campsite in just a few minutes, along with all of the sleeping soldiers. We need to find shelter before it reaches us; otherwise, we're goners."

I swallow, pushing down my rising panic as I look around for some sort of shelter. The gods seem to be throwing everything at us.

"There!" I announce, pointing to a small cave on the side of a pile of stones. Aiden turns the horse towards it, kicking us into a canter. I bite my lip to keep from groaning in pain at the bumpy movement, leaning forward against the wind. Already, it's stronger, whipping my hair about and blowing sand into my half-closed eyes. "There isn't enough sand here for a storm that big, right?"

"Not right now, but the storm is bringing sand with it," Aiden explains grimly as we grow nearer to the cave.

We pull up beside the overhang, kicking up pebbles, and Aiden jumps down from the horse before he helps me down, once again grabbing my hips and lowering me to the ground. I grab the horse's reins and lead it into the small cave, finding it is deeper than it first appeared. Aiden goes about preparing immediately, as he is the only one of us who has seen a sandstorm before. He takes his knife and cuts up the torn bodice I've long since stopped wearing altogether, the sun too hot for it. He cuts two ragged squares of fabric from it and douses them with water so that they are soaking wet before he hands one to me.

"When the sandstorm comes, hold this over your mouth if sand starts to blow in. You don't want to breathe it in." He advises darkly.

I nod, taking the makeshift handkerchief and sitting down beside him on the ground. The light beyond the cave has changed, growing dark as the sun is blocked out. The wind picks up slowly, a gentle breeze blowing outside. And then it hits, and the whole world grows dark. It happens so suddenly, the wind howling and roaring like a monster. The sound of the sand rushing by echoes through the cave and frightens me. Small streams of sand blow in on either side of the shelter, making the fire flicker and dance, but mostly, it continues to blow past the cave entrance. The horse stamps nervously and knickers, blowing hot air out of its nostrils. I lean back against the cave wall and shift closer to Aiden as the temperature grows colder, the sun being blocked along with its warmth. Aiden turns and glances at me out of the corner of his eye, smiling slightly.

"It's going to be fine; they pass as suddenly as they come."

I nod; the noises outside the cave combining with the darkness and sudden cold, making me begin to tremble in a combination of cold and fear. I pull my legs up to my chest and wrap my arms around them, setting my chin on my knees. Aiden looks at me again, concern gleaming in his eyes. He shifts closer and wraps his arm around my shoulders. I stiffen, my shoulders straightening, but relax against him, allowing myself to take advantage of his body heat.

"It'll be fine, you'll see," he says reassuringly, his hand rubbing my arm gently.

"You better be right," I mutter teasingly. He smiles, and we settle down, sitting in silence as we wait out the storm. Even the horse begins to calm, folding its legs and lying down in the ground beside us.

Then the wind changes, blowing in our direction. Sand sprays against us, making my eyes burn and water. Aiden jumps up, raising his hand in front of him against the spray of sand, and grabs the saddle pad off the ground.

"Cover your mouth!" he shouts at me, picking up the saddle pad and coming back towards me. I lift the wet cloth and held it over my nose and mouth, screwing my eyes shut. The cloth keeps the sand out of my nose so that I can breathe, but it still hits my skin, stinging and burning. Aiden and I move to sit beside the horse and he sits beside me, holding his own cloth over his nose. He lifts the saddle pad and covers us with it, huddling against me so that it covers both of us and the horse's face. His side presses against me, his head touching mine as he squeezes his eyes shut and covers us with the saddle pad. It stops the sand from peppering our skin, and despite the noise, the cold, and the pressure of the sand against the cover, we are safe.

I open my eyes now that the stream of sand is blocked and find Aiden with his already open. His gaze meets mine, and he nods slightly at me as he takes his damp cloth and wipes the sand from my eyes and face gently.

It will be fine, I read in his eyes. I choose to believe him, nodding in return before I move closer, taking comfort in his closeness.

I lose track of how long we sit there, maybe minutes, maybe hours. It all blurs together, whisked away by the sand and the wind. Aiden was right when he said it ends as soon as it starts. The winds die suddenly; the sand stops pelting against the saddle pad. Aiden lowers it carefully, dropping his wet cloth and blinking as the sunlight returns outside of the cave, bringing heat with it. I lower my own cloth, sitting up straighter. It ended so quickly, it feels surreal.

Aiden stands, leaving my side cold where we were pressed together. He walks to the entrance of the cave and peers out, checking to see what the sandstorm left behind. I stand up, patting the horse on his sand-covered back before I turn to face Aiden as I shake the sand out of my clothes and hair.

"Is it safe?" I ask, meeting his gaze as I bring my hair over my shoulder and run my fingers through it.

"Yes, it's gone now," he replies, walking over and picking up the saddle pad from where he let it fall. He shakes it out, sand falling down in a torrent. I take the horse's reins and lead it up, wiping it down with my scrap of cloth and getting all of the sand off of it.

Aiden lifts up the saddle and begins to redress the horse. Aiden leads the horse out of the cave and I follow, squinting at the light. Despite the thick layer of sand over the cracked, dry ground, there is no damage. The tree still stands, the rocks are still red, and the sun still glares brightly. Aiden steps back so that I can mount the horse before he swings up behind me, reaching around me to grab the reins. He nudges the horse and we start moving again as if nothing happened. I look around as we ride, fascinated that nothing has changed from such a terrifying storm. It is as if it never happened, but I know it did.

"You've heard of the calm before the storm?" Aiden asks me suddenly, making me jump. I nod, looking back at him out of the corner of my eye. He surveys the land around us with a calm, satisfied expression.

"The same can be said for after."

We're halfway across the Spás Folamh and will soon reach Darragh. I don't know what to expect, don't know what we'll find. But communications say seers are thriving in the South. And wherever the seers, we go.

—Field Journal of Aiden Lorian

Chapter Twenty-Five

Aiden

It has been two days since the sandstorm, and I am losing hope that we'll ever find my men. They've been ahead of us for a week now; how much farther can they have gone? I sigh heavily as I think of Morris, who is probably worrying for me. When will I find them? And how much farther can I risk taking Camari before it's too late for her to turn back?

I sigh again, and Camari twists to look at me, barely wincing at the movement. She's healing miraculously well. That, or she is good at hiding her pain, just like me.

"What's wrong?" she asks, concern weighing down her voice. I simply shake my head.

"Nothing, just thinking."

"About Morris?"

"How do you do that?" I ask, unable to fight my smile.

"Do what, know what you're thinking about? I'm a mind reader as well as a seer, didn't you know?" she teases, pulling her hair over her shoulder as she does so often. I stare at the strands for a few moments as she runs her fingers through them before I blink and look away, flushing. Something as simple as her hair being free and loose is extremely distracting as of late and I don't know why. I don't want to know why.

"It's okay, Aiden, we'll find them," she says, turning to face forward once more. I nod, hoping she's right.

The stream gurgles and bubbles beside us as we ride, still filled with water. I hope it stays that way all the way to Sutoran, but I know it won't. It's not the first thing I've hoped for that will never come true.

"Aiden, look!" Camari speaks suddenly, her voice tinged with fear. I look at where she's pointing and my heart lifts. Up ahead of us are two caravans and numerous men on horses. It isn't Morris and my men, no; it is more than that. It is the entire contingent of soldiers. My men must have caught up with them early, and they are waiting for me.

I grin but catch sight of Camari's face, and my smile fades. She's pale, all of the blood leaving her face so that her freckles stand out, and her eyes are wide with fear.

"Camari, it's going to be okay. We made a deal." I assure her.

"Yes, you and your men did. That entire group of soldiers didn't," she says, her voice shaking. I know she's right, and I try to think of something to do. I have no doubt they've already seen both of us, so I can't just leave her here to walk, not to mention she'd never make it, not walking. But, if they see her scalsen, she'll be arrested, no questions asked.

"Put your cover on, quickly!" I instruct her, slowing the horse so that it barely crawls, giving her time. She obeys, her fingers shaking slightly. After she's slipped it on and buttoned it up all the way, she takes out the fabric square I cut from her old bodice and wraps her hair in it, tucking in every strand with trembling hands until it is all out of sight.

"Okay, stay calm." My voice slips and rings with authority without my intention, and it seems to calm Camari to some extent. "Once we arrive, I'll introduce you only as someone who saved my life and who is going back to Krakent. They will see nothing, they will let you go, and you can return home. Understood?"

"Understood." She confirms, her voice still shaking. I release the reins and take her hands in mine gently, squeezing them slightly.

"It's going to be okay, Camari. I won't let them hurt you; I promise." I vow, squeezing her hands once more. They're soft and warm in mine, and it feels strangely natural to hold them. I shake the feeling off and return my grip to the reins.

Camari turns to look at me, her dark eyes warm as she smiles trustingly. "I believe you."

We are a few yards away from the contingent when I see Morris racing out to meet us. He pulls up beside us, grinning brightly, and we lean over our saddles and clasp hands.

"Brother, it's good to see you." Morris smiles, scanning me up and down for injuries. His eyes linger on my bloodstained shirt for a moment before he turns to Camari, warning in his eyes. "What exactly is the plan here?"

"We give her a horse and some supplies and let her go on her way, and we say *nothing*. We made a deal, and we'll stick to it." I state firmly. He nods in agreement.

"Sounds good to me, but what about Eben?"

"Even he won't go back on a swear."

Morris looks unconvinced, but he nods all the same, and we ride towards the contingent, Camari gripping my wrists nervously.

As we get closer, men come out to meet us, though a lot of them stay with the caravan. I remember what is in there, or rather, who is in there, and my stomach turns as everything comes back to me with sparkling new clarity. I was able to escape myself and what I had to do for the past moon and a half. Not anymore.

And now Camari sees what you've done. She sees you for the monster you are.

THE CURSE OF THE BLESSED

Camari stares at the caravan, folding her hands in her lap, and I place my hand on her shoulder in an attempt at comfort. I am the cause of their imprisonment; I *won't* be the cause of hers.

"Well well well; look who survived." Eben crows, walking towards us. He's followed by my men and some of the soldiers, including Lieutenant Gladwell, the man I left in charge. I grin, dismounting and clasping hands with each of them, patting them on the shoulders in greeting.

"You took forever to catch up, mate; we were worried something actually happened to you," Grant says, shaking his head.

"Well, nothing did," I reply, turning to Miller, who is smiling faintly at us. "You did your duty well, Miller; you should be proud."

"I am, and you should be, too," he says, still smiling.

"What's she doing here?" Eben growls. I turn and see that Camari has dismounted and walked up behind me, her fear completely hidden as she stands with her chin raised and her shoulders back.

"Oh, I'm here just to see you, of course," she says, glaring at him with venom. I give Eben a hard look before he can retaliate.

"We made a deal, Eben, and we will abide by it. She gets a horse and supplies, and then she's on her way."

"Are you insane? We can't do that!" he hisses, staring at me like I've grown a second head. Lieutenant Gladwell steps up to me, saluting.

"Lorian, good to see you well. You had us worried."

I nod to the soldier, trying to be polite while still glaring at Eben in warning.

"No need, Lieutenant, I am well and ready to continue."

Gladwell turns to Camari, who looks at him with slightly narrowed eyes. "And who is this young lady?" he asks, looking at me suggestively.

"This is-"

"Kazi. Kazi Malcolm," Camari says suddenly, holding her hand out to him and smiling brightly. Miller raises his eyebrows behind the lieutenant's back, and I fight back a smile. You can't say she isn't a good liar.

"Yes, *Kazi*. She helped us get out of a bit of a problem back in Krakent and in turn, we said we'd help her. She needs a horse and supplies, and then she'll be on her way," I explain, picking up where she left off. Camari smiles at me, her dark eyes gleaming, and I realize these are the last moments we'll ever spend together. After this, we'll go our separate ways, never to meet again. I swallow, filled with sorrow and something else I can't put a name on. Camari's smile fades as she continues to look at me, and she shifts slightly so that our hands brush together, linking our pointer fingers together. My hand feels warm when we touch, and I squeeze her finger once before I let her go like I should have the day I met her. Because someone as beautiful as her has no place in the life of someone as poisonous as me.

Lieutenant Gladwell nods, jolting me back to reality. "Of course, we'll be happy t-"

"Cut the crap, Aiden," Eben growls. Gladwell cuts off and frowns at him, confused, while Grant subtly stomps down hard on Eben's foot.

"I don't know what you're talking about, Eben. That is no way to speak to your commanding officer," I growl through gritted teeth. He ignores me, still glaring at Camari, whose eyes have gone strangely vacant, her face empty.

"She's a bleeding seer, and we owe her nothing!"

Grant winces, Morris facepalms, and Miller glares at Eben with an anger I've never seen on his face before. Gladwell turns to look at both Camari and I, frowning in confusion.

"Is this true?" he asks, looking at Camari. The strange expression is gone from her face and she shakes her head, still playing the innocent young woman with a surprising talent as well. Even I half believe her.

"No, Lieutenant, I have no idea what this man is talking about. He's been grumpy with me ever since I helped them in Krakent. You know, injured pride and all."

Gladwell nods, but his eyes narrow on her forehead, where a single strand of her hair is barely visible.

"I'm going to need to see your hair, *Kazi*," he says, his voice full of distrust. Camari pales, and I jump in, taking a step forward.

"Now, Lieutenant, is this really necessary? You know-"

"Oh, for the love of all that is holy!" Eben growls. Before anyone can react, he steps forward and grabs Camari roughly, making her cry out in pain as he pulls her toward him.

"Eben! Let her go!" I order, clenching my fists in anger as I advance towards him. Camari stares at me in fear, and my heart clenches in my chest. I promised her I wouldn't let them hurt her.

"This isn't Kazi or whatever crap she said. Her name is Camari," Eben says loudly, grabbing the cloth around her head and ripping it off. Her hair tumbles down her back, practically glowing in the sun. Gladwell turns and glares at me accusingly, but I'm not ready to give up yet.

"Lieutenant, Eben took one look at her hair and accused her of being a seer, refusing to listen. It's just red hair, that alone doesn't make a seer!" I snap, trying to twist his vision of Eben. I see the doubt in his eyes as he looks at Eben, seeing how he scowls at everyone and holds Camari in a painful grip. It is working. I don't even recognize him; the man I knew and loved vanished the moment I ordered them not to kill Camari, and he won't be coming back.

"Gladwell, ignore that son of a bitch, look!" Eben shouts at the lieutenant. He grabs the front of

Camari's cover, yanking her bad arm so that she cries out in pain when she resists, and pulls, ripping the already old and tattered cover off. Camari's scalsen are dark against her tan skin, standing out in beautiful shapes and patterns. But to Gladwell and Eben, they aren't beautiful. They weren't beautiful to me until a week ago, days ago.

Lieutenant Gladwell glares at Camari, disgust in his eyes, and Eben grins victoriously. I look at Miller helplessly, and he returns the look, as do both Morris and Grant.

What do we do now?

The lieutenant walks to Camari and grabs her chin, making her look him in the eyes despite how she quivers and shakes with fear. "You're a liar and a filthy seer on top of it. You're coming with us. Eben, take her to the caravan."

"No! Let me go! NO!" Camari screams, desperately pulling against Eben despite how much pain she must be in. She writhes and struggles, her hair flying about, and after she stomps down on Eben's foot in an effort to get away, he scowls, pulling her closer.

"Bitch!" he spits, striking her across the face. She whimpers, emitting a broken sound that I never thought I'd hear from her, and I am moving before I even realize it.

"Don't do this!" I hear Morris shout at me, but it doesn't even register. Eben's nose crunches as my fist makes contact, spurting blood. He lets go of Camari, who falls down onto the ground and scrambles to her feet. I punch Eben again, making him stumble back, and I go to hit him again and again, my anger spiking, but hands grab onto my shoulders and arms, restraining me.

"Lorian, stand down!" Gladwell shouts, his face red with anger. Eben wipes his face, his hand coming away bloody, and glares venom at me. Miller and Grant stare at me, obviously dying to help but knowing they can't. More soldiers grab Camari, holding her so that she can't run away. Gladwell walks in front of me, disappointment and anger in his eyes.

"Lorian, you could have been great, but you had to fall for a pretty face and a seer at that," he says, spitting the word seer out like it's poison. "You are under arrest for attacking your fellow soldier, not to mention aiding and concealing an enemy of the kingdom. Put them both in the caravan; they will ride with the other prisoners." He turns and walks away, striding over to Eben, who is smiling victoriously at Camari as she stands, pale with fear.

They begin to drag us to the caravan, my men watching on in horror. Morris looks at Eben like he wants to kill him while Miller and Grant stand frozen, watching as the events unfold like a nightmare come to life. The soldiers sneer down at Camari with disgust, seeing the blood on her clothes and pulling roughly on her injured arm. She cries out, and the soldier smiles.

"I thought seers were better than us. Why didn't you see any of this coming?" he asks, bringing his face close to hers.

"Because I was too busy laughing as I saw you hanging from a rope," she spits, pulling away from him. His face contorts into a scowl, and he strikes her again, right where Eben hit her.

"Leave her alone!" I roar, straining to get to her. The men holding me grunt with the effort, dragging me slowly towards the caravan where soldiers stand, ready to open it and throw us in.

"*Eben*!" Camari shouts, capturing everyone's attention. Even the soldiers dragging us slow down. She looks at him with such pure hatred that I get goosebumps, a bright red handprint glowing on her face. Eben turns to look at her, still looking pleased with himself, though unease glints in his eyes when he sees her expression. "We made a deal; you swore! You went back on that deal, and I just thought you should know; you *never* go back on a deal with a seer!" she hisses, hair hanging in her face and giving her the appearance of a wild animal. More unease shows on Eben's face, but she isn't done.

"I will kill you for this. It will be slow, it will be painful, and it will be by my hand. I know this will happen, and soon because I just saw it with my own eyes," she spits, her face already starting to bruise. As if to emphasize her point, the clouds shift, and sunlight hits her, making her hair shine and her scalsen almost seem to glow, but at the same time casting her face in shadows.

Eben pales slightly, but the soldiers come to their senses, dragging us to the caravan. They unlock the iron door and throw us in, slamming it shut behind us so that we are left in broken darkness on our hands and knees.

I scramble to my feet, moving to Camari's side and helping her up as she winces at her injuries, probably now torn open again. "Are you okay?" I ask softly, holding on to her elbow as she steadies herself. She nods; taking her arm back to shove the hair out of her face and pulls it over her shoulder, fear on her face again.

"No, but that's to be expected after being kidnapped. Again."

I wince, guilt flooding me. I promised I'd protect her, and I failed.

This is all my fault.

"Did you really see those things? The soldier hanging, Eben dying?" I ask quietly, unable to restrain my curiosity. This side of Camari, the seer parts of her, are new and unfamiliar. Alarming.

"The soldier will be fine unless I get out and have extra time. Eben, however," her eyes go distant, and her face becomes void of all compassion, void of anything but something dark and deadly. "Eben should look over his shoulder. *Often.*"

A noise in the caravan has both of us spinning around, our conversation forgotten. We forgot we weren't alone in the caravan.

Around fifteen children ranging from young to late teenage years are here, watching us. They look at Camari with curiosity, maybe even awe. They look at me with hatred, a thirst for revenge gleaming in their eyes.

I will probably stand trial when we reach Sutoran. But judging by their faces, I'll be lucky if I survive that long.

I still remember the day I first saw you in that tavern. I knew you were one I needed to have. You may not reply to these letters; I don't expect you to. These simply prove what I have always said. I will always find you.

—Recovered Artifacts from Krakent

Chapter Twenty-Six

Camari

One of the seers-a tall boy with curly brown hair and bright blue eyes-stands and walks towards us slowly. Aiden maneuvers in front of me slightly, unconsciously shielding me in case things get bad.

"Welcome to the caravan headed straight to hell," the boy says with a cold smile that doesn't reach his eyes. He crosses his arms, scanning us up and down and leaving me to do the same to him. His eyes are his trait, blue like the sky on a summer day. I spot his scalsen peeking out of the neck of his shirt from where they sit on his right shoulder. His clothes are rumpled and stained, torn in places and too big on him. He is tall, around my height, if not an inch taller. By my guess, he's sixteen or seventeen. Still only a boy.

I look past him and see the other occupants, my heart aching. There's a toddler, her thumb in her mouth, her bright white hair hanging around her face like a shield. There are little children, maybe eleven, who look at us as if they aren't sure we aren't going to hurt them. And there are people the boy's age, around sixteen or seventeen, in their early to late teens. They look at us with hatred in their eyes, or they look at Aiden with hatred. They look at me with curiosity and confusion as though they don't know where I stand. I am the oldest seer there, and they seem to be unsure whether they can trust me or not.

"I'm Alex, and as the oldest seer here, I'm in charge, which means you both answer to me," the boy quips, drawing my attention back to him. "You'll answer my questions unless, of course, you want to get hurt. Not all of us are children."

I can see Aiden tensing and sense the annoyance rolling off of him. He could have Alex incapacitated in a matter of seconds, and being yelled at about Alex being superior is probably doing nothing to help his temper.

I place my hand on his back, silently warning him to calm down. He glances back at me, his shoulders dropping, and I look at the boy and nod for him to go on. They've lost everything; I won't take his pride too.

"Who are you, and what are you doing with the assassin? You are a seer, aren't you?" Alex asks me warily, looking at my arms and my hair.

"Yes, I'm a seer. My name is Camari Dorsar. I'm nineteen years old, which I think makes me the oldest." I inform them, stepping out from behind Aiden. His eyebrows rise slightly, probably surprised that they caught someone my age and didn't kill me immediately.

"What are you doing with *him*?" he asks, jutting his chin out at Aiden.

"That's a long story."

"I don't see any of us going anywhere anytime soon," Alex says, raising his arms and gesturing to the mobile prison we are in. Not a request, then.

I sigh and plop down to the ground, tired and sore. Alex sits down, and several children scoot closer, interested in a story despite their fear. I smile at the little girl with white hair, trying to show that I'm friendly. She ducks behind another child but peeks out at me, listening. In fact, all of them have fallen completely silent and are listening. I pull my hair over my shoulder and run my fingers through it, smoothing out tangles.

"It all started over a moon ago."

I tell them everything. Every detail that makes it a good story. I tell them about finding Aiden in the woods and healing his shoulder. I tell them how he and his men stayed in the village and how Aiden and I became good friends. I gloss over the part where I felt more than friendship for Aiden, deciding they don't need to know that I almost let myself fall for the royal assassin. I tell them how Aiden and his men kidnapped me when they discovered I was a seer, making me go with them on the threat of my mother's death. At that part, Alex glares at Aiden with ferocious hatred and I hurry on. I tell them about the attack, how the seers ambushed us and tried to kill us, only stopping when they saw I was a seer. I tell them how they were going to kill Aiden and his men and how I didn't want to let that happen after getting to know them better and learning that Aiden doesn't actually hate the seers, so I set them free and let them escape. When I tell them about being shot, the boy and a girl around his age both walk around to my back, staying clear of Aiden, and look at the blood-stained bandages on my shoulder, their eyes wide. Finally, I tell them how Aiden saved my life, taking care of me when I was shot and protecting me during a sandstorm. And I tell them how he fought for me tooth and nail to get free, even though it meant him being arrested, too.

By the time I finish, all of the children have scooted forward and are listening eagerly, no longer afraid of me.

"And I know that no matter what happens to us, whether we escape before we reach Sutoran or we are sent to the facility, Aiden and I will fight to get us out. Aiden doesn't give up, and neither do I." I finish with a shoddy attempt at instilling hope in them, turning to look at Aiden over my shoulder. He meets my gaze, his eyes warm with surprise at my story, and returns my smile. I face the children again, and Alex speaks first.

"I guess, since you're the oldest now, you're in charge," he says slowly, looking somewhat relieved to pass that duty on to someone else.

"Actually, I think Aiden's the oldest," I tell him, turning to Aiden. "How old are you again?"

"Twenty-two."

In my mind, I immediately calculate how much older he is than me and then shake my head slightly, wondering why on earth that is the first place my mind went. Of all times, now is most certainly not the time for more delusions.

"Oh, so Aiden's the oldest then." I smile, turning back to the children.

"I meant the oldest seer," Alex snaps, glaring at Aiden. They might not kill him right away after my story, but they still hate him. I didn't expect otherwise, though I'd hoped. But look where hope has gotten me.

"Okay then, I'll take charge," I say finally, standing up and dusting off my skirts as I play along. It makes sense that they would want someone in charge; they're children and are used to having parents to turn to for answers. So if they ask me to fill that hole for them, I can't say no. "I want everyone's name and age please."

In total, there are eighteen children, eight teenagers, four preteens, and six little children ranging from three to seven. Some of them have bright, glowing eyes of shocking colors, others have colored hair and scalsen, and one even has blue-tinged skin. The little white-haired girl is four and is named Molly. The girl who looked at my back with Alex is named Addie. When I hear her name, I think of Adeline with a pang of grief and homesickness. Is she worried about me; is she safe and well?

I push those thoughts away and focus on the children, smiling at them as they crowd around me, touching my shiny hair or poking my scalsen, as almost all of the children only have small little bits here and there. I realize that most every seer I've met has smaller scalsen than mine, but I tuck that thought away to think about it later, Aiden's words from Onaydo echoing in my ears.

The more scalsen you have, the more powerful you will become.

"So, what do we do now?" Alex asks me, already looking to me for leadership.

"We watch, and we wait. We learn as much information as we can by careful observation, and when an opportunity presents itself, we strike." The children's eyes gleam as I speak, hope spreading like wildfire. I turn to look at Aiden, who is watching me as I address the seers. "How many days are we from Sutoran?"

"About three weeks, maybe less if they travel quickly," he replies, glancing behind him to where soldiers are visible outside the caravan, walking around and preparing to set out. "It can take moons to cross the Spás Folamh if you've never done it be-fore, but we do it countless times a year and know the fastest routes."

"And what do they do with the seer prisoners?" I ask, turning partially so that I don't have to crane my neck to see him.

"They're stuck in here for most of the journey. They get let out twice to see to their needs, in the morning and at night. They get fed a morning and an evening meal before we start moving and after we've stopped for the night. At night, after camp is set, they get to sit outside of the caravan for a few moments, but they're locked in after dark."

I nod, logging away all of his information, in-cluding how he speaks about the prisoners as *they* and not *we*. He hasn't yet comprehended just how much his situation has changed. He's gone from be-ing the royal assassin, the king's right-hand man and killer of all seers, to being a traitor to the crown and an accused seer sympathizer. And all of that hap-pened because of me, because he was trying to pro-tect me. Guilt shoots through me as I realize just how much I cost him, and I look down at my hands.

"Camari, are you okay?" Aiden asks, his hand resting on my arm.

"Don't touch her!" Alex snaps, standing up and staring at Aiden. Aiden looks up at him, his eyes filled with cold fire, but ever so slowly, he lifts his hand from my arm, laying it back down on his lap.

"Alex, that is not necessary," I say firmly, giving him a stern look before I turn to Aiden, who is still glaring at Alex with an expression on his face I can't quite read.

"I'm fine, Aiden, just thinking."

Aiden turns back to face me, frowning. "You're pale."

"I am tired, stressed, and in a large amount of pain. I think those are the proper grounds for pale skin," I reply, raising my eyebrows and hiding my embarrassment that he was looking at me close enough to notice in the low light.

"We have water?" Addie offers, jumping to her feet. She goes to a bucket in the corner before I can say anything, filling a tin cup with water and bringing it back to me. The water is warm but surprisingly clean, so I thank Addie before I drink it, thankful for how it cools me off in the horrible heat. Drinking half of it, I turn and offer the other half to Aiden, who gratefully accepts, downing it in one gulp before he hands me back the cup. I give it to Addie with another thank you, receiving a shy smile. Addie is an interesting seer, shockingly beautiful. She has dark brown skin and a mass of tightly coiled curls on her head that slink down to her chin. Her colorful trait, however, is her skin. She has patches of pale skin on her arms, face, neck, and basically everywhere else, making me think of when someone pours cream into a cup of chicory, the white and brown blending together partially. Her scalsen are small, a patch on her right collarbone. She is truly beautiful, almost as if the gods couldn't decide what color to make her skin, so they used both.

"So now we wait?" One of the twelve-year-olds, a boy named John with baby blue hair, asks me, leaning forward on the floor.

I sigh, rubbing at my aching face as reality fully sets in. "Yes; now we wait."

The Provinces of Zorda are split by the Spás Folamh, a desert in the middle of a kingdom with lush forests and greenery. It stands to prove that in this world, there is no true order or reason.

–Zorda: Aristocracy, Geography, and History

Chapter Twenty-Seven

Aiden

Spending three weeks in a caravan full of people who hate me is bound to be educational, and I know it is not going to be pleasant. While Alex, Molly, Addie, and all of the other children look at Camari with something akin to adoration in their eyes, they look at me with fear, hatred, or both. The guilt inside of me doubles every time one of them looks at me, terror on their face. It was different when I was just helping to escort the caravan, when I didn't have to look at them or talk to them, when I didn't know their names and ages. But now I have to know all of that. And it eats me up inside. I've destroyed homes and families; skies above, there is a *four-year-old* in the caravan. She probably won't even remember her parents, just the fear she experienced. All because of me.

I'm a monster.

"Aiden, they're stopping."

Camari's voice snaps me out of thoughts and I look over to where she sits beside me. We've been moving all afternoon, and while the children sit as far away from me as possible, Camari has sat down right beside me, wincing at the movements of the caravan. She stayed beside me the whole afternoon, talking occasionally but mostly staying silent, swaying with the caravan and occasionally bumping against me. I can tell that though she hides it from the children and from me, she is terrified. Her breaths are deep and controlled, and her limbs are relaxed, but I've seen her wringing her hands and worrying at her bottom lip with her teeth, her eyes flickering with fear. The controlled breaths aren't natural but forced, vain attempts to slow a racing heart. That is my fault too.

You fuck up everything. All of these people's lives would be better if you'd never been in them.

The thoughts that were gone during my time with Camari have returned in full force. Truth, terrible truth, echoing in my ears.

Camari is right; the caravan is slowing to a halt, the sound of people slowing their horses leaking into the caravan. All of the children fall silent, shifting eagerly. We all sit there for what feels like a lifetime, though it is probably only ten minutes, listening to the sound of tents being erected, fires lit, and horses fed. Four soldiers dressed in the all-black uniforms of Zorda appear beyond the iron bars, one of them flipping through the keys on the keychain. The metal clicks together as he pushes a key into the lock, turning it and pulling the door open.

"Alright, you have thirty minutes; come one at a time," the soldier says gruffly, beckoning us forward. The kids start forward eagerly and Camari and I fall into the line behind them, exchanging a glance. I jump down from the caravan and turn, offering Camari a hand down before looking to see what the kids are doing. They've split into two groups, boys and girls, and each group has gone to an opposite side of the caravan. Camari turns and follows the girls to the more secluded side while I go to the boys' side, relieving myself before I walk back to the back of the caravan. The girls come back around, and Camari walks back to me, her face tinged red with embarrassment at how the prisoners are treated.

"This is humiliating," she says to me, hopping up to sit beside me on the back of the caravan.

"I'm sorry." I don't have the heart to remind her that this is nothing to what will come if we don't get out of this. She already knows.

She turns and looks at me, her hair falling around her face and framing it in beautiful copper. "This isn't your fault, Aiden. I should have turned and walked the other way as soon as I saw the caravan."

"You would never have survived the Spás Folamh on foot, and they'd already seen you. I promised I'd protect you, I promised that they wouldn't hurt you, and I failed."

"Look around, Aiden." Camari gestures to the children sitting on the ground or pacing to stretch their legs. "No one here is without hurt; no one here is safe, not even you. We just have to deal with what's happening now."

She's right. But they wouldn't be hurt; they wouldn't be here if it wasn't for you.

Camari hops down from her seat, walking towards the children and drawing their attention.

"Alex, how long do we have left?" she asks, turning to the boy with a serious expression. He stands tall, proud that she asked him.

"Twenty-two minutes."

"Okay, that's plenty of time. How would all of you children like to help me?" she asks, crouching down and gesturing with her hand for them to walk to her. They all gather around her, excitement on their faces, and I notice just how good Camari is with them, speaking to them like they are her equals.

"You see them over there?" she asks, jutting her chin out towards the camp. It is a community of tents; the horses are put in a temporary paddock where they are eating from feed bags. The entire contingent of soldiers is only ten yards away, going about their evening. The four guards who watch us are several feet away, talking among themselves and not paying attention to us at all. They're used to defenseless children, not adults that know how to cause problems.

"We want to escape? We need to learn about them," she says, tucking her legs underneath her and facing the half circle of children.

"Learn what?" A nine-year-old named Stella asks, peering at Camari from beneath her thick eyelashes.

"Their routines and schedules for a starter. We need to learn what time the guards watching us shift; we need to find out who has what kind of weapon and what their favored hand is. Every bit of information is good information. How would you all like to be spies?"

Most of the younger children look excited, probably thinking that they are going to play a game, but the older children look excited for a different reason, a determined glint in their eyes. They finally have someone to tell them what to do to get the revenge they've been thirsting for.

"What do you want us to do?" Alex asks, smiling widely at Camari. She returns his smile, her eyes gleaming with mischief.

"Today? Let's start with a little sabotage."

The next morning dawns bright and early, but everyone in the caravan has been awake for a while, eager for their plan. I am among them, anxious to watch Camari's plan play out. Her goal is to slowly get under the soldier's skin, to make them nervous and jumpy. A nervous man makes mistakes, and mistakes will eventually be the fuel for a fire.

A shadow falls into the caravan as the soldiers walk in front of the caravan, temporarily cutting out the rising sun. Everyone sits up straighter, the whispers and murmurs ending abruptly.

"Let's go, thirty minutes as usual," the guard grumbles, throwing the door open. We line up and Camari whisper-shouts one last thing.

"Remember; eyes wide and fluttering!"

The children nod in almost perfect unison before they jump out of the caravan, older children helping the smaller ones. Camari lifts Molly down before she jumps down herself, her face lacking the signs of anything but exhaustion and boredom. I school my face, glaring at all of the soldiers as they bring each of us two camp biscuits and allow each of us a scoop of water from a bucket. Two of the soldiers look away guiltily, uncomfortable that one of their prisoners is their ex-commander. Camari wrinkles her face at the biscuit as she takes a bite, as it is really nothing more than hard porridge.

"What, it's not good enough for you?" One of the soldiers sneers, stopping in front of her. Camari shakes her head, lowering the biscuit to her lap.

"I doubt it's good enough for even a rat like you, but I'll eat it anyway," she mutters, crumbling part of it in her hand. He scowls and goes to hit her, but I stand and catch his wrist, glaring at him.

"Take a second, rethink that idea," I growl, taking a step forward. He steps back, scowling with pink tinted ears, and continues to hand out rations. Camari raises her eyebrows at me as I sit back down beside her.

"How gallant of you."

"Only a coward strikes the first blow against a woman," I spit. Camari snorts, taking a large bite of her biscuit.

"You're old fashioned in some of your beliefs, Lorian," she says airily, tossing the rest of her biscuit away with a disgusted look.

"No, I just respect that though we are equal, we are different."

"Hmm, interesting."

"What?" I ask, looking over at her. She smiles at me, raising an eyebrow.

"Just something I've noticed over the past few days. You have a surprising sense of honor for an assassin."

My smile fades and she blinks, guilt spreading across her face. "I'm sorry, Aiden, I wasn't thinking."

"It's fine, I am-was-an assassin."

"But reminding you of it certainly isn't helping matters."

"It's fine, Camari. You can call me an assassin all you want," I tell her, meeting her gaze with a smile. She nods, wiping crumbs from her skirt.

"Well, you can call me-"

"Obnoxious and stubborn redheaded woman?"

She grins at me, shaking her head. "I was going to say seer."

"I like mine better."

Our conversation cuts off as the soldiers walk back over, the man with the halberd waving it as us.

"Alright, back in the caravan," he orders. We all clamber to our feet, some of us stopping to dust off our clothes or finish our water. Camari shakes the sand out of her skirts before she stands up. She meets Alex's eye and nods subtly.

"Wait!" she exclaims suddenly. The guards stop and stare as one by one all of the seers freeze. Some of them tilt their heads, others stiffen in awkward positions as if they are frozen mid-step due to something they are doing. Or something they are seeing.

Camari tilts her head to the side, kind of like she does when she thinks hard, but this time it is much more eerie. Her hair falls to the side of her head as she stands there, frozen in a vision. At the exact same time, all of the seers begin to flutter their eyelashes as if they are in a trance, a shared vision. The guard's faces pale and they step back, glancing at me. I do my best to look nervous, widening my eyes and standing stiffly. I'm not a good actor.

It lasts maybe ten seconds, and then the spell breaks. Once again in perfect unison, all of the seers gasp loudly, unfreezing and falling onto the ground, some on their stomachs, others on their hands and knees. I pretend to be concerned, walking up to Camari and offering her a hand up.

"What did you see?" I ask loudly, looking around at the other seers as they all stand up, looking shaken and pale. Even the young ones are acting perfectly, Molly's eyes wide and filled with fear behind her curtain of hair. But maybe that isn't faked.

"We can't travel today; there will be an accident." Camari breathes, her eyes wide and her hands shaking. Several of the children around her nod, looking desperate.

"Nonsense!" snaps one of the soldiers, his eyes wide as he tries to dismiss the 'vision'

Exclamations of 'please, we can't go! 'and 'we can't, we saw it! 'echo around as all of the seers begin to panic. Molly bursts into tears, her white hair falling in front of her face as tears stream down, landing on the ground with a plop. The guards are all pale and one of them is shaking, looking around in desperation as all of the seers beg for them not to go. I notice Eben watching from a few feet away, his face chalk-white and his hands clenched around the hilt of his dagger. I know Camari has seen both him and his reaction when I see the little pleased smile spread across her face before she smothers it.

"Enough!" Eben roars, stalking over with two more soldiers. "Shut up and get in the caravan!"

The children all turn and file in, smiling at each other victoriously when their backs are turned to the guards. Molly walks up to Camari and Camari picks her up, balancing the toddler on her hip.

"You were amazing!" she whispers, smiling widely. Molly beams, her eyes still puffy from her forced tears. Camari sets her in the caravan before she climbs up herself. I pull myself up after her, and the door slams shut behind me, the guards still pale and doubtful.

Inside of the caravan, all of the seers huddle together on the ground, bracing themselves against the walls and benches. I sit down beside Camari, who has Molly in her lap. She glances over at me and nods before she looks back at the seers, whispering to them.

"You guys did amazing!" Camari exclaims, beaming. They all smile proudly, Alex jutting out his chest slightly. "Hold on tight; this is going to be a bumpy ride."

We all huddle together and wait, bracing against the wall as best we can.

I hear the horses get saddled up and the drivers climb up onto the front of the caravan. All of the children whisper excitedly, though a few look sick to their stomachs with nerves.

We hear the flick of the reins followed by a voice commanding the horses to move. The caravan jolts into movement. And then it falls three and a half feet down onto the ground, landing with an echoing thud. The children cry out in fear, all of us bumping up against each other painfully. Camari whimpers as her wounds are banged against the wall, and I look over at her in concern, seeing a dark, wet spot on the wall behind her.

"Is everyone okay?" Camari asks everyone, breathing deeply and obviously in pain. Everyone nods, confirming that they are fine, and I exhale in relief.

Children have small, delicate fingers, and are good at walking quietly. They're also good for loosening all of the bolts on the wheels of a caravan while 'relieving themselves.'

Camari smiles victoriously, and I smile too. We just instilled a high level of fear and belief in the soldiers. Next time, chances are they'll listen to the seer's 'vision'. And that is a victory for everyone in the caravan.

Anger will make one break things they value, reveal what should have remained hidden, and fail to act with reason.

–The Religious Texts: The Book of Wisdom

Chapter Twenty-Eight

Camari

Sabotaging the caravan was a strategic move, but not for the reasons normally used. Sabotaging the caravan, faking the vision, it was all a huge play, and one I am proud of myself for orchestrating. They have the wheels back on the caravan and screwed on tightly in just twenty minutes; they barely lost any time. But they are *scared*.

I saw the fear on their faces when we all froze, fluttering our eyelashes like we were having a joint vision. I saw Eben's face when we all fell to our knees, 'released from the vision. 'It was the sweetest thing to see him so scared, like the cherry on top of the cake.

I warned the children that it would hurt when we fell, and I warned them that they would need to lie like they'd never lied before. They exceeded my expectations.

THE CURSE OF THE BLESSED

They got the timing perfect, stopping when I stopped, falling when I fell, waking up when I woke. Molly's tears were a stroke of genius, one that Alex was quick to take credit for by the use of a pinch on the arm, and it all worked like a charm.

The guards led us outside and made us sit while they fixed the wheel, two guards watching us with the help of Eben. We sat compliantly, schooling our faces to look solemn, as if we warned them. Because we did.

Aiden was an incredible liar as well. As soon as I started faking the vision he looked at me with fear and concern, as well as a little curiosity. The soldiers ate it up. He sat by me as we waited outside, still playing the act to perfection. Then, I suppose I knew he was good at lying already.

At one point, Eben stopped in front of us, looking down at me with a scowl. "Did you see this happening? Not much of a danger," he sniped, trying and failing to sound confident. I smiled up at him with a knowing look, knowing it would scare him.

"We saw this, yes. But it was only the beginning of a whole chain of events. It's what starts it all."

"Starts what?" he asked, momentarily forgetting his hatred for me.

"Now, where's the fun in telling you that?" I replied, tilting my head and smiling sweetly. He growled and started forward but the other soldiers intervened, glancing at me fearfully before whispering.

"Don't; you could just be creating another link in the chain of events."

At that Eben paled several shades and hurried away. I swear, the soldiers are doing a better job of selling our lie than we are. I've realized that the lack of knowledge about us, the false beliefs, we can use them to our advantage. True we are persecuted because of the lies, but their ignorance can be used against them. We can scare them. Nothing is scarier than the unknown.

After the wheels are back on, we set off again, locked up in the caravan just as before. My whole body hurts from the fall, as does everyone else's, and I'm sure my wounds have split open again; my shift feels wet and warm on my lower back. But, no one else complains, and they are children, so I won't complain either.

"You said there was a whole chain of events, do you have them all planned?" Aiden asks from where he sits beside me, swaying with the motion of the caravan. I shake my head, smiling mischievously.

"We'll just have to wait and see what the gods give us," I say, genuinely excited to see how we will twist our little bit of power. Once you get that little bit of it; that hold on the rope, it is far easier to pull and gain more. And we definitely got our hold on the rope.

"Camari?"

I look up as several of the children scoot towards me, bored and tired from the caravan's swaying. The sun is already setting, and we sit in almost complete darkness.

"Can you tell us a story?" John asks, rubbing his head where it banged against the wall of the caravan when we fell. I sigh, not really wanting to do anything, but relent, nodding in agreement. The rest of the children scoot forward eagerly, and I begin my story.

It is a simple one Adeline told me when I was little, about a king that collected pens. One day he found a magic pen, and got into a lot of mischief. I embellish it, making it more entertaining for the children, and by the time I am done, several of them have dozed off.

I lean back against the wall as the children turn away, tired from such a stressful day. Aiden smiles at me, resting his arm on his knee. "You're a natural with them," he says quietly, jutting his chin out towards the kids. I smile sleepily, turning to face him.

"They're easy to talk to; just talk to them like they're your equals. Too many people speak down to children, treating them like they're stupid and delicate. They need people to treat them as they would want to be treated, so that they grow up and expect nothing less from anyone."

"Where did you learn that?"

"My...my mother."

"Did she raise you like that?"

"Oh no, she never quite trusted me enough," I say sadly, thinking back to how often we used to fight, how we even fought over Aiden. Although to be fair, she was somewhat right about him.

"You'll get back to her, Camari," Aiden says gently, undoubtedly feeling guilty that he is the reason I'm not with her right now. I've tried several times, but there is nothing I can do to ease his guilt. It is his cross to bear, his wound to heal. Some things you can't do for other people, no matter how much you want to.

"So, what now?" I ask, turning to face Aiden again, who looks surprised by my question.

"You're asking me? You're the one with the master plan."

"Well, assume my plan doesn't work. You'll be taken for an audience with the king. Won't he pardon you? He knows you; there are rumors that he's close with his royal assassin. He'll let you off the hook, won't he?"

Aiden's expression hardens into one carved from stone and I backtrack, wondering what I said wrong.

"You mean pardon me so that I can watch the rest of you go to the facility and not care? Is that what you think I'll do?" he asks, anger in his voice. Alex looks up from where he sits a few feet away, narrowing his eyes at Aiden warningly.

"No, that's not what I meant at all, I was just-"

"I might have done that before, but I wouldn't do that now!"

"I know that, Aiden, I wasn't saying you would! I was trying to think positively! If you get pardoned, maybe you can help us get out as well," I explain quickly. Aiden's eyes still burn with anger, but now it isn't directed at me.

"He won't pardon me, Camari. I'll be lucky if I get sent to the facility."

"What do you mean?"

"I was never supposed to help seers, yet alone befriend one! I've broken my contract; I've broken years of tradition, and he won't let that stand."

"Why would he care if you broke some stupid, disgusting tradition?" I ask, genuinely confused. I scowl as I see the wall come back down behind his eyes, blocking him off. We went so long with him being open, I had hoped it would last. "You know what? Keep your secrets. I'll be with the children, who are at least honest."

I stand, wincing at the movement, and walk away from him, going to the front of the caravan where Alex, Addie, John, and a girl named Gwen sit. They look up as I approach, smiling when I sit back down.

"That was genius, Camari! you're a much better leader than Alex," Addie says enthusiastically before blinking guiltily at Alex, who is scowling at her. "Sorry! But you know what I mean."

Alex harrumphs, looking away from her.

"I think Alex did well in keeping you safe for so long," I say tactfully. Addie relaxes and Alex's scowl falls away, replaced by a smug look.

"Who is the man with the ax?" Gwen asks, startling me.

"What do you mean?"

"When you saw him you looked at him all angry like. You don't like him very much?"

These kids are too observant for their own good.

"No, I don't like him."

"Why not? You like the assassin a lot, and they work together," Addie says, leaning against her knees.

"I think 'like 'is a strong word; Aiden and I share the same goal, but I don't think he likes me beyond that. As for Eben, he's just not a good person," I explain, doing my best to dismiss any assumptions.

Gwen nods seriously and I fight a smile at her serious expression.

"Neither is the assassin," Alex says, glaring over at Aiden. I glance over my shoulder and find Aiden watching us, though I doubt he can hear us.

"I disagree. He's made mistakes, but he's not a bad person," I tell Alex. "And I think he'll beat himself up for those mistakes for the rest of his life. We don't need to do that for him"

Alex still scowls, though his eyes change slightly as he muses over my words, obviously fighting against their logic. It's easier to hate.

"So, what are we going to sabotage next?" John asks excitedly, his eyes sparking.

"I think for now we are just going to wait and observe; we don't want to do too much at once. In a day or two, we'll strike again."

"And how many times will we strike before we can get away?"

"Until an opportunity presents itself," I reply, pulling my hair over my shoulder and running my fingers through it. A small part of me is worried that we won't have an opportunity, that even if we do escape we'll starve to death in the Spás Folamh. But I can't tell them that. They need to hold on to what little hope they have.

This caravan is not friendly on my wounds. The bumpy movements, the crash when we felled the wagon; it has impacted me painfully. When the wagon fell, I slammed against the edge of the bench attached to the wall, barely refraining from crying out in pain when I felt my healing wounds split open again. Now, a day later, I wake up and immediately realize the back of my shift is wet with blood. I sit up without thinking, inhaling sharply as pain stabs through my back. I carefully scoot to the door of the caravan where there is the most light. I touch the back of my shift with my hand, wincing at the movement, before I hold it up in front of my face. My fingertips are wet with blood, some fresh, some older.

Dammit! I must have torn them open yet again at some point in the night. After the caravan sabotage, they closed slightly only to open up again. I am doing my best to hide it from the others in the caravan, but Aiden has looked at me several times with concern, catching me mid-wince or flinching. He always seems to know when I'm in pain, it's unnerving.

Reaching down, I pull up my skirt and grab hold of the edge of my shift, carefully ripping it so that I have a long piece of circular fabric in my hands. Ripping it again so that it isn't connected in a circle, I twist painfully and press it against my shoulder, hissing in pain.

"Camari?"

I jump, spinning around to see who said my name. Aiden is sitting up, rubbing the sleep out of his eyes with the heel of his palm.

"Go back to sleep; it's still early," I whisper, turning back to what I was doing, carefully wrapping a piece of the torn fabric around my middle to act as another layer of bandages for my back.

"What are you doing?"

"Nothing!" I snap, turning in an attempt to hide my back.

"Gods, how long have you been bleeding?" he exclaims, shock in his voice. I turn and find him standing behind me, looking at the bloody fabric.

"It's nothing; calm down! You're going to wake the children."

"I will not calm down when you're soaked in blood!"

"I'm not soaked, I'm…" I grasp for a term that will make it sound less drastic. Doused? Coated? *Leaking*? I give up, letting my sentence hang open as I turn my focus back to bandaging my shoulder next.

The last thing I want is for one of the children to find me 'soaked 'in blood. It would probably just send them right back to the night their parents were killed, and that is the last thing they need.

I jump again when Aiden's hands take the ends of the fabric, pushing my hands away. "Stay still, I'll do it."

I sigh, relenting as he begins to carefully wrap my shoulder, pulling it tighter than I could have by myself. This is also his way of apologizing for yesterday's argument, so I let him.

"The sabotage?" he guesses, carefully weaving the ends into a sturdy knot.

"I just don't heal as fast as you do," I reply, toying with a loose string on my skirt. "Speaking of which, how are your wounds?" I asked, realizing I haven't seen them in a long while. He reaches up and pulls aside the neck of his tunic, revealing two pink scars on his broad shoulder.

"You weren't lying about healing quickly."

He nods, pulling his tunic back over his shoulder. "Always have, probably always will."

"Lucky." I sigh, pulling my knees up to my chest. We fall into an awkward silence, staring out the barred door as the camp beyond slowly begins to stir.

"How many days left until Sutoran?" I finally ask, desperate for something to say.

"Two and a half weeks, maybe three weeks," he replies patiently, aware that I already know that.

"Not long."

"To me it feels like forever," Aiden comments, watching as the soldiers begin to gather together, preparing to come and wake us. The soldiers walk towards the caravan and I stand slowly, stretching out my shoulder gently. "Time to face the music."

"Yeah, real nice music," Aiden mutters, standing up as well. The guards bang on the iron as they always do and the children begin to stir, sitting up and rubbing their eyes sleepily.

"Let's go. Thirty minutes!" they shout, opening the door and gesturing for us to step out. I jump out first, turning to help the little kids down, but Aiden gives me a look.

"Don't even think about it," he says sternly, taking my place and helping the seers down. That is, the seers that will let him, which are only five. The others jump down and walk away from him quickly, once again going to the two sides of the caravan to relieve themselves. It is necessary, but relieving myself in front of ten other people, even if they aren't looking and my skirts cover me, is completely humiliating. I can tell the other girls feel the same, blushing and going as quickly as they can. I hurry back to the front of the caravan, sitting down on the ground and pulling my knees up to my chest as I watch the sun rise. Part of me hopes the journey across the Spás Folamh will go on forever, because I know that once we reach Sutoran, things will be far worse. The other part of me wants to reach Sutoran as soon as possible, if only to end the horrible days spent locked up in the caravan and the humiliating way we are treated. My heart goes out to the children that will be scarred by their experience, never trusting another soul. And I can't honestly blame them.

I turn, looking over to where Molly sits with the other children her age. Her hair, pure white, reminds me a bit of Adeline's platinum blonde hair. Now that I know what she was trying to shield me from all of these years, I feel so much guilt over fighting with her so often. She was trying to keep me from the exact situation I am in, being persecuted for being a seer.

I frown, still looking at Molly's hair. Her colorful trait. I've been wondering how it is that I am a seer; I don't think that either of my parents are seers, and I never saw Adeline's scalsen. But her hair was just as unnaturally bright as mine, just a different color. Was she a seer, and she just hid her visions from me, just as I hid my 'episodes' from her? But where were her scalsen then? Every seer has them, no exceptions.

A mental picture of her burnt, scarred upper arm flashes through my mind and sears into my vision. My stomach twists nauseatingly and I lift my hand to my mouth as bile rises up my throat, as a terrible idea surfaces in my mind. As I fully comprehend what she must have done.

She burned her scalsen off.

Adeline took a flame or a hot iron, and burned off her skin. She set herself on fire to avoid the exact situation I am in, to protect herself from threats like…like Aiden. She did that for her, but also for me. She wanted to protect me from the life of a seer, and so she put herself through excruciating pain to do so. And I've thrown away her sacrifice, the pain she put herself through, for what? Because I tried to save someone's life and that someone turned out to be a murderer and a kidnapper? Because I let myself fall for a pretty face and kind words? I've completely lost sight of who I am. Am I a seer? Am I a human? Am I a fool or a healer?

I don't know who I am anymore.

I run shaking hands through my hair, tears burning my eyes as they slowly escape and trail down my face, surely leaving tracks through the dirt. A few moons ago I was lonely, bored, and miserably so. But I knew who I was, *what* I was, and what my place in the world was. I don't even know for sure what I am anymore, I still haven't truly accepted that I'm a seer if I'm honest with myself. Is my place in this world simply to be a prisoner, a pawn in a battle that has been waged for centuries? Is this the miserable existence I've been assigned?

And Aiden. Maybe these children aren't the only ones with trust issues now. Aiden may have changed, but he still keeps so many secrets, and he has told me so many lies, probably told so many more I'm not even aware of. Can I even trust him? Will I ever be able to trust him without having any remaining doubts?

I think back to his facial expression when he saw me bleeding, when the soldiers found out I was a seer and were dragging me away, hurting me. He defended me, fought for me, tried to protect me. I can trust him. But I need him to let down his walls, or that trust won't last.

I wipe my tears away with the back of my hand, pushing anymore back. A shadow falls across me and I look up, scowling when I see Eben.

Not what I need right now.

"Why the tears? Have you finally realized just how futile your situation is?"

"On the contrary, those were tears of joy. I was reliving my vision of your death," I say coldly, enjoying the fear that flickers through his eyes. It's not good to enjoy someone else's pain. But I still enjoy his.

"I can't wait to go back to that village of yours and kill your mother. I'm not a traitor like Aiden after all, and a seer is a seer, no matter how old."

"Good luck finding her. My mother knows how to hide," I snap, even as fear pulses inside of me. It's true; if she stayed hidden for almost twenty years with me, she'll have no problem hiding again.

"I'm good at finding people," he growls, leaning closer in an ominous way that makes goosebumps sprout on my skin, "I found you."

"What are you talking about?" I ask, leaning back slowly as I notice the dangerous gleam in his eyes. What does he mean, he *found* me?

Eben shifts and something flashes across his face that I can't decipher. "I'm spending too much time around you and your seer *rats*. I'm starting to spout rubbish as well," he snaps dismissively, dropping the camp biscuit that was my morning ration onto the ground, where it quickly gets coated in sand and grit. I pick it up and wipe it off, taking a bite and pretending it is delicious even as sand crunches in my teeth and I struggle to swallow.

"The only rubbish around here is you," I reply offhandedly, swallowing before I chuck the rest of the biscuit back onto the ground. Eben's eyes flash with anger, filling me with satisfaction, but I know I need to get my tongue under control before I go too far. He doesn't seem himself today, he's acting…unpredictable.

"Maybe I'll talk Aiden into giving me a turn with you before we reach Sutoran. I could use some female company, no matter how ungainly and ugly." He sneers, his eyes flashing with delight at what he said, knowing he hit a nerve. I see red as my rage spikes, and I abandon all pretense of holding my tongue. What he insinuates is horrible, disgusting, and the idea that I'd do anything of that sort makes my blood boil.

I hate this man.

"The day I go near you with anything but hatred and disgust is the day I die. You are a lecherous swine and I can't wait 'til my vision for you comes to pass," I hiss at him, spitting on his shoe for good measure. His eyes burn with anger and I see the moment he loses control of his anger. Good, I welcome his anger at this moment, seeing as no one else's anger can match my own.

"You little-" he grabs my upper left arm, dragging me up roughly and striking me across the face. My face burns, but I barely register it, too angry to care.

"It doesn't matter what you want, I can take anything I want from you," he hisses in my face. I twist in his grip, getting a cold feeling in the pit of my stomach from the look in his eyes. Lust, primal and fierce, having nothing to do with affection or love, but lust all the same. The idea makes me sick.

"You're a vial excuse for a man," I spit, driven on by my terror of him, of the memories flooding my mind. His grip on my arm tightens painfully and suddenly his mouth is pressed against mine forcefully, his other hand holding the back of my head so that I can't move. His kiss is wet and disgusting, his teeth knocking against mine as he tries to force my mouth open. I fight against him, trying to twist my head away with a cry, but he holds me too tightly, his hands holding me against him so that I can't move to fight back. I begin to panic, trying to push him away, but that only seems to encourage him. I gag as he forces my mouth open, trying even more desperately to get away. Panic fills me, this scene all too familiar, and despair makes my knees weak. Suddenly I hear a shout and then Eben lets go of me with no warning. I drop to the ground on my hands and knees, retching and sobbing in a combination of pain and disgust before I look up, wiping my mouth with the back of my trembling hand. Aiden is on top of Eben, pinning him to the ground with his arms stuck beneath him.

"GET THE HELL OFF ME!" Eben roars, trying and failing to shake Aiden off.

"You useless, disgusting piece of *shit*!" Aiden winds up, punching Eben in the face. Aiden's face is contorted with rage and his eyes burn so that I hardly recognize him. He hits Eben again and again, his knuckles turning bloody as reopens wounds Eben already had. Before I have time to react or do anything, two sets of hands grab me, one person on either arm, hauling me up from the ground roughly. Three more soldiers grab Aiden and pull him off of Eben, Aiden still fighting and lunging at Eben. Eben rises to his feet, his uniform covered in sand and dirt, cursing and spitting venom at Aiden.

"Lock them in the caravan, we set out now!" Eben roars, glaring at me one last time before he turns and stalks away, shaking off the other soldiers. We're pulled to the back of the caravan and thrown in roughly, the door slamming shut behind us with an air of finality.

Zordan Aristocracy is not as complicated as it is made to appear. It is a monarchy with three provinces, two duchies, three barons, and recurring but not permanent lords.

–Zordan Guide to The Aristocracy

Chapter Twenty-Nine

Camari

I push myself up onto my hands and knees, gasping at the pain of such movements. All of the children are huddled in the back of the caravan, watching Aiden and I with concern and confusion, but I ignore them for a second, turning to where Aiden is pushing himself up into a sitting position. He wipes at a stream of blood from the small cut above his eye that must have reopened and glares down at the blood on his knuckles, still breathing heavily.

"Are you okay?" I ask him, scooting closer. He meets my gaze and his eyes still burn with anger, incomparable to the hazel eyes I know so well.

"I'm going to kill him." He spits sand from his mouth, wiping again at the blood on his forehead with more force than is necessary, smearing it across his forehead.

"I already claimed that honor," I joke, though my stomach still rolls with nausea at what Eben tried to do, my shaking hands hidden in my skirt.

"How can you possibly pretend to be okay?"

"It's not okay, but scaring the children won't help anything," I say in a tone that is much calmer than I feel, glancing pointedly at where they sit, watching and listening to every word we say. The older kids who understand our conversation appear to be filled with anger at what they hear, and I see Alex look at Aiden with a newly founded respect. "Eben's day will come, Aiden, I can guarantee that. But now isn't the time."

"I look forward to that time. I can't believe I once thought of him as a brother!" Aiden spits, though his eyes are now hollowed out with grief and hurt at what he lost, what he found out to be a lie. He places his hand over mine, meeting my eyes. "I got you into all of this. I am so sorry," he whispers. I flip my hand over and squeeze his, smiling even though I've never felt more broken.

"It's not your fault, Aiden. You need to let go of your guilt."

His eyes flash with anger again and he pulls his hand away, clenching it into a fist. "Not until you are free; until the children are free. Maybe not even then."

I sigh, knowing that he is telling the truth. And there is nothing I can do about that.

When I wake from a nap brought on by a sleepless night and the caravan's rhythmic swaying, I hurt everywhere. My head and face hurt from Eben crushing it against him, my back and shoulder hurt from my wounds being opened over and over again, my wrists hurt from where Eben held them together so that I couldn't fight back. Even my scalp hurts from where one of the guards pulled out some hair in an attempt to restrain me. *Everything* hurts.

I force myself up with a groan, rubbing my eyes and resting my head in my hands.

"Welcome back to the land of the living," Aiden says from where he sits beside me, looking over with a faint smile.

"How long was I asleep?"

"An hour, maybe two. I figured you needed it."

"This caravan sways too much; it makes me tired," I complain, scooting back to lean against the wall. Aiden nods but says nothing. He still looks angry from the morning's fight with Eben, his shoulders stiff and his jaw tight. I shudder at the memory, embarrassed that I panicked and failed to get away by myself. The key to being able to defend yourself is to never panic. I've learned that lesson first hand; I should have known better. It's not the first time that I should have known better.

I push away thoughts of what might have happened if Aiden hadn't come when he did, and remember what I realized about my mother before Eben came, thoughts that are equally dark. "Aiden, I forgot to tell you, I think I figured out just how it is that I'm a seer," I say, turning to him. He looks back at me, his eyes gleaming with interest, but he doesn't ask, waiting for me to offer up the information.

"I think Adeline is a seer. She has a horrible scar on her right arm where she was burned, and I think she burned her scalsen off in an attempt to stay undetected."

"And her colorful trait?" Aiden asks, completely passing over the part where my mother permanently disfigured herself. *Soldiers.*

"Her hair, just like me. It has always been the brightest shade of blonde, like a buttercup or aged parchment." I reminisce, remembering how I spotted a faint line of gray at her temple the last time I saw her in the cottage. I wonder if it has grown longer, if she is okay.

No, I need to focus; one thing at a time.

"That would make sense, though it's both impressive and horrifying what she did to her arm," Aiden comments, picking at a callus on his palm absentmindedly. "The self control alone that would be required…if your mother was a man, she would be an impressive soldier."

"She had to!" I reply defensively.

"I'm not disagreeing! I know she had too. But are you sure your father wasn't a seer too? This just seems a tad…farfetched. I'm not saying you're wrong, just that there might be other possibilities besides permanently disfiguring oneself."

"No," I say quickly, looking away from Aiden and clearing my throat. "He wasn't a seer."

"How can you be sure? He might have-"

"I said he wasn't a seer, okay? Just drop it!" I snap harshly, crossing my arms over my chest. Aiden falls silent for several minutes while I stare at the wall, trying to stop unwelcome thoughts from creeping in. That's all today has seemed to be, one unwelcome thought after another.

"Who is your father, Camari?" Aiden asks eventually, his voice barely a whisper.

"My father is *dead*," I rasp, digging my fingers into my upper right arm as I fight against memories. He is dead, and that is the way it needs to be. Left in the past.

"Then who *was* he? You can tell me," Aiden speaks in a quiet voice that threatens to break me, tears burning my eyes.

I will not cry again today.

"It doesn't matter, because he's dead," I respond shortly, standing and walking away from him. I sit in the corner of the caravan, leaning against the wall and refusing to look back at him, afraid his concern will wreck what little self-control I currently have. I haven't broken in four years; I can't afford to break now. If I break anymore, I may never get myself back together again.

I need to be able to put myself together.

I sit outside the caravan, separate from everyone else, and watch the last sliver of sunlight fade. They've let us out for longer than usual, probably forgetting to lock us up again. Not that I'm complaining; the summer heat is starting to weaken and turn into autumn, and I enjoy the cool breeze that blows across the sandy ground of the Spás Folamh. Under different circumstances, this would be beautiful land. But now, it will forever be tainted by this experience.

Footsteps crunch behind me but I don't turn my head as Aiden sits down beside me, watching the sky blaze bright red for a moment before it turns to a dusty purple as the sun vanishes.

"I'm not going to judge you, Camari. I'm the last person that has the right to judge another. Talk to me; let me in. Don't block people out like I do. Don't be like me," he says quietly, still watching the sky. "Trust me, it is a dark, meaningless existence. The only thing keeping me going is a promise I made to myself because of this obnoxiously stubborn redhead I met. I don't see you finding another one of those, so don't be like me."

I fight back tears and sit quietly for several moments, taking controlled breaths until I'm sure I won't

cry, sure that I have control of myself.. When I finally speak, it is in a low voice, low because I'm not
sure I want to hear what I am about to say. Because
all I want to do is *forget*.

"My mother has always been beautiful, and when
she was younger, in her early twenties, she was stun-
ning. I remember being very little and watching her
work, thinking to myself she looked like a star.

"When I was fourteen, I grew sick of being
taunted that my father left me, and I asked who my
father was. She told me this story: she lived in a different village then, and she said there were many visiting nobles that passed through. One day, a noble-
man came into the inn she worked at and he took a
fancy to her. She was polite, but he gave her a bad
feeling, so she avoided him. He came back every
night for a week, and she said he would just sit there,
sipping mead and watching her.

"One night, when she was walking back to the
cottage she lived at, he stepped out of the shadows.
It was late; there was no one else in the street. No one
saw him grab her, and no one heard her scream." I
swallow hard against the lump in my throat. I can feel
Aiden watching me, but I don't dare to meet his gaze.
Now that I've started, I can't seem to stop, and the
words pour out of me. It's like purging an infected
wound; once you start, you can't stop until it's clean.

"She ran from that village two days later, terrified
that he would find her again. Later she found out she
was pregnant, and she gave birth to a child just before
moving from yet another village to Krakent. She had

a little girl with ugly birthmarks on her arms and shiny red hair."

"She had you," Aiden whispers, beginning to understand where it is I'm going. I nod, hugging my knees to my chest as I start to shiver uncontrollably.

"Then how do you know he's dead if you've never met him?" he asks me. I meet his gaze and my face twists into a cold, humorless smile, devoid of any emotion.

"I have met him. He found out she was pregnant when she ran; he was obsessed with finding her and claiming another thing he owned. That's why she left the village she was in before Krakent, because he found her there."

"And he found her again," Aiden concludes, appearing aghast at my story. He hasn't heard anything, not yet.

"I was fifteen; I had known about my father for just a year. One day, I got home from fetching water from the well, and he was there. I still remember what he looked like, every detail. He had pale ginger hair streaked with gray and it was tousled and dusty from his journey. He wore elegant, fancy clothes, though they were dusty too. I still remember the scent of the lavender soap he used, still clinging to his clothes. I haven't been able to smell lavender since without becoming ill.

"My mother was standing in the doorway of the cottage, screaming at him to leave and never come back. I watched from a few feet down the street as he threatened her, vowing that he would be back. Then he turned and saw me, and he recognized me. He smiled, and it made my blood go cold," I whisper, remembering the fear I felt at that moment as I realized who he was. Tears prick at the corners of my eyes and sniff, not to any avail.

"'You must be my daughter,'he said, and I was disgusted at the way he was looking at me. I'd never seen Adeline so angry, she shoved him and pushed him, yelling that I wasn't his and he could never come back. Some people in the village showed up and they escorted him away, seeing how upset she was. They knew my mother, and they knew she was never angry or scared, not like that.

"He shouted that he'd be back, promised it, but he got on his horse and rode away anyway. Adeline didn't calm down for a whole day, shaking and sick with fear. I had no idea what to do; it was horrible seeing her like that.

"Three days later, life was returning to normal, and I was walking through the woods like I always did. But he found me."

Aiden stiffens beside me and I see his hands clench into fists, but I keep going, needing to finish my story. I need him to know the truth.

He needs to know that he isn't the only monster in this caravan.

"He said he followed me, he said that I was even more beautiful than my mother. He said that-" I break off, a sob catching in my throat as I struggle to breath. "He said that if he couldn't have her he could still have *me*.

"You asked me why I was so calm after Eben attacked me? Well I wasn't, I was furious; I still am, because I panicked. In a situation like that you can't panic, *you can't lose control.* But I *did.*

"He grabbed me and shoved me against a tree. He held me there with one hand while he worked on the buttons of my cover with the other, hissing every vile thing he would do to me into my ear. I screamed, but no one heard," I whisper, tears streaming down my face.

"My mother made sure I knew self-defense and that I always carried a knife, but at that moment, I panicked. I couldn't think, I just hit him wildly and screamed as he unbuttoned the last button. It wasn't until he pulled my cover off and saw my arms that he stopped. He was shocked; I could see it on his face. At that moment my panic ended." I look over, meeting Aiden's gaze and holding it as I finish my story. Watching his reaction as he learns what I've done.

"I pulled out my knife and shoved it into his gut, twisting it to release all of the toxins, just as I'd been taught to do. He let go of me and fell down, bleeding out slowly, and I turned and ran the whole way home. I didn't leave the house for a week after that, and I've never returned to that part of the forest since."

My mouth is dry when I finish, looking up at the stars that have emerged. The soldiers will be coming soon to lock us up, in fact, I'm surprised they haven't already come.

I don't expect Aiden to respond, I expect my story to make him see just how horrible I truly am, so I jump in surprise when he does finally speak.

"So when Eben taunted you about how your mother might have…that's why you reacted the way that you did."

"Yes."

"And when we… when we kidnapped you in the woods," he says slowly, trailing off.

"All I could think of was how it was happening again, and there was nothing I could do to stop it," I whisper, pulling my hair over my shoulder and running my hands through it. "So, now you know. I'm a murderer just like you and all of your men. I'm worse; I killed my own father. And I'm a hypocrite and a liar-"

"Camari, you are nothing like me!" Aiden interrupts me, seeming shocked at what I said. "You killed in self defense, you had no choice! We killed because we were ordered to. And that man is not your father. He raped your mother and attacked you."

"I-I *killed* him!" I gasp, folding in on myself as I begin to sob. I can still remember the feeling of his blood on my hands, how I stood above him, shaking and panting animalistically as I struggled to think, to breathe. He just stared up at me, his green eyes filled with shock, like he couldn't believe what was happening.

"You defended yourself," Aiden argues. He grips my chin gently and forces me to face him, his brow set firmly in conviction. *"You are nothing like me."*

"You're not angry with me?" I whisper without thinking, more tears pouring down my face in a torrent. He lifts his hand to my cheek gently, his eyes filled with compassion.

"No, and I hope you know I never could be, not for something like that," he whispers. "I will say it one more time. Camari, you are not a monster. You are nothing like me. Now, breathe."

I close my eyes, sighing shakily. I scoot closer to him and lean against his side, leaning my head against his shoulder. He rests his cheek against the top of my head, and I don't try to stop the tears that keep sliding down my face. I doubt I could if I tried.

The nightmares have persisted all week. I've never had nightmares before, not even as a child. Not even after the assassination. But these persist, no matter how long I stay awake, no matter how I run. I can't outrun them.

—Field Journal of Aiden Lorian

Chapter Thirty

Aiden

Everyone in the caravan is asleep except for me. The children have been looking at me differently, and I am hoping that they are starting to get used to me. Alex, who hates me, met my gaze and nodded at me as I paused to let him climb into the caravan first. That surprised me, but also gave me hope that they could one day forgive me. Because if they can forgive me, then maybe I'm worth forgiveness after all. And then maybe I can forgive myself.

I look over to where Camari sleeps, her arms wrapped around herself protectively. It feels like we've been in this caravan for weeks, not days. We have two more weeks before we reach Sutoran, and then who knows what might happen. We could both be sent to the facility, or one of us could be executed and I might never see her again.

A pang shoots through my chest at the thought as I stare down at her, wondering how she has become so important to me in such a small amount of time. She is bossy, *dangerous*, and she is a seer. But she is also smart, compassionate, fierce, and the most beautiful woman I've ever met. I think back to that awkward conversation we had in the woods, where she waited and waited for me to tell her why I had lost my feelings for her and I didn't have an answer. What she didn't realize is that I have no answer because I never lost my feelings for her. There are times when I wish I had, when I tried to convince myself I had, but…it's more than a feeling, it's a knowledge of who she is and what she believes. It's infectious.

As I gaze at her, a small ray of moonlight comes through the barred window on the front of the caravan and lands on her, making her hair glow like a star.

I groan, rubbing my hand through my hair.

I am in so much trouble.

Flames burn in the distance, eating through house after house, uncaring if people are inside. People run screaming, some holding children. Men stand with swords, but the soldiers in black are stronger. The men fall, and the women follow, leaving the children wailing on the ground.

THE CURSE OF THE BLESSED

The sword in my hand drips their blood onto the ground. Blood that I wish was mine. The woman in front of me wails, her silver hair gleaming like a sword in the firelight. Please, *she begs me,* please let us go. *But I can't.*

I blink, and the woman is replaced. I stare in horror at Camari as she kneels in front of me, her dark eyes filled with terror. All of her courage and compassion is gone as she looks at me, visibly trembling. You were right, *she sobs,* you are a monster. *I shake my head, tears spilling down my face at her hatred, at what I've become.*

Please, you don't understand! *I beg her, but she shrinks in on herself in terror. My sword moves on its own, and I fight it, desperate to stop what is about to happen.*

The blade lifts above her head.

And then it falls.

I startle awake as the door squeals open, bringing the smell of rain in with it. Sweat drips down my back, and my hands shake as I breathe, looking around at the caravan. The caravan. Not a seer village.

"Welcome back to the land of the living," Camari says, smiling at her reference to our previous conversation. I stare at her, at her smile, feeling sick to my stomach, and slowly, her smile fades away. "Aiden, are you okay?"

I don't deserve her concern.

"Fine, just… tired," I reply, doing my best to push the dream to the back of my mind. I haven't had a nightmare like that since before Krakent, and then I would go and run until every trace of the dream was gone. But I can't run now. And Camari was never in the dream before.

I get in line with the children silently, Camari falling in behind me, resting her hand on my arm as she passes in a comforting gesture. One I don't deserve. Rain soaks into my clothing as I jump down and go to help Camari, but two of the four soldiers step forward, stopping me.

"She stays in the caravan," one of them says gruffly. I frown, looking back at Camera in confusion. She appears just as confused, if not a little scared.

"You called to let us out, so let all of us out," I say to the guard, the urge to protect her driving me forward.

"She doesn't get to go out; she lost that privilege yesterday," the second soldier snaps, glaring at me. I open my mouth to argue, filled with anger, but Camari cuts me off.

"It's fine, Aiden. I'll just wait here," she says, seeming resigned if not slightly angry. I nod, glaring at the soldiers one more time before I step back. They slam the door shut, and Camari is veiled in shadows.

I walk a few feet away and sit down, accepting my rations with a scowl. I am the one who attacked Eben, not Camari; she shouldn't have to pay for my mistake. Not that I regret it. Eben deserves more than a beating.

THE CURSE OF THE BLESSED

I look over at the children and spot several of them smiling up at the rain that hammers down on us, Alex going so far as to lay on the ground with his limbs spread, taking it all in. I can't help but smile at the sight of them all enjoying themselves, if only for a brief moment.

"Aiden?"

I turn, looking over my shoulder. Morris stands there, looking down at me, rain plastering his hair to his forehead. I rise quickly and pull him into a hug, relieved to see he's okay. Morris pats me on the back before he pulls away, blinking raindrops from his eyes.

"Are you okay?" I ask him, scanning him up and down for injuries.

"Better than you, it would seem. I'm sorry I haven't visited sooner; I haven't had a chance before now."

"It's fine; I didn't expect you to visit at all," I say honestly.

"What's going on, Aiden? They can't do this to you!" Morris exclaims, running his hand through his mouse-brown hair in aggravation.

"I went against my contract with the king-"

"We all did, even Eben! Aldred can't do this to just you; it's not right."

"He can, and he will. You know him, Morris, just as well as you know me. He has no compassion."

"That's not true. Maybe you can beg for forgiveness, you can promise you'll-"

"No."

Morris frowns, taking a slight step back. "What do you mean, *no*?"

"I can't do it anymore, Morris. Killing the seers is wrong, and I won't do it anymore."

"It's not ideal, but we don't have a choice; we signed the contracts before knowing what he had planned for us, and we can't-"

"I won't beg him for forgiveness, not after everything we've done for him," I say firmly, unwilling to change my mind. Besides, he doesn't fully understand the contracts, he doesn't know what it is that drove me to continue being an assassin.

Morris takes a half-step back, scanning my face before his eyes widen. Lightning flashes behind him, momentarily casting his face in shadows. "That's not all, is it? You care for her. Would you really leave us for her? You feel so strongly?" he asks, searching my face. I shake my head because my feelings on this matter have nothing to do with my feelings for Camari.

"I just know that what we've done is wrong, and I can't do it anymore. We slaughtered countless people, Morris, and for what? Because we were ordered to?"

"We had to! We signed those contracts, and we knew what would happen if we broke them."

"Enough with the contracts; that doesn't justify it!" I snap before I force myself to lower my voice. "I know you, Morris. I helped raise you, and I'm proud of who you've become. You're smart, kind, and positive. You know this is wrong. So does Miller, and so does Grant."

Morris blinks, looking down at his feet as his fingers flex and relax at his sides. He knows it, and he's just shoved it down too far, just like I tried to. The difference between us is that I failed.

"Well, what do we do now?" Morris asks finally, meeting my gaze with fear in his eyes. "The men feel the same way; we know they do, but we can't just let you out; we'll just be locked up with you."

"I know; we need a plan; we need to take it slow." I sigh, running my hand through my dripping hair again as I think.

"Did the seers really have a joint vision?" Morris asks, glancing over towards where the seers sit, Alex and Addie watching us as we speak.

"It appeared that they did."

Morris nods, receiving his answer. "Look, Aiden; Miller, Grant, and I want to help; there are even a few other soldiers here who don't like what they're doing. Imagine how many there are in Sutoran or in the base! But we don't know what to do. If we let you out, it will help no one."

"We need to come up with a plan to get everyone out, but we can't plan anything with Camari locked in the gods-damned caravan!" I snap, my anger rising again. Morris frowns, looking over at the caravan.

"Why is she locked in? I mean, besides the obvious."

"Eben attacked her yesterday, and I pulled him off of her. He's punishing her to get at me."

Morris nods, bowing his head in thought for a moment. Then he turns and walks away without another word. I watch as he walks over to the two soldiers, nodding as they salute to him. They aren't commissioned soldiers yet, only staff sergeants, and Morris is a first lieutenant.

"Why is the seer locked in the caravan?" I hear him ask them, straining to make out their words over the noise of the rain.

"Sir, we were given orders by Lieutenants Gladwell and Cass to keep her locked-"

"Lieutenants Gladwell and Cass might have been left in charge while we were gone, but now we're back, and both lieutenants report to me. Let her out now."

I grin as the soldiers fumble to open the door, proud once again of my kid brother.

Camari jumps out, squinting as water droplets land in her eyes, and the soldiers step away from her and Morris. They exchange a few words, and Camari grins brightly before they both walk back towards me.

"Whatever you plan, tell me how me and the others can help without blowing our cover because something tells me you might need a few friends in the army," Morris says. I nod at him, and he turns to leave but stops, turning to face me.

"And, Aiden, don't give up hope. He does have some compassion."

I nod grimly, not agreeing but knowing he won't be convinced otherwise, and Morris leaves, nodding at the soldiers guarding us as he passes.

"What was he talking about?" Camari asks me, frowning at Morris 'retreating back.

"Nothing," I reply, looking away from Morris. Camari frowns and anger flashes in her eyes, knowing I'm lying. I feel a pang of guilt about holding back, especially after what she told me about her father, but I push it away. There are some things Camari doesn't ever need to know.

R.C. Huye

It was made official law that seers were to be arrested or killed on sight, and anyone caught aiding a seer was to be given the same treatment.

–Retractions from the Royal Historical Documents

Chapter Thirty-One

Camari

After being forced to stay in the caravan two days ago, they haven't tried to force me to stay in again. Morris was great in getting them to let me out, though I wasn't surprised to see that Aiden put him up to it. I was angry, however, when once again, Aiden slammed his wall down. I am so sick of his secrets; the gods know I've told him a major one of mine. I don't know what I expected, though. Maybe after I opened up to him, I thought he'd open up to me. I should know by now that he won't; he's admitted it himself. And that hurts far more than I like to admit.

I've noticed that the children are far more relaxed around him, especially Alex. I guess that they heard how he helped me four mornings ago, and they decided that maybe he isn't going to hurt them after all.

I'm glad, for his sake, that they are slowly coming to that conclusion.

My wounds closed again two days ago, and they haven't reopened yet, so I'm hopeful they might finally complete the healing process. My clothes are all hopelessly stained with blood anyway, but it would be nice not to stain them again unless the blood is Eben's.

I shift as the caravan goes over a bump, and Molly looks up at me from where she sits in my lap. The little girl is as clingy as a spider web and has been sitting in my lap all week.

"What's wrong?" she asks, her young voice making the w's sound heavy. I smile down at her, pulling her hair out of her face and smoothing it back gently.

"Nothing at all," I assure her, gently braiding her hair so that it will stay out of her face and tying it off with a string.

She slowly begins to doze off on my lap and my mind wanders back to the same subject it has wandered to for the past few days. My mother told me his name was Duke Bidennore. His eyes were an ugly shade of green, almost yellow. His hair was red like mine, but while mine is the color of flames or even darker, his was watered down into a pale orange color that was barely ginger. He had a long jaw, and his teeth were unnaturally straight. I still remember how his bony fingers felt, digging into my upper arm hard enough to bruise my skin. For moons after meeting him, the smell of lavender made me throw up. Now, it just makes me nauseous.

I'll never forget the feeling of his warm blood pouring over my hands, how it smelled like iron and salt, how he reached for me as he fell, as I ran. Adeline was shocked when I ran into the cottage, my hands covered in blood and my skin a pasty white. I told her what happened, and she was horrified, but not with me. I have a feeling she was proud of me, maybe happy he was dead. Just horrified that I was the one who was forced to kill him.

"Camari?"

I jump, turning to Alex as he walks up to me, his brown hair hanging over his forehead. He crouches down beside me, glances at Molly, and reverts to a whisper.

"I wanted to ask you, when is the next sabotage?"

I open my mouth to tell him not yet, to tell him that I haven't thought of anything, but I hesitate. I might know *just* the person.

I smile up at him. "How about tonight?"

Sitting on the ground outside of the caravan, I look over at Alex and Addie, my two main helpers, and nod at them. As one, we all carefully rise, slipping into the shadows. I haven't told Aiden about our plan; he definitely won't approve. He'll say we are putting ourselves in danger recklessly. But he isn't a seer, and he doesn't fully understand just what has been done. Besides, our guards are horrible; it's amazing what we can get away with under their 'watch'. Maybe this will teach them to be more vigilant of their charges. Or maybe they're just not used to having charges that aren't broken.

With the sun slowly beginning to set earlier and earlier as autumn sets in quickly, we are able to sneak from shadow to shadow as we creep from the caravan over to the campsite where the contingent of men have set up for the night. They all sit around a fire, eating stew from metal bowls and drinking from tin cups.

We press against the side of a tent, Addie and Alex grinning with excitement.

"Alright, remember your jobs. Addie, all you need to do is grab a spare lantern. Alex, you're in charge of flint. Then you both run back to the caravan as fast as you can. Got it?" I order sternly.

They both nod and set off, each slinking in a different direction. I walk to my own destination, crouching low to stay in the shadows. I know that if any light hits my hair, it will gleam like a beacon, and we need to lay the next link in our 'chain of events.'

Reaching the tent I'm looking for, I peer inside to make sure it is the tent Eben and Lieutenant Gladwell share before I slink around back to wait for the others. When I told Alex and Addie my idea, they were eager to help. I think they know that I want revenge for what Eben did, and if they can help one of us get revenge, they will. Too many of us need revenge for what has been done; we crave it. And I have a feeling all of them want revenge on Eben, who has done something to each of us. It is a group effort and a group victory.

Addie appears on my left, breathless with excitement, and she hands me the lantern she stole, the inside still full of oil. I accept it wordlessly, and a second later, Alex appears, handing me two flint stones, saying, "You don't want to know how I got these."

"Thank you. Now, go back to the caravan!"

"Like hell! I want to stay and see the fireworks," Alex says with a grin. I scowl at him, knowing that if he stays, Addie will too.

"As soon as this catches, they'll be running towards us. I need you to go; otherwise, they might catch us."

"We're not leaving you," Addie whispers urgently. I sigh heavily, knowing they won't go anywhere, and nod curtly.

"Then stay here and get ready to run like you've never run before," I snap, slipping away without waiting for a reply. I open the lantern and turn it so that all of the oil drips out, coating the tent. I go to strike the flint but suddenly get a better idea. Darting into the tent, I grab the unlit lantern from where it sits on the ground and run back to where Alex and Addie wait.

"You wanted fireworks?" I ask Alex with a smile, remembering Onaydo and the start of my pyromaniacal tendencies. He grins as I set down the lantern, using the stolen flint to light it. "You're about to get a bonfire."

I stand, holding the lantern in one hand. "Run!" I order just before I throw the lantern straight at the tent. It shatters, oil goes everywhere, and the tent catches with a roar. I hear startled screams and shouts from the campfire, but Alex, Addie, and I are already running back to the caravan, grinning when we hear Eben roar in anger. Oh yes, revenge feels *good*.

Alex, Addie, and I reach the shelter of the caravan just in time, sitting down and grinning at each other in success.

"Okay, everyone in the caravan!" our guards shout, their eyes wide when they see the fire. We stand up and get in line, shaking our heads as we pass the guards.

"We tried to warn them," I say gravely. Alex and Addie nod along, and the guard's eyes widen comically, making it hard not to laugh. Once inside the caravan, we all grin and celebrate again.

"That was amazing! Did you hear how loud it was?"

"And the colors? It was so bright!"

"It made my eyes hurt! Did you hear him scream?"

"Oh, he sounded pissed! It was beautiful."

"What did you do?" Aiden's voice comes from behind me, and Alex and Addie share a look with me before they scurry away to where the other seers are huddled, most likely to tell them an exaggerated version of our victory. I turn to face Aiden, finding him directly behind me, his arms crossed over his chest.

"You set that fire?"

"Yes." There's no point in denying it. I cross my arms and shift my weight, not liking the annoyance in his eyes. I didn't do anything wrong.

"Dammit, Camari! That could have ruined everything!"

"How? And ruined what?" I ask, more annoyed than confused.

"What if you were caught? What if Alex and Addie were caught?"

"We weren't."

"But what if you were? What then? I wouldn't be able to save you."

"I don't need you to save me! If history serves me correctly, I've saved *you. Multiple times,*" I hiss, even more annoyed at his insinuation that I would put Alex and Addie in direct danger. I would never have let them be caught, and I had a plan in case we were.

"Let me guess, it was Eben's tent." He sighs, pinching the bridge of his nose.

"Yes. So?" I ask, raising my chin defensively.

"So you risked your lives for a petty act of vengeance?"

"Last I checked, you were saying how much you wanted to kill Eben. Why the sudden change of heart?"

"Oh, my heart hasn't changed a bit, Camari; I would still love to kill him. But was setting his tent on fire worth it?" he asks, raising his brow inquiringly.

I glare at him, hating that he's mad at me for taking a stand. He has no right to judge me.

"Yes, it was. Doing something to attack Eben will always be worth it. I may have only learned I'm a seer recently, but since then, I've had plenty of time to be treated like a seer. You will never understand the depth of how horribly we are treated. You will never understand what it is like to wake up every day and know that everyone on the continent wishes you dead. So yes, it was worth it. It will be worth it every day for the rest of my life."

Aiden's annoyance slowly fades, replaced by something I can't read, but I'm not patient enough to stay and figure it out. I am sick of him and his walls. I brush past him, my happiness at our victory depleted significantly.

Among the other seers in the caravan, we are celebrities. They're ecstatic to find out whose tent we blew up, and they are even more excited when they realize I've now blown up two tents.

Aiden is quiet for the rest of the night, and I have no idea what is wrong, but I try and fail not to care. I'm still furious at him for thinking he has to protect me. I saved his life when he was shot; I rescued him from execution at the hands of the seers not once but twice! I've proven I don't need to be protected, but he tries to protect me anyway. Part of me is warmed that he cares what happens to me, but another part of me is just put right back in Krakent, where Adeline tried to control everything I did. And I'm angry that he's annoyed by our attack. I expected him to be pleased, proud even. I didn't expect him to be angry.

And what right does he have to be angry?

I'm in a loop of angry thoughts, and I think the seers sense my mood because they all leave me alone. I sit against the wall of the caravan, frowning at the ground, as I go through my circle of thoughts again, and again, and again.

We could hear the soldiers struggle to put out the fire and the cheer when it was finally out, but I know that everything was destroyed. It will have been reduced to ash, and Eben will have lost everything just like I have, just like *all* of us have. Fitting. I'm sure Alex and Addie will agree.

The sun rises outside, and I can hear the soldiers walking toward our caravan, their weapons jingling as they walk. The key enters the lock with a clank, and the door opens, letting in faint streams of sunlight.

"Thirty minutes." They sigh, their voices heavy with exhaustion. They were probably up putting out the fire. I smile to myself, pleased that what we did has affected them too.

We file out, now completely used to the schedule we are forced to obey. I jump down, ignoring Aiden's offered hand down, and walk over to sit by Alex, plopping down heavily. He frowns over at me, taking in my dark expression.

"You and Prince Charming fight?" he guesses, rolling his eyes. I scowl at him, tugging on the end of my messy braid.

"No."

"Yeah, right. You always look like someone kicked you in the back when you two fight," Alex says, rolling his eyes again and taking a large bite of his biscuit.

"That's not true!" I object, flushing.

"Sure it isn't. What, he didn't like our fire experiment?"

"No, he did not." I scowl.

"His loss; that was bloody awesome! I can't wait to see the big guy's face!" Alex laughs.

"You might not have to wait very long," I respond, gesturing with my chin. Eben is walking towards us with a deathly gleam in his eye, his face and clothes covered in soot and his black hair a mess. I grin up at him as he stops in front of me, struggling not to laugh at his expression.

"Good morning, Lieutenant! You look well rested," I greet him in a loud, cheerful tone. Alex chokes on the water he had just swallowed, trying not to laugh, and Eben's jaw clenches, his fisted hand turning white at the knuckles.

"I know it was you," he says quietly, his hand resting on the handle of his new ax.

"I'm sure I don't know what you mean. Our guards can testify that I was here all night. Can't you boys?" I call out to them. They nod nervously, not wanting to admit how lax they are. Predictable.

"Cut the crap, Camari! I know you set my tent on fire!" Eben roars, his face turning red.

"On the contrary, my good sir, you have no way of knowing that. Besides-"

Eben pulls out his ax, his face manic with rage, and I jump to my feet, my snarky comment dying on the tip of my tongue. Alex ditches the rest of his breakfast as well and stands, slowly walking backward from Eben.

"You little bitch! You set my tent on fire!" he screams, spittle flying from his mouth. "What the hell is wrong with you?"

"You burnt down entire villages. You burnt down people!" I shout back, trembling with a sudden onset of rage. The entire camp has gone quiet, forming a circle watching us. The soldiers are too scared of Eben to interfere, and they stand and watch with the seers and the other soldiers that walk over. "You can't take a portion of what you dish?"

"Sorry, Cam. I'm out," Alex whispers quickly before he turns and bolts back to the safety of the gathering crowd. I can't blame him.

"*Eben!* Drop your ax!" Aiden is struggling to make his way through the crowd, throwing off Morris as he tries to restrain him with a growl of frustration. Eben ignores him completely, too focused on his prey.

"So you admit you did it?" Eben challenges me, his ax hanging by his side.

"No, I don't, because I *didn't*. I knew it was going to happen, but I just chose not to tell you. How does it feel to see everything you own *burn*?" I hiss, my breathing ragged. I see several of the seer children nodding along, and jeers fill the air directed at Eben. The guards shift on their feet, doing their best to silence the crowd, but their eyes widen with realization. The realization that they are vastly outnumbered.

Eben roars in anger, but before he can swing his ax, Aiden makes his way through the crowd and tackles Eben to the ground, driving his elbow into Eben's gut.

"You ass!" Eben bellows, struggling to throw Aiden off. He manages to reach over and grab his ax from where it fell to the ground, and I run over without hesitation and smash his hand with my foot. He roars in pain, and his grip loosens enough for me to kick his weapon away. Aiden pins Eben's arms against his back, grinding his face into the dirt, and then finally, the soldiers decide to act, realizing that the seer girl isn't about to be killed. They shove through the crowd, once again grabbing Aiden and I roughly and dragging us towards the caravan. More soldiers have to jump in to help contain Aiden as the initial two fail to keep him from lunging at Eben. The murderous look on his face chills my blood as four men manage to begin to drag him backwards, and the chill causes my heart to still. Not with fear, no. With awareness, as I finally begin to understand just what the man I call friend is capable of.

Eben rises to his feet, spitting sand and glaring murder at us both, his dark gaze sending shivers down my spine. No. I will not allow myself to even begin to feel afraid. I lift my chin and hold his gaze, refusing to be intimidated by the rage, of the promise in his eyes as he stares me down.

I will never be afraid of him again.

I cry out as I'm thrown into the caravan, my hip hitting the floor painfully. Aiden stumbles in a second later, landing on his hands and knees, his face still murderous. I lay there for a few seconds, listening as the seers are directed toward the caravan, and a smile breaks across my face. I begin to chuckle weakly, holding my hip gently where it throbs, and suddenly I can't stop laughing, my eyes beginning to water.

"Are you okay?" Aiden asks in bewilderment, staring at me like I've gone mad, his eyes wide when I turn to look at him.

"I think…we must be the…the worst charges they've ever had," I burst out, cackling like a madwoman as I lay on my back, amused beyond reason. Aiden grins, shaking his head at me in exasperation as he rises to his feet.

"Every time I turn around, you're about to get yourself killed, and every time, you refuse to run. You're insane." he chuckles, offering me a hand up, and I recognize it for what it is: an olive branch to leave our past argument behind.

I accept his hand, climbing to my feet as I continue to laugh. "Don't act like you don't love it."

An awkward silence falls between us at my words, and we both freeze, still holding hands. I drop his hand hastily, clearing my throat as the silence continues. His gaze burns into the side of my face like the sun, making a flush climb up my neck. We're saved from the awkward silence as the seers begin to climb into the caravan, all chattering loudly about what just happened.

"Nice save, Aiden." Alex snorts, patting Aiden on the back condescendingly as he walks past us. "You could make a career out of tackling brutes away from suicidal redheads."

"At least he didn't leave her," Addie says in a sing-song face, smiling at Alex over her shoulder as he glares after her half-heartedly.

"I'm glad Alex left. He doesn't need to get involved with my grudges," I relent, earning another side smirk from Aiden. Addie shrugs, and the conversation leaves us behind as they all go and huddle underneath the window, the one spot in the caravan that receives airflow.

Aiden sits down with a sigh, and I slide down the wall next to him with a groan, suddenly achy and drained of energy, my hip still throbbing slightly. I can guarantee the curve where my hipbone sticks out will be purple tomorrow.

"Are you sure you're okay?" Aiden asks, gently pushing a loose strand of hair out of my face and tucking it behind my ear, his movement casual as if he does that all the time. His hand remains behind my ear for a moment, sending tendrils of heat down my neck and making my cheeks heat. I open my eyes and find his face close to mine, only an inch away. He's so close that I can see each individual eyelash; I can feel his breath as he exhales. He holds my gaze, his hazel eyes gleaming gold as his hand slowly slides down to cup my cheek gently. My heart races in my chest, and he can probably feel my pulse speeding, can see my eyes widening as I instinctively lean closer. But that would be a mistake.

I lean back, turning my head away so that his hand falls away. He sits back up silently but stays beside me, his shoulder brushing mine. I lean my head on his shoulder, still wanting to be close to him for some inexplicable reason I don't feel like dwelling on, my cheek suddenly cold where his palm was moments ago. It occurs to me that I've stopped seeing him as the different Aiden, the real one compared to the one I knew in Krakent. In fact, I've stopped comparing the two Aiden's completely, the old and the new blending into one person. It's just him.

A few minutes later, my exhaustion takes over, and I fall asleep.

The gods have fallen silent. They do not answer my pleas or visit my dreams anymore. Whenever I reach out, there is a wall like a bramble bush in the way. I can't help but wonder what or who is to blame.

—The Religious Texts: The Book of Bryson

Chapter Thirty-Two

Camari

I wake to complete darkness. My mouth is dry, and I have to peel my tongue off the roof of my mouth as I sit up slowly, looking around. I guess I slept through the evening meal, as the moon is bright outside, casting its glow on the sand and giving it a supernatural appearance as we bump along, traveling straight through the night as the soldiers occasionally decide to do.

Everyone in the caravan is asleep; Molly is sleeping with Addie, her thumb in her mouth. Aiden is on my right, his face turned toward me but relaxed, more so than it ever is when he's awake. I wonder when the last time was that he had a good, full night's rest. When was the last time any of us had that?

Being sure to be quiet, I stand slowly and creep over to where the bucket of water and the tin cup sit, filling up the cup and draining it. I could probably drink more, but they didn't refill the bucket the previous day, and our water supply is running low.

I creep back over to my spot and ease back down, pushing my tangled hair out of my face. I turn towards Aiden—for warmth, of course—and scoot closer to him, finding comfort in his smell of pine, leather, and linen as I drift back to sleep.

The next thing I know, I'm waking up to faint sunlight, warm and well rested. I stir, yawning and rubbing my eyes, but then freeze. At some point, as I slept, Aiden put his arm over my waist and rolled closer, his face directly above mine and turned slightly into my hair. I lie still, unsure of what to do. Part of me wants to go back to sleep, to press against him, soak in his warmth, and pretend that he rolled closer on purpose. But, the logical part of my mind takes over before I can follow my temptation, spitting out facts. Aiden doesn't care for me, not like that, and it would be humiliating for him to wake up and find me pressed against him. He probably just did it in his sleep by accident, his body seeking warmth.

Holding my breath, I carefully slip his arm off of me and roll away in one smooth move, cheering myself on in my mind. I remind myself not to be disappointed that he held me in his sleep and didn't do it on purpose. Because that would make things complicated and change things. And I don't want that…

Life was so much simpler when I was convinced I was never going to find anyone.

THE CURSE OF THE BLESSED

Sitting up, I push my hair out of my face, running my fingers through it. My clothes still hold the faint scent of Aiden, and I stand quickly and walk to the front of the caravan, sitting down by the door and waiting for them to open it.

I need to squash these irrational urges; they are bound to be dangerous. I am nineteen, almost twenty, and I've never had a man show interest in me, at least, none but Walter. But then, I've never really been attracted to a man before; I wouldn't let myself be attracted to anyone. It's always too risky. I couldn't let them see my arms, and that would always be a problem. But Aiden has seen my arms. I've known him for moons, and in that time we've gone from acquaintances to friends to enemies to allies and back to friends again. And now my feelings are changing once more. I can't let it happen. Besides, it's not like they'll last long. They're probably just a passing thing triggered by him taking care of me over the past few days. Listening to me. Not judging when I confessed my sin-filled past, but instead understanding it in a way possibly nobody else could…

I'm doing it again! Gathering my hair, I part it on the left side and begin to braid it, giving myself something to do. My hair is the longest it has ever been, and it's becoming a tangled , filthy mess. The sun hasn't bleached its color, though that might have something to do with the fact that we're kept in the caravan all the time. We're due to arrive in Sutoran in just under a fortnight, and then, who knows what will happen. I have a feeling I'll be sent to the facility with the others, though I will be the oldest ever to be 'rescued 'by the king. I also have a feeling Aiden will be pardoned, this whole thing having been blown majorly out of proportion by Eben. He shouldn't be executed for striking a deal with me, not when it was necessary. The king will see that, and if any of the rumors about him knowing the royal assassin well are true, he'll spare Aiden.

But will Aiden go back?

The door rattles as the key enters the lock, the sound as familiar to us now as a rooster's crow. The seers stir, sitting up and rubbing their eyes. Aiden stretches up across the caravan and smiles at me groggily, running his hand through his sandy brown hair so that it sticks up in places. I return his smile, standing up and shaking out my skirts, which are hopelessly torn and stained by now.

See? Just a friendly smile, like always. Nothing has changed, and if I expect it to, I'll just get hurt. I shouldn't have wanted it in the first place.

We all file out just as usual, the routine now ingrained in us after over a week. The sun is covered in a thick layer of clouds that makes the temperature drop several degrees, providing a sweet relief from the usual blistering heat. Taking my rations, I set them down on the ground and ignore them, needing to move around. Shifting my weight back and forth, I carefully stretch out my arms, pulling them tightly across my chest before I shake them loose and pop my neck. After that, I stretch out my legs, sighing blissfully as my muscles ache pleasantly.

"Sore from being thrown about yet again?" Aiden asks, sitting down beside me with a faint groan.

"I'm sick of being still all day," I reply, my right knee popping as I walk over and sit down beside him. I pick up my rations and swirl the water around in the cup, hungry while at the same time lacking any appetite.

"I thought you were sick of being injured. Which is it?" Aiden teases absentmindedly, taking a large bite of his biscuit before he screws up his face in revulsion and forces it down. "Gods, these things just get worse and worse with each day."

I take one look at my biscuit and toss it behind me. I've lost weight over the course of our 'journey'. My shift hangs on me more than it did before, and my skirt's waist slips and slides on my waist. But nothing could ever make me want to eat those disgusting camp biscuits.

"You need to eat, Camari; you should keep up your strength," Aiden scolds gently, even as he forces his food down with barely concealed grimaces.

"I'm fine," I reply absentmindedly, scanning the camp a few yards away. There. Eben is walking through the tents, still looking enraged, his face so bruised he has more purple skin than healthy skin. I grit my teeth in anger, clenching my fists in my skirts. Of course, he wasn't punished; why should he be?

"What's wrong?" Aiden asks. I frown, realizing he was watching me closer than I thought.

Do not let that go to your head.

"Nothing, I just saw Eben walking around. I hoped he would be punished, but I should have known better. Why would they punish him for trying to kill a seer? Who would miss me?" I ask bitterly, downing my water in one swig. Because from the moment what I truly am was revealed to me, everything that transpired since has taught me one thing: A dead seer is tolerable; desirable even. A bragging right, that you aided in ridding the continent of the god-created plague. A living seer? We are the rats that hide in people's cellars and alleys, picked off one by one. No one mourns us; no one fights for us. We don't even fight for ourselves anymore.

"Adeline, Morris, Grant, Miller," Aiden begins, ticking off each finger as he lists the people that he assumes would miss me. "Alex, Addie, Molly, John, Ellie, Edmund-"

"Okay, okay. I understand; the seers would miss me; you don't have to name all eighteen of them." I smile softly, twisting my fingers gently. Aiden smiles back at me, leaning against his knees, and it is the same smile he gave me in Krakent, the one that made my mouth become very suddenly dry. It has not lost its effect.

"I would miss you," he says in a softer voice than before, the words rasping in his throat slightly. My heart stutters, and I feel my cheeks warm. I look away quickly, knowing my face and chest have flushed bright red. Damn him. Damn him and his pretty face and kind words, damn him and the chivalry and sense of justice that seem so out of place in an assassin. And damn my foolish heart for noticing all of it.

"Thank you, but I still wish Eben was punished," I say softly, tracing a shape in the thin layer of sand that covers the cracked and dehydrated earth beneath me.

"I think me beating his ass in front of all of his peers two days in a row was a pretty good punishment," Aiden says with a wry smile. "And it was a decent form of therapy for myself. I should have taken it up a few years ago."

I laugh, my bad mood lifting away as I spend more time with him. "I can only imagine."

The day is looking like it will go just like all of the others, with us stuck in the caravan and moving closer to Sutoran. I sit beside Aiden with Molly on my lap, and we play a word game to pass the time. Aiden keeps guessing crazy made-up words to make Molly laugh, and me smile.

"How about-" Aiden was about to guess another word but breaks off when the caravan pulls to an abrupt halt, the voices of the soldiers growing louder.

"What's going on?" I ask, setting Molly on the floor and standing up. I walk over to the door and peer out without waiting for an answer. The soldiers I can see have bright smiles on their faces and are talking, pointing at something eagerly. Aiden comes up beside me and peers out, frowning.

"What is it?"

"We must have moved faster this trip; we're a lot closer to Sutoran than I thought," he muses, still frowning as a dark look enters his eyes, memories from when he was one of them.

"How do you know that?"

He gestures with his chin at the soldiers. "There's a small village about a week from Sutoran called Bareilles. We always stop there for a few days; the soldiers get to rest, and we stock up on supplies. Judging by their stupid grins, my guess is we just arrived."

As I watch my sons grow, worry fills me. They are so similar, yet so different. And they are both so easily influenced by their father, I fear for what will become of them.

—Journal of Maren Landry

Chapter Thirty-Three

Aiden

Camari pales considerably at my words, and I turn back to the door, searching for any faces I recognize. There. Sergeant Gramwell rides by, grinning from ear to ear. He has a beau that lives in Bareilles so that just convinces me further that we are in the town.

How did we arrive so fast?

"What happens to us while we're here?" Camari asks, drawing my attention back to her.

"Well, the lieutenants will be drunk most of the time; they all come here for the top-notch brew. The soldiers catch up on rest, visit any relatives they have that live here, and are very lax about their control."

"So we get forgotten?"

"No, but they definitely give us more freedom. Last year, we were here at the end of summer as well, and they had a festival to celebrate the changing of seasons and to promote a good harvest. It was a sight to behold; everyone dressed up and danced all night." I remember how Grant had donned a flower garland and danced around with any young woman he could, how Morris drank too much ale and tried to kiss the proprietor of the pub. All things from my past, things I'd never truly been able to enjoy in the first place. Unlike the others, I had never been able to shake the feeling of the stares from outside. The knowledge that I was warm and surrounded by laughter while a dozen children were cold and drowning in a sea of misery that I created, that I shared in.

"I doubt we'll be invited to join the festivities," Camari says dryly, shrinking back as she sees our four guards approach the caravan. I step back as well as they unlock the door and call for us to climb out. We all cluster together, looking around and waiting. I can still see the desert stretching in the distance, but the houses started just a few feet behind us. We are on a dusty street, the caravan directly in front of us, and people mill about on either side of the street and watch us.

"You get five minutes to stretch your legs, then it's back in!" one of our guards yells at us. The children begin to move about, shifting their weight and looking around nervously, one girl's face crumpling with tears of fear. Camari must notice it as well because she claps her hands, drawing their attention to her.

"It's going to be okay; we're just taking a little break from traveling. This is a village called Bareilles, just a week from Sutoran."

"Why are we here?" a boy named Theodore asks, his brown eyes wide and frightened.

"Think of it as a vacation of sorts, just a nice break from the bumpy road," Camari says kindly, squatting down with her elbows on her knees so that they are at eye level. "We get a day or two to rest and play before we continue on our journey." The little children all nod, looking somewhat less anxious than they did before Camari spoke to them.

"You're a natural with children." I compliment her as she stands up, watching the kids begin to mingle and talk, some of them now appearing excited. She smiles, gaining a wistful look in her eyes.

"Yes, well, growing up, I wanted siblings to play with because all of the village kids avoided me. When I got older and started thinking about the future, I already knew I wanted kids. I still do. But that won't happen now," she says sadly, her dark eyes filled with a sadness that makes something within me rise, wanting to eradicate the source of her sorrow.

"What do you mean? You could still have children one day."

She shakes her head, still smiling sadly as she watches Molly chatter away with Theodore, the pair of them just a moon apart in age. "No, I won't. I am on my way to prison, Aiden. I will never marry, never have…that bond with someone. Never have the chance to bring life into this world. That dream flew out the window the second I learned what my markings are."

The injustice makes me feel ill. A wave of loathing seeps through me as I realize that everything she just confessed, it is all my fault. I took away that dream. "I'm sorry, Camari," I say softly, not sure what to say. She nods, still watching Molly and Theodore.

"It's not your fault. It's just the way the world is."

It is your fault.

"Well, maybe the world needs to change."

Camari turns to me then, her brow high in surprise. "That's an interesting thing for the royal assassin to say."

I know she doesn't mean it as an insult, just a fact, and I don't allow myself to be offended. "A few moons can change a lot, as we both know."

She hums in agreement, smiling. "Indeed."

"Time's up! Back in the caravan!" The guards call, opening up the door and gesturing for us to start walking back in. Camari and I sigh in unison, neither of us wanting to be locked up all night. Though, and I'll never admit it to her, I don't hate it as much as I should. I don't hate sitting next to her in companionable silence, or waking up with her scent in my nose, as if she had been in my arms only moments before. I may even enjoy it.

"Wait!"

We stop as a woman just past middle-age steps off of the road and begins to speak with the soldiers, just loud enough so that we can hear. "You have a woman with you this time. Let us take care of her."

I immediately step in front of Camari when I hear that.

Take her where?

The soldiers appear uncomfortable, and Lieutenant Gladwell walks over, addressing the woman. "Ma'am, how may I help you?"

The woman points at Camari, who raises her brow at the woman's abruptness, and speaks to the lieutenant in a calm voice. "We welcome you into our village every time, even those who don't agree with how you take care of the children on the way to the facility. But, now you have a woman with you, and she must be treated as such."

Lieutenant Gladwell frowns, turning to look at Camari. "She's still a prisoner, ma'am, we can't-"

"She is a woman and must be treated as such! You cannot leave her to rot in a wagon! I will not allow it!"

"We can't have her escape, it-"

"You can tell your king I forced you. Now, we will take care of her during your stay. She needs much work."

Camari scowls, leaning against me as she watches their interaction. My stomach turns as Lieutenant Gladwell folds, likely intimidated by the surprisingly bossy woman. Or not caring what happens to Camari. One less seer to look after if she is injured or killed.

"You can have her for the night, but in the day, she must be in the caravan with the others. And a soldier will be posted outside of your home so that she cannot leave. Understand?"

"Fine." The woman nods curtly before she glances over her shoulder and gestures to two other women. A soldier comes and shoves me out of the way, taking Camari's arm, and leading her toward the woman. She glances back at me, her scowl replaced with wide eyes.

"It's okay; you'll be fine," I assure her, even as I worry. She nods and follows the strange woman, leaving me with the children to wait for her return.

With every voyage between provinces, we stop in Bareilles, and this journey is no different. The men celebrate a job well done. I sit and watch, because I can't escape the feeling of the stares burning into my neck from the caravan.

—Field Journal of Aiden Lorian

Chapter Thirty-Four

Camari

What is going on? This bossy woman has had me dragged to her place of residence by a soldier, where two other women stand, not seeming at all surprised to see me. The soldier, surprisingly, leaves me alone with the three women, excusing himself almost immediately and positioning himself outside the door. The women give me their names curtly, putting their attention into leading me into a building and up a flight of stairs. The first woman's name is Jude, and her two companions are called Sarah and Zia. Jude has brown hair pulled back in a bun, olive skin, wire-rimmed glasses perched on her delicate nose, and a frame that speaks highly of her cooking. Sarah is rather beautiful, short with tan skin, freckles, light brown hair, and blue eyes that have rings of yellow around the pupils. Zia has dark brown hair, brown skin, and black eyes that reflect light in both a beautiful and eerie way.

They ignore all of my questions and lead me up a flight of wooden stairs before they push me into a flat rather roughly, slamming the door behind us. They lead me to a high-backed wooden chair and push me down into it before they step back and survey me.

"Good hair, though it's horribly knotted."

"Needs new clothes; is that *blood*?"

"Look at her nails!"

I looked down at my hands, the nails chipped and broken away in places, chewed down all the way in other places. *They have a point.*

The next thing I know, my clothes are being pulled off rather unceremoniously, and I am shoved into a metal tub filled with hot water. I pull my knees up to my chest as Zia begins to scrub my back with a cloth while Sarah picks out clothes for me to wear.

"Why are you doing this?" I ask when I finally find my voice. Jude comes and sits beside the tub on a stool, tugging my arm forcefully towards her so she can begin to smooth my nails. It's a lost cause, but I let her try.

"We do not agree with the king's treatment of the seers. I saw you, and you looked like someone who needed much help, so I helped," Jude says simply, her broken speech giving away that Zordan is not her first language. She must be an immigrant from Bheofraige, the kingdom across the sea.

"Yet you welcome his soldiers and let them stow a whole caravan of starving children here for a few days while they drink and party?" I can't keep the scorn from my voice.

Jude raises her eyebrows, looking up at me over the brims of her glasses. "We sneak them much food and water, and we help in other ways while the soldiers are occupied. We three own the pub, not the town. They use my pub for food and drink, so they must put up with some of my demands."

I raise my eyebrows in surprise at her. "Do you know what could happen to you if you're discovered?"

"That's why we are careful. We can't refuse to let the soldiers in; it's too dangerous. But we can help in second way without being caught by soldiers or the town. So, we do."

I gain a new sense of respect for these women and relax a little more as Zia begins to lather my hair with soap while Jude starts on my other hand.

"Well, why help me specifically?"

"They never had a woman before, and you look sad. You also look dirty and bloody, so I decide you need our help, and I was right," Jude says matter-of-factly.

After that, we all fall silent, and the women go about their work as if they take care of random seer women every day. After I've bathed, they sit me in a chair in front of a fire, wrapped in a warm towel for modesty. They work the tangles out of my hair and comb it with warm oil, parting it on the left side just how I like it. They clean my almost-healed wounds gently, rubbing them carefully with a balm to promote healing. At first, they gawked at the arrow wounds, and after I explained how I got them, they shook their heads in horror and offered a prayer up to the gods. Finally, they go about dressing me, holding up several clothing items and arguing about whether or not I should wear it, sometimes reverting to their first language and leaving me there, struggling to understand. Finally, they have an outfit put together, but dress me in a simple cotton shift to sleep in, for they said I'll be spending the night there.

They lead me to a table and sit down with me. They then give me a plate filled with food. Chicken, boiled and buttered potatoes, a dinner roll that is still warm, and a glass of water with actual ice. I hesitate to eat, feeling guilty for eating so well, but they assure me that the others are being given food just as good, so I give in and eat, though I don't resist nearly as much as I probably should have. The women talk merrily as I eat, going from speaking Zordan, to their own language, and back again. I barely listen, too immersed in my food. It has been over three weeks since I've had a proper meal, and I definitely show it. I don't think I've ever had such a delicious meal.

After my meal, I lean back in the chair and struggle to stay awake. I'm warm, clean, and I have a full stomach. My eyelids droop repeatedly and I'm unaware of how long it has been when Sarah gently wakes me with a touch on my shoulder, helping me up and leading me over to a small bed in the corner.

I fall into it and vaguely remember someone placing a blanket over me before I fall asleep.

I'm back in Krakent, running an errand for Adeline. I walk down the street and notice that I'm getting strange looks from people. Looking down, I see that my arms are uncovered and that I'm dressed in gray trousers and not my own skirts and bodice. I try to cross my arms to hide them, but suddenly there are shackles on my wrists. I begin to run, turning blindly down roads as I try to get away. Suddenly I crash into someone and almost fall over. Stumbling back, arms steady me and hold me close. I look up into Aiden's eyes and he stares down at me, his hazel eyes close. Then suddenly, he kisses me, his lips warm and soft against mine, igniting a fire in me. He pulls away too soon, and his eyes are cold and an ugly green. Duke Bidennore sneers down at me, and I try to pull away, but he holds me too tightly.

I can take whatever I want from you. *He hisses. Then it isn't the Duke in front of me, but someone I don't know, his dark brown eyes full of grief, an expression that seems uncharacteristic on his stern face.* The wounds are too deep; only the gods can fix this now.

I look down and find crimson blooming across my shift and spilling down onto the ground, warm, sticky, and smelling of iron and salt. Then darkness sweeps towards me, and I fall into it.

I wake with a start, sitting straight up in the bed with cold sweat beading my forehead. Jude, Sarah, and Zia all start, looking over at me with wide eyes.

"Are you good?" Sarah asks awkwardly as they all stand and walk a few steps closer. I nod, turning so that my legs hang off the side of the bed. Sunlight streams through a window, lighting up the loft and announcing the hour.

"How long have I been asleep?" I ask, rubbing my eyes with the heels of my palms and picking off bits of sleep sand from the corners of my eyes.

"Almost eleven hours now. We must get you dressed and fed before we bring you back to the caravan," Jude says, walking over to me and pulling me up from the bed. I obey them as they go about getting me ready, giving me a bowl of oats and cream for breakfast. After that they brush my hair again until it hangs straight down my back and gleams. They dress me in a pale yellow skirt that is thick but practical and pair it with a brown bodice. I put on my old boots, though they have been cleaned, and sit still as Sarah does my hair. She begins a braid at my right temple and braids all of my hair back into it so that it wraps around my head and drapes over my left shoulder.

"Okay, now we will bring you back. You will come with us again tonight, okay?" Zia confirms, her dark eyes glinting as she smiles.

I nod with a smile, grateful for their help. "Thank you. I appreciate what you've done for me."

Jude smiles brightly. "Come, let us go."

THE CURSE OF THE BLESSED

I follow her as she leads me down the wooden stairs we went up the previous evening, sighing at the idea of spending the whole day in the caravan. But I have no room to complain; at least I was able to sleep in a real bed the previous night; the other seers were not.

Leaving the building, Jude leads me down the street, walking quickly with her chin raised high. I follow her, as I am unsure of where we are going. The soldier from the night before falls in with an audible groan, obviously frustrated to have missed out on the festivities of the previous night.

The caravan was brought to a large animal pen of sorts, and rather than be kept in the caravan all day, the seers are allowed to sit outside, the four usual guards standing and watching them. We approach, and Jude nods to me before she turns and walks back the way we came, leaving me to walk up by myself. The soldiers raise their eyebrows at me as I walk towards them, gesturing for me to join the others. I probably could run in the opposite direction right now, and I'd have a good chance of getting away, but two things hold me back. One: Jude, Zia, and Sarah would be blamed for my escape and possibly harmed; I can't do that to them. Two: I can't leave Aiden, Molly, Alex, Addie, John, all of the seers. I can't just leave them.

I walk into the group of seers, smiling when Molly runs and gives me a hug.

"Where were you?" she asks, her eyes wide. I crouch down and push her hair behind her ear.

"I was with some friends, but I'm okay now."

"We had friends too!" she says with a smile, and that is when I notice the new, simple cotton dress she wears. Looking around, I see that all of the seers are wearing new, clean clothes, some of them too big or too small. Alex wears a shirt with baggy sleeves that he's rolled up so that he can use his wrists, and Theodore's trousers drag around his ankles.

"I'm glad," I tell Molly. She beams before she turns and runs over to Theodore. I stand up straight again and am looking around when I see Aiden walking towards me, relief apparent on his face.

"You're back! Are you okay? How did they treat you? What did-"

"I'm fine, Aiden; they were really kind. They said they brought you all food and clothes?" I ask, looking at Aiden's new shirt.

"Yes, it was a bit of a surprise, but they-" he cuts off, surveying my new outfit as if he only just noticed. His eyes linger on my face, now clean and visible, with my hair braided back. "You look..." he trails off as if searching for the correct word, and I flush, my dream suddenly coming back vividly.

"They gave me new clothes too and said they'll come back for me tonight." I explain. Aiden nods, looking slightly embarrassed for some reason as he rubs the back of his neck awkwardly.

"Well, we have the whole day to pass. What should we do?"

If I'm being honest, I think I just enjoy messing with the soldiers. Seeing them fill with fear so easily, after what they've done and how they've treated us, it feels good, especially when Aiden joins in.

The children are eager to have another 'vision', but the only problem is we need to think of something to see. In the end, it is Addie who comes up with the idea, surprising me.

"What if we 'see' them getting sick?" she suggests, tugging on a curl as she thinks. I frown, liking the idea but trying to figure out how we'd carry it out.

"But how would we get them sick? We don't have any access to their food or something to make them sick, for that matter."

Addie sighs, looking down at her lap as though she's embarrassed by her idea. I open my mouth to tell her it is a good idea, but Alex cuts in.

"We don't have access to their food, and they're not exactly eating while they're here anyway; they're just drinking," he says, wrinkling his nose. Aiden suddenly looks up, his eyes wide.

"That's it!"

"What's it?" I ask, confused.

"Jude! You said she doesn't share the soldier's views on seers. What if they help us? The soldiers guzzle brew; trust me, I was one of them. They'll be so drunk they won't notice if something is slipped into their drinks!"

"But what if they blame Jude!" I exclaim, horrified at the idea of them getting in trouble for us.

"That's a risk we'll have to take. I doubt they will, though; they trust the villagers completely. You saw how easily Gladwell let Jude take you. They're mostly immigrants, so the soldiers here view them as docile."

"But it's still a risk! Aiden, we can't make them do that for us!"

"We won't be making them, but we can ask if they'd be willing."

I go to object again, but Aiden cuts me off, understanding but stern. "It's their choice, Camari. We should let them make it."

I sigh heavily, knowing he's right. Besides, if we pull this off, it will be worth it to see one of the soldiers possibly wet his pants. They're already that scared of us.

"Fine. I'll ask her tonight."

The others grin victoriously, but I don't feel like celebrating. I can't stomach the idea of putting anyone else in danger.

The day goes by too fast, and Jude comes for me at dusk just as promised. Aiden nods at me as she leads me away, and I turn away from them quickly.

"You're very quiet; don't speak much," Jude comments as she leads me down the street, heading to her tavern.

"On the contrary, I talk too much most of the time as long as I have something to say."

"And now you have nothing to say?"

"I do, I just don't like it," I reply, staring down at the road as we walk. Am I willing to risk them getting caught if it means us making another chain and gaining a bit more control?

Cold fingers tip my chin up, and Jude smiles as I meet her gaze. "You have pretty face and strong presence; don't waste it on the road."

I smile, standing straighter with my chin up. Jude nods approvingly.

"Better. Now, speak your bad words," she instructs, leading me around the pack of the tavern and up the flight of wooden stairs. She takes them two at a time, and I scramble to keep up with her, the soldier, a different one this time, once again remaining at the door.

"The others-"

"The seers?"

"Yes, the other seers; they want me to ask you for a favor."

"And you don't like the favor? 'Jude asks over her shoulder, opening the door to the flat and leading me in. We are the only ones there, Sarah and Zia being absent, and Jude leads me to the table and bids me sit. She sits across from me and leans forward, listening intently. I sigh but explain.

"We have been messing with the soldiers over our journey, pretending to have visions and then making something happen so that they believe we saw it happen. It gives us a small amount of power in a powerless situation, and that's something we all desperately need."

"That sounds fun," Jude says with a grin. I continue, brushing crumbs from the table's surface.

"Well, we had an idea for another trick. We want to make them sick and have a vision beforehand so that they think we knew. But, to make them sick, we'd need access to their food, and we don't have that." There, I said it. Jude nods knowingly.

"But I do because they all eat and drink much at my tavern."

I nod, quickly adding, "But you can say no; in fact, it would probably be safer if you did."

Jude holds up her hand, stopping me in my tracks. "But I want to. I won't get caught, and it will help you."

"But you might get caught, and that's-"

"Worth the risk. Tell them I'll do it tomorrow evening.

Jude says with an air of finality. I sigh, knowing the others will be happy. But if she gets caught, I won't be.

After another miraculous night with a huge meal and a real bed, Jude leads me back to the other seers the next morning. I'm wearing the same clothes as the previous day, but she decided to do something fancy with my hair again. She said she's never met a seer with hair as vibrant and red as mine and enjoys 'making art with it'. She wove braids starting at both temples that go all the way back to the crown of my head before they tie off, leaving loose strands of hair to flutter around my face and trail down my shoulders. The wind blows as I walk, and I admit to myself that I enjoy the fancy styles; they make me feel strangely confident.

"Okay, you do your vision today. I will make the soldiers sick tonight, as we said," Jude confirms, stopping at the end of the road. I nod, knowing she's oddly eager to help us take a stand.

"Be careful."

Jude smiles and nods before she turns and leaves. I watch her walk and feel a pang in my chest. She reminds me of Adeline, her attitude mirroring my mother's, and my homesickness surges.

I turn and walk to the seers, as the guards have already spotted me and are waiting. "With the others," One of them orders, his hand resting on the hilt of his sword.

"I know, I know," I snap. I walk into the group, hugging Molly and saying hello in reply to all of the greetings I receive. Everyone is smiling, or they have an excited gleam in their eye, eager for the day's vision.'

I walk past all of them and sit down in a patch of shade, leaning back against the narrow trunk of a sycamore tree that is beginning to lose leaves. Despite the fact that autumn is supposed to have started a few days ago, the heat is still miserable, rolling off of the ground in visible waves. I close my eyes and lean my head back, dappled sunlight falling through the leaves and making a pattern on my closed eyelids. I can hear the villagers going about the hustle and bustle of their daily lives. A faint breeze blows, smelling of heat, humidity, and dust. My homesickness grows as the sounds and scents mingle together, almost exactly like Krakent. I can just imagine walking down Seller's Street, chatting with Greta, roaming through the forest and spending the afternoon collecting herbs for Adeline.

But home isn't perfect. I'd still have to cover my arms, hide who and *what* I truly am. I'd have Adeline, but no one else. I wouldn't have Alex, Addie, Molly, John, or any of the seers. I wouldn't have Miller, Morris, and Grant. I wouldn't have Aiden.

"For someone who is about to pull off the scam of the year, you look surprisingly sad."

I smile at his voice, cracking my eyes open and peering up at Aiden. He stands a foot or so away, looking down at me. The sun shines and hides most of his face from me, but I can see the sweat dripping down his neck, staining his tunic a darker color.

"Not sad, just contemplative."

"What about?" he asks as he sits next to me, unfazed by my evasion.

"I was thinking about home. Or what was my home, at least."

"Was?"

"Well," I shift to face him, meeting his hazel eyes. "I'm not sure it's really what I want anymore. Part of me wants to return and forget all of this ever happened. Forget you kidnapped me, forget I'm a seer, just forget it all."

Aiden's eyes flash in the shadows, but the emotion is there and gone so fast I can't decipher it, so I charge on. "But I can't do that. Being a seer is a part of me now, and I can't just pretend I'm not one, not after seeing how they're treated firsthand. And Krakent was never really welcoming to me; it was never truly a home. I think I'm just missing Adeline. She was my home, more so than Krakent ever was, but even that was far from perfect."

Aiden nods, listening, and I continue speaking. It feels good to get all of my thoughts out in the open. "And I realized I don't have a true home to return to, and even if I somehow found a place where I belong, I won't get to go there. I'm going to be dead in a week. That, or locked up in the facility."

"You're not going to die, Camari. I won't let that happen," Aiden says firmly, his eyes flashing again, this time with determination and something else, something protective.

"As much as it warms me inside that you don't want me dead, you don't truly have a say in the matter, Aiden. You're in the same situation I am."

Aiden opens his mouth to argue, but I stand up, ending our conversation. Shaking out my skirts to get out any sand, I hold my hand out to help him up.

"Let's go orchestrate that scam.

Secrets are like gold. The temptation to collect them is strong, and the temptation to trade them stronger yet.

—The Religious texts: The Book of Wisdom

Chapter Thirty-Five

Aiden

I sit back down underneath the sycamore tree, watching as Camari and the other seers get ready. They all act naturally, sitting and talking loudly, the hum of their voices rising up and blending together. And then it cuts off abruptly.

The guards turn to look at the sudden deafening silence, frowning in confusion. I'm prepared to play my part, and I sit up straight in surprise, looking back and forth between each seer. They all sit up straight, staring ahead into nothing. Their eyes are wide, and they are breathing fast, as if they're seeing something scary. The soldiers look back and forth between them, their eyes wide with fright.

I watch Camari as she plays her role expertly, fluttering her eyelids occasionally, sitting as still as a statue. She's incredibly convincing. And then the spell breaks and all of the seers gasp, falling forward or slumping to the side.

"What was it? What did you see?" One of the soldiers asks, earning angry looks from the other three men he serves with. But not angry enough; They want to know as well.

The other seers all turn to look at Camari, acknowledging her as their leader. She levels her stare at the guard who spoke and remains silent, just looking at him. The guard shrinks back slightly, looking to regret his question, but Camari seems to have pinned him to the spot with her gaze. I smile, watching her proudly. For someone who was hesitant to do this scam, she is mastering it.

"Nothing," she finally says loftily, her voice extremely unconvincing. The second soldier scowls in anger and starts forward, drawing his sword halfway.

"Now listen here, you little-"

I start up from where I sit, but the other three soldiers grab onto his arms and speak quietly to him, calming him down. He re-sheaths his sword with a scowl and walks a few feet away, turning his back on Camari.

The seers slowly start talking again, in hushed tones at first, slowly getting louder until they are back to normal. Camari walks back over to me and plops down with a sigh, rubbing her eyes wearily. "One vision, as requested."

"That was perfect. That one soldier almost pissed his pants."

Camari smiles but still looks away, her eyes distant. I know she's reluctant to draw Jude into this, probably because of how kind Jude has been to her, but if Jude is willing, it really is her choice. And we need her help.

"It will all go fine, Camari. By tomorrow, we'll have a bunch of sick soldiers and more power over them and their fears. Next time we tell them what to do because of a vision, they'll do it."

"We'll see." That is all she says.

"What's really bothering you?" I ask in exasperation, starting to get a little annoyed at her mood. No one is happy about our current situation, but acting the way she is won't help anything. She looks over at me, her eyes alight with the annoyance I would guess is also showing in mine.

"Nothing, I'm just thinking."

"You're a horrible liar."

"No, I'm actually a highly accomplished liar; I just don't feel like lying right now, or lying to you, for that matter."

I'm strangely flattered she doesn't want to lie to me, but something is obviously bothering her, and it frustrates me that she won't just tell me.

"Camari, whatever you tell me can't be worse than anything you've already told me," I say. Hurt flashes through her dark eyes, almost immediately swallowed up by her default emotion, anger. I instantly regret my words.

"Compared to you, who has told me absolutely *nothing* about yourself no matter how hard I try to learn, I'm sure I must seem to talk my jaw off. Screw you, Aiden, *and* your judgments about what I've told you."

She stands and stalks off, her fists clenching and relaxing at her sides as she walks. I sigh, sagging back against the tree. Why did I bring up her father? Why did I mention it?

I'm such an idiot.

She sits down all the way across the small court-yard beside a child named Edmund, who always sits by himself. He looks over at her, sees her face, and looks away, content to sit in silence with a companion. I watch as she stares blankly across the clearing, not seeing what she's looking at as if she's walled off all of her emotions and her thoughts from her face. It is a horrible thing to have caused that numb expression, especially to Camari.

"You two fight in basically every conversation you have," Alex says with a snort, surprising me as he comes and sits beside me.

"I don't know about that; we just don't agree about everything." I object, looking over at him as he leans against the tree trunk.

"No, you just fight. It's probably because you have about as much sense as an acorn," he replies, smirking. I scowl at him, and he turns and meets my gaze, his blue eyes twinkling. "It's been obvious to everyone here since day one that you two care about each other, and yet you keep ruining it by saying the wrong things."

"When did you become so wise in the ways of the world?" I ask dryly. He grins mischievously.

"I may be only sixteen, but I've seen a lot more of the world than you. That comes with the territory of being a seer."

I look away again, feeling another pang of guilt deep in my gut, but this time for things I can't seem to fix.

"And you've seen so much of the world that you have an endless supply of friendly advice?"

"*Romantic* advice," Alex replies with a wink. I raise my eyebrows, fighting against the flush creeping up my neck.

"I don't need any romantic advice for Camari; we're just friends if that even. I'm afraid you can't help with this."

"Yeah, keep telling yourself that." Alex snorts again, rolling his eyes. I scowl at him again, annoyed at how he takes pleasure in patronizing me.

"What's that supposed to mean?"

"It means exactly what you think it means."

"Cryptic. *Annoying*."

Alex grins at me again. "Those are the words my mum would use to describe me." Then his smile fades as he remembers what happened, what I did. He looks away again, and I can see a war waging in his eyes. Grief, confusion, anger; it's like a storm, an ocean where one emotion comes crashing after the other in repetitive waves that never let up.

And I'm the wind that created the tempest.

"What will happen to us in Sutoran?" Alex asks me, for the first time giving me a glimpse of his fears.

"You will be taken to the facility. It's a place where seer children are taken to be raised to use their gifts for the good of Zorda."

"But what is it actually like?" Alex asks skeptically. I frown, realizing I don't know. I've avoided the place like the plague, desperate to hold on to the belief that the facility is what the king says, a good place where seers are raised and treated well. Even then, I knew deep down it was a lie.

"I don't know, I've never been."

"Haven't you had to drop off prisoners?" Alex asks, frowning with confusion.

"Yes, but we just unload the caravan. Soldiers take them from there, and I've never been past the front gates."

"Wonderful." Alex sighs, leaning his head back against the tree with a sigh, "We have no idea what we're heading toward."

"Not true; we have a small idea. I may have never entered the outpost, but we have Miller, Morris, and Grant. They're going to help us."

"Wonderful; we have three allies against an army and a king. What could go wrong?"

I roll my eyes at his sarcasm, though he's once again right. It's obnoxious.

"We'll worry about that when the time comes." Because as scary as it is, he's right. I don't know what's going to happen.

Change name. Isolate from everyone. Save for covers. Burn any keepsakes. Tell her nothing.

—Recovered Artifacts from Krakent

Chapter Thirty-Six

Camari

Edmund doesn't seem to mind me sitting beside him; in fact, I catch him looking at me with a faint smile at one point. I only know his name because he comes from the same village as John, Molly, Judah, Gabrielle, and several other children who know his name. He hasn't said a word since his parents were killed, not a single peep. My heart aches for him.

It's nothing compared to what you've already told me.

I grit my teeth, clenching my hands into fists in the dirt. Why did I tell him about my father? He was so persistent, pushing and pushing until it seemed like the only option was to tell him. But then he just threw it back in my face.

I close my eyes and lean my head back to the sun, my eyelids burning red. But it isn't enough to burn the memories out of my head.

The leaves crunch under my boots as I run, the tree branches striking my face and drawing thin lines of blood.

The pain that shoots through my back and shoulders as he slams me against the tree, hands pinning me to the trunk painfully.

"I can't have your mother, but you're far more beautiful than she ever was. I can take my time with you."

My sobs and screams, my fear making me useless.

His rough fingers as he tugged and pulled at the buttons of my cover.

The sound of my heart racing as he paused and leaned closer, slowly stroking my face and sending chills deep down into my heart.

The feeling as my fear recedes, and I know I have to act; I have to save myself.

The shock on his face as my cover opens up, revealing the birthmarks on my arms.

The warmth of his blood as my dagger sinks into his flesh, sinking in up to the hilt so that I have to struggle to pull it out.

I shudder, scrubbing at my eyes with my hands to rid them of the memories. When I open them again, I can feel Aiden looking at me, but I ignore him, instead turning to look at Edmund. He meets my gaze, his brown eyes open and curious.

"Thank you for letting me sit with you," I say gently. He says nothing, simply nodding once.

"Are you friends with any of the kids here?" I ask him. He shakes his head, his black hair flying from side to side at his vigorous movement.

"Can we be friends?"

He shakes his head again, and I smile, fighting against a laugh. "Fair enough. How about sitting partners?"

He nods once before he looks away from me again, over to where the caravan is. I feel another pang of grief for how scarred Edmund is. He's six years old. He should be chattering and running, playing with other children. Instead, he sits beside me, a prisoner, and can't talk, *won't* talk. What did he see that could have taken his will to talk? Why does he believe he needs to remain silent?

I sigh, pulling my loose strands of hair over my shoulder and rubbing the back of my neck, prying sweaty strands of hair off of my skin. I wonder when autumn will officially start and when the heat of the summer will start to fade. It can't come soon enough.

The sun shines blindingly white against a clear blue sky, not a cloud in sight. I envision a gray sky, the blue hidden by a thick layer of clouds. White flakes of snow falling from the sky, getting stuck in my eyelashes and melting as they land on my skin, feather-light and cold. The ground coated in a blanket of white that glistens and gleams like crushed diamonds, crunching underfoot and making everything look like an enchanted wonderland.

I sigh, blinking once, and the barren landscape and blinding sun return to my vision, replacing my imagined paradise.

That evening I sit tensely, watching as the sun sets, waiting for Jude. The day passed in a boring blur, each second dragging on longer than the last. I sat by myself for the second half of the day; Edmund, tired of my silent company, went to sit by himself in the shade of the caravan. Aiden tried to talk to me at one point, but I walked away. I wasn't sure I'd be able to talk to him without punching him, and I didn't want to do something I'd regret. Though I'm not sure I'd regret it.

I spot Jude walking down the street before the soldiers do and jump to my feet, not bothering to shake out my skirt in my eagerness. I have to wait for her to get closer, and I stand impatiently, shifting from foot to foot.

"Camari, please, let me talk to you before you leave."

I scowl, turning to my right to face Aiden. He stands facing me, his hazel eyes apologetic and guilty.

Not good enough.

"If you feel like talking, talk. I can't promise I'll talk back," I say simply, watching as Jude slowly, so agonizingly slowly, gets closer.

"I didn't mean anything hurtful by bringing up your father; I was just trying to get you to talk to me. Honestly, you hide yourself with this wall of anger, and I was just trying to get you to let me in."

"That's rich coming from you." I spit, any pretense of not speaking abandoned. "I don't talk to you? I wall myself off? What can I honestly say I know about you, Aiden Balthasar Lorian? I know you're the king's assassin, I know your full name, and I know Morris is your brother. But I didn't learn any of that from you! I learned it by listening and putting pieces together. You've never told me anything about yourself, not a thing! Every time you get close, you slam down a wall! So don't you dare lecture me about not talking to you!"

Aiden's eyes spark with annoyance and anger, reflecting my emotions. Maybe it is the stress, the heat, the close quarters, but it would seem that both of our grasps on patience has slipped away completely. I'm yelling, and everyone is staring at us, but I don't care, and when Aiden starts speaking, he is yelling as well.

"You have a wall as well! Every time something happens that you don't like, you blow up! Your default emotion is anger because you don't want to feel anything else! You tell me just as little as I tell you!"

"I tell you nothing? I told you about my father!"

"Told me what about your father? See? You can't even say it!" Aiden shouts, throwing up his hands in agitation. "You said we were the same, but we're not! I know my demons; I'm repenting and trying to fix them! You're too afraid to even admit the truth, to say what you did! Why do you still allow him to maintain that power over you?"

"Admit what? Say what?" I growl, clenching my hands into fists. Skies above, do I want to bloody punch him now.

"That you killed your father!" Aiden snaps. Then his face falls, and all of his anger disappears. "Oh gods, Camari. I'm so sorry. Please, I am so sorry."

I feel weak and lightheaded. My breath rasps in my throat; my blood feels cold, moving sluggishly through my veins. I can feel everyone's stares; I can hear the whispers as they gasp and begin to talk about what Aiden just shouted to the whole courtyard, to the whole town.

"Camari, please, I-" Aiden tries to apologize again, reaching for me slightly, but I raise my hand and cut him off. I meet his eyes, fighting to keep my lower lip from wobbling, to keep tears from spilling down my face. I can barely comprehend what he just did. We are surrounded by soldiers, and they all just heard what he said. I could now be accused of murder and arrested for murder. I could be tried for murder, and as a seer, I'll be convicted. And it is all Aiden's fault.

"I hate you," I say quietly, unable to speak louder than a whisper. "You have single-handedly ruined my life, and you seem to find ways to make it worse every day. I hate you, and I wish I'd left you in that forest. I wish I'd left you to die." My voice wobbles on the last words, and two warm tears escape, trailing down my cheeks and blurring my vision. With shaking hands, I reach up and pull the rukh pendant from around my neck, the one he returned to me when I was asleep. Stretching out my hand, I drop it at his feet in the dust. Hands encompass my shoulders and then Jude is leading me away before I can see Aiden's reactions to my words or my actions. I bow my head as we walk, staring at the tear-blurred road as Jude leads me away from the whispers and jibes.

"Ma'am, I don't think we can let you take her. She's just been accused of murder by-"

"I have an agreement with Lieutenant Gladwell. She is not a child, not a boy; she is a woman and will be treated as such while you all take advantage of my tavern. If you have a problem with this, you can bring it up with the lieutenant." Jude speaks strongly, and the soldier backs down. We start walking again and Jude's hands rub soothing circles on my shoulders as we walk.

"It's okay, everything is okay. Just keep walking," she whispers to me. So I do. Tears slip down my face, my hands shake so much that I have to tuck them under my arms to keep them still, but I keep walking. The loose strands of my hair fall around my downward tilted face and shield me from any passing stares. The whispers follow us as we walk, making goosebumps sprout on my arms. But I keep walking.

I don't pay attention to where we are going, so I'm surprised when I find that we're already at the flat. The door clicks shut behind us, and it is like a switch goes off in my brain. I fall to my knees, my hands going up to cover my mouth as a sob breaks loose. My shoulders shake, and tears begin to stream down my face, warm and salty, leaving sticky trails in their wake.

You killed your father!

The feeling of his blood on my hands, soaking the sleeves of my cover. The burn of his eyes as he stared at me in shock. The sucking noise his flesh made as I pulled my dagger free.

My sobs become stronger, resembling more of a retch than a sob. Jude grips my shoulders gently but firmly, pulling me up from the floor and leading me over to where an empty chamber pot sits in the corner of the room. I hunch over it, fighting down vomit, and Jude holds my hair back gently, rubbing soothing circles on my back.

"Shhh, deep breaths. Take deep breaths, in and out."

I obey, forcing my heaving breath to slow down. I count as I breathe, making my exhales last longer than my inhales to help slow down my racing heart. The retching quality of my sobs fades, and after a few minutes, the sobs fade as well, replaced by stutters in my breaths.

Jude helps me up silently, leading me to the bed and sitting me down gently with a soft but firm push on my shoulders. I obey her, feeling numb on the inside. Aiden's words echo around my head.

You killed your father. You killed your father. You killed your father.

How could he have said that in front of everyone?

To think I cared about him. I more than cared about him. And he betrayed my trust. Again.

This is why I don't let myself care for people; this is why I don't let people in. I have a wall for a reason.

Jude drapes a warm knitted blanket around my shoulders, pulling my hair back and out of my face. She presses a warm mug of steaming broth into my hands before she sits down beside me, wrapping her arm around my shoulders and smoothing wrinkles out of my blanket.

"Do you want to talk?" she asks quietly.

"Last time I talked to someone about it, it didn't turn out too well," I whisper, staring at the steam as it curls above the mug, reminding me slightly of scalsen.

"I will listen, but I won't talk. Pretend I'm not here; just say whatever is on your head."

I crack a weak smile at her slight error in grammar, still staring down into the mug. It warms my hands, and my freezing-cold fingers start to feel better.

"I didn't want to kill him, but I didn't have a choice. He raped my mother when she was my age, and she got pregnant with me. When she found out she was pregnant, she ran. She told me what had happened to her when I was fourteen, and a year later, my father found us. He caused a huge scene, and some villagers finally helped my mother drive him away. He was angry, but he left. I thought that was that. But a few days later, he found me in the woods. He chased me and had me pinned against a tree, preparing to do to me what he'd done to my mother. Then he saw my scalsen, and I saw my chance. I stabbed him in the gut... He let me go, and I ran. I made the mistake of telling Aiden all of this after an incident caused all of the memories to come flooding back. I thought I could trust him, I thought he-"

I cut myself off, swallowing against a lump in my throat. Jude listens silently, leaning against me and lending me bodily warmth. She doesn't say a word, just as promised, and instead gestures for me to drink the broth she gave me. I obey, downing it before I hand her the mug. She twirls her finger and shoves my shoulder, and I obey, turning and laying back on the bed. She adjusts the blanket over me, and my eyes begin to droop, feeling oddly heavy. She must have put something in the broth.

"Now you sleep, and tomorrow, all will be better," Jude whispers, smoothing my hair off of my brow, her fingers warm against my skin. The exhaustion overcomes me, and I slip away.

When I wake up, the loft is bright with early morning sunlight. My eyes and limbs still feel heavy from whatever Jude put in my drink, and I yawn heavily before I sit up, placing my head in my hands. My head is foggy from crying, and my throat feels dry.

"Look, who decides to wake up?" Jude says cheerily, walking over with a glass of water that I accept gratefully. I choke on the water, however, when I remember what was supposed to happen the previous night.

"Did the plan work? Are you okay? What happened to the soldiers, did-"

"Hush. It went perfectly; at least half the soldiers are sick with a…passing affliction."

I smile at her joke, pleased that we succeeded and, more importantly, that Jude, Sarah, and Zia are okay. Speaking of which…

"Where are Sarah and Zia?" I ask, looking around. I meet Jude's gaze and get an uneasy feeling at the look in her eyes. "What is it?"

"There are three soldiers outside. They say Lieutenant Gladwell sent them to retrieve you and return you to the caravan. You are leaving today."

My eyes burn with tears as I realize I'll never see Jude again, and I see sorrow in her own eyes as she looks at me.

"It will all be well. The gods will bring us back together one day," she says kindly. I nod, a tear slipping down my cheek. She wipes it away with a smile.

"Oh, you have gone a great distance, Camari, but you have a greater journey yet to undertake. I can see it in your eyes, in your future. You will change the world!" she says softly, her hand still on my cheek. I smile at her faith in me, nodding and accepting her words without dwelling on them too much. Because the idea of a greater journey waiting for me just fills me with exhaustion.

"From the gods' hands to the earth's face to your lips, let it be so."

Jude is prepared to make the soldiers wait, and she takes her time brushing out my tangled hair before she braids it back in a braid that trails all the way down to my lower back, practical yet beautiful. She hugs me one more time before she opens the door and lets the soldiers in. They step forward, nodding at Jude, and gesture for me to put my hands together in front of me. Frowning in confusion, I obey. One of the soldiers steps towards me, and my heart stills as I hear the sound of metal clinking together. The shackles bite into my skin as he places them on my wrists, icy cold despite the late summer heat. I scowl in anger at him, but he returns my gaze indifferently.

I meet Jude's gaze one more time before I'm led away, and she nods at me with far more faith than I have in myself.

"Remember what I said, Camari!" she calls, and then I lose sight of her as I am led down the stairs with a soldier holding on to either arm, the third man leading the way.

"Why the shackles?" I ask as they lead me down the stairs. I notice the soldier wincing several times, and the one on my right holds his stomach as if it hurts. I smile in satisfaction, pleased that they're in pain. Does that make me a bad person? Maybe. Or maybe it just proves what a broken person I've become.

"You have been accused of murder by the king's former assassin and possibly future assassin if he gets reinstated. You will now be held on a different level than the other prisoners." The soldier in front of me answers my question with a grimace.

"What do you mean, a different level?" I ask, fighting against the sliver of cold fear in my abdomen.

"You will be shackled at all times. You will not be allowed in the same caravan as the other prisoners, and you will face trial with the king upon our arrival in Sutoran."

I force my breathing to stay slow as panic races through me. Shackles at all times, a separate caravan? A trial with the king?

I'm a dead woman walking.

The Royal Assassin puts the desires of the king above his own and no duty is more important than that of the king's demand. No life is precious unless the king declares it so.

—The Contract of Royal Assassin to King Aldred III

Chapter Thirty-Seven

Aiden

Our guards are pale and pasty the next morning, and I smile a small, satisfied smile when I see the cold sweat on their foreheads. It appears the seers' vision has come to pass. The soldiers seem to believe that as well, staring at the seers in anger and fear as they clutch their stomachs. But there is far more fear than anger.

My satisfaction is short-lived, however, when I hear Gladwell dispatch three soldiers to retrieve Camari, announcing we will set out as soon as she returns. We're in line to climb into the caravan when I see them approaching. The soldier leading the way steps to the side, and I get a clear view of Camari. Her clothes are wrinkled from her sleeping in them, and her eyes are still red and puffy from crying. Guilt eats at me as I continue to study her, desperate to ensure she's okay. Only she's not, and it's because of me. Again.

If you had died in those woods, she would be okay. But you had to live, and so many people have suffered because of it.

She has her hair braided again, but she stares down at the ground, thoughts flitting across her face with each twitch of a muscle, each blink. Then I see the shackles holding her wrists together. Anger flashes through me, and I don't realize I'm staring until she looks up and meets my gaze. Her dark brown eyes flash with hatred and rage when she looks at me, as well as hurt, and she looks away swiftly, instead turning to face Gladwell as he approaches her. Eben follows just behind him, a smug expression on his face. They stop near enough that I can hear them, and the whole line of seers stops as everyone pauses to listen, even the soldiers who are supposed to be watching us pausing to stare. Camari seems to catch everyone's attention whether she is trying or not.

"Well, look who turned out to be a murderous bitch after all." Eben sneers, grinning as Camari's jaw stiffens. I clench my hands into fists, angered beyond reason.

"Until you face trial in Sutoran, you can't be trusted with the other prisoners," Gladwell says with a satisfied smile, tilting his head and studying her. "So, you will ride on a horse tied to Lieutenant Eben's, just so that you don't get any ideas. Your hands will remain shackled no matter what, and you will be tied to a tree or a caravan at night so that you cannot run. Do you understand?"

"How does it feel to be so afraid of a nineteen-year-old woman that you have to have her shackled at all times?" Camari asks coldly, the chains on her shackles clinking together. Gladwell scowls, and in one quick motion, he slaps her. Camari's head snaps to the side, her braid flying over her shoulder as a whimper escapes her, and she only stays upright because of the soldiers holding onto her arms. I start forward, my fingers twitching with the need to wrap them around Gladwell's throat, but one of our guards steps in front of me. Gladwell looks over and smiles at me before he speaks to Camari.

"It would seem your beau would try to intercede on your behalf, even after betraying you. How romantic."

Camari raises her head, sporting a split lip and a scarlet handprint on her face, and spits at Gladwell's feet before she speaks, leveling him with a deathly glare.

"Let's get a few things straight, shall we? One, I don't need anyone to intercede on my behalf, Lieutenant; I'm quite capable. I've already dreamt up at least three ways to kill you, and that's with my hands shackled and soldiers holding me back." Gladwell's face twitches, the only giveaway that Camari manages to unnerve him, but she isn't done. She turns and looks at me as she says her next bit, spitting each word out like they're full of venom. "And two, Aiden Lorian is not my beau, nor was he ever anything of that sort. He is nothing but an entitled, lying, manipulative, two-faced coward, and it would give me no small pleasure to end his miserable existence right now."

The soldiers snigger, led by Eben, as he grins at me. I ignore them and hold her gaze even as she spits insults at me and glares at me with forced hatred. I deserve everything she says and more. And I won't give up on her because of her words. I can't give up on her.

She must see my resolve in my eyes because she turns back to Gladwell quickly, her wall of anger faltering and revealing the true hurt and betrayal that lurks underneath.

"Well, that's quite a lovers' quarrel you two have gotten into," Gladwell says with a cold smile. Camari just continues to glare at him from beneath lowered eyelashes, her stare so full of hatred I wouldn't be that surprised if Gladwell suddenly combusted.

"Not to worry. You'll have plenty of time to work it out over the next week and a half of our journey. Until then, I'm sure Eben will be wonderful company."

"Just like old times, love." Eben croons, his eyes gleaming. He scans Camari up and down in one long, lecherous look, and I see fear glint in her eyes. My rage spikes again, a beast unwilling to be quieted, and I start forward again. The soldier in front of me acts quickly despite how sick he must feel, unsheathing his sword and holding the point at my neck so that I can't move.

He was well-trained.

The cold iron presses against the hollow of my throat, and I hold my breath, glaring at him with just as much hatred as Camari used on me, even as I'm impressed that he would stand his ground against me despite the obvious fear in his eyes. He knows who I am and has seen what I am capable of. I am the best assassin there has been in many years and the best soldier as well; I could maneuver away from the sword and kill that soldier and two others in a matter of seconds, and I would if it wasn't for two things. One, this soldier, and all of the others have families that will grieve their passing. That gives me my initial pause. I probably would have acted anyway, my rage driving me on, if it wasn't for the second fact. Because of the guards holding her and her shackles, Camari can do nothing to fight against the dagger pressed against her own neck. Her eyes are wide as they flit between Eben, who holds the dagger, and me.

"One wrong move and she dies," Eben hisses, knowing my capabilities and my flaws. He presses the dagger harder, and a thin line of scarlet appears on her throat, dripping slowly down her neck. I can see her chest rising and falling rapidly with fear, though her eyes are as veiled as ever. Excruciatingly slowly, I step back, relaxing my fists and falling back into line, my eyes never leaving Eben's. His eyes flash with triumph, and Gladwell smiles as he steps forward, blocking my view of Camari.

"Good. Now get in the caravan."

Many regard the gods as folklore or legend. Their hand cannot be seen as it tills the soil and initiates the seasons, so it is easier to believe that they are not there all together. How could they exist, with all of the hate that coexists? How could they allow it?

—The Mythical, Magical, and Mundane: Folklore of Zorda

Chapter Thirty-Eight

Camari

My guards lead me to what is to be my horse. It's laden down with supplies, a pack animal. This means if I manage to disconnect my horse from Eben's, I won't be able to get very far before it tires out and the soldiers overtake me.

Damn.

Two of the soldiers tighten their grip on my arms and step toward the horse, obviously meaning to lift me up.

"Hey, hey!" I twist from their grip, turning back to face them. "I will mount by myself, thank you very much."

"Your hands are shackled together." One of them gestures to my wrists.

"Oh really? I'd completely forgotten that; this answers so many of my questions!" I snap in a bright voice before reverting back to a scowl. "I know my hands are tied up, but I can still mount by myself."

The soldiers shrug, stepping back to give me space, obviously beyond caring. I turn to face my horse, blowing a strand of hair out of my face. Stepping forward carefully, I stroke its neck before I grab the pommel of my saddle and hold it tightly between my hands. Slipping my foot into the stirrup, I count to three under my breath before I take a deep breath and pull myself up. I swing my leg over as fast as I can, my face pressing against the horse's neck, and then I'm up. I sit back, wiping my face awkwardly with my hands to rid it of any horsehair. "See? I'm up."

The soldier that spoke before raises his hands in surrender and they turn and walk away, leaving me on the horse.

"So hostile, one might assume you didn't want to be here!"

I scowl, turning to find Eben approaching, leading his black stallion behind him.

"How funny, I thought I was being obvious with my hatred for you. I guess I'll have to try harder."

Eben just grins as he stops his horse beside mine and pulls a coil of rope from one of my horse's packs. Tying one end to his saddle, he cuts it so that the rope is only two yards, maybe two and a half, and ties the other end to mine. "There, now we're forever connected."

"An eternity of living hell. I mean for you, of course, not me. I'll be happy making you miserable."

Eben mounts his horse, scowling at me. "I look forward to your execution."

"Ah, but remember? I have a trial with King Aldred. Who knows, he might pardon me."

Eben chuckles in a way that chills my blood. "The king? Oh, he won't pardon you. Don't worry, I'm sure your hanging will be quick."

I look away, swallowing to hide the rapid beat of my pulse as my heart races, my throat tightening as if there is already a rope against it.

It will be okay; everything will work out.

"Are we leaving or not? I'm tired of sitting here." I snap. Eben glances over his shoulder, his eyes following Gladwell as he rides his horse past us so that he is visible by all.

"Yes, we're leaving," he replies, nudging his horse into motion. I follow, not that I have much of a choice, seeing that my horse is connected to his. I glance over my shoulder as we ride, my eyes holding on to the last glimpse I can get of Bareilles. I'll probably never see Jude again, and that thought sends a pang through my chest. But she'll be okay; we both will be.

Steeling my spine, I face forward again as we ride, setting my gaze on the spot in the distance. Just keep looking forward; as long as I do that, everything will be okay.

THE CURSE OF THE BLESSED

The sun gradually shifts across the sky as we ride, the caravan rolling noisily behind us. Now that I'm riding outside of the caravan, I notice that the river we were following has dried up completely, not leaving a hint as to where it was. We're now riding based entirely on the soldier's mental compass. The thought does not inspire much confidence. At one point, I asked Eben how he knew where we were going, and he replied, "We just do."

So informative; it's mind-blowing.

I shift once again on my saddle, trying not to grimace in pain. I am not accustomed to riding a horse all day and am extremely sore from it. But I bite down my groans whenever my horse stumbles or skips on a rock because the last thing I'll do is let Eben know I'm in pain.

I glance over my shoulder at the caravan as it trundles behind us, pulled by a team of horses. I can't see anyone through the small barred window because of the glare of the setting sun in my eyes, but I can feel their gazes burning into my skin, though I don't know exactly who is staring at me. If I have to guess, it will be Molly, John, or Edmund. Or Aiden.

I face forward at the thought, gritting my teeth against the surge of anger. I finally was able to tell him how I felt about him all those weeks ago when he kidnapped me, even adding a few more adjectives to it. But he just looked at me with an expression in his eyes that did nothing but make me angrier. I wanted him to be angry with me; I wanted him to be hurt by my words. I didn't want whatever emotion he showed. I wanted to hurt him as he hurt me, more even. And at the same time…

I stop my train of thoughts abruptly before they go somewhere I don't want them to go.

Up ahead of us, Gladwell raises his right arm and signals for the contingent to set up camp for the night. The caravan's creaking stops behind us, and Eben slows his horse to a stop before he swings his leg over its side and jumps down. I stay on my horse, watching as, in just a matter of minutes, the soldiers have an entire camp set up. Tents are erected, a fire is started, and horses are taken care of and let off to graze. The three soldiers from before come over and gesture for me to dismount. I do so, smiling at them.

"It's funny that they think it will take three grown and armed men to take care of one shackled woman. They must have such faith in your abilities!"

They ignore my jibe, two of them grabbing my upper arms roughly and leading me away as the third man stays behind to tend to my horse. They take me toward the caravan, and I frown, wondering if they are going to lock me in there tonight after all. They lead me around the back and stop just in front of the door.

"I thought I wasn't supposed to go in there. I'm 'too dangerous'." I scowl. At the sound of my voice, there's a rustling inside the caravan as several seers walk towards the door and peer out at me. The soldiers ignore me, one of them reaching for his belt. I assume he's going for the key, but instead, I see him grab a small coil of rope. The second guard tugs me closer to the door and holds me there. The other guard ties the coil of rope around my waist, making sure the knot is in the back where I can't reach it. Taking the short end that is remaining, he ties it to the caravan's wooden wheel.

"Are you serious?" I ask as he ties it, raising my shackled arms and making the chains rattle. "What do you think I'm going to do? I can't use my arms!"

"We're following orders." The soldier with the rope snaps. I scowl at him, using my hands to awkwardly climb up to sit on the ledge of the caravan.

"So this is where I'll be tonight?"

"And the next night, and all the nights after that," Eben says, walking up with a grin. "After all, didn't you say you thought of several ways to kill Lieutenant Gladwell with bound hands? We can't be too careful."

"I can't wait until my vision about you comes to pass." I scowl at him, turning so that I can lean my left side against the caravan's door. He pales slightly, turning and walking away without another word, and the soldiers follow him. With their watchful gazes gone, I allow myself to sag against the door, sighing heavily. My wrists are red and raw from the shackles, and new wounds are starting to appear over the scars from my previous wounds. It seems I will always be injured to some capacity.

"Camari?"

I turn my head toward the door and smile when I see Molly pressing against the bars, her eyes wide.

"Hey, Molly, how are you, love?"

"Why are you tied up?" she asks me, her lower lip wobbling.

"Oh, it's nothing bad, I promise. They just wanted to give me a break from riding in the caravan, so they're letting me sit outside." I lie, relieved when she buys it.

"When will you come back in with me?" she asks, her little hands clutching the iron bars of the door.

"Soon, love, I promise." I smile. She nods, returning my smile, though it's hesitant. She turns and walks back to where Addie sits, climbing into her lap. Addie smooths back her hair and hugs her, nodding to me with a sad smile. An unspoken agreement passes between us, and I know that Addie will take care of Molly after I am…gone.

I blink rapidly as water rushes to my eyes, watching as Molly begins to doze off against Addie, soothed by the repetitive stroking of her hair. Everything will be fine. I repeat that mantra to myself, taking a deep breath and pushing my anxiety away. Everything will be fine.

But what if it isn't?

All is well; the child is a boy. The mother survived, though she is weak and will take time to recover. What do you wish to be done with them?

—Correspondence from the Royal Hospital of Zorda

Chapter Thirty-Nine

Aiden

"Are you going to talk to her or not?"

I turn and glare at Alex as he sits down beside me. "Mind your own business, why don't you?"

"Honestly, you're the king's assassin, but you're scared to talk to the woman you're in love with. Pathetic."

"Why do you even care? Last I checked, you hated me; what's changed?" I ask, purposefully ignoring the second half of his sentence. The kid is getting on my last nerve with all of his 'advice.'

"It's pretty irritating watching you screw up every time you talk to her, and I'm just trying to stop it and save all of our sanity," Alex replies dryly, running his fingers through his mop of brown hair and smirking at me. I ignore the temptation to punch him, raising my eyebrows at him.

"Save your sanity, huh?"

He nods, dropping his mask of sarcasm for a second and showing me his honesty, showing that he is actually trying to help me. I sigh, running my hand through my own hair before I brace my hands on the floor and push myself to my feet. "If only to keep the last bit of your sanity intact."

Alex grins as I walk away from him and the sleeping seers, the wood creaking underneath my boots as I walk towards the door. Camari is leaning against the iron bars of the door, obviously in the most comfortable position she could find, and it doesn't look very comfortable, for that matter. Her eyes are closed, her face is relaxed, and she appears exhausted, but I can tell she isn't asleep; her breathing is too fast for her to be asleep. She doesn't move as I sit down beside the door, leaning against it opposite her so that I am looking into her face.

"Go away," she says quietly, her voice sounding drained of any strength and just empty. It nearly breaks me.

"You should know by now it is not nearly that easy to get rid of me. I did kidnap you, after all."

She doesn't open her eyes, and I drop that tactic to get her to talk and revert to another. "Plus, I can't really go far. I'm kind of stuck in the caravan."

"And I'm shackled and tied to the same bloody caravan with only a foot of slack!" Camari snaps, her eyes flying open and burning with anger. I'm both happy that she's talking and showing emotion, even if it is anger, and filled with even more guilt when she shakes her wrists so that her shackles rattle together.

"So then you agree that we're kind of stuck to-gether; we don't have to argue."

"I may be shackled, but I can still reach through the bars and strangle you," Camari growls, her dark eyes shining in the night like dying embers.

"That would be quite a feat, especially with the shackles being so wide that they can't fit through the gap," I reply lightly. Camari sighs again, the fight leaving her just as quickly as it came, and she sinks against the door again, her face only a foot from mine.

"I don't want to talk to you, Aiden; I don't want to see you, I don't want to know you. Just leave me alone to my shackles and rope so that I can plot ways to escape before I'm executed."

"Well, maybe I can help you with your plotting?" I offer, still trying to keep my tone light even as my heart grows heavier with each thing she says. She just sounds so broken; it's killing me. Camari looks up at me from beneath her eyelashes, raising her eyebrows slightly.

"You're the reason I'm in this mess in the first place; you're the reason I'm going to be taken to trial when I reach Sutoran. Secondly, I told you very clearly this morning just how I feel about you. Why can't you just understand that and leave me alone?"

"First of all, I know all of this is my fault, and nothing will make me happier than helping you get out of the mess I made. Secondly, I heard everything you said this morning, but I'm fairly confident that it was just hot air, and I'm not giving up on you that easily. And thirdly, I will work as hard as I have to if it means I earn your forgiveness. I don't know why I said what I did, Camari; the words just flew out. If I could go back in time and stop myself from saying them, I would. I never want to hurt you, and I'll do whatever it takes to convince you of that." I speak honestly, never breaking away from her gaze as I tell her a small part of what I should have said ages ago. She sighs in resignation, as if she's finally realizing I won't be leaving anytime soon.

"Fine. Just know that I still hate you."

"Understood." I consent, smiling faintly at her. She closes her eyes again, shifting on the narrow ledge she balances on in an attempt to get more comfortable.

"Why don't you sleep on the ground? It might be a bit more comfortable."

"Jude gave me this skirt; I won't ruin it by rolling around in the dirt," she says softly, her eyes still closed. Camari formed a surprisingly strong attachment to Jude in a short period of time, and part of me wonders if it isn't so much Jude she's thinking about but her mother. Yet another thing that is my fault. Skies above, the list just keeps on growing. Should I even hope for forgiveness at this point?

No. You are a monster. Monsters don't deserve forgiveness. They deserve death and death alone.

I can tell she's slowly falling asleep, her breathing becoming slower, her face relaxing, and her body drooping against the bars more. I shift on the ground, leaning against the iron bars as my own exhaustion slowly grows stronger. I look at Camari one last time. Her face is peaceful, and her red hair glows in the moonlight, her skin appearing pale as porcelain, contrasting strongly with the deep fire color of her hair. Then I fall asleep, still leaning against the door so that she won't be alone.

The Royal Assassin is a servant of the king and not a threat to the people, but rather only a threat to enemies of the kingdom. Any other guilds that are constructed will be treated as a threat, and dealt with accordingly.

—Excerpt from Zordan Laws and Commandments

Chapter Forty

Camari

I wake with a crick in my neck, and my entire body aches from the awkward position I slept in. I sit up carefully to avoid falling off the ledge, popping my neck and stretching as I yawn. My shoulders and elbows pop as well, and I grimace at the noise. Something stirs on the other side of the door, and I turn, my eyes taking a second to adjust to the shadows of the caravan. Aiden is still asleep, pressed against the bars. His face is relaxed, and his hair has fallen over his face. I frown, annoyed at the emotions that surge forward. I force them back with a scowl, sliding down from the caravan and landing on the ground with a small thud.

The camp is beginning to stir, and I watch as tents are collapsed and put away expertly, the beginning of their breakfast being made. Eben crawls out of a tent, a smaller one than before, I realize with a small smile. He stretches and yawns before he spots me watching him.

"Sleep well?" he asks, sauntering over with a grin.

"Like the dead," I reply with a smile, if you could call it a smile. It is more of a bearing of the teeth. His smile slips slightly but comes back when he sees the bags under my eyes.

"You look the part."

"You have nothing better to do than taunt me? Your life really is meaningless."

Eben shifts his weight from foot to foot and looks towards the caravan. Spotting Aiden still asleep and pressed against the bars, his grin grows wider than ever.

"Look who made up." He jeers, walking towards the caravan and pulling out his sword. I stiffen, unsure of what he might do, but he simply runs the blade along the bars. The noise echoes loudly, and Aiden jerks up, his eyes bleary with sleep and the side of his face still bearing the imprints of the bars.

"Good morning, sunshine, glad to see you and the enemy are still getting along so well!" Eben says loudly, sheathing his sword with a metallic whine. Aiden scowls at him, running his hand over his eyes to wipe away the last traces of sleep.

"Glad to see you're still an immature ass," he retorts, straightening his rumpled shirt and running his hand through his hair. Eben scowls, his fist clenching on the hilt of his sword.

"Remember which one of us is in prison for being a traitor. You still have the imprint of the cage between us on your face." Eben spits. A shadow passes over Aiden's eyes, hiding any emotions, and his jaw clenches.

"You're right, there is a cage between us, and you are on the inside," he says coldly. Eben's face goes blank with shock for a second, and then it contorts in rage, turning mottled and red. He turns and grabs my arm, dragging me roughly to my feet.

"Then how come I can do whatever I want to her, and you can do nothing to stop me?" he snarls, twisting my arm roughly. I whimper slightly, gritting my teeth to keep from crying out as the edge of my shackles cut deep into my flesh at the position of my arm, drawing blood. Aiden's face contorts into something unrecognizable, so filled with rage he looks positively manic.

"Let. Her. Go," he says slowly in a voice as cold and hard as ice.

Eben just sneers at him. "Or you'll do what? Yell at me?"

"It's not what I'll do," Aiden replies cryptically. His eyes flash to mine, and he holds my gaze, ignoring Eben completely, and I know what he is trying to say. *Defend.*

Lifting my foot, I stomp down as hard as I can on the arch of Eben's foot. He roars in pain, and his grip on me lets up slightly. I use that and twist, getting free of him, before I finish the spin all the way around and use the momentum to swing my arms towards his face. The iron of my shackles hits his jaw hard, and I feel the force of it reverberate up my arms painfully. Eben falls to the ground from the force of it, pushing himself up slowly and bringing his hand to his jaw. It immediately begins to bruise where I hit it.

"It's what she'll do to you that you should worry about." Aiden finishes, staring coldly down at Eben. I'm still panting, my heart racing, and I stare down at Eben with hatred. He returns the stare, his nostrils flaring. Pushing himself up and still holding his jaw, he spits blood on the ground.

"No rations today. There are consequences to your actions," he snarls, turning and walking away. I almost laugh out loud. None of us would have eaten the camp biscuit anyway.

He should have learned by now I feel no guilt over getting revenge on him.

I turn back to the caravan, and Aiden's eyes seize my gaze again. "Are you okay?" he asks softly. I nod, gently rolling my wrists to help relieve the ache building up.

"Yeah, that was actually pretty satisfying."

Aiden snorts out a laugh, raking his hair away from his face again. "I bet. I can't wait 'til I get my chance to do that."

I nod, tilting my head to either side and popping it. He isn't forgiven, not yet. That would be too easy for him.

Almost as if he senses my thoughts, his smile fades, and he closes off once more. That is what I both love and hate about Aiden: he knows what I am thinking almost as soon as I've thought it.

"How are your wrists?" he asks, gesturing with his chin. I look down to where a trail of blood has dripped down my hand.

"Sore. As I said, I always seem to be injured. One would think I asked for it," I say wryly. Aiden raises his brow, and I glare at him. "Don't say it. I didn't ask for this."

At that, he falls quiet, leaning away from the bars. "No. No, you didn't."

And with that our conversation ends.

Riding along beside Eben, the purple lump on the side of his face fills me with satisfaction. He doesn't look at me once; he just stares straight ahead with a scowl on his face. I have a feeling it causes him pain to talk, which is just another bonus, like the cherry on top of the pudding. Not having to hear his voice will always be a win. Not to mention it makes it far easier for me to continue getting a little bit of revenge.

"So, I've been wondering, for someone who claims he despises seers, why are you so obsessed with me?" I ask, looking over at him. His eyes glint, but he doesn't reply. I meant the question as a taunt, but now that I think about it, it's a valid question. He does seem to have a vendetta against Aiden and I, and I'm beginning to wonder why.

"I mean, honestly, I saved your life twice, and yet you refuse to abide by our deal. Now, one could believe that was because you just hate seers and didn't want to see one get away, but I'm starting to think it was me specifically that you couldn't stand letting get away. Why is that?" I tilt my head to the side as I speak, thinking carefully. He hasn't reported Onaydo to Gladwell; he hasn't mentioned it at all that I know of, which means he kept to that part of the bargain. So why hasn't he let me go?

"I mean, there has to be a reason. What's the matter; lose your voice?" I ask in a soft, concerned voice. Eben huffs a breath heavily out of his nose, and his hands grip his reins so tightly his knuckles turn white. His jaw would probably be clenched if he wasn't in such pain, yet another reason to smile.

"I guess I'll get my answer another way," I say with a nonchalant shrug. Eben looks over at me, curious despite himself, just as I guessed he would be.

"And what ways would that be?" He grinds out, moving his jaw as little as possible. I turn to face him, swaying with the movement of my horse and smiling in what I hope is a confident way as I tap my temple.

"With the gift I was born with."

Eben scowls, facing forward again. I copy him, smiling to myself. Oh yes, getting to him is easy. At least, it is for me.

Two days after Eben and Aiden's clash, I am falling into a new rhythm with the camp. The fact that I am getting used to being a prisoner is both sad and, in an odd way, amusing. I've been keeping count of the days that have passed since Aiden took me from

Krakent, refusing to allow myself to lose track of time. Twenty-two days. To Adeline, I've been missing for twenty-two days. I've been a prisoner for twenty-two days. It's expected that I get used to it, right? Or have I found another way that I'm abnormal? Camari Dorsar, the adaptive captive.

The men are just starting to set up camp for the evening, and I'm sitting beside the caravan, already tied to the wheel. I sleep on the narrow ledge at night, even though it is far more dangerous. The ground sucks the warmth from me as I lay on it, and I spend the entire night shivering until I get the guts up to climb up onto the ledge and lean against the bars, trying to get as warm as I can despite the iron bars separating Aiden and I. Aiden has started sleeping against the iron bars, whether I start the night on the ledge or on the ground. He hasn't said why, hasn't even brought it up, and so I say nothing lest he responds with something that will piss me off. Part of me enjoys waking up and having his face be the first thing I see, and the other part of me is mad at that part of myself. He ousted my secret to an entire village; he is the reason I am in shackles. Yet no matter how many times I remind myself of that fact, part of me is still drawn to him like a magnet. And I can't escape the little voice in my head that whispers, saying it wasn't on purpose and that if the positions were reversed, I might have done the same thing. Saying that neither of us can control our mouths and tempers at times.

I pull my knees to my chest and wrap my arms around them, watching as the fire starts across the campsite, keeping the growing darkness at bay. I can't feel its warmth from where I sit, my cold bones begging me to draw closer to its flames. Waves of cold tingle down my spine, and I hug my knees tighter to myself. The noise around me seems to fade slightly, slowly disappearing altogether. I frown, blinking as the fire seems to flicker and dance slower than normal.

Look.

I shake my head slightly, but nothing changes. My hearing and vision are still slowing, fading away.

Look and learn. Listen, Camari.

I blink, and suddenly I'm not in the campsite anymore. I sit in a wide-open field, dark pine trees visible in the very distance. The ground is covered in a thick layer of snow, pure white and perfect. The sun glints off of the icy crystals, making it glow a pure white, almost an unnatural shade. Far in front of me on the icy plain stands Aiden and another man I don't recognize. They're so far away that they wouldn't be able to hear me if I shouted, and I stand still, watching to see what will happen.

Aiden is dressed in different clothes. Both him and the other man are wearing the same pants and loose cotton shirts, both dyed slate gray. Both men have swords and are dueling, their blades clashing against each other's loudly. I try to step forward now, sensing danger, but my body pulses in sudden agony at my movement, and all I can do is watch as they duel. Suddenly, Aiden's head turns toward me for no reason, heartbreak on his face, and he loses his concentration. The second man drives his blade forward and pierces Aiden's flesh between his ribs. I scream as I see the sword impale Aiden, doubling over and clutching my hands to my stomach as grief strikes me like an arrow, the pain visceral.

This can't be happening.

The second man pulls his sword back and stabs it down into the ground. Aiden staggers back a few steps, and suddenly, all I can see is the snow on the ground at my feet, white and spotless. I stare at it, unable to look away and see a drop of red appear on the otherwise spotless surface. Another drop appears, and another, until suddenly, there is a pool of red-tinted snow beneath me.

Look and learn; listen.

I hear the voice again in my head, the same voice I've been hearing since I was a child walking to the monastery on a winter day. I try to think back to it in my head, but I am unsure if it hears me. *I'm listening; I'm learning.*

The bloody snow still glints in the light, and I study it as it gleams and shines, smelling heavily of iron and salt. Aiden's blood.

Camari.

The blood begins to freeze over into one solid pane of ice, still crimson red, and I picture Aiden's body lying a few feet away, spilling his life force out onto the ground for me to stare at.

Camari!

The ice shatters and suddenly, the snowy field is gone, and I'm aware of someone gripping my shoulders and shaking me gently. I gasp for air, realizing that I've been holding my breath, and blink, my eyes refocusing on my surroundings. I'm back in the darkening campsite, still chained to the caravan, and a small crowd of seers surrounds me, with the four guards staring from behind them all. Aiden is crouched in front of me, his face mere inches from mine and his hands gripping my shoulders.

"Are you okay?" he asks me softly, his hazel eyes wide with concern. Seeing his face, I flashback to the snowy field with the sword in his gut. My stomach turns, and I scramble to my feet. The seers all back up as I turn from them and stumble as far away as I can and fall to my knees as my arms are tugged to my side by the taught rope, emptying the contents of my stomach onto the ground as I heave. I gasp for air, my body shaking and convulsing as I vomit onto the desert floor. Cold hands brush my neck, and I flinch, but it's only Aiden gathering my hair back away from my face gently, crouching beside me silently. I force myself to take deep breaths through my nose, fighting back against my rising nausea as I spit, clearing my mouth out. Once I'm confident I won't be sick again, I sit back on my heels and run my hands over my face, wiping away warm tears.

"What did you see?" Aiden asks from beside me, his voice low and deep. I swallow against the bitter, acidic taste in my mouth, thinking quickly. I can't tell him; I just know I can't.

So what do I say?

"How do you know I saw something? I could just be sick from lack of nutrition." I stall, turning to face him and pulling my hair from his grip, running my violently shaking fingers through it. My entire body is trembling, vibrating with a combination of adrenaline and terror, my teeth chattering as my heart races.

"We both know that's not what it was. You were sitting as still as a statue, shivering uncontrollably, and at one point, you let out a scream that made my heart stop. Your eyes…you've never had a vision with your eyes wide open like that. They were white, Camari, like spiderwebs had been put over your eyes. What did you see?" His voice is firmer, more demanding the second time he asks, and I swallow again, wringing my fingers together on my lap.

"I saw– I saw someone die."

"Who?" he asks, his eyes wide with concern and urgency. And fear.

He thinks I saw my own death.

"I'm not sure; it was no one I know. I just saw a duel and saw someone get stabbed." I lie, forcing my face to remain stoic as I talk about Aiden's death like it is nothing.

It is far from nothing.

Aiden buys my lie, sympathy spreading across his face. "I'm sorry you had to see that. Are you okay?"

It seems ironic that I just saw Aiden die, yet he is asking me if I am okay. "Yes, I'm fine. I think I'm just tired," I reply, rubbing my eyes with the heel of my palm. My hands won't stop shaking, and I hold them out in front of me, watching them. Aiden reaches over and takes them gently, his own hands warm and steady and immediately calming my racing pulse.

"Camari-"

"Back in the caravan, your time is up!" The guards call, swinging the caravan's door open and gesturing the seers in. Aiden scowls over his shoulder at them, annoyance flashing in his eyes, before he turns back to me, releasing my hands.

"You're sure you're alright?"

"I'm fine, Aiden. Go back in the caravan before you give them an excuse to pick on you even more," I say, forcing a weak smile even as I feel like I'm about to fall apart.

Aiden holds my gaze for a few seconds, his eyes flicking back and forth as though he's searching for something. Then he nods, turning and walking back into the caravan without another word. I sigh heavily once the door to the caravan closes, running my hands awkwardly through my hair. Whatever I just saw, I need to find a way to stop it from happening. I can't let Aiden die, not like that. The scene replays in my mind over and over, the shock on his face pure and extreme. Tears pour down my face, and I hug myself as I try to rein in my sobs, biting my fist to muffle them. It's going to be okay; I won't let that happen.

Aiden is going to die.

I watch as the soldiers begin to crawl into their tents, retiring for the night. Their lives are so simple. They have no worries, no fears. They do what they are told and don't think about it twice; they don't wonder if what they are doing is right. They don't have a gift that makes no sense and fills them with fear; they don't have the weight of the world on their shoulders. And yet, I don't envy them for a second.

Standing up, I shake out my skirt before I climb awkwardly up onto the ledge. Aiden raises his eyebrows when he sees me, as I usually don't climb up until he is asleep. I simply settle against the bars silently, soaking in whatever warmth I can. As much as I want to stay angry with him, I just can't seem to. At some point, I have to quit trying to stay angry and forgive him. And now I don't truly know just how much time we have together.

"Good night," I whisper, keeping my eyes closed. I'm dozing off, falling into that space between wakefulness and sleep, when I hear him whisper back, "Good night."

I smother my smile and let blissful sleep take me.

Seers were chased from the kingdom at threat of death. Women and children, mother and son alike abandoned everything and ran from the army that descended upon them.

—Retractions from the Royal Historical Documents

Chapter Forty-One

Aiden

Everyone in the caravan groans as the wheels go over yet another rock. The trail is getting more and more bumpy with each day, a sign we're nearing Sutoran. The others in the caravan have come to the same conclusion and we all sit in silence as we're jostled this way and that. We go over another bump and everyone groans again, being thrown against the walls and into the people next to them.

"How much longer?" A boy named Matthew growls, rubbing his elbow where it is beginning to bruise.

"Three days, maybe two," I reply, rubbing my neck. It's starting to ache from being thrown back and forth.

"I shouldn't be looking forward to reaching the facility, but if it means getting out of this caravan, then gods, let us arrive sooner!" Alex exclaims, raising his hands to the sky. Several seers mutter their agreement, shifting on the hard floor.

"When will Camari be allowed back in the wagon?" Addie asks, lifting her head from where it was leaning against the wall. I swallow back my annoyance at the question. I've been asked the same question at least twice a day, for the past five days. Every time I give the same answer.

"Soon."

"When is 'soon'?" She counters, her eyes flashing.

"I don't know, Addie, whenever Camari comes back. That's when soon is."

"You're just going in a circle. Soon is when Camari comes back and Camari comes back soon. Give us an actual answer!" Addie snaps, throwing her hands up in the air.

"I don't have an actual answer, Addie! I don't know when she's coming back; I know as little as you! The guards said she'll ride with Eben until we reach Sutoran, where she'll face trial with the king. That's all we know!"

"And whose fault is that? Who shouted out her secret to the entire village?" Addie spits with more anger than I've ever seen the girl use.

"I know it's my fault; I'll never deny that! It is my fault that you all are in this situation; so repeating it will help with nothing! All we can do now is help her in any way we can," I growl, struggling to refrain from shouting at her. She huffs out a breath and leans back against the caravan, looking towards the door rather than me. Her multicolored skin is coated in dirt and grime, just like all of us, and is almost the same shade. My anger fades and is replaced with pity. She's just scared, like everyone else.

"Everything will be okay, Addie, you'll see," I say in what I hoped was a kind manner. She turns and looks at me, nodding once, before facing the door once more.

I sigh, pushing myself up from the ground. Being stuck in the caravan makes me restless, so I tend to move around a lot. I begin to walk back and forth, swinging my arms and popping my neck to help loosen up my stiff muscles. Stretching out my legs, I turn and look out the barred door. The desert is beginning to fade away slowly behind us, and I spot a few patches of grass growing here and there, though it's mostly brown. I used to get excited when we started nearing Sutoran, eager to return home. Now I dread it. It isn't Sutoran I don't want to see; I've missed my home desperately. It's my job, how I was known, what the people thought I was, that I don't look forward to returning to. The loneliness. Even with Morris and my men around, I was still alone in Sutoran. Now, I've grown accustomed to having the seers around all the time. I've grown accustomed to having Camari with me all the time.

Finished with my stretches, I continue on with my exercises, determined to stay fit.

I keep having the same thoughts spiraling around in a circle, repeating over and over. I had the answer; I was just fighting against it as hard as I could. I was the royal assassin, I didn't feel compassion; I didn't care for anything except for my men and myself. I'd prepared myself to live my life like that; I'd wanted to live my life like that. How has everything changed in just a few moons?

I sit back down, leaning against the wall of the bumpy caravan. My shirt has a half circle of sweat around my collar, and my hair is sticking to my forehead. I shove it back with a scowl. I've never kept it this long; it needs to be cut.

"Why the face?" Alex asks wearily. He's leaning on the wall across from me, the bags under his eyes making him appear exhausted. I have a feeling I look the same, and taking a quick look around, I see that everyone else does as well. We're all tired of this caravan.

"No reason; just thinking," I reply. A lock of hair falls onto my forehead again and I shove it back aggressively, annoyed beyond reason. Alex raises an eyebrow at me, smirking weakly. It's funny how over the course of our journey to Sutoran, he's gone from hating my guts to being an ally of sorts.

"Yes, you're as relaxed as can be."

"What about you? We reach Sutoran in two days; how are you coping?"

Alex looks towards the door, his jaw clenching and his eyes darkening. "Oh, I'm very excited to begin my lifetime of enslavement to the king. Doing great."

"We'll figure it out, Alex. We'll think of something." I sigh. Do I truly believe that? Alex looks at me, his dark eyes glinting in the low light.

"Think of what? Figure out what? You don't even know what we'll do; you don't have a plan.

You've been arrested. If you can't save yourself, you sure as hell can't save us."

I bite back my retort, knowing it will only anger him further. And besides, he has a valid point.

"Let me worry about myself. I'll figure out a way to get all of you out of this," I say, leaning forward against my knees so that Alex has to hold my gaze. He hesitates, but then nods, leaning back against the caravan. Now I just have to keep that promise.

Because I'm so good at keeping promises.

"Now, back to what we were talking about before you changed the subject." Alex sighs, turning to face me again, his signature smirk present once more.

"Which was?"

"Your miserable attitude."

"Everyone's in a mood; look around. We're stuck in a caravan and going over every rut and hole in existence."

"Why do you do that?" Alex asks, frowning curiously, a new expression for him. I scowl at him, not in the mood for games.

"Do what?"

"It's like you have a wall and as soon as we start talking about anything you're feeling or thinking, you slam it down. Why do you do that?"

"You sound just like Camari."

Alex grins. "I'll take that as a compliment; she's funny. And she's right."

"I told you that you sound like a woman and that's a compliment? Also, you're only saying that because if she's right, you're right too."

"Now you're avoiding it!" Alex says in exasperation, throwing his hands up in annoyance. I grin, crossing my arms and stretching my legs out in front of me.

"My thoughts are my own and no one else's."

But that's not true, is it? If you could control your thoughts, you wouldn't constantly be afraid of yourself.

Alex rolls his eyes. "Obviously. But sometimes it's nice to talk to someone; it helps to voice your thoughts. Makes them easier to work out. That's what my mom always said at least."

"I'm good," I say firmly, shifting again on the ground. Alex just raises his eyebrows and holds my gaze, not blinking.

"Aiden, I am bored, tired, and avoiding the future. Do not confuse my desperation for entertainment for me caring about your feelings. That being said, I am not dropping this beautiful chance at an entertaining distraction."

I groan, running my hands through my hair for the third time. "I'm just trying to think out every scenario of what could happen when we reach Sutoran."

"Nope, that's not it."

I scowl at him again. "How do you know?"

"My seer, witchy powers. No, I've just been stuck in this caravan with your melancholic, brooding ass for weeks; I know too much about you by now, it's disgusting. Almost all of your scowls and moods circulate around one problem."

"Which is what, oh-wise-one? Please enlighten me on the source of *my own problems.*"

"Camari."

"Camari isn't a problem!" I snap immediately. Alex grins and I realize that I fell right into his trap. If I could scowl anymore than I already am, I'd be doing it.

"You've got it *bad*, man," Alex says in a lilting, sing-song tone, still grinning as he raises his eyebrows suggestively.

"Shut your mouth. You don't know what you're talking about. Go talk to Addie; the other girls might enjoy talking about their feelings with you, but I'll pass."

"No, seriously. Have you at least told her-"

"I said shut up!" I snap. Alex falls silent, his smile fading. I groan, rubbing my face with my hand. "I'm sorry, I don't mean to yell. It's just..."

I trail off, shaking my head and silencing my train of thought, But Alex persists with a returned grin. "It's just what?"

"She complicates everything!" I snap. A few seers look up from the back of the caravan and stare, but Alex waves them off. I am vaguely aware of the caravan being pulled over for the evening, but Alex gestures for me to keep going and I do, words exploding out of me. "I'm a soldier! I don't have to worry about anyone because I know my men and I know they can take care of themselves, and we take care of each other. That's how it was before; it was easy, simple. Or it was simple, before I became the assassin."

"But…?" Alex broaches carefully, prodding me on. I exhale raggedly, running my hand down my face.

"But then I became an assassin. And even then, I hated what I was doing and I longed for something else. And then Camari came into my life and changed everything. I went from being a member of the king's army and hating myself to being stuck in a caravan filled with people I'm supposed to hate; who hate me almost as much as I do. Everything's gone wrong."

"How has she changed your life?" Alex asks. He reminds me heavily of a doctor treating a patient, only he's too judgmental. Not that I care; now that I'm talking, I can't seem to stop

"She flipped it completely. I never wanted to-" I cut off abruptly, staring down at my hands where they sit on my lap.

"You never wanted to what?" Alex asks in a surprisingly gentle voice. I think he realizes that I've never talked to anyone like this, and is trying to let me get it all out. I feel so stupid, talking the way that I am, sharing all of this, but at the same time, it also feels so good to just let it all out.

Just say it, get it out of our system, and never speak of this conversation again.

"I never wanted to care for anyone, not like that. I don't deserve it after everything I've done, and no one has ever felt a semblance of love for me except for Morris. But then Camari came into my life, and changed everything. And I've done nothing but cause her pain since I entered her life. Her life would be better if she had left me to die in the woods. Everyone's life would be."

Alex raises his brow. "Aiden, that is not a good train of thought to have."

"But it's true. If…if I was dead-"

"Someone else would have taken your place and done what you did, but perhaps been less merciful." Alex cuts me off, his voice harsher than I've ever heard it. "Do not let your mind go any further down that road."

"If it was someone else, they would have left Camari alone that first day, and not followed her like a moth to a flame, like a damn fool." I spit. "She wouldn't be here. I don't want her here and yet at the same time I do. It's disgusting."

"Why do you want her here?" He prods, skipping over the rest of my statement, his gaze flicking over to the door for a moment before returning to me as he smiles.

"Because she's my rukh," I say quietly, almost to myself. "Camari… She's a complication, a huge one. If she hadn't entered my life, I'd still be the royal assassin, working with my brother and my men. But I don't want to change anything that's happened. I'm… I care for her a lot, and that complicates everything."

Alex is smiling in a calm way, completely different than his usual grins and smirks. "Look at that, the big oaf has feelings."

I scowl, rolling my eyes at him. "The big oaf just wanted to sit in silence, but you needed entertainment."

"But seriously. You better tell her how you feel before it's too late," Alex says, his voice taking on a serious edge.

"Sixteen and filled with worldly knowledge. You weren't lying," I say with a faint smile. Alex grins again, opening his mouth to reply, but he's cut off as the soldiers open the door and call for us to file out. I push up from the ground with a sigh, feeling lighter somehow, and get in line, more than ready to get out of the damned caravan.

The Royal Assassin, Aiden Balthasar Lorian, will be held responsible for the actions of his men, and their lives will be his responsibility in all that they do. All that he does will be a reflection on them and all that he earns, they will also earn.

—The Contract of the Royal Assassin to King Aldred III

Chapter Forty-Two

Camari

I tilt my head side to side and pop my neck, sore and tired from riding the horse. My wrists are raw and weeping from the iron shackles and I have a feeling I couldn't be more uncomfortable if I tried. Thankfully, just as I'm seriously contemplating strangling Eben with the chain connecting my shackles, I hear the order for the caravan to be pulled over and for camp to be set for the night. I sigh in relief, slumping against my horse's neck as I resist the temptation to cry from pure exhaustion. I hear my guards walking toward me. They cut off their conversation when they reach me, but I hear enough for my heart to start racing.

"-Sutoran tomorrow?"

"Yeah, sometime mid-morning."

They reach me and gesture for me to dismount, and my thoughts are flitting around too fast for me to say anything. We will reach Sutoran tomorrow. I'll face trial tomorrow. I gulp against my rising panic and let the guards lead me toward the caravan. I walk quickly, eager to tell Aiden what I've learned. My guards tie me to the wooden wheel and I walk as close to the door as I can with the ropes short length, waiting eagerly for the soldiers to open the door.

"-would have left Camari alone that first day, and not followed her like a moth to a flame, like a damn fool. She wouldn't be here. I don't want her here and yet at the same time I do. It's disgusting."

I pause at the door as I realize it's Aiden speaking, and about me as well. Alex's gaze flickers to me and I flush, caught eavesdropping, but he just grins and turns back to Aiden who is scowling obliviously.

"Why do you want her here?" Alex asks as he smiles.

"Because she's my rukh." I almost miss Aiden's whisper, but once his words register, my stomach drops and my breath catches in my throat. "Camari... She's a complication, a huge one. If she hadn't entered my life, I'd still be the royal assassin, working with my brother and my men. But I don't want to change anything that's happened. I'm... I care for her a lot, and that complicates everything."

I quickly step away from the door when I see the soldiers walking toward the caravan, my face flaming. I sit in the shadows of the caravan, leaning against the wheel I'm tied to. The door is opened and seers begin to file out. Molly immediately runs to me, climbing into my lap and giving me a hug. I smile and hug her back, still watching the line of people exiting the caravan over her head. Alex jumps down, adjusting his shirt as he walks. He glances over at me and grins, winking before he saunters over to where Addie sits. I flush again and look away, starting a conversation with Molly and spacing out as she goes into a long description of a dream she had. Aiden jumps down from the caravan and glances toward us. I quickly look back at Molly, but watch him out of the corner of my eye. He hesitates as if he's going to walk towards me, but then changes his mind and walks over to Alex and Addie, sitting down closer to them. Alex glances over at him and shakes his head, rolling his eyes before gesturing for him to join their conversation.

"Camari?"

I start, looking back down to where Molly sits on my lap. "I'm sorry, what were you saying?"

Molly's smile fades and she tilts her head to the side. "Are you okay?"

"Of course, I'm just tired," I say immediately. She nods wisely, as if that explains everything.

"Will you braid my hair?" she asks me the same thing every evening, and I always say yes. She turns on my lap so that I can reach her hair. I run my fingers through it, gently easing out any tangles or knots. My gaze wanders again as I do it and I find myself staring at Aiden again. He's saying something to Alex and Addie, and Addie is nodding enthusiastically. Suddenly Aiden glances over his shoulder at me and I look back at Molly quickly, my face flushing. I internally curse myself. I can't blush every time Aiden looks at me just because of what I overheard. It just won't work.

I'm...I care for her a lot, and that complicates everything, but I don't want to change anything either.

I'm...

All I can think about was what he said. And what he stopped himself from saying.

I care for her a lot.

I hear his words again and again as I weave Molly's hair into an intricate braid. That was the most I've ever heard him say about what he thinks; how he feels. Usually we get so close, and then he slams down that wall again and again, shutting me out.

I care for her.

I've been keeping track of the days, and it has been over thirty days since I was kidnapped by him. I've known him for moons, multiple moons. Sometimes it feels like a week; sometimes it feels like a year. And in that span of about three moons, he's gone from my friend to my enemy, then to an ally, to...I don't know what he is anymore. Can I honestly say I don't care about him in that way? Can I honestly say I don't feel anything?

I risk another glance at him and find him looking at me. Our eyes connect and I can feel my face turning red. He smiles faintly, his overlong sandy brown hair sweeping across his brow, and I look away, turning back to Molly's hair and tying it off before I lay

my hands into my lap, my heart racing at the ramifi-
cations of what I must now admit to myself.

No. No I can't.

R.C. Huye

Chapter Forty-Three

Camari

We reach Sutoran at noon. The sun shines directly above us as I amble along on my horse. Eben keeps glancing at me and smirking, as if he knows what fate awaits me. He probably does. I keep my fears hidden beneath an impenetrable mask of indifference, and it works, because after yet another smirk that provokes nothing out of me, his smile fades and he looks away with a huff.

The desert finally faded away the previous evening, and the city is framed in rocks and tall, brown grass. There are trees, but they are scarce at first, though it looks like they eventually thicken up into a forest that looks so familiar and safe it makes my eyes burn with homesick tears. Despite my fear, I can't help but admire the city that rises up in front of us. It has a large stone wall that is both intimidating and striking. I can see soldiers stationed at the gate where there are lines of people either entering or leaving. Beyond the wall, the city rises up in peaks and structures. The stone buildings are intimidating even from far away, with glass windows that gleam in the sun and dark rooftops, some of them with turrets. The citadel is visible in the far distance, big and made of dark stone. A chill races across my arms that has nothing to do with the early autumn chill that is finally descending on us. Beyond the wall, way to the right, there stands one rooftop all by itself, the only building for miles in that direction. I know without asking that it is the facility. All eighteen of the children in the caravan behind me will end up there, and, hopefully, me as well.

I turn my eyes away from it, choosing to instead observe and take in any information that could come in handy. We're close enough to the wall now for me to make out details. There are six soldiers at the gate, deciding who is allowed to enter their capital. They each have a sword buckled around their waist, five of them on the left side and one of them on the right. A few of them also have assorted daggers, knives, and one of them has a small hatchet. *Wonderful*.

I'm pulled from my thoughts when I hear the driver of the caravan woah and we all suddenly stop.

"What's going on?" I ask Eben, glancing over my shoulder and watching as four soldiers walk to the back of the caravan.

"You and Aiden aren't going to the same place as the rest of them. He'll come ride on another horse while the seers are taken to their new home," Eben replies with a sneer, curling his lip on the word seer.

"Where will we be taken?"

Eben turns to face me, smiling widely. "To the citadel. You have an audience with the king. I expect he's especially looking forward to seeing Aiden again."

"What does that mean?" I ask, a quiver of fear affecting my voice.

"You'll find out." Eben dismounts and gets another short coil of rope off of his saddle. Another packhorse is led up beside mine, and he ties the rope so that my horse is now connected to it as well. I hear a clacking sound and twist in my saddle. Aiden is being led between two guards, his hands shackled in front of him. His eyes glow with rage, and he glares at Eben as he pauses in front of him.

"Look what you've become. A traitor, chained and led like an animal in front of our king." Eben crows, taking far too much pleasure from Aiden's humiliation.

"And yet a drop of my blood has more honor than a pool of yours," Aiden replies coldly.

"Get on your horse. I can't wait to watch you hang!" Eben snaps. He aims the last part at me and I see Aiden's jaw clench from where he now sits on the horse beside me, but I just smile toxically, unwilling to let him have the last word.

"I think you've forgotten who saw who hanging from a rope," I say coldly, even as I swallow against nausea. Eben blanches and turns, quickly walking back to his own horse. The soldiers walk back to the caravan, and I muffle my smile, facing forward on my horse again.

THE CURSE OF THE BLESSED

We start moving again, and Sutoran gets closer and closer. We take our place in the back of the line of people moving forward to enter the capital, but the line moves far too quickly. I glance over at Aiden again, but he's staring straight ahead, his eyes dark and calculating. We both know what is coming.

Far too soon, it is our turn to be evaluated. We slow to a halt as two of the six soldiers walk up. They stop beside Gladwell's horse and they confer. They're close enough that we can hear their conversation.

"Lieutenant Gladwell, welcome back to Sutoran. Is this the new load of prisoners?" the lead soldier asks, his eyes flicking to the caravan before he turns back to Gladwell, completely overlooking us.

"Yes sir. Eighteen new seers to be rescued." Gladwell's reply sets my teeth on edge. *Rescued.*

The soldier's gaze comes to rest on Aiden and I. He glances at our shackled hands before looking at Aiden's face. His eyes widen and he turns back to Gladwell. I'm puzzled by his reaction; the identity of the royal assassin is kept hidden, isn't it?

"Why are those two shackled sir? That's-"

"I know who it is, Mose. The girl's a seer and he's a bleeding supporter, tried to free her and everything. I sent a messenger ahead and they have an audience with the king. "

"Alright, go on through then sir," The soldier says, taking one last look at Aiden before stepping back and letting us pass. We ride forward, entering the city. I glance back at the soldier, Mose, as I pass, and his eyes meet mine. They're filled with wonder and fear, and he looks away quickly, rubbing the top of his head. Just what do these people think seers are capable of?

My horse's steps are muffled on the dirt roads, the shadow of the gate passing over us as we ride beneath it. The streets are loud and bustling with people going about their daily lives. We're at the very edge of the capital, but already there are buildings on either side of us. There are stands where merchants stand babbling and advertising their products.

Fresh fish, we catch 'em, you buy 'em!

Charm necklaces, wards to protect you from a seer's mind powers!

Daggers and hidden knives; never be defenseless!

I look around at all of the people, not bothering to try and hide. We certainly attract stares. A contingent of soldiers, a caravan of prisoners, and two people shackled on horses. People stare openly at us, some of them pausing mid-step to stare. A little girl tugs on her mother's hand and points at me, speaking loudly.

"Mummy look! Her hair is so red!"

The mother pulls her away quickly, bending down and speaking in a low voice to her. Probably filling her head with more lies about seers. That's when I realize just why we're moving so slowly; Gladwell is putting us on display.

At that moment, something dark flies by my head, close enough for me to feel the air near my cheek move and I lurch, my heart racing. *What was that?*

"Was that-"

"A rock," Aiden growls, searching the crowd. His face is purely murderous and several people step back as his horse nears. A man towards the back of the crowd catches my eye, dressed in ragged clothes and staring at me with complete hatred in his eyes as I pass, never looking away. My heart races and I force myself to breathe slowly, not letting myself dwell on how close I just came to death, all due to one rock.

We slowly pass through streets, and I notice that as we go on, the buildings get nicer and the streets go from dirt to cobblestone with sidewalks. My fear grows steadily as we get closer and closer to the citadel. Finally, we stop at a fork in the road where the road to the right turns back to dirt and there are no buildings. Three soldiers ride up beside us and Eben turns our horses onto the left road. I glance over my shoulder and see all of the other soldiers go right, bringing the caravan with them. Right goes to the facility. Left goes to the citadel.

I glance over my shoulder as we ride, catching sight of the caravan just before it goes around the corner. Then it disappears from sight. I swallow against the lump in my throat, my vision going blurry, and force myself to face forward once more, my eyes burning.

"They'll be okay." Aiden's voice draws my attention, and I turn to face him. He's looking at me, his eyes filled with compassion. I nod, but something makes me stop, something makes me say more.

"Aiden, I need you to make me a promise," I say quietly. He looks uneasy, knowing me well by now, but nods all the same. "If anything happens to me; if I'm sentenced to death…promise me you'll take care of them. Promise me you'll take care of all of them."

"Nothing's going to happen to you, Camari; I won't let it!" he snaps harshly.

"You can't control what happens to me any more than I can. Promise me." I order, my voice wobbling slightly. He still scowls angrily, and he clenches his jaw without replying.

"Please," I whisper, my voice coming out quieter than intended. He hesitates but then gives me a curt nod, sitting stiffly on his saddle.

"Thank you."

He nods again, his expression softening. "I won't let anything happen to you, Camari. I promised, and I don't intend to break another promise to you."

I nod, but look away. He has no way of keeping that promise, and he hasn't had any luck keeping any of his other promises either.

We continue to ride, and the buildings and streets slowly pass, blurring together in my mind. Eben and the soldiers slow their horses to a halt as we enter a large stone courtyard, surrounded by columned hallways and soldiers. I'm pulled roughly off of my horse and thrown to the ground with no warning, my knees and palms scraping painfully on the stone ground. Aiden is treated the same way, and he lands beside me on his elbows and knees with a grunt.

"Take them to see the king, but take your time. There's no rush!" Eben calls, smiling. He turns and rides away, leading our two horses with him. Six guards come over, three for me, three for Aiden. I'm pulled up from the ground, and my wrists are grabbed by one set of hands. One of the soldiers unlocks my shackles, letting them fall onto the stones beneath me with a clatter. I snatch my wrists to my chest immediately, my hands shaking as adrenaline pumps through my veins. This is it. This is my last chance to run and have the slightest chance of getting away. I don't have to look at Aiden to know he's thinking the same. Spinning around, I turn and bolt across the courtyard, my heart pounding so fast I fear it may explode. I make it all of eight steps before someone grabs me by my hair and pulls me roughly back. I scream in frustration and rage as my feet fly out from beneath me and I fall back, landing on the hard stones painfully.

This is it.

I press my hands against the ground, pushing myself onto my feet, my knees shaking as the guards start towards me again.

"Get away from her!" I heard Aiden bellow. He pulls roughly against the soldiers holding him, and I run towards him just as he gets free. His arms wrap around me and hold me against him, shielding me from our harsh reality. I press my face into the crook of his neck as I struggle to hold in my sobs of fear and panic, wrapping my arms around his neck and holding onto him. His face presses against my hair and for a moment, for one perfect moment, it's just him and me. There is no danger, there are no guards, there is only us. Then hands are gripping my arms and pulling me away, the moment shattered. In the final seconds before I am pulled away, I bring my hands up to the back of Aiden's head. His eyes meet mine, and then suddenly, his lips are on mine. Fire shoots through me as his lips press against mine, his fingers digging into my waist. Then, we are separated as the soldiers drag us apart, ending our last moment together.

"No!" I scream, writhing and fighting against them. Aiden fights just as hard, his gaze never leaving mine. One of the soldiers pulling him away plants his fist in Aiden's stomach, and Aiden doubles over with a grunt.

"Leave him alone!" I scream, pulling and kicking my feet. The third soldier dragging me snarls as I kick him in the shin. Letting go of my arm, he swings around and slaps me. My head flies back and I see stars as my vision goes black. My lip splits and bleeds, and my cheek burns.

"Don't touch her!" I hear Aiden bellows.

"Come along willingly, or we will take you to see the king in a coffin. Your choice." The soldier who seems to be in charge speaks sternly, his low voice rumbling like thunder. I stop fighting, licking the blood off of my lip and glaring at him from behind my hair as I pant, probably appearing like a savage animal. I don't want Aiden's death on my hands. Aiden glances at me, sees the blood on my chin, and must come to the same conclusion; his eyes alight with anger. The soldier smiles.

"Good. Let's go see the king."

King Aldred II gifted his name to his eldest and only legitimate son, King Aldred III.

—Zordan Guide to the Aristocracy

Chapter Forty-Four

Camari

While they've stopped beating us and we've stopped trying to run, Aiden and I are still dragged along roughly. The soldier's fingers dig into my flesh, and I scowl at them, tossing my head to get hair out of my face. I hear a muffled curse as Aiden is dragged along behind me, probably causing more problems than is necessary. We're both good at that.

We're led through the entrance of the citadel and into the building. The hallways are made of dark marble with inlaid patterns of different shades of gray. There are black iron candelabras along the way that light the hallway, and while the left wall has occasional windows, the right wall has several sets of mahogany doors. Instead of entering any of the doors we pass, the soldiers keep leading us down the hallway. We turn right, then left, then left again. I have a feeling we've taken so many turns because the soldiers are trying to keep us disoriented, but it isn't working. Besides, Aiden probably knows this place blindfolded.

Finally, we turn to the right and the hallway leads to a set of double doors, already open. We enter the room and I look around, taking in as much as I can. The room is huge, and the first thing I notice is the large wooden chair across the room with iron embellishments. No, not a chair. A throne.

To the left of the throne is a smaller wooden door which I guess the king will enter through. The walls and floors are marble, just like the hallways, though in this room the walls are white and the floors have far more intricate patterns. There are windows on the wall to my right, tall and crisscrossed with iron. Iron candelabras sit between each window and line the opposite wall. There are also candelabras on either side of the throne, and the entire room glows brightly.

The soldiers lead me roughly to the middle of the room before they throw me down onto the floor. My knees and palms hit the ground and I hiss in pain, pushing back onto my knees and shoving my hair out of my face once more.

"There are other ways to let go of a prisoner!" I shout at their retreating backs. Four of them leave the room, closing the doors behind them, while the other two stay with us, stopping us from moving. I glance at Aiden and find him already looking at me, his eyes calm and still. I draw strength from his gaze and straighten my back, my hands ceasing their shaking.

My head turns quickly enough to make my neck hurt as the door beside the throne opens up. A man walks out, followed by two more soldiers. The man is tall, I guess around six foot three inches. He has black hair that is brushed back and curls around the nape of his neck, as well as black stubble on his strong chin. He is wearing nicely tailored clothes with elegant embroidery, and on his head gleams a simple beaten-gold circlet.

King Aldred in all his glory.

He is handsome, and younger than I thought he'd be, appearing to be maybe thirty years of age, but his eyes are cold and such a dark brown that the iris and the pupil appear to be one and the same, and his smile is even colder. This is not a compassionate king.

As if that was ever in question.

He walks confidently to his throne and sits down, resting his arms on the armrests and simply exuding regality. His two guards stand on either side of the throne, out of the way. King Aldred studies both of us in silence for a few minutes. He studies Aiden first, and whatever he sees there, he shows no emotion. Then he looks at me. I meet his gaze and glare with as much hatred as I can muster. His smile widens briefly, and pleasure flickers through his black eyes. He leans back in his chair and presses his fingertips together.

"Now, forgive me, for I don't have all the information here. Aiden Baltasar Lorian I know well, better than most in fact. But you… you, I don't know," he says, his gaze alighting on me and staying there. His voice is deep and thrums with power and confidence, and he speaks slowly, like I'm an amusing puzzle he's looking forward to deciphering. I'm entertainment to him. "What is your name, my dear?"

"I am not you're anything." I spit, my hatred surging. This man who is responsible for thousands of deaths, this man who is responsible for my mother's burned and scarred arm. Aiden is not to blame; this man is.

I will kill this man.

"I didn't ask what you aren't; I asked what you are," the king says with a faint smile. "I'll reiterate; I should have assumed you'd be slightly slower due to your background. What is your name?"

The soldier holding my left arm digs his fingers into my flesh until I'm sure he's drawn blood. "Camari." I force the word out when the pain becomes unbearable. The pain fades and the king's smile widens as he leans forward on his throne.

"Kamri. Kamri what?"

"Kuh-mar-ee. Camari Dorsar," I say slowly, figuring he mispronounced my name on purpose.

"An interesting name. I don't think I've ever heard it before."

"My mother is creative." I give him a hostile smile. His grin widens and he looks at me with a new interest, finding a competent foe.

"Where are you from, Camari?" he asks me, still talking pleasantly as if I'm not his prisoner, as if I'm not on my knees before him while Aiden stands awkwardly to my right. I ignore his question and keep my mouth shut. If I tell him, he'll know where to find Adeline. I'd never do that.

He holds my gaze for several more seconds before waving his hand dismissively, leaning back in his seat as if bored. "Oh well, we can talk more in a minute. For now, I want to speak with my royal assassin."

Aiden is brought forward and kicked down onto his knees beside me, five feet of space separating us. He doesn't look at the king with the same hatred I do, but rather with something else that I can't decipher. A sort of… sorrow.

"Aiden, my how you've changed in the four moons you've been gone. Where to start!" the king says with fake enthusiasm, smiling at Aiden. There's an undertone in his voice that gives me chills. "You return a prisoner, accused of being a seer supporter? What happened; did you fall in with the wrong crowd?"

Aiden meets his gaze, his face like a stone. That something in his gaze I can't decipher; it's accompanied by forced courage. Does Aiden fear the king?

"I grew a backbone; I acknowledged the truth."

"Let me guess, it was this young woman who showed it to you?" King Aldred's words are sarcastic, waving his hand in the air, but Aiden shakes his head.

"I've known all along. She just made me face it."

"My, you have changed. The Aiden I watched grow up had sworn off love of all sorts. Do you love this woman, this seer filth?"

Aiden's eyes burn with anger at the slur, but he's saved from having to answer as the king continues. "Is it true you attacked my soldiers, your brethren, in an attempt to free her?"

"Yes."

King Aldred frowns mockingly. "And you don't regret it? You don't plan to repent and ask for forgiveness? Because now would be the time."

"No," Aiden says darkly, once again using a monosyllabic answer. Something in the king's expression changes, something I don't like, and he looks back and forth between us, his eyes lighting up.

"Gods above, the seer returns your feelings! Oh, I love this. Obviously, she doesn't know who you are, otherwise she'd despise you."

"I know who he is!" I snap, speaking for the first time in minutes. "And I don't care. What he did in the past doesn't define him; it's what he decides to do now that does."

The king's eyes glint and he smiles widely, victoriously. "Oh, what a heartfelt speech. So touching, so inspirational! *So* misguided."

He turns his grin on Aiden and I turn as well, my throat tightening in anxiety as the wrongness of the situation hits me. Aiden appears regretful and guilt flashes in his eyes as he looks at me. The unease in my stomach grows and I swallow. *What don't I know?*

The king smiles, tilting his head to the side. "Why didn't you tell the woman you love who you are? *Brother.*"

A buzzing noise fills my ears and I feel numb. The word repeats in my ears, echoing. *Brother. Brother. Brother.*

A thousand pieces melt together to form a whole picture. The secrets he kept, his refusal to talk about his past in detail, his competitive family, the rumors about the king knowing the royal assassin closely, the soldier's shock at the Sutoran wall. He didn't recognize the royal assassin, he recognized the king's bastard son.

Brother.

I blink, swaying slightly, and everything comes together into a picture that is bright and clear. And terribly, terribly painful.

Aiden looks at me with guilt and sorrow on his face, completely ignoring the king. "Camari, I am so sorry. I wanted to tell you, but-"

"Oh. this is wonderful!" King Aldred interrupts with a grin. "She had no idea. Well, Camari, my brother might not be willing to share the intimate parts of his life with you, But I am more than happy to do so on his behalf, so allow me to fill you in. My father, the dearly departed king, was fond of women. You can imagine a bastard child or two would be inevitable. Aiden here is my half-brother, and so is Morris."

I stare at the king, keeping my face blank. Show no emotion, feel no emotion. That is the mantra I repeat to myself to block myself off. It isn't working this time. Rage fills my body, and I see red. Lies. Everything was just the result of lies. Every time I trust Aiden, he reveals more lies and betrayals.

"Camari, please, look at me. Camari, I am so sorry."

I can hear Aiden's voice, but I don't turn to look at him. I keep looking at the king. He is smiling as he returns my stare, seeing right past my mask and peering into my soul where all of those broken parts are fractured even more. And then he smiles, and I know he isn't done yet.

"Now, forgive me if I'm wrong, but I do know of an Adeline Dorsar who lives in Krakent."

The blood drains from my face.

"One of my associates knows her very well; he's actually one of my council members. He said he visited your mother a few years ago."

I blink, turning his words over in my mind. We were never visited by a council member; what is he talking about?

"He said he didn't get the best greeting. Your mother kicked him out of the house, and when he tried to connect with you, his only daughter, you stabbed him and left him for dead."

I hear Aiden's sharp intake of breath, but I can't breathe. I can't move.

No. Please gods, no. Merciful gods above, let this be another lie.

"His name is Duke Ralph Bidennore."

No, no, no, no, no. I can hear my breathing as it speeds up and can feel my heart race. This isn't possible. I killed him.

"He's actually here today and is eager to see you again. I was so excited to be able to make this family reunion take place. Let me bring him in," the king says smoothly, my reaction giving him nothing but pleasure.

I can do nothing but kneel there numbly as one of the king's guards turns and walks to the side door, pulling it open. And into the room walks my father.

The man I stabbed and left for dead in the woods four years ago. The man that raped my mother and stalked her across the continent.

Duke Bidennore walks into the room, his eyes connecting with mine and sending fear through me. He walks with confidence, and his hair is still the faint ginger shade, though there is now some gray at his temples. He stops in front of the throne, bows to King Aldred, and then turns to face me. A slow, pleased smile spreads across his face, and panic pulses through me. No, merciful gods, no! He is supposed to be dead!

"Well, daughter, it would seem we meet again."

I recognized the tenor of his voice, and the way he phrases his vowels. Terror shoots through me, and I begin to hyperventilate, making panicked, animalistic squeaks.

"Though, I'm in much better health than I was last time we met. I'm fully healed, as I'm sure you're relieved to find out, and I'm happy to see you again," he says, each of his words having a bite to them. *Remember what you did. I will make you remember. I will make you pay.*

"Stay away from me." I breathe, my voice shaking and filled with terror. He smiles and begins to walk closer to me. I pull against the soldier holding me in place, desperate to get away, but his grip is like iron, and I can do nothing but kick and scrabble around on the floor uselessly, watching the duke approach. He comes closer and closer before he stops directly in front of me and crouches down.

"Oh daughter," he murmurs in a low voice that only I can hear, a voice that makes me freeze like a deer. "how I've dreamt of seeing you again. I paid your mother a visit recently, and you weren't there."

I tremble in place as he whispers in my ear, unable to move as terror riddles me defenseless. All I can smell is his lavender soap.

"I can't wait for the fun we'll have when I visit you in the facility. Visitors are allowed once every three weeks, you know. I look forward to our meetings."

"What are you saying? Get away from her!" Aiden shouts, anger coating his voice. The Duke pulls back and turns to him, but all I can do is stare numbly at the floor as they speak. He is alive. He is alive.

"And you, the man that took my daughter from her home and broke her heart. We have many things to discuss."

Aiden snarls at him, but King Aldred raises his hand, cutting their conversation off. I snap out of my reverie and pay attention, my body vibrating with fear and adrenaline. The Duke's time is up, and as my father returns to stand beside his chair, the king looks down at both of us, choosing to speak to me first.

"Obviously, my dear, as your charges of murder have been proven false, you won't stand trial. Instead, you will be sent to the facility where you will be trained to use your powers for the good of the kingdom." The king turns to Aiden, still smiling pleasantly. "Aiden, as my brother, I am prepared to give you a second chance. You will be pardoned and your title of royal assassin will be returned. If you do something for me first."

My stomach squirms at the tone the king's voice has taken on, and, glancing at Aiden, I can see he hears the danger too.

King Aldred raises his right hand and one of his soldiers steps forward and drops a long leather whip on the floor two feet in front of Aiden.

"If you will prove your loyalty to the crown, you can be pardoned. Take this whip and give the seer five lashes. That's all you must do."

My stomach fills with cold fear and anger. To be whipped is to be treated as an animal, and it is painful. Adeline and I treated a slave that escaped their master after they'd been whipped countless times. I'll never forget his screams of pain as we cleaned his wounds or how deep the lacerations went.

Aiden looks at the whip, looks at me, and then turns back at the king. "Never," he says softly, appearing sick to his stomach at the very idea. The king loses his smile and his act fades. His face relaxes into a cold glare, and I realize that this is the real Aldred.

"Well then, know that what happens next is your fault and no one else's. Your Grace?"

"It will be my pleasure," the duke says with a smile. He steps forward and picks up the whip, looking at Aiden with a cruel glint in his eyes.

"Don't. Leave him alone," I say weakly. He may have betrayed me, but that doesn't mean I want him whipped. No one deserves that kind of punishment.

King Aldred smiles at me and a chill sweeps down my spine. "Oh no, my dear, the whip isn't for him."

And then the duke is walking towards me, his right hand clutching the whip tightly. I panic and pull against the soldier who holds me again, but I am weakened by fear and escaping is impossible.

"Stay away from her, you son of a bitch!" Aiden snarls, pulling against the man who holds him so strongly that another soldier comes forward to help keep him down.

Duke Bidennore smiles down at me as I quiver on the floor before he steps slowly around me until he is at my back. I hear the sound of ripping as my bodice is cut off of me from behind and the fabric falls into my lap, leaving me in just my shift. I tremble and shake at the sound, at the cold air hitting me.

"Five lashes, as ordered by Your Majesty," the duke says to the king, who smiles and tilts his head graciously.

The first hit is like lightning. A stream of fire down my back that burns beyond belief as the whip's bite sears through my shift. I bite back a cry; the only thing keeping me up is the guard holding me. The second strike is worse than the first and I feel warm blood begin to leak into my shift from where the whip made contact with the bare skin of my shoulder

"I'll take the whip; stay away from her! Leave her alone!" Aiden is screaming at the king. I can hear him still fighting to get away. The duke stills behind me, and though I can't get myself to look up, I hear the king's voice, cold and amused.

"Oh, Aiden, it will be much worse for you to have to watch the woman you love in pain. Whipping you would get me nowhere. This is *your* punishment."

The third strike hits directly over the first and the pain multiplies beyond belief. I whimper, a sob catching in my throat. My heart races so fast I half expect it to burst.

"Stop it! Hurt me, kill me, just leave her alone!" Aiden is still screaming and fighting, but all I can focus on is the pain and the duke.

The fourth strike tears open both my shift and part of my back. I sob loudly, the pain unbearable, and the drumming in my ears increases as I begin to see spots. I barely acknowledge the duke's pause, and he bends down and speaks in my left ear.

"See how it feels to be left for dead!" he hisses. He is close enough that I can only smell the lavender on his clothes and I retch. He straightens up again, and I brace myself for what is coming.

"I'll kill you! I'll kill you, you bastard!" Aiden roars at the duke, his voice filled with rage and desperation. "Don't fucking touch her!"

The duke simply whips me for the fifth and final time.

The whip hits my back and splits my skin, sending fire into my very blood. My guard lets go of my arm and I tumble to the floor in a pile, shaking and bleeding. I can hear my ragged breaths in my ears, but I make no effort to slow them down. I make no effort to do anything. Death would be a mercy.

I hear the king speak to Aiden again, his voice is now as cold as ice. "You are a traitor to the throne of

Zorda and will be persecuted as such. You betray the ideals of this kingdom for the seers, choosing them over your king. So, you will be sentenced to the same sentence a seer would receive."

I manage to bring myself to look up at the king as he speaks Aiden's sentence. I can see the similarities now, the facial structures, the strong foreheads. "You will live out your days in the facility, receiving the same treatment as your inmates. You will not be protected, and if I recall correctly, you have many enemies in that facility. Good luck, brother."

Aiden doesn't blink, but I know what that means.

The seers will tear him apart.

King Aldred turns back to me, his mask back in place seamlessly. "I look forward to hearing more about you from your father, Camari; he said he plans to visit you often. Enjoy the facility."

The soldier beside me drags me to my feet, and I whimper in pain, my back still screaming at me. We turn, and he drags me towards the door, practically carrying me, and the last glimpse of the throne room I get is of my father, the Duke, smiling at me as I am led away to my sentence.

*The betrayal I feel is nothing short of heart-breaking.
As a courier, it is my sole purpose to communicate
with the gods. They are my life, the very thing I live
for. And they have cut me off completely.*

—The Religious Texts: The book of Bryson

Chapter Forty-Five

Aiden

Everything happened so fast. Aldred telling Camari who I am; the blank look on her face as she tried to hide her emotions; the duke coming out; Camari's terror; the whipping. When we were in the throne room it felt like years, but at the same time, mere seconds.

Her screams still echo in my ears. All I can think about is how much I want to kill the duke. She told me he was important, a member of the king's court, but she never told me his name. But I know him. I've known him my entire life. And now I will kill him.

The soldiers drag us towards the door, Camari barely stumbling along, and I am being dragged after her when Aldred calls out, "Wait."

The soldiers are holding me slowly, turning and bringing me back to where I previously was. I stare up at Aldred, my half-brother, without attempting to mask my hatred. A glint of red catches my eyes and I glance over at it. Droplets of blood gleam on the white marble floors.

Camari's blood.

More seer blood on your hands, and not just any seer's. Her's.

"Well, brother, I hope you're happy with the fate you've chosen for yourself," Aldred says, leaning back on his throne and smiling. I recognize all of his faces, and this is the mask he wears for every audience. No one knows what he is truly like.

"You will pay for everything you've done," I say quietly. Aldred raises his brow at me, his eyes gleaming.

"Threats. Wow, she really has done a number on you. What is it about her? Her hair? Her anger? An ungodly fetish for her hideous birthmarks? What is it that draws you to her?" He seems to be honestly curious. I remain silent, meeting his gaze and holding it. It is none of those things, but he doesn't need to know that. After everything he's done, he has lost any right to know anything about me, just as I have lost any right to know anything about Camari.

No. I'll fix it. I'll explain everything. I won't lose her again.

"Are you truly willing to sacrifice everything for her?"

"Careful, Aldred, you're beginning to sound desperate." I smile coldly. He knows the answer to his own question; a minute ago, I was begging him to kill me if only he'd leave her alone. But he hurt her anyway.

I won't forget.

Aldred scowls at me, dropping his mask. "This is your last chance. Repent, Aiden. Don't disappoint our father even further. Don't do this to Morris"

"Disappointing our father was and always will be a proud birthright of mine. I will not repent to you, never."

Aldred's eyes flash with anger and he waves his hand at the guards on either side of me. They begin to pull me away again, but I hear Aldred call something as I walk away.

"I hope you live to regret this, brother. She hates you now. You gave up everything for nothing."

I don't look back as I am dragged away, but I do get a sinking feeling in my gut. For once, my brother might be telling the truth.

The facility is a creation of King Aldred I in the year 589. It had become evident that despite the laws, seers refused to leave Zorda and were breeding and spreading like a plague. And so, King Aldred I created a hospital just for them.

–Zorda: Aristocracy, Geography, and History

Chapter Forty-Six

Camari

My back burns as I am dragged away from the throne room, my feet stumbling as I try to keep up with the soldiers. If either of them are horrified by the king's treatment, they don't show it.

I heard the king call for Aiden to stay back and wonder what they need from him.

Probably some long chat between brothers.

The smell of lavender is still stuck in my throat, in my nose. Every time I inhale, I smell it again. It's horrible.

We exit the citadel and enter the large stone courtyard once more. The sky is overcast and gray, perfectly suiting the events of the day. As I am led through the courtyard towards the two small caravans that sit in wait, I stare at a spot in the center. Just there, not thirty minutes ago, I kissed Aiden. Oh, how everything went so wrong after that, I'll never understand.

The soldiers throw me into one of the caravans roughly, slamming the door shut behind me. I manage not to cry out as my back pulses agonizingly but whimper slightly as I feel more blood soak into my shift. Pushing myself up, I crawl to the door and grab onto the bars, calling out after the retreating soldiers.

"Wait! What about Aiden?"

One of them turns and smirks at me over his shoulder. "Don't worry, your lover will follow after you in another caravan. He's having a private audience with the king."

The caravan jolts as it starts, and I stare at the citadel as it slowly fades into the distance. Once it is out of sight, I retreat to the back of my caravan and sit in the corner, pulling my knees up to my chest.

He is alive. How is he alive? I stabbed him in the gut; I twisted the blade. His insides would have been shredded; he would have had toxins and poisons in his bloodstream. I felt his blood on my hands, warm and sticky. So how is he still alive?

The questions swirl endlessly in my head. I lay my cheek down on my knees, not bothering to try and stop the tears that make their way down my face. Every time I think I have things figured out, my entire life is flipped again.

I can't wait to visit you.

I shudder violently, my breaths turning ragged. Everything has gone horribly wrong.

The sound of the caravan door opening wakes me with a start. I lift my head from my knees and open my eyes blearily, blinking away the sleep that fogs my vision. Two soldiers climb into the caravan and approach me, each grabbing an arm and pulling me up roughly. I whimper as the partial scabs that formed on my back rip open again. They drag me roughly out of the caravan, and I squint against the brightness of the sun, my eyes taking time to adjust.

We stand outside a huge stone building surrounded by guards and soldiers. There is a large wall behind us that obviously surrounds the building and surrounding area, and soldiers stand on the top of the wall as well. I grow cold as I see all of the soldiers in their black uniforms roaming everywhere in groups of two at the minimum. This place is more protected than the citadel. No one can get in. Or out.

The soldiers lead me toward the building, nodding at certain guards as we pass them. The sound of metal armor echoes through the air and the sun makes the shadows of the guards look like giants, looming over my hunched and broken form. I try not to tremble as I am led closer and closer to the facility. We step through the doors and the sun disappears behind me as the doors slam shut.

We stand in a stone hallway, dark and ominous. There are no windows and the hallway is lit purely by weak candles. There are doors and hallways that branch off, the hallways just as dark and the doors appearing decrepit and heavy. The guards drag me towards the doors at the end of the hallway, old wooden doors with water stains and rust on the iron handles. The soldiers at the doors push them open as we near, and I am led through. We enter a large stone room with no windows. In the middle of the room is a row of plain cots with wool blankets, a large wooden table with all sorts of things on top, and three women. I resist slightly as I am led toward them, and when I see the leather straps on the edge of the cots, I pull and fight as much as I can, but that does nothing but cause me more pain. I am shoved forcefully down onto the cot, and the leather straps are tightened around my wrists and ankles, preventing me from kicking and punching anymore. I continue to fight, pulling on my arms and legs, bucking my torso. One of the women approaches me with a metal syringe, a device I have heard of and read of but never used, and I struggle harder.

"No! Get away from me!" I shout, trying as hard as I can to resist. The metal tip of the needle sinks into my arm, just where the veins are visible, and I feel them inject me with something bitterly cold. The world begins to go hazy. I can hear the soldiers and the women talking, but their voices are deeper than is natural and they blend together. The candle's flames burn far brighter than they did before, and then suddenly, the lights go out and are replaced with darkness.

I can hear voices talking faintly, low and femi-nine.

-Strange.

There are far more than usual. Garish, ugly things. I'll never get used to them.

Apparently, she and Aiden Lorian are in some sort of relationship. But I heard he whipped her, so he must have been pardoned.

Did she know who he is?

She couldn't have. The question is, what was he doing with a peasant seer? A peasant is one thing, for the gods know his father never cared about class, only anatomy. But a seer? A rat?

She's not a peasant though; her father is a duke, the one close to the king.

That makes her aristocracy!

She's still a seer.

I open my eyes, blinking the haziness out of them. The room slowly comes into focus and I turn my head from side to side, trying to get my brain to focus. I am in the same room I was in before, and I can see the women's backs on the other side of the room, holding some sort of gray fabric and sewing it together. What is that?

I remember the leather ties with a start and im-mediately tug on my arms and legs at the same time, finding them free. I shoot up from the cot, jumping to my feet only to fall back against the cot, my head spinning. I hold it in my hands, shutting my eyes against the swaying lights and forcing my breathing to still. The women's voices cut off abruptly and I hear footsteps clicking on the stone floors as they approach me.

"If you resist or endanger us, we will call the soldiers waiting outside and have you forcefully restrained," one of the women says coldly. I look up from my hands, my head no longer spinning. The woman who spoke has brown hair braided down her back and wears a simple silver dress. The two women behind her have their hair done in similar styles, though one is blonde and one has hair the color of iron. They all look at me coldly, lacking any compassion. And why should they feel compassion towards me? I am just a seer.

The first woman holds out the gray lump of fabric and drops it on my lap. Upon closer inspection, I find that it is clothing. A men's shirt and a pair of trousers dyed the same stone color. I realize with a start I am wearing nothing but my breastband and my undershorts. My other clothes, the ones Jude gave me, are nowhere to be seen. I ignore the pang in my heart at the loss of Jude's clothes and dress quickly in the gray uniform. It is scratchy and slightly too small. The pants hang an inch or two above my ankles, and the shirt hugs my thin frame too tightly across my chest and shoulders, showing just how bony I am. As I am dressing, I realize that someone has treated my back. The fierce ache remains, but I feel no blood as I move, and the initial burn isn't there. That is a small mercy and one I am happy to accept.

Finished dressing, I shove my tangled hair out of my face and face the women in silence. The first woman eyeballs my waist-length hair before gesturing to the iron-haired woman behind her, who steps forward and walks behind me. I stay still as I feel her roughly yank out the tangles with a comb, sometimes bringing water to my eyes. I feel her gather it together in her hands and expect her to tie it back, but instead, I feel a slight prickling and hear a slicing noise. She releases my hair, and I gasp as I see hair all over the floor, partially covering my bare feet. I lift my hands to my hair and find it now barely reached past my shoulders, some of the strands curving around my face. The loss of my hair, absurdly, is the final straw that brings tears to my eyes, and two escape, leaving watery trails down my face. That was the last thing I had left from my previous life, from before. And now it's gone as well.

The first woman ignores my tears and walks over to the door on the far side of the room, banging on it three times. The door opens with a groan and the soldiers from before walk in. I shove away the urge to run; it will serve no purpose. I have no weapons, no plans, nowhere to go. I have nothing.

They grab me by my arms and I am led roughly from the room, the women still not saying another word to me as I leave them. Exiting the room, I stumble as I fight to keep up with the soldier's brisk pace, still slightly drowsy from the effects of whatever they injected me with. We take many turns and many hallways and I struggle to keep track of them. Right, left, right, right left, left, left. Then, up a flight of stone stairs. We come out onto a long wide hallway that doesn't seem so much like a hallway as it does a wing. Both sides are lined with prison cells. Each cell looks to be about ten feet by ten feet, and each cell on the left side has a small barred window that provides light. I am led roughly past cell after cell, and seers come and peer out at me as I pass, some no more than eight or nine years old. Finally, we stop at a cell and one of my guards opens the door, throwing me roughly inside. I fall to my knees, my newly cut hair falling all about my face in a curtain. I shove it away and stand quickly, spinning to watch the guards as they lock me in and leave. One of the soldiers pauses and speaks to me coldly.

"Don't worry, your cellmate will be here soon," he says darkly. Then he walks off, leaving me in the darkening cell, wondering just who my cellmate will be.

I know what is coming tomorrow. I have a hearing with Aldred and have been summoned to court. He will offer me the job as the next Royal Assassin. I will never have to prove myself to anybody ever again.

—Journal of Aiden Lorian

Chapter Forty-Seven

Camari

I only meant to lie down on the cot and rest while I waited for my cellmate to arrive, but whatever they injected me with was obviously still in my system because before I knew it, I was half asleep. I was awake enough to take off my shirt, the scratchiest thing in the kingdom, and I climbed under the blanket, falling asleep almost immediately with it pulled up to my nose. At one point, I stirred, thinking I heard something, but I wasn't able to stay awake. Now, I wake to the sound of whispers and voices. I squint my eyes open, inhaling deeply, but see only gray. I remember the blanket over my face and shove it away, stretching my arms above my head to work out the knot in my back. My back twinges and burns with the movement, drawing a gasp out of me, and I remember my new injuries.

THE CURSE OF THE BLESSED

I sit up slowly, shoving my hair out of my face. The short strands fall right back around my face and I remember with a pang of sorrow my clipped hair. I rub my eyes with the heels of my palms, rubbing away sleep dust and grit. The whispers are still there, and it seems like they've gotten louder. I frown, shoving my hair away again, and look around.

Every seer in the vicinity is pressed against the bars of their cells. They are all buddied two to a cell, some partners of the same sex, others a male and female, and all of them are whispering and staring at me.

I look around hesitantly, and sure enough, even the seers in the same row as me are peering in at me. I can't see any seers in the cell to my right due to the stonewall, but the ones in the cell to my left both sit on the floor, leaning against the wall behind them as they stare at me. They're a boy and a girl. The girl looks to be younger than me, with blonde curls, eyes that shine like emeralds, and a patch of scalsen on her neck. The boy is maybe a year or two older than me, with short brown hair and dark red scalsen on his left hand that wraps around his fingers and ends at his wrist.

"Why are you staring at me? Why are all of them staring?" I ask with a scowl, refusing to allow myself to shrink underneath their gazes. The younger girl's eyes widens, and she shrinks slightly, but the boy holds my gaze, narrowing his blue eyes at me.

"Since when are we not allowed to stare?" he asks in a challenging tone, his voice coming out deeper than I expected.

"It's an incredibly unpleasant way to wake up." I snap, ignoring his challenge. I tilt my head both ways and pop my neck before I swing my legs around the edge of the cot so that my bare feet touch the stone floor. The boy's lips tug up at the corner, and he tilts his head slightly to the side, studying me even more than before. I remember with a start that I'm wearing just my breast band, though it covers at least half of my torso. Refusing to be embarrassed, I lift my chin and meet his gaze.

"What are your names?" I ask, scooting back on my cot and folding my legs up in front of me.

"This is Tina; I'm Tristan," the boy–Tristan– says. Tina smiles shyly at me and waves. I return the smile but stop smiling as soon as I meet Tristan's eyes again.

"Okay then. Why is everyone staring at me, Tristan?" I ask, glancing again at all of the other cells.

"Don't you think that information's worth something? Maybe a name?" he asks, raising his eyebrows. I huff out a breath, tucking my shorn hair behind my ears.

"Camari."

"That's pretty," Tina says, her voice coming out higher and quieter than anticipated.

"Thank you," I say softly. The only other person that has ever said that to me is Aiden.

"Well then, Camari," Tristan says with a smile, "your cellmate was delivered last night. They aren't staring at you; they're staring at him." He gestures with his chin and I turn to look. On the second cot, almost completely hidden in shadows and his blanket, someone sleeps. I stand up from my cot, letting my blanket fall to the floor, and walk over to see who it is. Unable to see their face because of their blanket, I kick them in the leg to wake them up. A collective gasp from the seers watching rings out, almost comedic in its intensity. I kick his leg again; I refuse to be scared of my cellmate, whoever it is. I'm done being afraid, at least for the day. Even Tristan inhales sharply and he watches with wide eyes as the person stirs, rubbing their eyes. They sit up slowly, their blanket falling down, and I scowl, turning back to Tristan and Tina.

"This is who you're all afraid of?" I scoff, placing my hands on my hips. "Seriously?"

"Do you know who that is?" Tristan asks urgently, his eyes wide.

"Yes, I know who it is; he did kidnap me and drag me across the Spás Folamh."

Tristan raises his eyebrows, and realization flashes in his eyes. "You're her."

"I'm who?"

"You're the duke's daughter that turned out to be a seer."

I flinch, taking a half step back from the bars. "How do you know about that? Who told you?"

Tristan seems surprised by my reaction, raising his hands slightly. Before he can say anything, a voice breaks the heavy silence.

"What happened to your hair?"

Tristan and Tina's heads snap to the left, and I roll my eyes at them before I turn to face Aiden, who has pushed up into a sitting position and is studying me with a frown, obviously still waking up. "It's all gone."

"Great observation; you should be a spy in the army. Oh, wait, you were!" I snap. Aiden still frowns, concerned about me despite the fact that he is in a prison full of seers. It both flatters me and makes me angry. He has no right to care.

"Did you *kick* me?" he asks, rubbing his face with his palm.

"Twice. But I know three is your favorite number. Three lies, Three betrayals, Three sons. I'd be happy to kick you again?" I offer sarcastically.

Aiden's eyes flick over to where Tristan and Tina are watching us, his shoulders caving in slightly at my words. Tina appears to be scared, and while Tristan seems angry, he also looks slightly frightened.

"Who are your friends?" Aiden asks, running his hand through his hair. I notice that it is shorn as well, a stark difference from what it was when I last saw him, where it was hanging at the nape of his neck. Everyone must get their hair cut when they get here for easier management. Just another way this is a prison, not an estate.

"I think neighbors is a more accurate term."

"Do I get to know them?"

"How well do you ever really know someone? I mean, you think you know someone, and then yet another rug is pulled out from underneath your feet. It never ends," I say, narrowing my eyes at him. Aiden looks away, guilt flashing in his eyes.

"Camari, look, I need to explain-"

"Don't. It doesn't matter." I snap, shifting my weight from leg to leg. "You're a liar and can't be trusted. I know that now, and I won't make that mistake again. But I won't abandon you to all of the seers that want you dead either if that's what's worrying you."

Aiden's face shows surprise, gratitude, and something else that I do not welcome, that I do not *want* to welcome.

"But know that I do not trust you," I say coldly. "You ruined that. Many times."

Aiden opens and closes his mouth, his face so torn it almost makes me feel guilty. Almost.

"Soooo…what's up with you two?" Tristan breaks the silence, raising his eyebrows at me.

"Nothing, just a disagreement," I say shortly.

"No, I mean why are you on such good terms with the royal assassin?" Tristan asks coldly. I sigh, already weary. I just made it clear that I barely tolerate Aiden; how are those good terms?

"Not everybody is as they seem." I sag onto my cot, shoving my hair back. It falls right back into my face and I scowl darkly at it, picking up one of the short strands and shoving it back forcefully. "And I hate my hair!"

Tristan and Tina jump at my outburst and I rest my head in my hands, fighting against tears with a few deep, controlled breaths. Everything has gone so wrong. I don't have even a semblance of control over anything going on, and the one person I thought I could rely on has more than proved I shouldn't. And now I am in the facility. We were supposed to escape before we ever reached Sutoran, we were never supposed to be here. If I hadn't been separated from the others after Bareilles...

"I like it," Aiden says softly, sitting down on the floor across from me. I scoff, annoyed once again at how his words make me feel. My heart is an idiot, and I can't afford to listen to it anymore. Look where that's gotten me.

Aiden's eyes trail down to my torso, where the majority of my stomach is visible, and he flushes brightly, looking away awkwardly. I blush as well and quickly reach for my shirt, pulling it over my head awkwardly and trying to adjust it so that it isn't quite like a straight jacket. It isn't much better than the breast band as it is so tight that it leaves nothing to the imagination, including how bony and flat I am.

"What time do we get let out of our cells?" I ask, changing the subject.

"Any minute now," Tristan says, still glaring at Aiden. I rest my head in my hands again and heave a sigh. This is going to be a fun day.

"Why do they allow men and women to be placed in the same cells? That seems rather counterintuitive, seeing as they want less seers, not more," I say, pulling my excuse for a pillow onto my lap and hugging it against my chest.

Tristan raises an eyebrow at my bluntness, the corner of his mouth curving up in what could barely be called a smile. "Because often enough, the men kill the women in their cells and it's one less seer to have to deal with."

THE CURSE OF THE BLESSED

My heart stops for a moment, and I force myself to take a deep breath. "Are there repercussions for such actions?"

Tristan scoffs, absentmindedly rubbing his scalsen. "Let me help you out, Camari. The soldiers in here? They aren't here for your protection; they're here to keep you in line. If you do not show up to your cell, they don't care. If you wander all over the facility, they don't give a shit because you can't escape. There is no way out. That is why they are here, to ensure that you stay inside or you leave in a sack. They don't care about anything else."

I squeeze my pillow tighter, swallowing as my throat constricts with fear. "But aren't most of the seers in here children?"

"The facility has been around for almost 300 years. There are people here that have grown up here. Most of them kill themselves or are killed by others before they get too old, but not all of them do. And there are a good amount of seers that are brought here when they're borderline adults, you for example. But, a fair warning. If they don't kill you, don't be surprised if a child does. There is no such thing as innocence here; I've seen a twelve year old child kill a seer four years their senior."

I swallow, imagining John or Matthew with bloodlust in their eyes, and my stomach heaves. Aiden is so deep in his thoughts that he doesn't even hear us.

The rattling of keys alerts us of the guard's approach and I look up with a start. Six guards walk up the stairs, two of them with key chains. They begin to make their way down the rows of cells, unlocking them and letting the seers out. The seers walk out of their cells and continue on past me, down the row of cells until they reach the other staircase and disappear down it. I stand up and begin to pace, waiting impatiently to be let out. I need to try and find the children from the caravan, to make sure they are okay.

Make sure they aren't dead.

"They're on their way; relax," Tristan mutters, pushing himself up from the wall and standing. He is taller than I thought he was, taller than myself, and his shirt pulls tightly across his shoulders; the cuffs of his pants not quite long enough. Something about him looks familiar, I just can't place it.

"I am waiting; I'm just waiting impatiently." I counter though I stop pacing. The corners of Tristan's mouth twitch upwards as he shakes his head.

"You don't do anything halfway, do you?"

"You have no idea," Aiden mutters under his breath, standing up and tugging on the collar of his shirt, which is obviously too tight, squeezing his broad shoulders. I raise my eyebrows at him, even as I mentally berate myself for the direction my thoughts have run.

"What's that supposed to mean?"

"Nothing, I was just agreeing with him," Aiden says, nodding in Tristan's direction. Tristan just scowls, obviously disturbed that Aiden agreed with him.

"I hope you're well-rested, assassin." He spits at Aiden. "I doubt you'll be alive come nightfall."

With that last remark, the guards let Tristan and Tina out, opening the cell door and gesturing wordlessly for them to exit. Tina glances back at me as she walks away but is soon blocked from view as the guard opens our cell door next. Aiden's face is unreadable, but from the way he flexes his fingers, folding and unfolding them, I know that he is preparing for anything. I doubt there will ever be enough preparation.

Our cell door opens and I walk quickly down the hallway, catching up with the end of the line of seers going down the staircase. Aiden falls in behind me, but I don't acknowledge his presence, too busy scanning the seers in front of me. Their ages and sizes differ from older than me to a few toddlers, but I see no one that I know. I heave a sigh, falling back down onto my heels and moving along slowly as the line moves. I figure that there are many more cell blocks, ours is too small to be the only one, and the others must be in different ones. Will we all be in the same room at any time? Or will I never see them again?

We finally exit the staircase and I follow the seers as they walk, relieved I didn't slip on the moist, mossy stone stairs and fall to my death. Not that the regular floors are any better, or even the walls for that matter. Grime and moisture coat everything, rust dusting all visible iron, stains patterning all of the doors, green sprouting in the cracks between stones. This place is rotting from the inside out.

Soldiers are everywhere, watching us and every move we make. I make eye contact with one, and he rests his hand on his sword, his black leather armor creaking with the movement. I immediately look away

There are several staircases off to the sides of the hallways, and more seers walk down from those, proving my theory of there being more cellblocks. The groups merge together as we walk until finally we reach the end of the hallway, where there is a huge set of open double doors. Past the doors is a large room, at least five times the size of the room I was tranquilized in. There are barred windows on the north and left walls, and there are four long tables on one side of the room, each table seating maybe one hundred people. Guards line the walls of the room, watching us just as vigilantly as they had before, all in leather armor. I assume only the guards that patrol outside wear metal suits. They don't think us enough of a threat to warrant them inside.

The seers split up once inside the room, going for the people they know or sitting down at the table to wait for food. No one speaks above a whisper, and the stress level in the air is tangible. One wrong word, move, breath, and you will regret it.

I rise back onto my tiptoes, scanning the room desperately for anyone I know. Molly, Alex, Addie, Edmund, John, or any of the children. Suddenly my eyes catch on a familiar mop of brown hair, and my breath catches in relief. I turn and find Aiden standing beside me, also surveying the room.

"Aiden, I found Alex!" I say, my voice filled with relief. Aiden's eyes flash to me but I've already turned and am hurrying across the room, dodging seers. Alex turns at the last second and sees me approaching. His eyes flood with relief, and he runs towards me as well. I throw my arms around him, hugging him close, and he wraps his arms around my waist and buries his face in my shoulder, still walking that line between being a man and also sometimes being a child.

"I was so worried about you!" I exclaim, drawing back slightly and making sure he's okay. He smiles, his bright blue eyes slightly damp.

"I-we…we weren't sure if you would…" he leaves his sentence unfinished, but I get the gist.

"We're okay; we both got life sentences like you lot." Aiden cuts in behind me, grinning at Alex in what I can only guess is a brotherly way. Alex's eyes flash with relief again and he and Aiden clasp hands, doing some sort of one-armed man hug that I find idiotic.

"Alex, where are the others?" I ask desperately.

"They're all here, don't worry. They're just not all in the same group. Look, there's Addie with Molly right now. Oh, and there's Edmund, and there's-"

He cuts off as Addie barrels into me, tears streaming down her face. "I didn't think you were still alive!" she cries. I wrap my arms around her and hug her close, rubbing her back.

"I'm okay, everything's okay," I reassure her, stroking back her curly hair. She pulls away, wiping her face and smiling at me. As soon as she retreats to stand beside Alex, I turn to Molly, who is beaming up at me.

"I knew you'd be okay. You promised you'd come, and I knew you wouldn't lie," she says innocently. I swallow a lump in my throat, my eyes burning as I realize how close I'd come to breaking my promise. I quickly pull her into a hug, stroking her white hair.

"That's right; I don't break my promises," I whisper thickly. I hear Aiden shift behind me as he and Alex confer quietly, but for once I hadn't meant my words as a blow at him.

Molly steps back and I stand up, wiping my face and smiling at Molly and Addie. Addie frowns at me, tilting her head to the side. "Where did all of your hair go?"

I finger the short strands in front of my face, having forgotten for a second what happened.

"Oh, they cut it off. They didn't like how long it was."

"You look good with short hair; it makes you look scarier!" Molly declares, putting her tiny hands into the pockets of her gray pants. I grin at her, surprising myself as I laugh out loud. It feels good to laugh.

"Well, that makes it all worth it." I tease, still laughing slightly. Looking around, I catch Aiden's eye and find him smiling faintly at me. I shove away the warm feeling I get and look away quickly, returning to looking for other kids I know. I notice all of the stares we're attracting, and my smile falters, slowly fading away. We're the only ones here with a smile, and my laugh echoed loudly. I meet the gaze of an older seer, and the hatred in his eyes chills my blood. Happiness does not seem to be welcome here.

"You better fill me in on what's happened." I hear Alex say quietly. They move away, walk over to one of the tables, and sit down. The whispers that follow Aiden echo obviously, and I wonder what will happen once everyone realizes exactly who he is. I wonder just how long that will take.

Ten minutes later, I have found, hugged, and talked to seven more children from the caravan, though Edmund didn't exactly talk back to me. We all make our way to the same table Aiden and Alex sit at and find seats. As I walk, the hairs on the back of my neck stand up and I feel a chill. I frown, rubbing my neck as I sit down across the table from Alex. Another wave of cold goes down my spine and I shiver, crossing my arms.

Watch and listen.

I frown, shaking my head slightly. Watch and listen to what? I look up and down the table, and for some reason, my gaze sticks on Tina, who sits at the far end of the table beside Tristan.

Watch. Don't interfere.

I blink, forcing my vision to quit being blurry as I watch Tina, seemingly unable to turn away. My eyelids feel heavy and beg to close, but I fight it.

Look.

My eyes close, and the sound around me fades away.

Tina is laughing and talking as she walks towards the doorway.

Stop. She stops.

Her eyes close and her face goes still.

The soldiers see her.

No. No, don't see her.

The soldiers grab her. She screams, her eyes flying open.

No, let her go. Stop it.

Camari?

They drag her away while the other seers are forced to stay back by the other soldiers.

Screams suddenly fall silent.

Camari.

What happened to Tina?

Look. Don't interfere. Hide yourself.

"Camari!"

I jolt back into reality, my heart racing as I turn towards the sound of my name. Aiden is looking at me in concern, and Alex, Addie, and all of the other children are watching me too. How long was I in that vision?

I wipe my brow, finding it damp with cold sweat.

"Are you okay?" Alex asks, looking confused. I nod once, quickly looking away and pretending not to feel Aiden's gaze burning into my face. I'm okay; everything is okay.

I glance down the table at Tina and find her still talking to the other seers. But Tristan is staring straight at me. His eyes are narrowed as he studies me, intrigued and annoyed. He saw; he knows what happened.

I look away, staring down at my lap. I know I saw that vision for a reason. But I don't know what the voice meant when it said 'hide yourself.' Just what or who do I need to be hiding from?

R.C. Huye

I am being reassigned, and I have yet to be told where. I have my suspicions that wherever it is, it will be far from the castle. I am a hazard, so I must be silenced.

—Journal of Maren Landry

Chapter Forty-Eight

Aiden

The hostility in the facility is so thick that it is almost visible, floating off of the seers and hovering above me like a storm cloud. As Alex and I sit down at one of the four tables, all of the seers in the vicinity immediately turn and stare at me, silence descending. My shoulders tense up defensively as they glare and begin to whisper once more. Some of the seers that have been in the facility since before my time and survived this long are my age or older, and their eyes fill with hatred when they see me. Not hatred for me necessarily; I did nothing to them. Hatred for what I stand for and what I did after them, for what I've become.

I can't blame them.

"Well, this is a friendly atmosphere!" Alex jokes dryly as we sit down at the end of the table. I scoff in agreement, shifting on the wooden bench.

"How long do you reckon before someone tries to kill me?"

"I'll give you twenty minutes. They'll need time to sharpen their chives." It's obviously a joke, but Alex's expression turns grim for a moment and I nod, looking down at the table. It's not a matter of if, but when. And how I'll respond when it happens.

"So," Alex prods seriously, "what happened at the trial?"

"Camari and I got sentenced here, same as you," I say simply. 'My punishment for being a seer supporter is to be treated like a seer."

Alex clicks his tongue, shaking his head. "That's not what I meant, and you know it. I want details, not a summary. What happened between you and the hair-hater over there?"

"How do you know something happened?" I ask in exasperation.

"Well, after Camari eavesdropped on our conversation in the caravan where you poured your heart out-"

"She heard that?" I exclaim, horror and embarrassment flooding me. Alex laughs loudly at the panic in my voice, earning even more looks from seers and guards alike, enough that I elbow him to shut him up. Laughter is most likely a rare commodity here. I don't want to know what happens to those who obtain rare commodities in this place.

"Oh yeah, she heard it, and judging by how she stared at you for the entire night, the feelings weren't one-sided."

I blink, my mind wrapping around his words and how they change my view of what happened. I immediately flashback to our kiss, but I shove the thought away. I've ruined things yet again, and this time, I have little to no hope of ever fixing them.

"Now she's refusing to look at you at all. What happened? Why are either of you even here? I expected you to be pardoned and her to be executed and didn't think I'd be seeing either of you again."

"Don't sound so disappointed."

"That is not remotely funny, and you know what I mean. I'm like a squirrel, Aiden. I am persistent," Alex says in a serious tone. I stare at him incredulously, unsure whether or not I want to laugh at him.

"Squirrel was the only animal you could think of? Seriously?"

"Quit stalling and spill before I stick some of these seers on you," Alex says, jutting his thumb over his shoulder at the masses, giving me murderous gazes, the murmurs echoing across the room as they speak incoherently, most likely about me. I have no idea what's holding them back from making a move, but something about this classroom seems relatively safe.

"Fine!" I close my eyes, reliving that one perfect moment in the middle of chaos. "We kissed."

Alex raises his eyebrows suggestively. "I'd think that would be a good thing."

"It was. Until we were dragged away to the trial, where Aldred-"

"-Aldred?"

"Yes, the king. He told Camari who I am." I sigh and drop my head into my hands, preparing myself mentally for Alex's reaction. *This is going to be a shit show.*

"And who is that? I'm guessing it will explain why you call the most feared king yet 'Aldred'," Alex says skeptically, picking at a splinter on the table absentmindedly, obviously not concentrating on my words too much.

"He's my half-brother."

"WHAT?" Alex bellows, shooting to his feet and shaking the table, drawing even more stares as everyone falls silent for a moment.

"Shut the hell up! I'm hated enough already; no one needs to know anything else about me." I hiss, grabbing his shoulder and shoving him back down onto the bench as the muttering resumes even louder than before. "Gods above, Alex; if you're trying to get me killed then you're going about it the right bloody way!"

"What the hell, man?! Do you have a backlog of secrets and you just drop one every week? What's next, you're secretly a woman?" Alex hisses at me furiously, his eyes wide. "Gods have mercy; the drama with you two never ends!"

"I will punch you in the face, I swear to the gods-"

"Let a man wrap his mind around this." Alex snaps, pinching the bridge of his nose as he exhales slowly and loudly, dramatic as always. "So you're a prince? Gross."

"No, I'm just the king's bastard s-*gross*? Were you *dropped* as a child?"

"It's up for debate." Alex rubs his temple as if he has a headache. "Well, that explains why you're here. How did Camari stay alive; was that you? Did you make a royal request or something?"

"What the fuck is a royal–you know what, it doesn't matter. No, I didn't make a *royal request*. She was whipped because of me." I scowl, clenching my fist. Alex's face darkens, and he glances over to where Camari is speaking with Edmund and John from the caravan. As we watch, Edmund hugs her, and she winces sharply, giving away her concealed wounds.

"Who whipped her?"

"Her father, who turned out to be alive, which is why she wasn't killed. You can't be sentenced to a murderer's death if you aren't actually a murderer."

"He's still alive?" Alex's eyes widen as he tries to take in everything I'm saying. "Didn't she stab him?"

"As he attempted to rape her, yes." My vision begins to turn red with anger, and I struggle against a violent impulse. One day, I'll get my revenge on everyone who's hurt her. I have to stop hurting her first though.

Alex's eyes widen and his jaw clenches in disgust. "But he's her-"

"Father, yes. How do you think her mother got pregnant?" I snap, turning and looking at Alex. He rests his head in his hands and stares down at the table, looking sick to his stomach.

"The drama with you two never ends. Bleeding hell, I thought my childhood was traumatizing- thanks for that by the way. And what about Camari; how is she taking it?"

"I don't know; we haven't exactly talked beyond her telling me she no longer trusts me," I reply, shoving aside a fresh wave of pain.

"Well, at least she can't be mad at you for outing her as a murderer anymore."

"Yes, I'm sure she'll take that fun fact into account." I shake my head and our conversation ends as Camari and some of the children from the caravan come and sit down across from us. Camari avoids making eye contact once again, and has a strange facial expression as she sits down, staring into the distance. She's staring at the opposite end of the table, and I would have left her alone if it weren't for her facial expression. I've seen that expression before, when she is seeing something that isn't there. When she's seeing something only she can see.

"Camari?"

She continues to stare down at the other end of the table where the two seers from the cell beside ours sit, talking to others. The guy glances at her and catches her staring, narrowing his eyes.

"Camari," I repeat quietly, glancing at the guards to make sure they aren't seeing her. Alex and Addie look over, frowning at her.

"Camari!" I hiss, urgency sweeping through my veins. She can't be seen having a vision; this is the worst place for her to be seen. I don't want to know what they do to seers who have visions while in the facility.

Camari jumps violently; her brown eyes are flooded with fear as she turns to me.

"Are you okay?" Alex asks her, seeming confused. I doubt he realized what was going on. Camari blinks, her eyes refocusing. I watch in frustration as a wall comes up, blocking off whatever she just saw.

"I'm fine," she says distantly, glancing down the end of the table again before staring down at her lap, her eyes wide. I want to ask what she saw, to push her to talk instead of closing herself off like me, but I can't, not with everyone else around.

Alex and Addie start a conversation as food is brought out. I was hoping for real food, but I'm not surprised when I'm given a tin of water and a bowl of gray stuff that could be associated with porridge. While it looks like something that came out the backside of a donkey, I am starving, and begin to eat. It is slimy and lacks flavor, but once I get past that, it is decent enough. I ate worse in the army.

For the following minutes, the only sounds are those of spoons against bowls and tins banging against the table. I look up from my bowl when I am almost done and glance at Camari again, worried about what she saw. She is staring into her bowl without really seeing it, and her hands still rest in her lap. When was the last time she ate?

"Camari, are you okay?" I ask quietly, though I know she isn't. How could she be?

She looks up at the sound of my voice, her eyes regaining focus. "I'm fine. Just not hungry."

"You need to eat; it will help you keep your strength up." I try again. I can't explain it, but I am desperate for the distant look on her face to go away. It scares me.

Camari's eyes flash with anger, and she looks at me coldly. "I said I'm fine, *Prince Aiden*. Mind your business and leave me be."

I look away quickly as her words hit me like a punch to the gut, swallowing hard. But, at least I got her to speak.

I listen in on Alex and Addie's conversation, not really paying attention. A few minutes later, Camari begins to eat slowly, and I allow myself a small smile of victory.

The identity of the Royal Assassin is kept a secret for one reason and one reason alone: you cannot seek vengeance against someone that you do not know.

–Excerpt from the Zordan Laws and Commandments

Chapter Forty-Nine

Camari

Look. Don't interfere. Hide yourself.

Those words echo in my ears over and over, always in that same mysterious voice that I've been hearing since a particularly snowy day when I was a child. I turn them over again and again in my mind, trying to figure out their meaning. I try to understand them together, but when I learn nothing, I separate the words.

Look.

I looked; I watched Tina get dragged away.

Don't interfere.

Interfere with what? How? The guards or with Tina?

Hide yourself.

How on earth am I supposed to hide myself? I am in a glorified prison; my every move is scrutinized by five guards and twice as many seers. How in the name of the gods am I supposed to hide myself?

I scowl down at my half-eaten bowl of sludge and push it away, doing my best to push the words away with it. I can feel Aiden's gaze still burning into me, watching my every move. It is almost as annoying as the undecipherable vision.

I peer through my curtain of hair at Tina all the way down the table. Instead, I catch Tristan's eye. He is watching me with suspicion and curiosity, not even bothering to hide it.

Well then, why should I?

I shove my hair back and turn my head, meeting his eyes straight on with a raised chin. Surprise flickers briefly in his eyes, but then he smirks at me. Shifting in his chair, he rests his arms on the table and leans forward slightly, never breaking eye contact. I swear I can hear his question as if he is speaking out loud right beside me.

What did you see about Tina?

I turn away, dismissing him. It's none of his business what I did or didn't see.

My attention is caught on a group of men entering the room, followed by three more guards. Just how many guards are there?

"Breakfast is over; split into your groups," one of the men says, his deep voice carrying across the huge room. The seers immediately react, standing and pushing their benches back with an ear-splitting screech. I turn to the seer next to me, a girl a year or two younger than me with pale pink hair.

"What's going on?" I ask quietly, standing with everyone else. She glances at me curiously as if I should have known what is going on.

"It's Ayone; we have 'class'," she says in a Northern accent, making air quotes with her fingers.

"Can you explain further? I'm new; I only just arrived last night."

"Oh, that explains your whole wide-eyed demeanor," she says with a wave of her hand. I bristle slightly but remain silent as she continues to speak. "I'm Gale by the way. We have a schedule here in the facility, and it's best that you memorize it. Ayones, Tries, and Súvigs are class days, which means we spend most of the day getting remade. It's not that bad as long as you pretend to agree with the doctor and ignore all of the seers who actually agree. They scare me. After class, we are 'free' for the remainder of the day until the evening meal, and then we are to be in our cells by ten, not that they actually give a shit if we're in them because if we're not then chances are we're dead! Dhás', Ceaths, and Beis' are free days. We each have assigned jobs to do around the facility; I'm sure you'll be given yours shortly, but that's basically it. On Seachs, we are forced to go to three hours of service where some entitled priest shoves his 'given knowledge from the gods' down our throats, basically telling us how we are vermin and rats and how the facility is our chance at rebirth. And yeah, just follow the schedule and don't look anybody in the eyes for too long. And avoid the men. Do all that and you may make it."

"And this schedule never changes?" I ask as we walk over to one of the groups. I notice that the men and women are separated on opposite halves of the rooms and frown as Alex, Aiden, and even horrid Tristan are led away.

"Well, every third Beis of the cycle is a visitor's day where anyone can come and see a seer. It's ironic, seeing as they've already slaughtered all of our families so we don't exactly have anyone to come visit." Gale sounds grim as she says this, but I feel my blood pool at my feet at the mention of visitor's day.

I can't wait for all the fun we'll have when I visit the facility.

"When was the last visitor's day?" I ask weakly.

"Two Beis' ago, so this upcoming Beis will be a visitor's day."

I look forward to our meetings.

Gale must see something in my face because she speaks again. "You don't have anyone to visit either, huh? Don't worry, it gets better. The grief dulls."

"No, it's worse. I do have someone to visit me," I reply quietly, feeling sick to my stomach. Gale frowns in confusion, but is stopped from asking any more questions as we're separated and guided to our seats.

There are twelve of us in my group and we sit in a circle, the man who is supposed to be our doctor sitting on a single chair between two seers with ample space between him and them. I look around the circle as I sit, but my gaze rests on the supposed doctor. He does not look anything like any healer I've ever met. He wears elegant clothing, richly made, and he has a dagger tied around his waist. His golden-brown hair is brushed back flat against his scalp and curls around the nape of his neck, and his eyes are cold and lacking any emotion. He has wire-rimmed glasses that sit on the bridge of his nose, and he peers through them at us with a sense of superiority.

I know immediately we aren't going to get along very well.

"I see we have some new faces," the doctor says, his eyes scanning the gathered girls slowly, passing over me without a second thought. "I'll have each of you stand up, one at a time, and introduce yourselves."

I shift on the ground, looking around at the girls. I recognize three other girls who were in the caravan with me; Addie, Lisette, and Vicky.

"Why don't you start?" the doctor says, nodding at Vicky. Vicky stands, her emerald eyes flashing with nerves.

"My name is Vicky; I am thirteen years old," she says hesitantly, obviously unsure of what she should say. The doctor nods at her in a way that could almost be interpreted as assuring. Almost.

"Good. Thank you, Vicky."

Vicky nods and goes to sit down, but the doctor speaks again. "You will now be known as patient 4563." He says, looking down at a piece of parchment he has, scanning it for something.

"Wh-excuse me?" Vicky stammers, her eyes going wide. The doctor looks up at her with cold amusement in his eyes.

"Upon arriving everyone is assigned a number. You are no longer the person you were before; you have the chance to be better. And for now, you are patient 4563."

And so it goes on. Addie becomes 4487, and Lisette is 4572. When it comes to my turn to stand, the doctor motions to me with his right hand, not even bothering to look up from his parchment.

"My name is Camari Dorsar and I'm nineteen," I say, forcing myself to stand tall despite the fear that quivers inside of me.

The doctor looks up at my name, and his eyes meet mine, narrowing slightly. "Ah, so you're Duke Bidennore's daughter."

I manage to hold in my flinch at the sound of his name, though the smell of lavender still fills my nose and makes me sick to my stomach. I shove aside my nausea and raise my chin.

"I'm sorry; I have no father by that name," I say clearly, breathing slowly through my nose. The doctor looks down at his piece of paper again. He folds it up slowly before crossing his legs and leaning back in his chair, taking off his glasses and looking at me.

"And yet, somehow, your mother conceived a brat with the duke, and here you are. Nevertheless, you are now called patient 4567." He finishes dismissively, looking away. I grit my teeth and sit back down, pushing aside the urge to lash out. It won't do any good.

"Now that we have everyone cleared let's begin with today's correction. For those who are new here, the corrections are our lessons on how to use your powers for the good of the kingdom and the king. Since we have newcomers, we will do a review today." The doctor announces. I hate referring to him as the doctor; he is nothing but a brainwasher. Does anyone actually fall for this?

"As you know, a seer has occasional views into the future, and as they age, they can control their powers and change what they see."

I frown. Where do they get their information? Do they actually believe this, or is this just them trying to lie to us about ourselves?

"What we do is help teach you to gain control of your powers and change the future for the better, not for the worst as your families would have had you do."

"How do you know our families would have us change the future for the worst?" I ask during one of his pauses. He turns slowly to face me, his face blank.

"Excuse me?"

"How do you know they'd have us change the future for the worse if you kill them without any evidence of their so-called treason? Do you have any proof? And who are you to decide what's for worse and what's not? When did the gods give you that privilege?" The entire group stares at me as I speak, and the doctor's face gets colder and colder with each word. Yet I can't seem to stop the flow of words. "What makes you so special that it is up to you to decide what is proper befitting our nation? How do we know for sure what is truly better or worse for-"

"Enough." The doctor speaks quietly and coldly, but his voice cuts through mine and stops me immediately. "You will be silent and you will listen to our lessons, and hopefully, you will learn."

I hold his gaze, my eyes just as cold and hard as his. "Or what?"

The doctor smiles, sending a chill down my spine that has nothing to do with a vision. "Or you will be treated as an uncooperative resident, and that will not be enjoyable for you. Am I clear?"

I hold his gaze as his words sink in. I was right. He is no doctor.

"Crystal," I reply coldly. He smiles at me for a second before he turns back to the rest of the group.

"Now, where was I? Oh yes. As you get older and your powers grow, your parents would have you use them to harm the kingdom and its residents, as we have seen happen many times in the past. It is our job to ensure you learn how to properly control yourselves and to resist all visions so that we can release you back safely into the world."

"What happens to those that fail to prevent their visions?" Vicky asks quietly, biting her lower lip. The doctor levels her a look that could maybe be mislabeled as compassion, and fear curls up in the pit of my stomach.

"Oftentimes, they go mad from the strength of their powers and what they see and they take their lives before we can aid them. Suicide is common amongst seers. And if we reach them in time and we cannot aid them, then they are dealt with accordingly."

I ball forms in the pit of my stomach as his words register, and I find myself questioning his logic and wondering if others are doing the same. Are seers suicidal because their powers ruin them? Or are they considered suicidal because they are young and trying to understand who they are, and the 'doctors' that are supposed to help them take that confusion and use it brainwash the seers into believing they are something they're not, that they never could be? Are we suicidal by nature, or are we trapped in a cycle created and completed right here by our supposed doctors?

And how exactly are we 'dealt with?'

The class lasted for almost the entirety of the day. By the time we're done, my brain feels fuzzy and I'm having trouble keeping my eyes open. I have no idea how so many lies can be shoved down your throat, disguised as truths. What scared me the most was that a few of the seers in my group were nodding along with him, agreeing with him. Lisette was one of them, though she caught my eye at one point and looked away guilty.

The doctor leaves after a few words about remembering and thinking on what he said, and the other groups split up at the same time. I stand and watch as the group of 'doctors' leave, followed by their guards. I try to catch Lisette but she turns and walks away quickly, leaving me watching after her.

"Hello 4576; what did you think of that meeting?"

I scowl and turn to face Tristan, who stands behind me with a smug look on his face. "How did you find out my number so quickly?"

"My group was next to yours, and everyone heard you get at it with the doctor," he says, shoving his hands into the pockets of his uniform.

"We didn't 'get at it'. and my name is not 4576; it's Camari. Call me that or don't call me anything," I say coldly, crossing my arms over my chest. To my surprise, Tristan smiles, or the corners of his mouth barely twitch into what I assume is a smile, and his eyes warm for a second, something I didn't think was possible.

"None of us use the numbers, at least, none that aren't already brainwashed."

I blink in surprise at his sudden change of demeanor. Is he…being nice?

"But it would be a good idea for you to learn everyone's number anyway. for when we're talking in front of guards or anyone who will listen in on us. Mine is 4494. Better be safe than sorry." Tristan adds. I nod, seeing the logic in his words.

"But it's a horrible thing. They're not just taking away our names; they're taking away our identities, everything that we were before we arrived here."

"But what can we do about it?" Tristan says with a dismissive shrug. I level a look at him.

"Something. We can always do something."

Tristan snorts, looking away. "Useless words from a romantic."

"No. Words from a realist. You always have a choice, Tristan," I say. He turns and meets my eyes again, but I can tell by his expression that he is no longer interested in our previous subject.

"Like how you have a choice to tell me what it is you saw about Tina?"

"Why do you even care?" I ask in exasperation, turning away from him and surveying the room. Addie is talking with Alex across the room, their heads bent close together. Very close together. I smile faintly to myself as I watch them talk to each other. They deserve to find some happiness in life. How fitting that they've found it in each other.

"Tina is my cellmate and best friend. If you saw something about her, I deserve to know." Tristan's voice is cold and it snaps me out of my thoughts. I look back at him, and to my surprise, I find desperation in his eyes.

"I'm not even sure what it is I saw, Tristan." I lie, keeping my face smooth and hiding any hint of my fib.

"I don't believe you," he growls, stepping closer.

"Back off, Tristan," I warn him, clenching my hands into fists. He scoffs, taking yet another step closer.

"What are you going to do, punch me? No offense Camari, but I doubt you know the first-"

He is interrupted as a shout sounds off across the room. I look over and spot a throng of seers circled around four people. Three seers are beating and kicking one person.

Aiden.

The guards are doing nothing but watching calmly. They won't interfere. I look over at Alex and catch his gaze. Then I turn and begin running towards Aiden, desperate to get there before he's hurt too badly. I shove past people and through groups, ignoring people asking what I'm doing and Tristan's calls for me to stop as he gives chase. Aiden needs me, and at this moment, that is all that matters.

I break through the circle of seers and pause for just a second, taking in the scene that lies before me. Aiden has been forced back against the wall, and though he has his arms up to block blows, he never actually seems to serve one. I'm hit with a realization and a wave of pity shoots through me. He won't hit them because he feels he's already caused them enough pain. He thinks he deserves this.

I run forward again just as Alex appears in the corner of my eye, also running towards Aiden.

"Hey!" I shout, trying to get the seers' attention. They're three men, all taller and bigger than me. I am good at self-defense and better with a weapon, but I have no weapon, and these men are huge.

But what choice do I have?

One of the seers pulls his arm back and aims for Aiden's face, so I resort to the most desperate and effective, if not slightly pathetic, method.

I kick him in the balls.

He releases a high-pitched whine and slowly crumples to the ground, curling up into a ball.

"What the hell are you doing here?" Aiden shouts at me, anger and annoyance lacing his tone. Blood drips down his cheek from a cut on his temple, an old wound reopened once again.

"You better get off your sorry ass and fight, Lorian, or they'll have both Alex and I bleeding as well!" I snap.

"You shouldn't have gotten involved!" he says angrily.

"When it comes to you, I'm always involved! Now fight back dammit!" I shout, tempted to punch him myself. One of the seers turns to face me; his eyes alight with anger at my interference. I'm his new target. Wonderful.

He swings at me, obviously not worried about the ethics of punching a woman. I duck underneath his arm and return the blow, one punch straight to the face. His nose cracks satisfyingly, although so does my knuckle. He shouts and brings his fingers up to his face, pulling them away with blood covering them. He bellows in rage animalistically and swings out blindly at me again. These men, while strong, are neither quick nor smart. Aiden could have beaten them in seconds.

I dodge his arm and go under it, but I don't see his second swing coming until it hits me in the side of my face, sending my flying sideways. I stumble, barely managing to stay on my feet as my jaw begins to throb sharply. He advances towards me, ready to finish what he's started, but Aiden gets between us suddenly, his split lip dripping blood down his chin and making him appear even more menacing. The man doesn't back down, and Aiden levels a punch straight to his face. The man stumbles back, and before he can recover Aiden is there with another blow to the face. He then grabs the man's head and brings it down onto his knee with a resounding crack that makes me cringe, my healer's instincts screaming in protest. The man crumples to the ground, out cold, and the fight is over. I gape at the three incapacitated men, Aiden's skill still surprising me. But my view of the room is cut off as Aiden steps up to me, his hands cradling my face.

"Are you okay?" he asks me urgently, his eyes scanning every inch of my face.

"I'm fine!" I insist, trying and failing to push his hands away as he examines my face, neck, and arms. I don't need him touching me like that; it awakens a swarm of feelings I don't want to feel.

"Your jaw is bruising," he says darkly, turning my head gently so he can see it better. "Does it hurt? Are you bleeding?"

His thumb brushes the underside of my jaw gently and I jump away from him, a flush rising up my chest. "Aiden, I'm fine. As a healer, I can attest that I know what I'm talking about."

"I'm fine too, thanks for asking," Alex gasps from where he stands with his hands on his knees, breathing deeply. "I got socked in the stomach, but I'm fine."

"Stand up straight. Breathe in through your mouth and push your stomach out, and suck your stomach in when you exhale." I order, watching as he obeys and the pained expression on his face begins to fade. I turn back to Aiden and find him slumped against the wall, a pained expression now on his face.

"Idiot," I mutter. "Stand up straight; let me look."

He obeys with a grunt and I lift his shirt, holding back a cringe as his bruising torso. I begin to prod not-to-gently at his sides, ignoring his hisses of pain as I feel his bones. My eyes fall closed as I continue to feel, working my way slowly up.

"What are you-"

"Shhh." I interrupt him, frowning slightly. "Let me focus."

I imagine this is what a musician must feel when they play their instrument, a soldier must feel when he fights. The feeling that you don't really have to think about what you're doing or how to do it; you just do it. It's an instinctive, trained action that is part of you. I could never forget how to heal.

"Possibility of cracked ribs, definitely bruised," I mutter to myself, lowering his shirt and starting on his jaw where it is bruising. "Can you open and close your jaw without pain? All of your teeth are still in there?"

"Yes and yes."

"Then your jaw is fine. Your head, I'm still not convinced, But it wasn't okay to begin with, so nothing has changed." I tease him, earning a smile. "You just need to wrap your torso tightly and you'll be fine."

"You shouldn't have interfered," Aiden says; his words still sounding slightly annoyed. "You could have gotten hurt."

"I said I'd help you not die, and I don't break my promises," I reply, pulling him away from the wall so that he's standing.

"I shouldn't have needed your help; I should have fought back!" he snaps, sounding angry with himself.

"Well then we agree on something." I snort, shifting underneath his arm as both Addie and Tristan walk over, Tristan having hung back and watched the entire fight. Addie flies straight to Alex while Tristan walks up to Aiden and I.

"I can't grow to rely on your help, Camari; it's not fair to you," Aiden says quietly, his voice deep and full of feeling. "You won't always be there."

I turn my head and look up into his eyes. He's already looking at me with something akin to gratitude and sorrow as well as frustration.

"Yes I will," I say quietly, even as my mind tells me I shouldn't have said it, even as it tells me it's a lie. "I'll always be there."

Promises unkept are the same as lies. They hurt and fracture the bond of trust until there is nothing left of it.

—The Religious Texts: The Book of Wisdom

Chapter Fifty

Aiden

The fight was expected, in fact, I'm surprised I went as long as I did without getting beaten up. My only guess is they were waiting until after the doctors had come and gone. One minute I was looking around the room and trying to spot Camari; the next thing I knew, someone was shoving me back against the wall as another guy punched me in the face. They spat at me, insulted me and goaded me. I have a feeling they wanted me to fight back so that they could better justify what they were doing, but I refused. I've caused them enough pain. I've created enough death.

But then Camari was there, practically spitting venom. And then not fighting wasn't an option because Camari might have gotten injured. She made it her fight too, and it was apparently decided for me a while ago that all of her fights are mine as well.

I'll always be there.

Her sentence, spoken softly, holds so much meaning. Does she mean that or is she simply trying to get me to fight back next time? Would she say that if she didn't mean it?

I still have my arm around Camari's shoulders, as she thinks she is helping me. In reality, it is making my chest hurt even more, but I'm not going to tell her that. The guy from the cell next to ours walks towards Camari and I, only looking at her. His eyes are narrowed as he looks at her in an angry way that immediately makes me defensive.

"I don't understand you," he says to Camari, looking down at her with a frown. "Why would you help him?"

"I'm right here you know," I mutter. He just ignores me, though Camari appears annoyed or maybe uncomfortable at his attention.

"You feel good with just standing to the side as three men beat on one? Good for you. I still have a sense of humanity," Camari says haughtily. I fight against a smile at the look on his face. He looks at me for the first time, then he looks back at Camari, and his face changes into something I don't like. He grins at her, though his eyes gleam like poison. But there is something else there, a feeling that he tries to hide. Is he...jealous?

I glance at Camari, but she doesn't see it and is watching him with a pinched expression on her face.

"Oh, I get it now. You're just another woman who's fallen for his pretty face, right?" Camari bristles, her eyes sparking, but the guy keeps going. "After all, you did say you'd always be there. How sweet."

"Here's a suggestion, how about you-"

"No, here's a suggestion. Tell me what you saw," he growls, taking on a threatening tone. I take a step forward, my hands curling into fists. He flinches back a step, and embarrassment floods his face but he recovers quickly. "Call off your pet and tell me or I will report you."

"Shut up!" Camari hisses. Judging from that hidden gleam in the guy's eyes and the way he's looking at her, he's not threatening her so much as challenging her. Testing her.

I don't like it.

Camari seems to have no idea what he wants and simply glares at him. Something in my chest stirs, and I want nothing more than to punch his face in and get him away from her once and for all. He's playing a game, and I do not like this game.

"Tell me." He orders, his smile disappearing as he looks at her in anger. "Now. Or I tell them."

"Not now!" Camari says through clenched teeth. Her eyes flick to the guards lining the walls and I see fear flash through her eyes. While it's obvious that I am missing something as this conversation is confusing the hell out of me, I don't miss the fear in her eyes. That's all I need to see.

"I may be bruised, but you just saw what I did to the seers back there," I say coldly, my threat obvious as I gesture to the three men still lying on the ground alone. "Back off or join them."

He holds my gaze for several seconds in complete silence, challenging me. I take another step closer to him and he just barely flinches. I smile coldly and he scowls, taking a few steps backward. I suppose it can be useful at times to maintain my act as assassin.

"You have to tell me eventually. The funny thing about having a sense of humanity? Everyone in here loses it," he says coldly before he turns on his heel and struts away.

"What the hell is going on?" I ask Camari, watching him leave the room, his blonde friend by his side.

"He saw me have the vision, and he wants to know what I saw," she says darkly, watching him saunter away.

"What did you see?" I ask her. And just like that, she remembers that she hates me and a wall slams down behind her eyes. She steps away from me, shoving her hands into her pockets.

"Nothing important," she says stiffly. " I'll see you back in the cell."

I watch as she walks away, sighing. There was a moment when she didn't hate me, a moment when she cared. If I have to spend the rest of my life, I will help her remember that moment.

R.C. Huye

In 382, a revolutionary group called 'The Blinders' was founded and led by a 21-year-old man named Keegan.

–Retractions from the Royal Historical Documents

Chapter Fifty-One

Camari

I sink down onto my cot, my head cradled in my hands and groan. What am I doing? I need to be avoiding him, pushing him away, hating him, not helping him in fights and letting him touch me. Not saying stupid things.

I'm pathetic.

I lay back on the bed, my head resting on my thin pillow. I kissed him. That shouldn't mean anything anymore since he's lied repeatedly to me, over and over and over again. I don't even know why I kissed him, it just happened. One moment, I was running and then the guards had me on the ground. When I got up I could have stayed still and been agreeable, I could have cooperated and avoided a beating. But I was terrified, and at that moment, I ran towards the only person that has ever truly made me feel safe and whole, desperate to escape my situation. I thought I was about to die, put to death for my father's murder, and I wanted to stop being afraid. I didn't want to waste my last moments with Aiden. So I kissed him, and for just a moment, the world stopped turning, the soldiers stopped coming, and time stopped moving. But that second ended, and he betrayed me. Again.

"What are you doing?" I jolt in surprise at Tina's quiet voice, sitting up with a start. She's peeking at me from her bed through the bars separating us, hugging her knees against her chest.

"I was just thinking," I reply, turning to face her. "Tina, why didn't the guards or soldiers break up the fight?"

"They don't care what we do to each other as long as it doesn't affect them. It's easier if we kill each other than it is for them to kill us; if they kill too many of us they get a write-up," she explains quietly. "But there are always more of us."

I swallow, staring down at my feet. If the guards will never intercede on our behalf, staying alive will be incredibly difficult. For Aiden, maybe even be impossible.

"How long have you been here, Tina?"

"Five years, maybe six. It's easy to lose count sometimes," she says lightly, staring out at all of the other empty cells. "Tristan will know exactly how long though; he never forgets."

"You two came here together?" I ask cautiously, trying to get more information on both of them.

"Yes, we're from the same seer village. We've been friends for as long as I can remember. It's hard sometimes; Tristan is so angry. But it wasn't your assassin that brought us here."

I piece together her puzzling words, slowly getting used to her confusing way of speaking. It makes me think of my visions, confusing and enlightening. And there's one more question I'm dying to ask.

"Tina," I hesitate, my heart pounding, but force myself to ask, "What happens to seers that are seen having visions by the guards?"

She bites her bottom lip, the picture of innocence and fear, and a chill races down my spine as she looks at me with her wide eyes, captivating my attention as my breath hitches in anticipation.

"I don't know. We never see them again."

As the week goes on, I gain a much better grasp on how things run in the facility. By the fifth night, I have the schedule memorized.

We are released from our cells at exactly seven o'clock every morning and then led down to our classrooms. Something that can't really be called food is served at seven forty-five, and then the 'doctors' arrive.

Ayones, Tries, and Súvigs we are in 'class' from eight o'clock to six o'clock, where fake sentiments are shoved down our throats.

The king wants what's best for you.

Your powers were given to you so that you could serve your kingdom with them.

THE CURSE OF THE BLESSED

If control is impossible, an end must be taken.

Pure rubbish.

Dhás', Ceahs, and Beis' we don't have classes, but rather we have duties to perform around the facility. The duties are basically glorified chores, and if we don't complete them, there will be consequences. My duties change depending on the day. Dhás' and Beis' I have to make the beds in each cell in my cellblock. There are fifty cells in my block. I make one hundred beds every Dhás and Beis. *One hundred.* And they're obviously pointless tasks, as on class days the beds do not get made and not a single guard gives a damn.

When making the beds, I find some pretty interesting things that seers have hidden from the guards and their cellmates. A handkerchief, a bejeweled pen, a small switchblade. I leave the things where I find them, not wanting to take more from anyone than has already been taken, but the switchblade I took with only a twinge of guilt. I might need it, and besides, if one of the seers used it against Aiden one day, I'd never forgive myself.

My Ceath task is slightly better than making the beds; I am given a mop and a bucket filled with water with strict instructions on what halls and rooms to clean. I then spend the entire day mopping floors, dusting candelabras, and imagining a gruesome death for each guard I pass. Because of this chore, I am able to explore a large portion of the facility as I cleaned, establishing a partial layout in my mind's eye. It's how I know that my classroom is one of eight, each one belonging to roughly three hundred and fifty seers. I estimate how many seers are in my classroom. That means there are roughly two thousand five hundred seers. All of us are literally cleaning our own prison.

Some seers don't have permanently assigned duties and are moved around to wherever they're needed. This is good because it meant I got to work with Alex on Dhá, both of us working together to do two hundred beds. He's always joking and happy despite where we are and how we're treated, and that makes my own heart feel lighter.

I wake up on the morning of Beis with what feels like a stone in my stomach.

Every third Beis is a visitor's day.

I look forward to visiting you in prison.

I shudder, sitting up slowly in my cot and hugging my knees to my chest. It is visitor's day. The duke would be coming to see me.

I take a slow, shaky breath, shoving my hair out of my face and pulling my shirt back on. It is early, earlier than when I usually wake up, and the sky outside of our small window is a dark, dusky gray, the sun nowhere in sight. Tristan, Tina, and Aiden are still asleep in their cots. I turn on my cot, leaning against the wall behind me. Cold seeps from it, through my shirt, and onto my back, soothing the lashes there. It has been six days since I was whipped and I am healing, just not fast enough for my liking. The wounds are now itchy and they burn, so the cold is a welcome relief.

Thinking of my back just brings my mind right back around to Duke Bidennore. I shudder again, hugging my knees tightly to my chest. I hate that I am scared of him. I hate him. But he is coming to see me. What if the guards leave me alone with him? What will he do? What if I freeze? What if he tries to-

"Camari, are you okay?"

I jump, whipping my head around to where Aiden is blinking at me blearily, his arm propping him up partially on his pillow.

"Yes, I'm fine," I say quickly, my voice coming out weaker and shakier than I would have liked. I realize I have tears on my face and I wipe them away quickly with shaking hands.

Aiden pushes himself up in his bed and rubs at his eyes with the heel of his palm, the blanket sliding down to reveal his bare chest and broad shoulders. I look away, down at where my hands lie in my lap, shaking. I fold them together, but they continue to shake anyway, betraying my fear.

"What's wrong?" he asks softly. I continue to stare down at my hands, hating the tears that threaten to escape as my lower lip begins to tremble.

"It's Beis." My voice comes out low and raspy, filled with fear.

"What does that mean, Camari?" His voice is steady and gentle, and a tear slips down my cheek, escaping. I wipe it off on my shoulder quickly, still staring down at my hands.

"Every third Beis is a visitor's day, where any seer that has a non-seer family can have visitors. Today is a third Beis." My voice shakes and two more tears escape. I wipe them away quickly, my eyes flitting up to Aiden before going back down to my shaking hands. My breaths are shaky and as hard as I try, more tears escape my eyes and trail down my cheeks.

I know he'll come; there is no doubt in my mind. It's what he'll do that has me so terrified. Because this time I won't be able to run.

I jump in surprise yet again when my cot creaks and dips down. I look up through my curtain of hair at Aiden as he sits beside me on my cot, leaning back against the wall. "It will be okay. Nothing can happen to you because the guards will be with you, and if he does hurt you, I'll kill him. Rest assured. It is going to be okay," he says, his voice rumbling in his chest. I nod, taking purposefully deep breaths. It will be okay.

Aiden places his arm over my shoulders carefully, giving me the choice of pulling away. Instead, I scoot closer to him, resting my cheek on his shoulder. His breath catches slightly, but then he pulls me against him, wrapping both of his arms around me and resting his cheek on the top of my head. Warmth leaches from his skin into mine and my racing heart calms, my lungs relaxing and allowing me to breathe deeper and better. I close my eyes and wrap my arm around his torso, allowing myself to fully relax.

"I'll go back to hating you tomorrow," I mutter, my shaking slowly getting under control.

Aiden sighs in exasperation, his breath warm on the top of my head. "I figured."

A silence descends between us for a few moments. "I hate being afraid," I whisper to no one in particular.

"I know." Aiden's chest vibrates under my cheek as he speaks, and his arms tighten around me slightly. "And you have no need to be afraid. You are the bravest person I know, and you should scare the duke, not be scared of him."

I huff out a laugh, turning my head slightly so that I can look up into his eyes. "I don't think you aristocrats are scared of anyone."

Aiden's eyes are gentle and open, staring into mine with such force that my heart speeds up slightly. "We should be."

I look away quickly, lest I do something that I might regret later. But I don't pull away.

Aiden hugs me closer, resting his cheek on my head with his nose just barely grazing my hair. My skin feels warmer, my blood rushes faster, and my heart skips a beat. Every inch of our touching skin comes alive so that I am aware of everything, and yet I am the most relaxed and comfortable I've ever been. I just feel safe.

Warm and comfortable, I'm not sure when exactly I fell asleep. I wake up with a start at the sound of a metal key rattling in a cell door. I blink at the bright light, trying to remember why I am asleep sitting up, why I am so warm. Aiden shifts beside me and it all comes rushing back. I sit up slowly, Aiden's arm falling down to my waist, and rub at my eyes to push away the fog before I look around again. The guards are still several doors down from us, and seers stream by on their way to the classroom, staring at me unashamedly. I look over at Aiden, who is sitting up and looking at me with a slight flush. There are sleep marks on his cheek from my hair, which means he fell asleep as well.

"Are you okay?" he asks quietly, rubbing the side of his face slowly. I nod, suddenly feeling embarrassed. Not so much about the fact that we fell asleep together, and not because he isn't wearing a shirt, but rather because part of me wants to lean back against him and fall asleep again.

"Thank you," I say, smiling at him before looking away. Which is a mistake, because Tristan is awake and is staring straight at me. Tina is awake too, but is too busy watching the guards outside to pay attention to anyone else.

"Well, looks like the puppy got let into the bed," he says with a smug look. Almost a week, and he is as cold and snobbish as ever.

"Can it, Tristan." I snap, not interested in fighting with him. It isn't worth my time. Perhaps he sees my disinterest because he seems to get even smugger, if not slightly angry.

"If you were cold at night, you should have told me, Camari, I'd have been happy to help warm your bed."

"Shut your mouth," Aiden growls, immediately on his feet. He's an inch or so taller than Tristan, and Tristan has to look up at him through the bars.

"Or what? In case you haven't noticed, you're enemy number one around here. If someone's angry, if something bad happens, you'll be held responsible, whether you caused it or not. But you know that, after all, were you not 'corrected' by the guards two days ago? You still have the bruises on you." Tristan spits.

I look over at Aiden sharply, scanning him up and down. Sure enough, there were semi-fresh bruises on his torso and jaw, ones I hadn't noticed in the dark. He didn't tell me.

"It's nothing serious." Aiden deadpans, still glaring at Tristan.

"Nothing serious? I told you I'd keep you alive; I can't do that if you don't tell me when you've been hurt!" I exclaimed, throwing my hands up in agitation. "The guards did that?"

"They knew me from basic training and aren't pleased with where I ended up so they thought they'd express their concerns to me. And I don't need you to keep me alive; I can do that myself," Aiden retorts but then immediately cringes. I scowl at him, our former closeness is gone, but I choose to instead deal with Tristan. I turn to face him, annoyed at his smile, as he watches Aiden and I fight. It is exactly what he wanted. Why?

"Tristan, I wouldn't care if the world was ending and we were the last two people in it, I would rather let a snake into my bed."

"Perfect, because that's exactly what you're doing." He smiles. I hate that I flinch, and I hate even more the pleased gleam in his eyes as he acknowledges that he's won this argument. "One day, once he's betrayed you and almost gotten you killed, you'll realize I'm right. And I'll be there to gloat."

The guards reach Tristan's door and unlock it, gesturing for them to walk. He does so without looking back, leaving Tina to scamper after him. They unlock our door next, and I walk out without looking

back at Aiden, my head bowed. Because everything
Tristan just said has already happened.

And I still haven't learned.

*Dorsar, Camari/ 4567. F: Duke Ralph Bidennore II.
M: Unknown. ~784*

–Recovered Artifacts from the Facility

Chapter Fifty-Two

Camari

The morning passes far too quickly, and before I know it, breakfast is over, and I am going from cell to cell, making beds and hoping to find something interesting. Eleven cots down, eighty-nine more to go, and I am stopped as two guards walk up. I subtly slide my feet into a better position, fingering the pocket of my pants where I have the stolen switchblade.

"You have help today." One of them says shortly, pulling someone forward. Aiden.

Of course.

"I'm good, thanks though!" I say with forced cheer, still fingering the switchblade. The guard scowls, taking a step forward. I refuse to concede even a step to him and lift my chin, though fear stirs in my belly as his watery eyes peer down at me.

"It isn't an offer; it is an order. You have two hundred beds to make now; get to work. Do you understand?"

"Yes, I understand." I grind out, clenching my hands into fists. The guards turn and leave, their steps echoing down the hall. I turn back to the second cot in the room, pulling the blanket straight before I pick up the thin mattress and tuck the blanket in while also looking for anything an inmate might have hidden. Nothing. I huff in annoyance, letting the bed drop before I turn to walk to the next cell, pushing past Aiden. I hear him follow me, and as I start on one of the cots, he starts on the other. We work in silence, the only noise being that of the bedsprings creaking and the mattresses being dropped. After three cells, Aiden is the first to break the silence.

"You know I didn't mean what I said, at least not how I said it."

"On the contrary, I don't know anything. I never know what you mean; you're the most confusing man I've ever met!" I snap, tucking in a blanket. Aiden turns to look at me, scoffing.

"Me, confusing? You're–that's–hold on, how many men have you met?"

I can't help but snort in laughter, fluffing a pillow. "Of course, that's what you focused on."

Still, the look of curiosity, as well as unveiled jealousy, for some reason, makes me say, "Don't worry, most men I know are fifty or older."

Relief flashes in his eyes, or at least I think it does; he cuts off my view by turning back to the cot he's working on. "Except Walter."

"Yes, except Walter." I concede. "Wait, this was not our original topic of conversation!"

"That's not my fault. You started it by saying I'm hard to understand," he says nonchalantly over his shoulder

"You are!"

"No I'm not!" he exclaims incredulously, turning to face me, his cot forgotten. "Ask me a question, and I answer it-"

"Please!" I drop my cot as well, turning to face him and crossing my arms. "You hide everything! Nothing you say makes sense!"

"For example?" he prods, taking a step closer. I lift my chin, once again refusing to back down.

"You didn't tell me that the king is your brother."

"You need to come up with another point; that one's getting old," he says, daring to scoff. I gape at him, taking another step.

"Getting old? You're a bleeding prince!"

"Technically, I'm not, I'm just a bastard son."

"Same difference."

"No, it's really not. One has value, one is disposable from birth," Aiden says, taking yet another step closer. "Another example."

"Seriously?"

"Deadly serious," he says, a small smile gracing his lips. I resist the urge to smile back, choosing to retaliate instead.

"You choose to talk to Alex about me rather than talk to me yourself."

Aiden's smile fades, and he takes a half step back. I grin at my small victory and take a large step towards him, gaining ground.

"What are you talking about?"

"I-" I stop, remembering just what that conversation was about. Of all points, why did I bring that up? "I heard you talking with Alex right before we reached Sutoran."

"Oh?" Aiden's voice is low, and goosebumps sprout on my arms. "What exactly did you hear?"

I blink, suddenly feeling flustered. What were we arguing about again? I can't remember. The way he's staring at me, his hazel eyes so intense, I forget everything else.

"Just…talking," I say lamely, grasping and failing for a way to change the subject.

"I'm sure you heard something of more value than that." Aiden challenges softly. "What did you hear?"

"I heard…I heard you telling Alex how you felt. About me. But that was over a week ago, and a lot has happened since then, so I doubt it holds precedence anymore," I say, looking down at the stone floor. Aiden takes another step forward so that there is barely an inch of space between us, and I look up but immediately regret it. His eyes ensnare me and I find it impossible to look away. It's like I'm drowning in him.

"I don't know, I think it still holds precedence," he says, taking yet another step closer. Now, there is only an inch of space between us. His hands brush mine, but instead of pulling away, he reaches out and laces his fingers through mine. I inhale sharply, my heart racing. His smell of linen and cedar soap fills my senses and I breathe deeply despite myself.

This is wrong; he lied; he can't be trusted. I need to step back and break whatever is going on; I need to end this now.

I need to want to end this.

"Maybe to you," I say carefully, taking a step back and pulling my hands away, "but not to me."

Aiden studies my face, his eyes shuttering as I put more space between us. "Are you sure about that?"

I can't forget what he's done, and I'd be foolish to try. "I can't just forget that you lied to me, Aiden. Over half of our conversations, of our entire relationship, have been based on lies. The entire time we were in Krakent together, lies! I can't just look past that!"

Aiden opens his mouth to say something but snaps it shut at the sound of footsteps in the hallway. I take a deep breath and smooth my shirt, relieved that our conversation is over. Then I remember just why the guards are coming, and all of my blood drains to my feet.

Three guards walk into the cell and focus on me, ignoring Aiden completely. My heart drops at the sight of them and my hands begin to shake as I remember. It is Beis.

"You have a visitor, 4567. We are here to take you to meet him.

My breath catches in my throat. "I don't want to meet him; you can send him away."

Aiden steps in front of me as if he senses my terror, reaching out for my hand behind his back and threading our fingers together again.

"It wasn't an offer, seer; it was an order. You will be coming with us," says one of the guards coldly. They step forward in unison, shoving Aiden aside and grabbing one of my arms in a painful grip each. I pull, trying to twist away, but they just squeeze tighter. Aiden starts forward, anger burning in his eyes, but the third guard steps in front of him, his hand resting on the hilt of his sword. Aiden stops, and his eyes meet mine for a brief moment as the guards take me away. I can almost hear his thoughts in my head, reassuring me and making my fear weaken. Almost.

It will be okay.

I nod shortly, and then I'm dragged away and am not able to look back at him.

As the guards drag me down the halls, my mind is in a flurry. I'm going back and forth between fear and shock. The duke is here to see me, and I don't know what he wants; I don't know what he'll do to me.

With all of these thoughts spinning about in my head, I haven't paid attention to what direction we're going in. I force myself to snap out of it, reminding myself harshly that I need to pay attention and get a better mental layout of the facility. I'm led down a seemingly endless hallway before we finally turn onto a flight of stone stairs. After climbing those, we come out on a small floor with a wooden door in front of us. Trepidation rises in my veins as I am led towards the door, but I don't try to get away again. It would just be a waste of strength, and there is no way I'd be able to get out of their grip.

And if worst comes to worst, I have a knife in my pocket. And this time, I won't leave until I'm sure he's dead.

The door is open and I am shoved inside so viciously that I fall onto my hands and knees. The door shuts behind me with a bang that echoes through my core, and my fear is confirmed; there won't be a guard in here with me. I push up from the floor with a scowl, wiping my hands on my shirt and shoving my hair out of my face. I swear, guards don't know how to simply let go of a person.

The room is small and has only three things in it. A heavy-looking wooden table with a wooden chair on either side of it rests in the middle of the room. And in the chair across from me sits the duke.

My breath catches in my throat at the sight of him and I clench my hands into fists so that they won't tremble. He smiles up at me, his pale ginger hair raked back away from his face. "Hello, daughter. I know it's only been a week, but it feels like so long since I've seen you."

"Not long enough," I reply shakily, my eyes flicking around the room for potential weapons. Chair; table leg; switchblade in pocket. I'd feel better with a sword. Or Aiden. Both actually, would probably be best.

"Come now, that's no way to greet your father," he says with a smile, pushing the chair on my side out with his foot and gesturing for me to sit down. He is purposefully speaking in an educated, elusive tone, emphasizing his title. Rather than frighten me, surprisingly it pisses me off. I ignore the chair, opting to stay on my feet.

"I don't have a father."

"You wound me. Come now, you don't truly mean that, do you?" he asks me, raising an eyebrow in a way I'm sure is supposed to look concerned. It comes across as demeaning. "Your mother and I got along so well; I'm sure she would be glad that we're getting to know each other better."

"Do not talk about my mother!" I spit, clenching my fists tighter so that my knuckles turn white. The duke raises his eyebrows at me, and his smile flickers away.

"My my, someone's testy today. You must get that from Adeline. She was always in a foul temper, avoiding me and talking to me as little as possible. It was a wonder I managed to get her alone."

"You raped her, you son of a bitch!" I scream, my fists shaking. His eyes gleam and he smiles up at me, sending chills down my spine.

"Would it make you feel better to know she didn't put up much of a fight? If she would have just-"

"Shut up!" I feel sick to my stomach and I'm not so sure I'll be able to hold off stabbing him if he says one more word. He stands slowly, like a hunter locking onto his prey, and prowls around the table towards me.

"I see you have not been taught to respect your superiors," he says slowly, trailing a finger along the table's edge. Fear unfurls inside me like a flower, and

I hate the way I tremble, hate the power he has over me.

"Respect is earned!" I spit. He asks slowly and stops, leaving a foot of space between us.

"Or instilled. Which would you rather I do?"

The door behind me opens with a click, saving me from answering, and the duke's mouth turns down in annoyance as he looks at the guards behind me. "*What*?"

"I'm sorry, your Grace, but we have another group of visitors here for another prisoner; she needs to be escorted back to her duties," one of the guards says, seeming apologetic.

"You can't be serious. Simply have the other visitors wait; I have-"

"I'm afraid I can't do that, your grace; these are…important people," the guard says carefully, although it's clear what he means is they are more important than the duke. The duke scoffs angrily, but I don't stay to listen. As fast as I can, I slip out of the door and run, ignoring the shouts for me to stop. Down the stairs, down that hall, back the way I came. I run as fast as I can, desperate to put space between the duke and I. And yet I swear I can still feel him behind me as I run.

There is a Zordan legend of whose origin I cannot find, that at a moment of dire need for salvation, if blood is shed on stone, the stone will yield and produce a saving grace.

—The Mythical, Magical, and Mundane: Folklore of Zorda

Chapter Fifty-Three

Aiden

I continue to slowly make cots, folding the blankets and straightening the pillows without really seeing them. I almost kissed Camari. She wanted me to kiss her. Or so I thought before she told me quite clearly that it, that we, will never happen.

I grit my teeth, tugging on a blanket too tightly and accidentally ripping it at the seam. Uttering a curse under my breath, I sit down on the mattress, resting my head in my hands. She is right; I don't deserve her. I lied; I've hurt her. But I never thought I deserved love at all, let alone loving someone like her. And now that I know her, now that I feel what I feel…I'll never stop fighting for her. I may finally be starting to come to peace with my past, as I think she did a while ago. It is my final betrayal that she just can't forgive.

But I won't stop trying.

And you won't stop failing, just as you failed eve-ryone here.

I'm shaken from my thoughts when footsteps echo down the hallway. I look up, expecting guards, but spot three seer men instead, and my heart sinks.

Not again.

"Look at the royal assassin, all on his own." One of them croons, grinning at me. They know how this is gonna go, the same way it has gone with each group of seers or guards since I got here. I'll defend myself, but I won't fight back. I won't hurt these people any more than I already have. I deserve the pain I receive. And that's why they keep coming back. They know I won't fight back because if I did, they wouldn't be able to come back at all.

"Did you ever think that maybe without all of your swords and weapons, you're just as pathetic as the rest of us?" One of them, a man with a shorn head and a patch of scalsen on his forehead, sneers at me, shoving me back a few steps. I refuse to let my fingers fold into fists.

"I don't just think it, I know it," I respond, slowly shifting my position. If they're surprised by my response, they don't have the chance to show it as more footsteps echo down the hallway, breaking us apart before anything truly begins. I scowl as the same three guards from earlier arrive, remembering the look of panic on Camari's face when they grabbed her.

"4581, you have visitors."

I frown, even as hope sparks in my chest. I haven't let myself hope that Morris would find a way to visit me; he was purposefully kept away from me as we crossed the Spas Folamh, as were Grant and Miller. But maybe he's found a way; maybe I'll get to see my little brother.

I walk with the guards willingly, not looking back at the seers I leave behind, though I feel their gazes burning into the back of my neck until I turn the corner. They'll be sure to find me later.

As the guards lead me down the halls, I make sure to focus on what direction we go and which turns we take. It will be important later for me to have a good mental layout of the facility. Because I sure as hell don't plan on staying here longer than I can help.

They laed me up a flight of stairs to a small platform with a wooden door, opening it and gesturing for me to step inside. I do so and they shut it behind me, leaving me alone with my visitors.

Miller, Morris, and Grant all stand, watching me. Grant is grinning so widely that he looks like he might split open. Miller is observing me with his usual calm and quiet demeanor, and Morris is trying to be calm too, but his eyes are shining. I grin when I see them and start forward. We all meet in the middle, and I greet each one of them. Clasping hands with Miller, hugging Grant and Morris.

"Gods above, your ugly mugs are beautiful." I grin, knuckling Morris' hair.

"Enough of that," Miller says almost instantly, though his lips are twisted into a faint smile. "Tell us what you've been doing."

"Oh you know, living the life. Four-course meals every morning and night. That kind of thing." I joke, leaning back against the edge of the wooden table that sits in the middle of the room. I don't miss their eyes as they flicker up and down, taking in my form and prison uniform. I've been keeping up with my exercises every day, refusing to allow myself to get weak, but the lack of proper sustenance is showing, and I know I've lost weight.

"How are you really?" Morris asks quietly, his voice filled with concern. I sigh, raking a hand through my short hair.

"We're surviving. They've taken away each of our names and assigned us a number instead; I'm 4581. They feed us sludge twice a day, and on certain days, we have work to do around the facility, while on other days, we sit in a circle for eight hours and are force-fed lies about Aldred. What's funny is I was echoing those lies not two moons ago, and now that I got the guts up to stop, they just seem even more vile." I comment dryly, looking down at my feet for a moment before I look back up at them. Morris seems angry, while Grant just looks shocked. As usual, Miller's thoughts are completely veiled.

"So everyone just calls you 4581?" Grant asks me, frowning.

"No, actually. The soldiers and the doctors do, and a few of the inmates want to kill me, but everyone else here who I'm friends with still calls me Aiden. Alex called me-"

"Who is Alex?" Morris interrupts with a frown.

"He's a seer I met in the caravan. He's great; he has an interesting sense of humor. He hated me at first, just like everyone else, but now almost everyone from that caravan is fine around me. Now, if we're talking about number names, you should have seen Camari's face when she received hers. I was sitting across the room, but-"

"How is Camari? Is she okay?" Grant asks at the same time that Miller asks quietly, "What's her number?"

"She's okay, and her number is 4567," I reply, not wanting to get into everything that's happened. Morris raises an eyebrow but it's Grant who speaks.

"Okay? That's the least you've talked about her since you met her. What's going on? What happened?"

"Okay, that's exaggerated." I snap with a scowl. Grant raises an eyebrow at me.

"Is it?"

"Fine. She's okay. We're surviving, and she's been taking care of the young children while also observing everyone. There's this jackass named Tristan who has been driving her crazy. She's healing from my punishment, and I think I'm slowly getting her to stop hating me."

"Your punishment? Why does she hate you? I thought she loved-"

"No." I interrupt Grant, not wanting to hear the rest of his sentence. "She doesn't. But that's beside the point. We were taken to a hearing with Aldred and he told her that we're brothers. Obviously, she didn't take it well. Then he revealed that her rapist father is still alive. Then he offered to pardon me once and for all if I whipped her five times. I refused; I didn't want to be pardoned, not by him. So he had the duke whip her and made me watch," I rasp, my hands curling into fists. Just thinking about it, remembering the duke whipping her…my stomach churns, and I take deep breaths.

"Wait, he offered to pardon you? To let you go?" Morris asks, staring at me. I return his stare, confused by his question.

"It wasn't real, Morris. I would have had to renounce all seers, continue killing innocents, and hurt Camari. It was never an option; I could never go back to the way things were, and I could never do that to her." I snap. Morris nods, looking away, but I'm kept from explaining it more as Miller speaks up.

"How are you going to get out of here?" he asks, a small smile on his face. "Don't tell me you don't have a plan."

I blink in surprise, looking back and forth between them. "First off, this is supposed to be the most impenetrable place in Zorda. What makes you think I can escape? And if I have a plan for escape, I can't tell you."

"Why not?" Morris exclaims indignantly.

"Because if Aldred orders you to tell him what you know, you'll have to. This way, you can honestly say you know nothing." I explain. Miller nods, but he exchanges a glance with Morris and Grant that has me on edge. "But what aren't you telling me?"

"Aldred's focus isn't on you, or anyone in the facility for that matter. Your escape shouldn't be impossible."

"Why?" I ask slowly. What is he focusing on then?

"He's gone crazy!" Grant bursts out. Miller scowls at him while Morris punches him in the shoulder defensively, but the damage is done.

"What do you mean, gone crazy?" I asked with narrowed eyes. Morris glares at Grant again before he turns to me with a sigh.

"He's not crazy; he's just…he's decided to start searching other villages and cities for seers. Forcefully."

"Miller?" I turn to my second in command, needing the unbiased explanation that Morris simply can't give.

"After finding out that Camari and her mother managed to hide themselves in a village and nobody knew they were seers, he's convinced there could be other hidden seers. He's determined to weed them out." Miller explains calmly, ignoring Morris' bitter expression.

I rest my head in my hands, taking in what they're saying. How many more innocent lives will he take?

"Is anyone doing anything to stop this? Is anyone speaking out against him?" I ask, looking back up at them.

"Don't be a fool. You know he controls the council, and the council controls the people. They spit seer propaganda left and right, and the people lap it up like starving dogs. He's obsessed, Aiden," Miller says, standing up from where he was leaning against the wall. "I think your betrayal was the last straw."

I snort bitterly, shoving my hands into my pockets. "Yes, because I betrayed him."

"That's how he sees it. That's how the entire kingdom sees it. We don't know what to do, Aiden. He's sending a contingent of soldiers out in two moons. That's in nine weeks. What do we do?" Morris asks, his eyes desperate.

"I don't know. I'm stuck in here; I can't do anything! You are my only contact with the outside world, and you shouldn't even be here in the first place!" I exclaimed, throwing my hands up in the air. I feel helpless. I hate feeling helpless. I was helpless once, a long time ago, and I vowed to never be that way again.

"No matter what, you cannot come back here again," I say slowly, a lump developing in my throat at Morris' stricken expression. "If you are seen consorting with a criminal of the crown, the consequences…it's nothing you'll want to deal with. Don't come back."

Morris slumps back against the wall, his eyes pained and full of distress. "We know. I don't know what to do."

I look up at them, each of them looking as defeated as I feel.

Neither do I.

R.C. Huye

Today is my last day at the castle. All of the other servants have said farewell and wished me luck, but I know the truth. I will not see my boys again after this.

Knowledge only leads to death.

–Journal of Maren Landry

Chapter Fifty-Four

Camari

A man named Gideon is brought in to help me finish the cots, Aiden having disappeared. He leaves as soon as the last bed is made, not having spoken a word the entire time, not that I minded or expected otherwise. As Aiden's cellmate and 'friend,' I am lucky I haven't been attacked or killed yet. Though maybe Aiden is the reason for that as well.

I make my way to the classroom, starving and desperate for food as well as company. The room is silent when I walk in, just as it always is. The day I walk into the sound of voices and, well, just noise in general will be the day something terrible happens. And for that reason, I enjoy the silence.

I ignore the hostile stares I receive as I walk, keeping my head down and staying as invisible as I can. It's like being back in Krakent, except here I am far more likely to be killed.

I stand in the corner of the room, watching the other seers. Alex is with Addie, Molly, and Edmund, talking to the children with a gentle expression on his face while Addie watches on with a soft look in her eyes. Tristan is with Tina and two other seers, Walsh and Benji, talking quietly. His eyes meet mine once but he looks away quickly, a dark look in his eyes. Obviously still maddened by our earlier argument.

I sigh, leaning back against the wall and crossing my arms. A huge wave of loneliness sweeps through me, and I sink deeper into the shadows. I miss Adeline. I miss Walter. I miss Greta and Mikael. But most of all, I miss not being alone. A tear makes its way down my cheek, and it is soon joined by several more. I wipe them away quickly, angry with myself. The other seers here have lost everything. I have no reason to grieve; my mother is still alive.

And yet, I'm still alone.

It is the second day of my second week when everything goes to shit.

I am just finishing dinner, which consists of a gray soup that I refuse to think too much about and some sort of vegetable mush. It tastes as bland as it looks, and I can only stomach a few bites. I feel Aiden's concerned looks but ignore them. I've lost a lot of weight, and my shirt is looser than it was when I arrived. But I doubt the food would help in any way.

It is disturbing that our diet consists of gray on gray on gray, that we wear gray and live within gray stones. Silver's depressed cousin; ugly, depressing gray.

I'm just about to push away from the table and go to my cell before it gets too late and the more dangerous seers start feeling brave when I feel it. A cold trickle down my spine, a whisper in my mind.

Watch. Don't interfere.

I inhale sharply, looking around with wide eyes. Aiden says my name, but I ignore him. Please, not tonight. Please no.

I finally find Tina, and my heart drops. She's sitting by herself at the end of the table, just a few feet down from me, and there is ample space around her so that she is visible to all. And she is having a vision.

Don't interfere.

The guards see Tina. I know as soon as they do. They peel from the walls and make their way slowly towards us. At that moment, I decide one thing.

Fuck the stupid warning.

I jump up from the bench and bolt towards Tina, ignoring the shouts and gasps, the people calling my number. Her vision ends right as I reach her and she gasps and shakes with tears at what she saw. I glance over my shoulder at the guards, terrified that they'll be upon us. But the seers have all gotten up and formed a crowd between Tina and them, slowing them down remarkably.

Praise the gods.

I grab Tina's chin and make her look at me, my heart aching at the fear in her eyes. "What did you see, Tina? I need you to tell me."

"They're…I…They'll take me; I don't want to go!" She panics, her breaths coming in short bursts. I take her hands in mine, squeezing them gently.

"Tina, look at me. It will be okay, but only if you tell me what you saw. I need you to tell me, please."

Tina looks at me with wide eyes, but she nods, and her breathing slows slightly. "I saw armies. They were burning people, killing them."

"Where? Who was doing this?" I breathe. The guards are almost upon us, shouting at the unresponsive seers to move.

"The king. He was killing everyone. Everyone!" Tina sobs. My blood goes cold. Everyone, as in nonseers?

But it is too late for more questions because the guards have made it through the crowd forcefully, their swords out. A seer that remained in the way for too long lies on the ground, bleeding out slowly. Tina screams when she sees them, a scream filled with such utter terror that it fills me with ice. I move to stand in front of her, desperate to shield the poor girl from them. One of them snarls at me to move aside, but I ignore him, spreading my arms and trying to form a shield. It doesn't make a difference though; he's a huge hulk of a man, and I'm an underfed woman who is weak and tired. One slap has me falling to the stone floor painfully, and I feel the lashes in my back rip slightly, eliciting a yelp. I scream at the guards to back away from Tina, to leave her alone.

It's no use.

They grab Tina roughly and begin to drag her away. She kicks and screams, tossing her blonde curls side to side as she thrashes desperately. I jump up despite the pain, ready to attack the guards if it means freeing Tina. Arms grab me from behind and wrap around my middle firmly but gently, pinning my arms to my sides.

"There's nothing you can do, Camari! Stop, you'll only get hurt!" Aiden says fiercely in my ear. I fight against him anyway, trying to get free.

"Let me go! Let go, you bastard!" I scream, thrashing about. I pull my leg up, ready to smash the arch of his foot and cripple him, but he knows me too well. He wraps one of his legs around mine so that I am thoroughly pinned, preventing any resistance.

"I am so, so sorry, Camari," he whispers in my ear. I sag against him, a tear rolling down my face.

I failed.

My heart cracks down the middle as Tina is dragged across the classroom and out the door, her face the depiction of terror as she screams for help and fights.

Then her screams cut off.

*We have returned from our first raid from up in
Clodagh, near Solas. I was treated like a hero, but
that feeling disappeared when I watched facility
gates close behind the caravan. I never want to
know what happens inside those walls.*

–Field Journal of Aiden Lorian

Chapter Fifty-Five

Camari

After Tina's…after Tina is taken away, the class-room is abuzz with conversation. Two hours creep by with everyone crying, shaking, or talking. Aiden apologizes for restraining me, but I'm too numb to say anything in reply. When the warning curfew is called, I walk back to my cell without waiting for anyone to follow to speak.

Tina is gone. And I don't think I'll see her again.

I rake my hair away from my face, exhaling heavily as I reach my cell. I pause in the doorway, looking over at Tristan and Tina's cell. Tristan is in the corner of his cell on the floor; his knees pulled up to his chest with his arms wrapped around them. He stares off into the distance without really seeing anything, and his eyes are veiled in shadows.

"Tristan, are you okay?" I ask quietly, taking my hand off the rusty metal bar and taking a step back into the hallway. He doesn't reply, and I'm unsure whether or not he even heard me.

"Tristan?"

He still doesn't reply and the broken look on his face breaks me too. I'm filled with fear suddenly that he's having a vision as well, and I panic.

"Tristan!"

He jumps sharply, jolting as if I shocked him. He looks up at me, his eyes wide. I walk into his cell and sit beside him, leaving space between us.

"Talk to me." I request, resting my cheek on my knees and looking over at him. Tristan continues to stare down at the ground, his face still vacant. I'm surprised when he speaks quietly.

"She was my best friend. We grew up together. I've known her since I was two years old." His voice sounds tired and broken. My eyes water slightly, and I swallow against a lump in my throat.

"I'm so sorry."

He turns and looks at me, his eyes wide and open for the first time. "You tried to help her. Why?"

"I…I saw it in a vision. I wasn't sure what it meant at first, but now I realize I should have known; I should have told you. And no one deserves to be treated like that. I'm tired of us being abused. Someone needed to take a stand." I explain softly, lifting my head up from my knees.

"And it had to be you?"

"Why not?"

THE CURSE OF THE BLESSED

A tear slips down Tristan's cheek, and he turns away from me again, staring down at the floor as more flow from his eyes. My heart cracks a little more and I scoot closer to him, wrapping my arm around his shoulders and pulling him closer to me. He gives up any pretense of being okay and sobs, breaking down in a way I've never seen a man cry. Tears pour down his face, and I begin to cry as well, all the while rubbing his back gently, trying to bring him even the semblance of peace.

Two hours later, when Tristan is asleep with his head leaning back against the wall, and I have woken up briefly, I find that my anger is still there. And it is burning stronger than ever.

The next morning, I feel like everything has slowed down. Walking down the halls and eating breakfast, it is all slow and…wrong. No one mentions Tina. No one speaks about what happened yesterday or where they took her. It is like she never existed. Only Tristan's silence and empty stares remind me that the entire thing wasn't a nightmare.

Aiden keeps looking at me strangely out of the corner of his eye as if he can see the storm brewing in my mind.

I knew what was going to happen. But I selfishly forgot, and look what happened. Aren't seers supposed to help people with their visions? What good is knowing the future if you can't change it?

As I walk into the classroom, I overhear the whispers of other seers. A seer did not return to her cell last night. She was discovered this morning, hanging from her knotted blanket that had been tied to one of the candelabras mounted on the wall. She hung herself.

She was thirteen years old.

I heard a seer mention that something similar happened last moon. I think of Tina being dragged away, of the seer the guard killed for standing in his way too long. Of all of the seers before them that I don't know about.

These thoughts and others plague my mind as breakfast is finished and the doctors enter for our classes. I walk to my group, watching as all of the men are led to the other side of the room. Again my anger is fed, their control acting as a bellow to my flames. What more can they take from us?

The doctor begins the lesson and I zone out as I always do, completely prepared to pay absolutely no attention. But this lesson is different.

"Now, I know that there was a disturbance yesterday involving 4497. I thought we might address it first," the doctor says without looking up from his chart. I lean forward at the sound of Tina's number, finally wanting to hear something he has to say.

"I know that to some of you, it was a frightening and confusing experience, so I'd just like to help you understand what happened. 4497 had a vision."

There is a collective gasp from my group, and I resist the urge to scowl. We're seers; what do they expect us to do?

"Her screams and outbursts came from the terror she was feeling, as she did not understand what she saw or what was happening to her. 4497 was then taken by our helpers to a special part of the facility. There they will help her understand her vision better, as well as how to use it for good."

Now I scowl, my stomach turning as I think of what they might have actually done to her. The flames grow higher.

"4497 was delusional at the time, scared and disoriented from her vision, that's why she was screaming. I can promise you she is being treated with the utmost kindness and compassion." The doctor finally looks up from his papers, and oddly enough, he looks straight at me. I hold his gaze, making no effort to hide my hatred and disbelief.

"4567, if you have something to say, please do so." His voice is cold and filled with what might be a warning, but the last thing on my mind is caution as I stand up to address my group.

"You said that she was being treated well. Then why was she dragged away kicking and screaming, and why have we not been able to see her? How could we ever believe that anyone here could ever be treated well? Look at what we are fed, at what we are forced to wear and listen to. Two seers died last night! How is any of this good for us?"

"4567, you raise some interesting points," the doctor says, crossing one leg over the other and looking up at me calmly, almost bored. The condescension in his voice makes my blood boil, and my hands curl into fists at my sides. I suddenly became aware that the entire room had fallen silent and is listening to the doctor and I. Wonderful, let all of the seers that have been brainwashed see how fake this truly is.

"I'm sure that once you take some time to calm down and think things over, you'll be able to see how everything we do is to help you be the best that you can be. All we want is for you to thrive, and we are doing everything in our power to help that come about."

Every word he says just incenses me further. My fists begin to shake from me squeezing them so hard. I'm sick of this. I am sick of hiding, of lying.

"So if you would please sit down, 4567-"

"Camari."

The doctor breaks off and frowns at my interruption. "Pardon?"

My 'name' is the final straw. I am not a number; I am a person. And so, like a person, I snap.

"My name is Camari, not 4567," I say coldly. Several people around me inhale sharply, but I ignore them. The doctor smiles at me coldly.

"Maybe it used to be, but not anymore. Now you are 45-"

"No, I am not. I am and always will be Camari Dorsar. You can call me that or nothing at all." I grit my teeth. Something in the doctor's eyes shifts, and whatever I see sends a tendril of fear into my stomach.

"Well, Mistress Dorsar. I believe the events of yesterday were too much for you to handle. I think I will have you transferred to two days of solitary confinement so that you may recover and become open to healing." He gestures to the guards, and four of them peel off the walls, walking towards me. I notice several people in the corner of my vision starting forward, but then they stop.

"Solitary confinement won't suddenly make me believe your lies!" I hiss, taking a step towards the doctor. He smiles and stands from his chair, walking towards me. When he speaks it is in my ear so that only I can hear him.

"No, it won't. But the rewriting sessions might."

I recoil as if I've been stung, searching his eyes. What does he mean, by rewriting?

His eyes reveal nothing and neither does his smile. I have no more time to ask any more questions however, because then the guards are there, dragging me away.

R.C. Huye

Chapter Fifty-Six

Aiden

I know as soon as I see Camari's face at breakfast that I won't like what she is going to do. Not that she'll go out of her way to cause trouble, but with the mood she is in, she won't go out of her way to avoid it either. She'll probably welcome it.

She purposefully avoids my gaze throughout breakfast, staring at the table without seeing it. I have no idea how, but somehow, she knew what was going to happen before it happened last night. I didn't see her have a vision, but I never know anymore; she tells me nothing. I can't blame her; I've been distant the past few days as well.

Her expression is mutinous as she goes and sits down with her group and I hesitate half a step, knowing that face. That is the face she was wearing minutes before Eben betrayed her to Gladwell.

"Lurking won't make her like you." A smug voice comes from behind me, and I turn with a scowl to face Tristan. What Camari sees in him, I'll never know, but something makes her treat him with far more kindness than I feel he deserves. He may be grieving, though if he is he doesn't show it, but if he goes out of his way to pick a fight, he deserves the consequences.

"Besides," Tristan continues, looking over at where Camari sits, shooting daggers at her doctor with her eyes, "if anything, you're going to make her feel stifled. That's why she likes me; I give her space."

I ignore the roaring in my veins that encourages me to bash his face in, to show him just how stifling I can be. The memory of walking in on Camari and him asleep in his cell, leaning against each other, rises up in my mind, but I push it away. Instead, I take a step closer and clasp his shoulder with a bright smile, earning an uneasy look from Tristan that makes my efforts worthwhile.

"Don't ever assume you know anything about my relationship with Camari," I tell him quietly, maintaining my bright composure. "We have saved each other's lives countless times and gone through more traumatizing bullshit together than you will ever comprehend. You have foolishly put yourself in the position to give me advice; do it again, and I will cut out your fucking tongue. Understand?"

Tristan nods once, something akin to fear gleaming in his eyes beneath his usual loathing as he remembers just who I am. Good. It won't hurt for him to remember just how capable I am.

I let go of his shoulder and turn to walk over to my group, mentally bracing myself for eight hours of lies being shoved down my throat. I make it all of three steps before every group falls silent. I look around and find Camari standing up, her hands clenched at her sides and her eyes glowing like hellfire.

Shit.

I take a step towards her, careful to avoid catching the eye of the guards and watch their interaction carefully. She's exchanging heated words with her doctor, spitting them out like venom coats each syllable. To his credit, the doctor just listens calmly, barely blinking as she speaks. No, instead, he closes his book and lifts his hand, flicking his fingers in a movement that is barely visible. But I see it. And so do the guards.

Four guards peel off of the wall at his gesture and walk quickly through the room, the seers making way for them instead of blocking them as they did for Tina. Why won't they do the same for Camari?

The answer hits me in the stomach like a brick, making me feel sick. It is because she associates herself with me.

I start forward, my heart racing, but someone grabs my upper arm, pulling tightly.

"Don't be a fool!" Alex hisses from behind me. "Joining her will help nothing."

The guards grab onto her upper arms and begin to lead her away, the phrase 'solitary confinement' echoing through the air and turning my blood into ice. I can't protect her if she is locked away. Hell, I can't even protect her now!

They begin to drag Camari away, ignoring her as she tugs against their grip. She isn't strong enough to fight back properly. The entire room is silent as they watch, no one saying a thing to help her. Because it won't matter anyway. Camari's eyes comb through the room, looking for someone. Her gaze lands on Tristan, pausing, but her gaze moves on from him almost immediately and she continues searching until she sees me. Her eyes meet mine, blocking everything else out. I return her gaze, willing her to see the thoughts in my mind.

I'll find a way out of this.

She blinks, and I know she understands. Then the guards have her out of the room and down the hallway, and our connection is broken. The room breaks out in noise as people talk about what just happened, staring after where Camari disappeared. Alex releases my arm and sidles away, guessing correctly that I don't want to talk with him. I stare after where Camari disappeared, purposefully keeping myself calm. She'll be okay.

She has to be.

And the doctor has now been added to my ever-growing list.

A man sidles up on my right, big, bald, scarred, and muscular, with what looks like a tattoo peeking out of the collar of his shirt. He shakes his head at the exit, scratching his ear nonchalantly.

"Girl's a feckin' eejit," he mutters in a deep voice, his Northern accent heavy. I bristle, looking over at him and pushing away the initial surprise that he deigned to speak to me at all.

"No more than the rest of us for getting stuck in here."

His eyes flash with surprise, but he looks away with a scowl, shifting away from me. "You are far more of a fool than I am, Aiden Lorian. More of an arse too."

I grunt, running my hand across my face wearily as I stare at where Camari disappeared, wondering where solitary confinement is. "I won't argue with that, I almost even agree.'

"Almost? You really want to disagree?"

"People change. I should be allowed to as well," I say coldly, remembering when Camari told me exactly that. I didn't believe her then. I do now.

I don't bother asking his name, fully expecting him to stalk off and find me later with three friends to give me a beating; it won't be the first time. Or even the fifth.

But he stays standing there, observing me out of the corner of his eye. I turn away from the exit to face him, crossing my arms over my chest. "What is it you want?"

"To tell you something that you might find important," he replies, still not looking at me. But maybe it is for a different reason than I thought. I turn my back on him and make it look like I'm studying the room again, still listening attentively.

"What would that be?" I mutter, eying the doctor who summoned the guards on Camari. He is watching me plainly, something on his face making me uncomfortable. There's something off about him; he's different from the other doctors. More calculating and observant.

"I might be the only seer here who isn't a fool, and you and 4567 are not nearly as discreet as you think, and neither are your two friends, 4472 and 4487."

Alex and Addie's numbers. *How long has he been watching us?*

The man continues on quietly and I school my face into nonchalance, looking away from the doctor's continuous stare. "If you two are planning something, I think we can help each other."

"I have no idea what you're talking about." I readily deny it, ignoring how my heart begins to thunder in my chest. What does he know? We haven't technically planned anything; at least, Camari and I haven't. I am still looking for a way out, and not just for Camari and myself, but for Alex, Addie, and Molly too.

"Cut the bull, we're both smarter than that. You've seen my face; I'm two cell blocks down from you, and my number is 3913. I want out of this shite hole, and something tells me that you're my ticket. Find me when the time comes."

Then he's gone, walking across the classroom leisurely. I don't look back at him but rather stay where I am, staring at the exit without really seeing it as my mind spins.

I still have to figure out where solitary confinement is; I have to make sure Camari is okay. I have to find a way to stop Aldred from killing millions of innocents, his bloodthirstiness making him crazed. But at this moment, I can only focus on one question.

Did I just gain an ally or an enemy?

I leave these journals here in the hopes that my boys will find them. My oldest, don't lose yourself in your lust for respect. You are more than they ever will be. My youngest, don't let your love for your brother blind your judgment. He is not all that he seems.

—Journal of Maren landry

Chapter Fifty-Seven

Camari

The guards drag me down the halls roughly, digging their fingers in hard enough that I know I will have bruises come morning. I stop trying to pull away after a few minutes, deciding it might be better to save my strength. Not that I have much left.

Two days of solitary confinement.

I curse myself, inwardly admitting I was rash, angry, and acted on my anger. If I keep behaving like this, acting on my anger and morals without thinking first, I'll get myself killed. Or worse, I'll get someone I love killed. I refuse to be the reason Alex, Addie, or Aiden get taken away like Tina. No, I won't let that happen again.

At least I'm gaining a better mental map. Indeed, I can now tell where most of the places are. All of the cell blocks, my classroom, the visitation rooms, and now the solitary confinement.

The guards and I turn to the right, and at the end of the hallway is a large door. The hallway is dim, and an ominous feeling stirs in my gut as we walk, my hands turning clammy with fear.

I know I'm sentenced to solitary confinement. But I don't know what their solitary confinement is.

My breathing speeds up and my heart races as the door draws near. I don't want to go in there.

We stop at the door and one of the two guards not holding me in place steps forward, a large key ring in his hand. He places a key in a keyhole and turns it with an echoing click. And then he unlocks another. And another. There are three locks.

I swallow hard, watching as the door is pried open with a groan and I am led in unceremoniously. It is a large room, about the same size as the room I was taken to upon my arrival. It is lit by the sunlight that comes in through the glass windows, each one protected by iron bars. On the left wall there are four more doors, each with two locks and a guard beside each one. In the middle of the room, there is a fancy chair with leather straps in the armrests and the feet. There is also what looks like a leather cap of straps that most likely strap one's head into place.

It is a torture device.

I begin to fight again, tugging and pulling desperately, even going as far as to pick my feet up completely and kick. It doesn't matter. It doesn't matter how hard I kick and scream and hit; the guards refuse to let go. They drag me steadily into the room, nodding at the guards along the wall. One of them peels away and leaves the room, leaving me to my punishment. To my doom.

The guards go to throw me in the chair, but to do so, they have to loosen their grip on my arms for a moment. I use that, pulling my right arm free and driving it into that guard's gut. He barks a curse, letting go of me completely. Triumph flares through me, amplified by adrenaline, and I surge forward, only for another guard to grab me by my hair and pull me back, my neck getting whiplashed by the movement. I cry out as hair is pulled from my head and my feet fall out from under me. The guard I elbowed steps in front of me, scowling darkly.

"Scraggly bitch!" He spits, backhanding me across the face. My head shoots to the side and I blink stars out of my vision, the right side of my face burning white-hot. All four of the guards now grab onto me, having realized that I am going to put up a fight, and they heave me off the ground and towards the chair. I don't struggle, still trying to blink dark spots from my vision and push away the pain on my face and scalp. Then they shove me into the chair, and I snap back to my senses, writhing and twisting. I scream bloody murder at them, telling them to let me go, spouting filthy words that would make Adeline's ears bleed if she was present. Terror pulses through my veins, my heart surges in my chest, and I release animalistic pants.

It is to no avail. One by one, they strap my ankles and wrists to the chair, pulling the leather so that it bites into my skin. I pull against it, tears pricking at my eyes.

No. No, no, no, no, no.

The leather rubs against the scars on my wrists from the shackles, bringing back memories that flood me with even more fear. What are they going to do?

The guard that slapped me forces my head back against the rest as a second guard pulls the leather contraption onto my head and straps it in place, prohibiting my movement. I strain against it but can only pick my head up an inch or so.

The guard that left returns, walking right back to his post and standing against the wall as if nothing is amiss. As if there isn't a young woman strapped to a chair and primed to be tortured, sobbing in terror.

A man follows him in, holding a black leather bag that is weighed down at the bottom. What is inside it, I don't want to know. But I have a feeling I am about to find out.

He smiles widely at me, showing uneven, yellow teeth. I begin to tremble and hate that I can't control myself enough to make myself stop. He walks up to the wooden table that I failed to notice rests beside my chair and sets his bag down on top of it before flicking it open.

"You must have been naughty to be sent down here for me to play with!" he says in a teasing tone that is completely at odds with my situation. He begins to dig through his bag, setting things out on the table as he speaks. A candle, a hollow needle, a small metal bowl, a vial of black ink, a small mallet, and a small, shiny blade.

"Never mind what you've done; I'm just glad I have a new person to play with." He smiles at me, his eyes wild, and I can't help the whimper that escapes.

This man is delusional.

"I don't want to play!" I choke out, my voice shaking. He looks over at me, his eyes gleaming.

"Well, we don't always get what we want," he says quietly, darkly, turning back to the table. He lights the candle with a scrape of his knife on a small piece of flint, wiping the blade on a small towel he produces from his bag. As the flame grows larger, he turns to the small metal bowl and pours in the vial of ink. He then reaches into his bag yet again and pulls out a small charcoal pencil. He gestures to a guard, who steps forward, bracing his hands on my shoulders and holding me down. He presses the charcoal pencil against my skin, writing something on my skin that I can't see. When he is done, the guard lets go of me, wiping his hands on his pants like I'm filthy.

"Before I get to have fun with you, I'm going to give you a little memento, just something to remember me by. Then, depending on how you behave, I'll let you enjoy your confinement. If you don't behave though, we're going to have fun together for your entire two days with some rewriting sessions. Understood?"

I nod once, gulping in fear. What does he mean, memento?

The man turns back to the table and holds the bowl of ink over the flame, swirling it slowly so that it is heated evenly. Once he is satisfied that it is warm, he sets it down on the edge of the table carefully, pushing the candle next to it. Dragging a small wooden stool to the side of my chair, he sits down and reaches for his needle. He holds it in the flame, cleaning it of any dirt or grime, before pulling it out and dipping it into the bowl of warm ink. He holds it there for several seconds, and I watch as ink goes up the needle slowly. Finally, he takes it out and picks up the mallet in his other hand. He approaches my skin with the needle and mallet, lightly pressing the tip of the needle over where he wrote in charcoal.

"This won't take me long."

Then he taps the needle with the mallet, driving it into my skin, where it releases the ink. I inhale sharply through my teeth, partially from the pain and partially from surprise. The man smiles at my reaction, his eyes flicking over my screwed-up features before he returns to his work. He pulls the needle back out, only to push it back into my skin a millimeter from the original hole. And then he does it again and again. He stops occasionally, either to refill his needle or wipe away any blood that has collected on my skin. I eventually stop tensing up at each stab of the needle, lying limp on my chair and enduring the pain. I bite my lip whenever he goes particularly deep or hits an especially sensitive spot, and he always smiles at any sign that I am in pain as if it brings him joy. He is sick and enjoys my pain.

And I hate him for it.

Finally, he withdraws the needle and lays it down on the table with the mallet beside it. He takes the towel and wipes my skin in a surprisingly gentle manner, getting rid of any blood, sweat, or ink. Then he gingerly unstraps up my arm and holds it up so that I can see my wrist.

4567.

My number. The thing that has replaced my name. The thing that has replaced me, making me nothing more than another redundant prisoner in the stone hole that is the facility, left here to be killed or to rot here until I kill myself.

And it is now permanently etched onto my wrist.

After I am finished receiving my tattoo, the man decides that I behaved well. "She can have the rest of her time to herself, " he tells the guards, clapping his hands and saying the last part with a grin that makes my blood freeze. The guards step forward and pin me down while the man slowly goes about unstrapping my limbs and my head, his fingers icy cold as they brush against my skin. I don't try to fight back once I am free; I'm drained both mentally and physically.

4567. My skin now reads in bold numbers across my wrist. It is a mark, a brand; it is a claim on my life. The facility saying that I belong here and I will never fully escape it.

I wonder what Aiden will think when he sees it.

I banish the thought almost as soon as it surfaces, annoyed with myself. It doesn't matter what he thinks; I shouldn't- don't. I don't care what he thinks, and there is no reason as to why I should.

And yet a small part of me still wonders what he will think; a small part of me still worries he'll take one look and curl his lip in disgust. And that immediately convinces me to hide my tattoo once I am released.

The guards grip me roughly as they pull me up from the chair, supporting most of my weight as my legs shake and wobble beneath me, adrenaline and malnourishment weakening me visibly. One of the guards stationed along the wall pulls his key ring from his belt before walking to the last door on the row and unlocking all of the locks. The guards pull me toward the door as the one with the keys pulls it open. It leads to a small room, maybe six feet by six feet. There is no furniture, no windows, nothing. Just dust and darkness. I begin to fight and kick again despite my exhaustion, terror coursing through my veins. I do not want to go in there.

The guards throw me in roughly, and I land hard on my hands and knees, ripping the fabric of my pants. I push myself up immediately, running for the door, but it is already slamming shut. The last thing I see is the face of the young guard with the keys, watching as the others lock me in with something akin to pity and guilt in his eyes. And then the door slams closed. The sound of the keys turning in the locks echoes loudly throughout my room, the only thing in the darkness besides me. I stand there for a few seconds, my breathing loud, my heartbeats echoing.

I can't see.

I can't hear.

I can't breathe.

I can't breathe.

I turn and begin to bang on the door with my fists, punching and screaming. "LET ME OUT! LET ME OUT OF HERE! *PLEASE!*"

I don't know how long I stood there attacking the door. I only stop when I feel the wetness of blood sliding down my fists and when I can no longer shout, my throat so torn up that I can barely make a sound.

"Please," I whimper to no one, sagging against the door, broken.

No one answers.

I retreat to the corner of the room, my eyes as adjusted to the darkness as they will ever get. I sag against the wall, sinking down to the floor and hugging my knees to my chest as I shiver and shake from a mixture of cold and fear. I look around the room for a moment, trying and failing to make anything out. My throat is tight, my terror visceral. I lay my head on my knees, choking on sobs and closing my eyes against the warm tears that leak out as I come to a frightening conclusion.

There is only darkness in this room, and it has consumed everything. Including me.

I am beginning to wonder if the gods have gone si-lent because of what we have done. If they have shut me out because they are ashamed.

—The Religious Texts: The Book of Bryson

Chapter Fifty-Eight

Aiden

Camari has been gone for a day, and it is killing me. I can't sleep; too worried about what she's being put through. When someone says solitary confine-ment, I think of a cell block somewhere consisting of one cell with her locked inside. Camari doesn't do well with being alone; I think one thing she secretly enjoyed about the caravan was that she was con-stantly surrounded by people. And now she's locked away by herself for two days.

"What's wrong with you?"

I scowl over at Tristan, finding him glaring at me already. "You mean besides your presence?"

"You've been staring at the wall for half an hour; did you hit your head, or is the puppy having with-drawals?" he asks snidely, picking at a callus on his palm absentmindedly.

"I don't know how Camari puts up with you." I groan, not feeling like getting into it with him.

"I could say the same, only she doesn't put up with you. She drives you away with a sharpened stick and still you come chasing after her with your tail between your legs."

"At least I have something between my legs."

"Shut up!" One of the seers across the way snaps, though it's too dark for me to make out who it was.

"If only he could," Tristan mutters, staring out his barred window. "Then maybe we'd all have some peace. Camari must be in heaven."

"Shut your damn mouth!" I snap, my ire rising.

"Ooh, someone's testy. Or possessive. But who am I kidding? You can't be possessive of something you don't even have in the first place."

"What did I say would happen the next time you tried to give me advice on my relationship with Camari?" I ask him slowly, turning to face him.

"I'm pretty sure you need something sharp on you to cut someone's tongue out, and the sharpest thing you have is your toenail," Tristan smirks at me through the bars, leaning one arm against them. "Although Camari's wit may be sharper. But again, something you don't have."

"Don't pretend to know her. You're just using her as a means to an end!" I snap, my hands curling into fists. He grins suggestively at me, crossing his arms.

"Aren't you doing the same? Guessing by how cozy you were a few days ago, I wouldn't be surprised to wake up one night and find out exactly how you're using he-"

I reach through the bars, grip the front of his shirt, and pull him forward so that his face crashes against the bars with a reverberating clang that echoes through our cellblock, effectively shutting him up, along with everyone else in the cell block.

"Say another word, and I'll end your miserable existence," I spit, pulling him even tighter against the bars, "you disgusting, lying piece of filth!"

I release him, and he stumbles back, swearing, and I see dark wetness on his nose before he hides it from view with his hand. "You son of a bitch!"

"No, son of an asshole. My mother was a saint," I reply coldly, walking back over to my cot and lying down with my back to him. "Insult either her or Camari again, and you'll meet her."

A bargain, one rebel for 4497.

Approached by 4494.

—Recovered Artifacts from the Facility

Chapter Fifty-Nine

Camari

I blink as my door is yanked open with a deafening metallic screech, my eyes watering and burning after days in just darkness. Or at least I assume it's been days; I truly have no way of knowing. The darkness was consuming and completely silent, and I went between waves of terror and shock to being completely numb. Twice, I woke up from sleep or a daze and there was a tin of water and a plate of stale, rock-hard bread at my feet. I only found them because I almost knocked them over the first time and lost my water. I had dozens of nightmares that had me waking up screaming, only for me to wake up in utter darkness, completely disoriented and confused. There were a few points where I thought I could hear the darkness speaking to me, could feel it strangling me slowly. I haven't moved from my corner where I wedged myself against both walls; my knees hugged against my chest in an attempt to comfort myself. But now, I have a reason to get up.

The guards walk in and grab my arms, not even giving me time to stand up on my own. Yanking me to my feet, they lead me out of my cell and into the room beyond. My legs wobble and shake weakly beneath me and the guards end up dragging me out. I manage to stay on my feet as they let go, though I sway from side to side and shake uncontrollably, my head pounding.

"Strip," one of the guards says gruffly, gesturing at me with his chin. I blink slowly, my mind slowly catching up.

"Ex-excuse me?" I ask, still shivering.

"You need a new uniform; yours is filthy. Strip," he explains slowly, embellishing each syllable. I know he's not wrong; I have many unidentifiable materials on my uniform, some left unidentified on purpose.

One of the guards steps forward, and I raise my hand to stop him, indignation flashing through me. I can at least undress myself; I'm not completely useless yet. I pull my shirt and pants off quickly, letting them drop into a filthy pile on the floor while I stand there in my breast band and undershorts, my arms crossed over my torso as I continue to shiver, my cheeks burning with humiliation. No man has ever seen me with this little clothing on, and it's incredibly embarrassing. Aiden saw me without a bodice when I got shot by the seers of Onaydo, but I at least had my skirt on.

THE CURSE OF THE BLESSED

The second guard comes forward, a bucket in his hand, and before I can do anything to prepare, he throws its contents on me. I gasp as the icy water hits me, soaking my underclothes and flattening hair immediately while knocking me back a step.

"Put these on." The first guard hands me a new uniform which I accept with shaking hands, my teeth chattering. I dress quickly, pulling on the pants first and then the shirt. The shirt is too big and has long sleeves that hang down to my palms, but I am grateful for it as my hair drips down my back, leaving trails of icy-cold water.

"Good. Let's get you back to the other vermin." The first guard nods to the second and they both take one of my arms, dragging me out the door and back the way we came two days ago. I struggle to keep up, my knees wobbling and shaking beneath me, and I trip and falter repeatedly, my limbs simply too tired to obey me.

Finally, after what feels like a lifetime, we reach familiar territory, and after a few more minutes of stumbling along, we arrive at my classroom. I'm immediately bombarded with the sights, smells, and sounds all at once and I flinch, nausea and panic swelling inside me. It's overwhelming all at once and tears prick at my eyes as I try to take it all in, to adjust back to everything after two days of nothing, two days I can barely remember.

The guards release me and walk away, their duty done, and I stand in the doorway, cowering like a fool, blinking against tears and the painfully bright light. Slowly, my senses start to readapt, and I take a few steps into the room, looking around. Someone bumps into me and I stumble, barely catching myself with my shaky limbs. I look around desperately for Aiden, suddenly wanting nothing more than to see him for just a moment. I know without a doubt that with him, I am safe. And gods above, I would love to feel safe again.

I hug myself as I look around, my heart still racing, and then I see him. He's standing off to the side with Alex beside him, both of them talking with serious expressions on their faces. As I watch, Aiden turns from Alex and scans the room urgently, hope in his eyes. Then his gaze lands on me, and a beautiful smile breaks across his face, making my heart flip over in my chest. I start running towards him, unsure whether I want to smile or cry, and he begins to shove through the crowd, abandoning Alex. Right before I reach him, he reaches out to me, and then I'm in his arms, and for the first time in two days, I can breathe again.

I wrap my arms around Aiden's neck and hold on tight as he holds me against him, my feet lifting off of the ground entirely. I inhale deeply, stress falling off of me like shackles as his scent of cotton, leather, and pine fills my lungs, bringing with it comfort and security.

"Camari." His voice rumbles in my ear, his chest vibrating beneath my cheek. I just hold on tighter, tears sliding down my face unrestrained as I cry. I don't care that I'm supposed to be angry with him. At this moment, I don't care about the past. For these few minutes, all I let myself care about is that I'm safe in his arms, out of the dark.

Finally, I loosen my grip, and he lets me go slowly, if not reluctantly, though he keeps his hands on my waist, and I keep mine on his shoulders only because my legs are still feeling weak.

"Are you okay?" he asks me, searching my face, which I'm sure looks as gaunt and exhausted as I feel. He reaches up and wipes away my tear tracks tenderly and I smile, more tears making their way down my cheeks.

"I am now."

Fifteen minutes later, I'm sitting at the table, slowly spooning gray sludge into my mouth as my hand shakes like a baby bird. Aiden hasn't left my side and his hand rests on the small of my back, a comforting presence, even though I'm sure he is watching me eat with concern in his eyes. Alex and Addie sit across from me, both of them watching me like I'm a baby about to take its first steps.

"I'm not going to disappear; you can blink, you know." I smile, taking a sip of my water.

"Blinking is overrated," Alex replies, waving his hand in the air. "I prefer my eyes dry and useless. Are you feeling okay?"

"I'm fine," I tell them for the fifth time. "I'm tired, shaky, weak, and cold, but I'm fine. Let's talk about something else, please. What happened while I was…away?"

As soon as I ask, all three of them exchange a dark glance, and my suspicion rises. "Tell me or I'll stop eating."

Aiden clears his throat, his thumb moving absentmindedly against my back in an extremely distracting manner. "While you were gone, we were…approached."

I look back and forth between them, finding their caution comedic. "Well, was it consensual?"

Aiden smiles, shaking his head. "Funny. A man approached me and said he's seen us four together, he knows we're trying to escape, and he wants us to key him in on our plans."

"We're trying to escape?" I ask, earning shocked looks from the others. I shake my head, realizing my error. "No, I mean, do we have a plan? Because I was unaware."

"Not yet, but I've been working on one, and something tells me he does," Aiden explains.

"And we want to…steal his ideas?" I prod, finishing my breakfast and pushing the bowl away. There's nothing like starvation to make you really appreciate a bowl of indescribable mush.

"No, but-" Aiden is interrupted as the doctors walk in and call for everybody to find their class. He scowls murderously as my doctor walks in, his head held high in confidence.

"After class, all of us meet in Alex's cell. I'll tell you then," he says quickly before he turns and walks away, the absence of his hand leaving my back suddenly cold. We all disperse; I give Addie one more forced smile before I return to face the doctor who banished me to two days of hell.

The doctor smiles smugly at me as I take a seat, his spectacles showing my partial reflection. "Well, look who has returned to our lessons! Let us all give a warm welcome to 4567."

Everyone murmurs a greeting or smiles at me, a few simply waving. I ignore them all, never looking away from the doctor. He seems to know exactly what is crossing my mind and holds my gaze, still smiling. Oh, this man is far more intelligent than he lets on. And far more cruel.

"How was your stay in solitary confinement? Did all go accordingly?" he asks smoothly, prodding me on. I fake a smile that probably looks more like a grimace. It would be a lie to say I'm trying to make it look like anything else.

"I suppose it did. I certainly had time to think, just as you advised, and I will say you were right. I will be thinking things over far more than I was before."

And watching every word I say and everything I do around you.

I know without a doubt the doctor picks up on my message because his smile tightens slightly and he reclines in his chair. "I should hope so. And I hope your memento will remind you to do just that."

I stiffen slightly, my right hand going to my left sleeve and pulling it down more, even though it already hides my tattoo. I almost forgot about it; it was not a concern when I was trapped in the dark by myself. But now…

The doctor tracks my movement with a smile, and he isn't the only one. Addie frowns at me, studying me with questions in her eyes. I look away, knowing that I won't want to answer any questions she has to ask. My tattoo is something I am incredibly ashamed of, and I will never let her see it if I can help it. I will never let any of them see it. Especially Aiden.

The doctor finished with his interrogation, opens his notepad with a snap and smiles out at all of us. "Well then, let us begin. Who here can recite the history of Zorda?"

I, His Royal Majesty King Aldred Ignatius Lorian III, hereby order that the focus of the Royal Assassin will be to decrease the seer population within the borders of Zorda.

–The Contract of the Royal Assassin to King Aldred III

Chapter Sixty

Aiden

Eight hours of lessons later, we're finally dismissed. As usual, I leave the lesson wondering how anyone could believe the crap the doctors are spouting. There are two kids from the caravan in my group. One of them, Peter, listens in disdain. But Joseph, as well as two other men in my group, listen with dead eyes, nodding in agreement with what the doctor says. And it makes me sick to watch, knowing if I say anything, I'll just get thrown into solitary confinement like Camari was. And yet, I also know that they are likely to end up like the girl who hung herself with her bedding. There is no right decision.

After a quick scan of the classroom tells me that Addie, Alex, and Camari are already gone, I turn and walk towards the entrance, ready to go meet them and explain to Camari what she missed. But then I see the man from before, standing right in my plain view. And making eye contact with me.

This could be interesting.

I stop beside him but don't face him, instead turning and looking at the tables where seers are gathering for their evening meal.

"What do you want?" I ask, moving my lips as little as possible.

"I saw that they released 4567, and I'm assuming you're on your way to meet with your friends right now. I want to ask you to tell them what I've said to you, as well as what I'm about to tell you now. I'm not the only one."

"What do you mean, not the only one?" I ask, hope to stir in my chest.

"I know at least five seers who want out of here just as badly as me, no matter what it takes, even if that means trusting the royal assassin."

"Ex-royal assassin," I say through gritted teeth, my old title chafing.

"Same difference. My acquaintances have agreed that if you and your…allies are willing to meet with us, we're willing too."

"And how do I know that when we get there, your acquaintances won't be guards ready to take us to the executioner's block?" I hiss, my anger rising up as I picture a guard dragging Camari toward the wooden block, already slick with others' blood.

"I could ask you the same thing, and the answer will be the same. Sometimes, you have to take a leap of faith," he replies, sounding enraged by my question.

"I'm not that big a fan of leaping," I say dryly, ready to end our conversation and go meet the others.

"Look at my left collarbone."

"What?" I ask, confused at his sudden change of tone.

"Turn around and look at my left collarbone," he repeats, his voice calm, the kind of calm a voice is when they are telling a story or repeating a piece of history. I turn slowly and glance at his left shoulder, still confused as to what the point is. There's ink on his skin. No. Numbers. My blood chills as I see what is tattooed on his shoulder.

3919

"Those bastards locked me up in solitary confinement for five days. The first thing they did was give me this, a memento he called it, so that I'd always remember to behave. That's not the real reason though. The real reason is that they know what the numbers mean. They take away our identity, our personalities, and our individuality. They replace us as people. And I have my number permanently branded onto my skin. So don't think that even one day goes by when I don't think of the face of every guard, every doctor in this hell hole that has done me wrong so that when the day comes, I can kill them all." He spits those words with such venom as if he can already see their deaths and craves them. "I've been here for twenty years, Lorian. I was out looking for my older sister after she ran away, and instead, I was caught by soldiers and brought here. I haven't been outside since I was twenty-eight, and my parents lost both of their children. If you give me the same chance I'm giving you, we could help each other."

My mouth runs dry and the picture of his tattooed shoulder stays in my mind long after I've turned my back to him once more. "I'll talk to them tonight and tell them what you said. If we all agree, we will meet with your group," I rasp. He sighs behind me, a sigh of relief.

"Thank you."

"I have just one more question."

I felt rather than see him tense up behind me. "What?"

"You know my name; I feel it's only right I get to know yours."

"You know my number."

"Your number isn't your name." He is silent for several seconds, and I think he isn't going to answer. When he does, his voice is so low I flinch.

"Jax."

I nod, knowing our conversation is over. Turning, I leave the classroom and walk to Alex's cell, my mind still swimming with everything I just learned.

Everyone is there when I arrive, and they look up when they hear me before relief flashes in their eyes.

"Took you long enough," Alex says, tension visible in the lining of his shoulders.

"Sorry, I'll explain in a minute," I tell them, walking in and taking a seat on the cot beside him. Addie and Camari sit on the bunk across from us, their arms linked together.

"We were about to start without you," Addie says crossly, her head leaning against Camari's shoulder.

Camari shushes Addie, though her eyes crinkle slightly with a smile.

"Well, we can start now." I sigh, leaning forward and bracing my elbows against my knees. I look at Camari, who looks nervous about what she is about to be told. I can't blame her; I don't like what I am about to say. Only Aldred would.

"We do not yet have a plan for how we are going to get out of here; that much is clear. But we do now have some support for when we do. Jax approached me, telling me that he wanted to help us get out if we took him with us, and now, he approached me again when I was on my way here. He told me that he knows a group of seers who are trying to figure out a way out, just like us."

"Okay, hold on," Alex says, lifting his hand. "First of all, since when did you learn his name? And second, how many people?"

"I learned his name today, and he didn't specify how many people. He said at least five."

"But how do we know we can trust him? How do we know those five people aren't guards waiting to catch us?" Camari asks, picking at her nail beds as she listens.

"I asked the same thing, and he told me some reasons he has for hating the guards that made me believe him," I reply. Camari raises her eyebrows in skepticism.

"And what would that be?"

"He told me about his five-day stint in solitary confinement. The doctor there, or whoever it is that watches the seers, tattooed Jax's number onto his shoulder," I say, looking at each of them in turn.

Camari blinks, looking down at the floor. Alex scowls, his blue eyes darkening.

"Tattooed, as in permanently inked into his skin?"

"Yes, I saw it myself. 3913 in big, bold numbers across his collarbone. It's horrible, and he'll be stuck with it forever. He said the doctor called it a memento so that he'd never forget."

"That's horrible," Alex whispers. I look at Addie, expecting her to say something, but she isn't looking at me. She's picked her head up from Camari's shoulder and is staring at her, something akin to horror on her face.

"Camari," she whispers, her voice cracking. Camari returns her stare, shaking her head slightly.

"What's going on?" I ask, looking between them in confusion. Addie opens her mouth, but Camari beats her to it.

"Nothing, we just need to talk for a moment. Excuse us, please," she says quickly. Then she is up, grabbing Addie's hand and pulling her from the cell. Alex and I look after them, Alex looking unsure whether he should follow or not.

"What's that about?" I muse, watching as they stop several yards down the hall and begin to speak in hushed tones, Addie looking at Camari with this strange look, a combination of anger and sorrow.

"Women," Alex says, shaking his head. I can't help but agree.

There is no curing or isolating it. It is not of this world.

—Recovered Anonymous Correspondence

Chapter Sixty-One

Camari

I drag Addie out of the cell without another word, pulling her down the hallway and not letting go until I am sure we're out of earshot. Only then do I release her, crossing my arms over my chest. She steps in front of me, her eyes shining with a mixture of anger and grief.

"'I hope your memento will remind you to do just that?' That's what the doctor said to you this morning, and you flinched. Where is it?"

"Addie, please, you need-"

"Where is it?" she repeats, her voice breaking again. I swallow against a lump in my throat, blinking as my eyes begin to burn. I lift my left arm between us and tug back my sleeve, revealing the numbers. 4567 in dark, bold letters, marring the scalsen on my wrist permanently.

A tear falls from Addie's eye as she looks at it. I pull my arm back quickly, tugging my sleeve down to hide it.

"Camari, how could they?" she whispers, another tear joining the first.

"It's not that bad, Addie," I reply, hating how my voice breaks. "It's just a tattoo."

"You and I both know that if that was just a tattoo, you wouldn't be hiding it," she says. And, of course, she's right. It isn't just a tattoo. Nothing is just anything in this facility.

"Addie, I'm begging you, please don't tell Aiden or Alex. Please!" I ask imploringly, taking her hands in mine and squeezing them. She looks unsure, but she nods, taking her hands away to wipe the tears from her two-toned skin.

"Okay," she whispers, meeting my eyes and nodding. I exhale in relief, a weight lifting off of my chest as she promises.

"Thank you." I breathe. Addie simply nods, turning and leading the way back to the cell. I follow after her, smoothing my face and hiding any betraying emotions behind a mask.

Aiden and Alex look up at us as we enter the cell, clearly puzzled by our behavior. Alex's eyes catch on the dampness on Addie's cheeks and narrow, immediately turning to me accusingly. Addie shakes her head at him, taking a seat on the cot beside me and leaning her head on my shoulder again.

"Everything okay?" Aiden asks cautiously, his eyes searching my face. I keep my mask intact, nodding.

"Yes. Now, you've told us we might have trust-worthy allies in the facility, but we still don't have a plan for escape. When do we meet with these people, and what are you not telling me?" I ask, raising an eyebrow at him. Addie snorts slightly, probably thinking it's funny me to ask what he is hiding when I am hiding something as well. I jar my shoulder, sending a clear message.

You promised.

Addie's hand finds mine, and she squeezes it, sending her own message.

And I'll keep it.

Aiden looks at both of us questioningly but shakes his head slightly, deeming it unimportant. "I'm not keeping anything; I just haven't gotten to that part yet," he says, taking a deep breath. Unease floods my veins at his expression.

"What is it, Aiden?" I ask, my voice coming out quiet. He exchanges a glance with Alex, who looks just as cautious as him, before looking back at me.

"Last Beis, my men visited me."

"Grant and Miller? Morris? Are they okay?" I ask, smiling as I think of Grant and his accent, Miller and his sternness. But Aiden isn't smiling.

"They're fine, but they brought some bad news. Aldred is kicking his seer hunt up a notch."

The cell seems to suddenly be very quiet. "How so?"

"He's going to start searching non-seer villages. And we all know what it means when Aldred 'searches a village'."

A rushing noise fills my ears and I flash back to the classroom the night of last Dhá.

I saw armies. They were burning people, killing them.

The king. He was killing everyone.

"Tina knew." I breathe, staring at the floor. I'm vaguely aware of Addie lifting her head from my shoulder, of Aiden asking me what I mean.

He was killing everyone. Everyone.

"She knew what was going to happen. She bloody knew, and she told me!" I shout, standing up. "But I forgot because I went and got myself locked up with a doctor that likes to 'play!' I could have done something!"

My anger is white-hot, rushing in my ears and turning my vision red. Aiden stands up and puts his hand on my shoulder, looking me in the eyes.

"There was nothing you could have done to warn us sooner, Camari. Tina had her vision on Dhá? Well, Morris and the guys told me about this on the previous Beis. There's nothing you could have done, and there's nothing we can do until we get out of here. Morris said Aldred won't be moving out for another nine weeks. We have time to figure this out, so calm down, and we'll figure this out."

Aiden's logic and calm help cool my rage, and the rushing in my ears fades. I take a deep breath, nod and sit back down. Aiden sits back down as well, taking a deep breath before continuing.

"I can talk to Jax tomorrow and arrange a meeting with his group, and after that, we will move forward with how to get out of here. One step at a time."

"That sounds good to me, but I want to include Tristan," I say distantly, picking at my cuticles so I can avoid meeting his gaze.

"What?" Aiden exclaims, startling me. "You've got to be joking."

"Why on earth would we help him?" Alex objects, crossing his arms.

"He wants out of here just as much as we do, and I think we can trust him," I say over their exclamations. "And he has lost the only person he had."

"We cannot trust him; he'll betray us the first chance he gets!" Aiden argues, annoyance is visible in the set of his shoulders.

"He won't betray me; I'm pretty sure he's started to…care for me," I say, flushing. Jealousy sparks in Aiden's eyes for just a moment, but he pushes it away so quickly that I'm not sure whether or not I just imagined it.

"He'll betray us immediately. He hates me, and the feeling is mutual." Aiden snaps, leaning back and crossing his arms. His sleeves ride up, and I notice fresh bruises on his arm and a heaviness fills my heart. He's getting attacked so often that he's stopped telling me about them completely.

"Aiden, Tristan deserves a chance to get out of here just as much as we do." I say softly, speaking in a gentler tone. "Everyone does."

Aiden groans, resting his face in his hands, and I know I've won.

"Fine, Tristan can come," he says through gritted teeth. I smile, relieved. I don't like Tristan, but I can't just leave him behind. I don't want to leave anyone behind.

"Alright, let's all return to our cells and meet up again on Seach after chapel since we'll be working all day tomorrow," Aiden says, standing up and popping his neck before gesturing for Addie and me to exit first.

Aiden and I wait for a few minutes with Alex so that it looks less suspicious to the guards we'll pass. Aiden and Alex exchange another look before both of them turn to face me simultaneously, crossing their arms.

"What were you and Addie talking about, and why was she crying?" Alex demands. Aiden winces at his tone, placing a hand on his shoulder.

"What he means to say is, what is going on?"

I bristle, crossing my arms. "It was a private conversation, and it's fine now."

"It is not! You made Addie cry!" Alex snaps, still angry.

"No, I didn't!" I retorted, equally angry now, "We were just talking about a subject that she didn't like!"

"What subject?" Aiden asks, frowning heavily. I pause for a second, trying to think of a way to explain to them without telling them about my tattoo. But every explanation I come up with leads to more questions that will eventually out my 'memento.' And that is the last thing I want.

"Look," I say, staring at Alex, "if you want to know, just ask Addie." I know she won't tell, which will shut Alex up. Some questions are better left un-answered.

I turn, spinning on my heel, and begin to walk down the hall. I hear Aiden say a few more words to Alex before he jogs down the hallway after me to catch up, slowing to a walk when he reaches my side. We walk in silence, the only noise being that of our steps on the stone floors.

"He doesn't mean any harm," Aiden says quietly, breaking the silence. "I'd act the same way if the roles were reversed."

"He needs to mind his business!" I snap back, tugging at the sleeve of my shirt self-consciously.

"Why can't you tell me what it is you and Addie were talking about?"

"Because it doesn't concern you!"

"But it does." Aiden steps in front of me, cutting me off. "If it concerns you, then it concerns me too."

In any other circumstance, his words would be sweet, maybe even flattering, but not at this moment, not when the tattoo is still in the forefront of my mind.

"Aiden, the moment I deem it important, I will tell you, okay? But for now, I just need to not think about it," I say, my voice dropping as I speak. Aiden's eyes search mine for a moment before he fi-nally nods, stepping to the side so that I can pass. I begin to walk again and he falls in beside me, this time remaining silent.

I step into a cell and take a deep breath, relieved to be back. Then I snort a laugh, shaking my head. I'm happy to be locked up in a small cell with Aiden all night. Solitary confinement has made it seem like a gift.

"Look who's back."

I spin around, smiling, when I find Tristan sitting on his cell's floor, reclined with his legs extended in front of him and crossed at the ankle. I sit down on my cot, listening as it squeaks beneath me. "Yep, my vacation is over."

"Oh yes, being locked up for two days is a vacation. I'm kind of glad I haven't had the chance to go on one then," Tristan says with a wry twist of his mouth. I roll my eyes, sagging back on my cot. Aiden sits down on his cot and watches our exchange with mild interest. Tristan juts his chin out in the direction of Aiden, his voice coming out bitter. "I see you found your puppy again."

Aiden scowls, raising his right hand and giving him a rude gesture. Tristan simply returns the gesture. I roll my eyes at them, already sick of their bickering.

"And on that note, I'm going to bed," I say dramatically, lying down and pulling my covers to my chin.

"What happened to sleeping without a shirt?" Tristan asks.

"Watch it!" Aiden growls at him.

"It's just a question!" Tristan snaps back.

"I'm cold, that's all. Good night," I say firmly, rolling over so that my back is to them. I can feel their stares burning into my neck the entire time I lie there until I fall asleep.

Two days later, Addie has kept her promise. No one knows about my tattoo; no one looks at me in disgust and pity. I plan to keep it that way.

On Seach, we're woken up an hour earlier than usual. Seach is a holy day. Well, it would be a holy day if I could go to an actual monastery. The services we're forced to attend in the facility are little more than jokes, just excuses to talk about the disgusting creatures that are seers.

I jolt awake as the guard unlocks our door, leaving it open before walking to the next one. The light outside is a pale gray as the sun begins to slowly rise. I groan, sitting up and rubbing my eyes with the heels of my palms before I shove my hair out of my face and stand up. Aiden is already up, stretching with a groan and popping his shoulder. I tear my gaze away from his bare chest, though not before I see the bruises marring it, the lacerations on his ribs, and am filled with a surge of pity. Thankfully, he pulls his shirt back on and I loosen the leash on my self-control back to its previous length, my face burning. I've been sleeping with my shirt on for the past two nights, and it is miserable. The fabric is unbearably scratchy and chafes wherever it touches my skin. I can barely fall asleep, and I wake up if I roll over in my sleep, the fabric scratches me more. But it's a better alternative than letting my tattoo be seen.

Over the past two days, the skin on my left wrist has gone from sore and achy to purple and bruised to irritated and itchy. Now, it is finally returning to normal, the puffing and irritation having gone away at long last.

I stretch my arms over my head, popping my lower back and relieving an ache there. "Why do we have to attend these idiotic services?"

"Because we don't have the option of not going." Aiden points out, shoving his hair out of his face and scratching the stubble that will soon be gone. Oh yes, we seers are forced to be groomed before we can enter the monastery. Every Seach is the same humiliating process. The guards will take us in groups to the room that I was first taken to upon my arrival. Many other women and I will have to put up with people pouring icy water over our heads, shoving us back into our old clothing, brushing our hair so roughly that they yank out half of it, and many other things. I imagine it is what cattle feel like as they're lined up for slaughter, but then, we are nothing more than animals to them. I'm not sure how it goes for the men, but I do know that whenever Aiden comes out, he is freshly shaven and his hair has been trimmed back to the shorter length it was when we met, making him look younger. Not that I've noticed.

After this Seach's version of abuse, I am in line with the other seers as we file into the monastery. The guards and workers of the facility are allowed seats for the three-hour service. Seers are not. We all stand in the back or along the sides of the large room, shifting from foot to foot and waiting for the service to be over.

The monastery is a huge room but extremely plain. Dark stonewalls with a few blandly colored tapestries depicting the favored gods of the priest, candles lighting the room and casting shadows, a few windows at the front of the church that let in sunlight, and a large wooden table at the front of the monastery where the priest stands to give his sermon and offers his weekly sacrifice to the gods. I miss the monastery back in Krakent; it was a work of art where you immediately felt a connection with the gods as soon as you walked through the doors. This is just a room. A bleak, dark room. The stone is darker and older than the rest of the facility, and I've deduced that this 'monastery' was here before the facility was built, and the facility was added on room by room. Not that that fact helps us in any way, but counting the stones helps pass the hours.

I stand in the back with Alex, Addie, Aiden, and Molly, the little girl balanced on my hip. If the guards look, I'll have to put her down, but they never look, not unless there is a noise or a racket. And there never is; we make sure of that.

Tristan stands a foot or two away from me, sticking by me without being 'part of the group.' He's made it clear he wants nothing to do with Aiden. We'll see how long he keeps that idea when I offer him a chance out of the facility if he helps us.

The first hour of the service passes with us chanting prayers and hymns, each duller than the first. I stifle another yawn, shifting Molly on my hip. She's fallen asleep, the steady chanting knocking her out like a light. And gods, has the kid gotten heavy. I shift her again, my legs aching. I don't want to wake her up and put her down, but an hour of holding her while just standing here has taken its toll on my already weak limbs.

"Give her to me," Aiden says quietly in my ear. I smile at him gratefully, carefully handing the sleeping child to him. She stirs slightly before falling asleep again, her head on his shoulder and her hair in her face. Aiden is gentle with her, holding her against his chest with care and rubbing small circles on her back, possibly without realizing he is doing it. I smile again, this time to myself. Moments like that reveal his true character. And are thawing me to him once more.

My arms now free, I shift my weight from foot to foot and watch as the priest finishes up his last prayer. Next comes the moment we all hate: the sermon.

"Good morning, brothers and sisters!" he calls out, projecting his voice powerfully. All of the gathered guards and workers echo back, "Good morning."

The seers do not.

"And what a beautiful morning it is! The autumn chill has gotten stronger and brought hints of the coming winter with it, chilling our bones but warming our hearts."

I roll my eyes at his metaphors. Tristan catches my eye and does the same, shaking his head at the priest with a look of disgust.

"Today, I would like to talk about corruption, a subject the gods have told me to broach. As we all know, corruption is a living, breathing thing, just waiting to sink its fangs into any unsuspecting and innocent heart, which is why what is done here is so marvelous. What you people do is take in the corrupted and ill, and you heal them."

Now, it is Aiden who is scowling, probably angry about the lies being spewed.

"And the sad thing is, these people don't even know they're corrupted. They speak blasphemy to the gods, saying it was the gods that gave them their abilities when it was really the Disrupters. They do things only the gods should be able to do, and they claim they do it naturally. They claim it is a gift they are given." At this part the priest breaks off and slams his hands down on the wooden table in front of him, the boom echoing and making several people flinch. "They are not a gift!"

His shout echoes throughout the cavernous room, making Molly stir slightly.

"They are a curse! A horrible, filthy curse that you must pray to be rid of! And we must do all that we can to help these poor, ignorant human beings find the light."

I look over at Aiden, Alex, and Addie, at Molly, still sound asleep in Aiden's arms, and even at Tristan, scowling at the priest with distaste. We've already found the light. But maybe we will do what the priest recommends because he is right about one thing. We need to help others find the light as well.

R.C. Huye

The earth whispers its secrets to its inhabitants, and if they are clever enough to listen, then they will never lack answers to their questions.

–The Magical, Mythical, and Mudande: Folklore of Zorda

Chapter Sixty-Two

Aiden

Camari is hiding something. I don't know what it is, but I know, I feel it in my bones. Her conversation with Addie, the way she continually tugs on her left sleeve, a newly developed nervous tic. How whenever anyone calls her 4567 she flinches as if she's been struck. I notice all of this and more, but I don't ask her about it. Asking her about it might just push her even further away, and she is already distant.

It is Ayone, and our classes have just ended. I think it is ridiculous that I am forced to sit through the lessons as well; I'm not exactly a seer. But I am also grateful because it means I can keep an eye on my friends most of the time.

I spot Jax standing by himself a few feet away and immediately start heading towards him, making sure my steps look casual, as if I am just moving about to stretch my legs. I know he sees me coming because he immediately relaxes, trying to make himself look casual. I stop behind him, making sure my back is turned to him.

"We want to meet you and yours as soon as possible. After that, we'll decide what we do next," I say quietly, keeping my mouth from moving too much.

"Tonight."

"Where and when?"

"For tonight? My cell in fifteen minutes. I'm two cell blocks down from you, third cell on the left."

"See you there," I say shortly before walking back the way I came, keeping my steps light and casual despite how much I want to run and grab everybody. I reach Alex first and tell him what is going on. He nods once, saying he will inform Addie. Then I go and find Camari. She is sitting at the table with Molly, picking at some sort of dried fish and bread. She looks up from forcing Molly to eat a bite of fish, her own face skinnier than it should be. I sit down across from them, getting a piece of bread and forcing it down despite how dry it is.

"Jax's cell, ten minutes," I say as soon as I've swallowed it. She nods subtly and I stand and leave, walking out of the classroom. I go down the hallway and check to make sure there are no guards near before I stop and lean against the wall, waiting. Two minutes later, Camari appears with Alex behind her. We don't risk words; I simply stand from the wall and lead the way to Jax's cell, praying silently to any god, listening that he isn't about to betray us. Every time we near a hallway that we know has stationed guards, we separate, going by one at a time and waiting for the others before continuing. This caution makes us a few minutes late, but when we all file into Jax's cell, he is the only one there. He stands when he sees us, eyes flitting from one to the other as he scans each of our faces and assures himself of who we are. His eyes linger on Camari, and I resist the urge to step in front of her, to shield her.

"You're the one that was taken to solitary confinement." He doesn't ask but rather states it like a fact. Camari nods, holding his gaze.

"Did you get it too?" Jax asks quietly, his eyes, which are a light shade of orange, filled with compassion. Camari's eyes shut the way they do when she is shutting herself off from everyone.

"What does he mean?" I ask, looking between them. Does he know what she is hiding?

"I have no idea," Camari replies coolly, never lifting her gaze from Jax's. They stare at each other, and the silence grows heavy. Finally, Camari looks away, crossing her arms over her chest and adjusting her shirt's sleeve. Jax looks back at me, his face devoid of any answers about whatever the hell just happened.

"The others will be here any minute."

"How many are there in total besides you?" I ask, frowning. I hope to meet them all at once.

"Two. We're currently working on finding other ways to meet and communicate," Jax explains, scratching at his scalp.

"Just two? Not an outstanding number." I frown, disappointed.

THE CURSE OF THE BLESSED

"If we play our cards logically, our numbers will grow." Jax counters, sitting back down on his cot with his arms crossed. I'm stopped from replying by the sound of footsteps. All of us are immediately on our feet, ready to fight or flee, just in case. In walks a seer, making the already crowded cell an even tighter fit. He looks at us five in hostility as he files in, going to stand beside Jax rather than us. He even looks at Addie suspiciously, something I find completely unnecessary, and then stares at Camari coldly, his black eyes and tall nose giving him a hawkish appearance.

"This is a serious discussion, not a place for children," he says, jutting his chin out in Addie's direction. To her credit, Addie meets his stare without shrinking away. Camari does as well, her dark eyes cold as ice.

"Then why are you here?" she asks coldly, slowly stepping in front of Addie. The man scowls at her, annoyance flashing across his face. Alex coughs into his elbow, a move I suspect he used to hide his grin. I'm having trouble hiding my own, and I'm not the only one.

Jax stands up from his cot, his eyes giving away his grim expression as they glow with amusement. "Well, as lovely as this is, let's get to it. This is Isaiah." We introduce ourselves as well, though Camari and Isaiah don't stop glaring at each other the entire time.

What a great start to our alliance.

Jax seems to have the same thought, looking between Camari and Isaiah with annoyance on his face.

"We're missing one," Alex says, also glaring at Isaiah.

"Rob is on his way," Isaiah replies, his voice laced with annoyance. Sure enough, footsteps once again echo down the stone hall, alerting us of another's presence. Seconds later, another man walks in wearing a guard's uniform.

"You!" Camari gasps, fear crossing her face. The man looks at Camari, blinking in surprise. I step in front of her, glaring at both him and Jax.

"You said we could trust you." I spit, mentally calculating the best way out of the cell. Jax raises his hands, gesturing for us to calm down.

"Relax. Rob is on our side. I probably should have warned you ahead of time that a guard was coming."

"You think?" Alex snaps, still glaring at Rob. Rob, to his credit, only blinks at him, once again turning and looking at Camari.

"I am so sorry for what they did to you. I couldn't help you; that would have blown my cover," he says, his voice weighed down with guilt. Camari is still staring at him, traces of fear visible in her eyes. What does he mean; who did what to her?

"Hold on, you were one of the guards in solitary confinement?" I ask, trying to make sense of the jumbled mess everything is. Rob nods, sticking his hands into the pockets of his uniform.

"I got placed there two moons ago. It's horrible. I can do nothing but watch as they do disgusting things to helpless people. Most of them are lucky and don't get a tattoo, but there are a few that the wardens decide need a more permanent lesson. They don't get off so lucky. And then there are the rewriting sessions…"

I can't keep my eyes from straying to Jax, to where I know his tattoo is on his shoulder underneath his shirt. How many others have those tattoos? How many others have been branded? I sincerely hope I will never find out and am grateful it didn't happen to any of my friends, to Camari.

"You said we were meeting with more potential allies; you didn't mention the royal assassin is one of them!" Isaiah hisses, looking at me in distrust. I return the look, sizing him up. I do not like this man.

"He is a potential ally, him and his friends here," Jax says, looking weary already.

"He's the reason half of us are in here in the first place!"

"And I'm doing my best to right that wrong." I interrupt. Isaiah snorts, making my fists itch to punch him in the face just once. Camari elbows me gently just once, almost as if she knows what I am tempted to do.

"Now that everyone is here, I have some questions," I say, changing the subject. Jax nods, gesturing for me to go ahead.

"You approached me saying you wanted our help to get out of here. Do you have any idea just how to accomplish that?" I inquire, asking what I think is the most important question.

"We're going to use the monastery," Rob says. I exchange confused looks with Camari, Addie and Alex.

"What do you mean, use the monastery?" Addie finally asks.

"It has passages, tunnels that I only know about by accident. We can use those to get out unnoticed."

"Why would they have built tunnels in the facility?" Alex asks, still looking confused. Rob opens his mouth to reply but Camari cuts him off, surprising all of us.

"Because the monastery isn't part of the facility, is it? It was built years before, and the facility was just added on."

Rob nods, looking surprised that Camari knows this. He's not the only one. I look at Camari questioningly, and she shrugs.

"I noticed the stone is older and has a different shade and texture. It is different altogether, which led me to realize the monastery was built first," she explains. Alex snorts, and Addie rolls her eyes, shaking her head with a small smile on her face. Leave it to Camari to notice that kind of thing.

"The monastery was built during the time of the persecution when priests and worshippers were being slaughtered for their faith and loyalty to the gods. Most monasteries and sanctuaries built back then had secret tunnels or passages so that the priests could easily escape if they needed to. This monastery is one of them, and I don't think many know that."

"Let's hope so because otherwise we're stuck here," Jax grumbles.

"What charming positivity," Alex comments dryly. I frown as I try to calculate just how we'll pull this off and what we will need.

"There's no way all of the seers can get to those passages without attracting attention. We'll need to cause a distraction of some sort and we will also need weapons so that we can defend ourselves. How-"

"What are you talking about? We're not saving all of the seers; we're just saving us!" Isaiah interrupts loudly. I turn a confused look on Jax, who has the decency to look guilty.

"We can't leave without getting as many people out as we can," Addie interjects, looking horrified at the idea.

"There are two thousand, four hundred and fifty-two seers currently in this facility; we can't possibly get them all out," Isaiah says, rising off of the wall he was leaning against.

"You'd rather leave them here to die without even trying?" Camari asks angrily, her dark eyes flashing.

"Look who's talking!" Isaiah replies, looking just as angry. "You're partners with the man who stuck us all in here in the first place!"

"Aiden is twenty-two years old; this facility has been around for centuries. He didn't put every seer in here unless he's somehow immortal and that's another thing he's failed to mention to me." Camari scoffs, rolling her eyes at Isaiah.

"It doesn't matter anyway. How do you know every seer here is going to die?" Isaiah snaps, looking ruffled by her insult. At this, both Jax and Camari get a distant look in their eyes.

"For most of them, it might be better that they are killed. Rather than what they will be forced to face,"

Jax says quietly, his voice raspy. Isaiah has the decency of looking guilty, and Camari's face slowly returns to the present, much to my relief.

"If we have a chance of getting out of here, we need to give others that chance as well," she says quietly. The room is silent for several seconds, and we simply watch Jax, knowing the final decision will come from him. If he doesn't agree, I figure we can just work by ourselves with the information they've given us. Whatever it takes.

Jax finally looks up at us, his face heavy. "Fine. We get everyone else out too. It's not like we don't have a big enough stash."

Camari grins, her eyes lighting up and knocking the air out of me. Even Isaiah's scowl lessens slightly.

"But," Jax says suddenly, making our smiles fade, "if we find out that for some reason we can't get everyone out, then that's it. I'm gone, with or without you."

In the army, there were opportunities to make allies out of your enemies. Now we just kill them.

—Field Journal of Aiden Lorian

Chapter Sixty-Three

Camari

I do not like Isaiah. He is smug, arrogant, rude, and cold-hearted. And a small part of him reminds me of my father.

An elbow to my side courtesy of Aiden brings me back to the present, though I return the jab anyway. Jax is speaking, explaining a basic plan that we can build off of.

"-Need weapons. That's where Rob comes in. On the day of our escape, we will raid the barracks."

"They have a barracks in a prison?" Aiden asks doubtfully. "That doesn't seem very wise."

"It's over two thousand seers and less than five hundred guards. No one is supposed to know about the barracks, and it's there just in case the seers revolt. Not that they expect us to fight back. The seers cower under their power, and they now believe we hold no threat."

"I look forward to changing their minds," Alex says with a grin.

"Where is the barracks?" Aiden asks before the conversation goes too far off-topic.

"A few hallways down from our cell block, basically in its own vicinity," Rob says, rubbing his face and appearing tired. That will make it harder to reach.

"Are there enough weapons in there for all of us?" Addie asks, surprising me. She isn't one for weapons or shows of force of any nature.

"It's a glorified stronghold. Yes, there will be more than enough," Rob says.

"That leaves supplies, seers, and a distraction," Alex says, counting off of his fingers. "Anyone got any ideas?"

"Getting more seers on board will be far trickier than the other two issues. We could talk to someone only for them to turn around and turn us in." I sigh, pinching the bridge of my nose.

"You risked it with me," Aiden says to Jax, shifting his weight from foot to foot.

"That was a calculated risk. I saw you and your group talking when you thought no one was listening, and I noticed the way you look at that one," Jax explained, nodding at me. Pink stains Aiden's cheeks, something I find oddly adorable, and he doesn't look at me despite how I turn and stare at him, instead continuing to stare at Jax as he speaks. "Plus, I saw how often you were getting beaten up and still are. I figured you have the appearance of a man who would do anything to get out of here. You have the appearance of someone who has somewhere to be, something to do. So, a calculated risk."

"A risk nonetheless," Isaiah mutters. I shoot another glare at him, only to receive another elbowing from Aiden. I turn my glare on him, and he returns it.

"We can't afford more enemies!" he hisses under his breath so that only I can hear. I know he's right, but I can't resist muttering, "he started it."

A smile tugs at the corner of his mouth, but he pushes it away. "Then be the bigger person and end it."

Once again, he's right. I don't mind him being right; I just mind it being at my expense. But I make a mental effort to avoid sending any more scowls in Isaiah's direction. But if he says one more thing that rubs me the wrong way...

"What's the least risky way of going about recruiting more?" Alex asks, glancing over at Addie.

"Every time we talk to a person, it will have some level of risk, lad, that's inevitable," Jax replies, shaking his head.

"What if we focus on observing different seers this week, maybe see if we notice any that, I don't know, act like us or something," I say, stumbling over the last part. "Besides," I continue quickly, "I already have someone."

Jax looks up in interest while Aiden scowls, crossing his arms and looking away from us both.

"Who?"

"4494. His name is Tristan and he occupies the cell next to ours."

"And you think he can be trusted?" Jax asks intensely, his eyes boring into mine.

"Yes," I reply, pushing past my hesitation. He can be, I know it. Aiden snorts, rolling his eyes. Jax turns to look at him with raised eyebrows.

"But you don't?"

"Not by a long shot," Aiden replies, ignoring my glare. "His loyalty is to himself and possibly Camari, no one else."

"Exactly, he's loyal to me. That means he won't betray me!" I argue, angry that he would undermine me like this.

"Why is he loyal to you?" Jax asks me, looking confused.

"Because I helped his friend with something important," I say at the same time that Aiden scoffs, "Because he fancies himself in love with her."

Almost everyone immediately begins to look uncomfortable, Addie looking away hastily, Alex coughing into his elbow and averting his eyes. Even Jax looks slightly uncomfortable, which I didn't think was possible for him.

"He is not in love with me," I tell Aiden angrily, flushing despite my efforts to stay calm.

"You're right, he's not. But he thinks he is, and that's enough to make him do something stupid," Aiden replies with a forced calm that I see through, finding the anger underneath.

"That makes no sense!" I spit, ready to hit him. Aiden opens his mouth to reply, anger finally showing on his face, but Isaiah cuts him off.

"Take your stupid lover spat somewhere else and let us get back to the matters at hand," he says dismissively, speaking in an oh-so-holier-than-thou voice. I bristle even more, turning towards him with fists ready to punch. Aiden, quickly forgetting our argument, steps between Isaiah and I quickly.

"We can meet again in a day or two, but for now, let's look for trustable seers and try to recruit more," Jax says firmly, effectively ending our argument. Aiden nods, and just like that, our meeting comes to an end.

Seach comes around, and I have a plan. Granted, it's a stupid and dangerous plan, but at least it's a plan. I'm going to sneak out of the service and look for the tunnels. Rob told me they were in the monastery somewhere behind the altar. After that, it's just a guessing game. The thing is, there's a partial wall behind the altar that conceals what Rob says is the priest's quarters and the preparation rooms. And of course, the tunnels are in the priest's quarters.

I haven't mentioned my plan to anyone else yet, I figure if I get caught, I don't want to incriminate any of them. Besides, Aiden would be angry and try to talk me out of it, Alex would call me crazy, Addie would be anxious, and Jax would…I don't know, but I'm not willing to take the risk. This is something that has to happen, and if something happens to me, the revolution can still happen. If something happens to

Aiden or Jax, we're screwed. So, to put it frankly, I'm expendable.

I get in line with the seers heading into the monastery, spotting Aiden's head a few places in front of me, his hair freshly trimmed. He's far less bruised and bloody than usual, and that's all due to one thing: two more seers were caught having visions this week. Two more seers were dragged away, screaming about fire and blood and death, their screams cutting off as soon as the doors closed. One of those seers had a lover here in the facility with them, and that lover threw themselves down the stairs the next morning; poor Alex was in the cellblock that was being led to their classroom at the moment she fell and saw everything. He didn't speak much that day. And now, everyone is paranoid of having a vision and being turned in. Because of this, we're all avoiding each other like the plague, turning and running the other way if approached. The problem with that is we haven't been able to enact our plan of approaching seers about our escape because whenever we try, they flee. It was a bad idea in the first place, maybe even a stupid one, but it was all we had, and now it too is gone. But at least Aiden doesn't keep returning to our cell bloodied and bruised. It hurts my heart to see him in such a shape, still unwilling to truly fight back. I am slightly haunted by the woman who killed herself, by all the pain she must have experienced, and I am horrified by the two seers that were taken away for their visions, but I will never be unhappy that Aiden is no longer wounded constantly.

"Ready for three hours of misery?" I ask when I finally catch up with him, ignoring the glares I get from the people I elbowed past

"It won't be too miserable," he says, smiling over at me. I flush as red as my hair, ducking my head and tugging on my sleeve.

"Should we try to approach anyone while we're here?" I ask, changing the subject. Aiden scowls, his eyes darkening.

"No. Everyone is too afraid of being taken away; they might make a scene. The last thing we want is to draw attention to ourselves."

Especially today.

I remain silent as we walk into the monastery, standing in a large crowd against the back wall and watching as the officers and workers take their seats while a few guards stay standing to watch us, though not very attentively. A few minutes later, the priest makes his entrance and the chanting begins. Only the seers that have been successfully brainwashed chant with the workers, smiling and looking at the priest with something akin to awe. It makes me sick.

Aiden is a few places over from me, with Jax beside him. Tristan is behind me, huffing sighs every few minutes. I need all three of them to be distracted while I sneak out, otherwise they'll follow and cause a scene. One is stealthy, maybe two, but four is a distraction. If I wanted a distraction, I would just fake another vision. I'm pretty damn good at that.

An hour passes and I shift anxiously from foot to foot, watching as the chanting ends and the sermon begins. Aiden and Jax are conferring quietly, but I can still feel Tristan's attention on the back of my neck. I need something to distract him for just sixty seconds! The priest's sermons last around forty-five minutes, and then there's thirty minutes of praying, and then worship is over. I need time to search for the tunnels because I have absolutely no idea where they are. And Tristan is ruining everything!

More time passes, and I look around casually for something, anything that might serve as a distraction, when suddenly the gods smile upon me. One of Tristan's acquaintances, Derek, comes quietly to stand next to him, and they start a whispered conversation that I can barely hear. I wait several minutes so that I'm sure they're deep into their conversation before I slowly take a step to the side. No one notices a thing. I continue to sidle to the side, waiting for someone to say my name. No one does. Giving up any pretense of going slow, I begin to carefully walk through the crowd of seers; stopping whenever I think a guard is looking my way. A few minutes later, I make it to the wall and begin to squeeze through the thin rows of seers. A few of them glare at me or give me sideways glances, but most ignore me. And then, with one quick set of steps, I'm behind the partial wall and in the concealed area.

I can still hear the priest prattling on and do my best to listen so that I know when my time is running out. I appear to be standing in a dark stone hallway with one open doorway on my right and one at the end of the hallway. Walking quietly, I enter the first room and look around. It's simple enough, with a wooden table littered with books, paper scraps, ink-wells, and quill nibs. There are two bookshelves on the left wall, filled with books and leaflets, papers falling off of the shelves in places. On the right wall is an iron bar that stretches across the wall. There are multiple priestly robes hanging upon it, varying in color and detail, with some embroidered with what appears to be real silver and gold. The far wall has a painting of King Aldred that gives me goosebumps when I first see it. I do my best to ignore it and begin to look around the room while being uncertain what I am looking for. I look under the table, rifling through the books and papers before carefully putting each back where it was. I pull out each book on both bookshelves before making sure I put those back where they go as well, checking each leaflet to see if they hold any important information. When that yields nothing, I do my best to pull the bookshelves out an inch or so and peer behind them but find nothing. Scowling, I push them back with a grunt and go to carefully rifle through the priest's robes, peering behind them and also finding nothing. Thirty minutes have passed and I'm beginning to feel anxious. After taking the painting off of the wall and checking behind it, I decide that there are no tunnels in the room and to move onto the next one. Hanging the painting while doing my best to avoid looking at it, I turn and walk back into the hallway, still listening to the service as it goes on, which is why I noticed the priest ending his sermon and starting the prayers. I take a deep breath and move quickly to the next room, my hands shaking slightly. I am running out of time.

The second room is roughly the same size as the previous one, with no windows. A small cot sits in the far corner of the left wall, neatly made. There's a small wooden bedside table beside it with holy scripts messily stacked on it and a half-full glass of water. Finally, there is a messy bookshelf on the right wall and beside it is a wardrobe that I assume holds the priest's personal clothing. Otherwise, it's strangely empty. I begin my search anyway, rifling through everything. I pull out each book before tucking them back in once more, groaning as they each reveal themselves to be useless. Once that proves fruitless, I check under and behind the bed, in the wardrobe, under it, and behind it. Nothing. Scowling to myself, I turn slowly and scan the room for anything I've missed. And my eyes catch on a stone on the empty portion of the wall below the foot of the bed. It's slightly lighter than the others, more worn, and I see a deep scratch or two on its surface. I approach the wall and touch the stone, feeling along the edges of it. It's definitely scratched on the edges and just appears older than the other stones. Bracing my hand against it, I push with all of my strength, digging my heels into the floor. Nothing. It doesn't budge a millimeter.

Frowning, I tilt my head and study it again, looking at the scratches on the sides. Maybe I've got it all wrong. Instead of pushing…

Doing my best to wrap my fingers around the edges, I dig in my fingertips and pull. It slides out as if it's been greased with butter, dropping heavily into my palm so that I almost drop it onto my foot. Setting it aside, I crouch down and peer into the square hole I've made, roughly five inches long on each side. Not seeing anything, I stand up and stick my free hand into the hole, feeling around cautiously. It goes up to my wrist before my fingers brush against something cold. Iron. I touch it again, tracing it to learn its shape. It's not just iron, no. I've found a latch.

I rotate my wrist, grip the latch, and pull as hard as I can, gritting my teeth. The latch moves. And the wall moves with it.

In front of me stands a doorway about six feet tall and three feet wide. Peering into it, I find a tunnel that goes on further than I can see, made of old stones similar to the monastery. I grin widely, my heart racing as I stare into the darkness.

I found the tunnels.

But then my smile disappears as I realize what I can hear. Nothing. The prayers are done, and I can hear shuffling feet as people rise from the pews and the seers are filed out. The priest will be coming any minute now.

Crap.

I quickly place my hands against the door and shove it back into place, grunting at the effort. Once that's in place, I slide the stone back into its hole, making sure it is uniform with the others. Taking one more quick scan of the room to make sure everything is as I found it, I turn and hurry towards the door. Only to run right back the way I went.

Footsteps echo down the stone hallway, only one set, and I duck into the wardrobe hastily, pulling it shut behind me and burrowing behind the rows of clothes. My breath echoes loudly in the wardrobe and my heart thuds loudly in my chest as I crouch, peering through the small crack in the door. The priest walks into the room, bedecked in his elegant robes that are so big they dwarf his small frame. He sits on the bed and begins to undress, pulling layers of purple fabric and white under robes off one by one. I shrink away from the crack, cursing myself in my head. I'm stuck in a wardrobe with a naked priest right outside who will kill me if he sees me.

Wonderful.

Whole minutes pass, and I finally gather the guts to peer out of the crack of the wardrobe, and to my immense relief, the priest is dressed in the clothes that were at the foot of his bed. I watch as he picks up the robes, folds them over his arm, and walks out of the room.

It's now or never.

I slowly crack the door open, stepping out and shutting it behind me. I walk quietly to the doorway and listen for a second, making sure no one else is coming. Once I'm sure, I take a deep breath and stick my head out just to be sure it's all clear, and step out of the room. And then I run.

I keep my footsteps as quiet as I can but run as fast as I can as well, holding my breath. I pass the doorway of the first room, go down the hall, and stop at the end of the partial wall, peering around the corner. I can still see the seers waiting in a huge group, slowly shuffling out. And the guards aren't looking, thank the gods. Taking another calming breath, I walk quickly and quietly towards the group, my hands shaking slightly as I join the edges and melt in with the other seers. I release a heavy breath, my heart stuttering still, and relax. I can't honestly believe I pulled that off.

A hand grips my elbow, and my heart jumps up my throat, racing with adrenaline as my lungs stop working.

"You sure know how to scare someone half to death!" Aiden's voice is harsh and quiet in my ear, and I sag against him, clutching my chest where my heart still races.

"Right back at you! I thought you were a guard!" I hiss, trying to still my quivering hands.

"And I had no idea what to think, because you just disappeared," Aiden growls angrily, tightening his grip on my elbow. I cast my gaze down, feeling guilty.

"If I told you what I was doing, you would have tried to stop me," I object weakly.

"Or I might have helped you with whatever it is you had to do, but you didn't give me the chance. I guess we'll never know now, will we?" he asks bitterly, releasing my elbow and moving away from me as we walk with the other seers. I'm flooded with even more guilt at that because I hadn't honestly considered him helping me. Why do I always assume the worst?

The gods know and see all. They alone can decree what is right and what is wrong. For a human to do so would be akin to stepping on the toes of the heavens.

—The Religious Texts: The Book of Heresy

Chapter Sixty-Four

Camari

Aiden and I walk into the facility, but I say nothing as he leads us away from the classroom. After a few minutes, I realize we're heading to Jax's cell, and I grimace. The last thing I want at this moment is to see Isaiah.

After checking for guards, we enter his cell and find everyone else is already there, including Tristan, who looks extremely uncomfortable and hostile. Probably not the best feeling for a secret meeting about escaping prison.

He appears relieved when he sees me, but then, so does everyone, and I'm reminded once again of my fight with Aiden. I smile at everyone and stand beside Aiden, but he goes over to stand beside Addie, leaving me with Tristan. I swallow and mask my face, shoving down any inconvenient emotions. Now is not the time.

"Well, look who's back. I'm gonna start calling you trouble, lass," Jax says, his deep voice tinged with amusement. I smile, pleased that someone appreciates what I've done. Tristan looks like he wants to yell at me, Alex seems annoyed and maybe slightly impressed, and Addie appears to be pissed off.

Wonderful.

"I kind of like that nickname," I admit, shoving my hands into my pockets and ducking my head. Alex snorts in laughter while Aiden rolls his eyes, but I ignore them both.

"What did you get for us? Anything useful, or did we all worry for nothing?" Isaiah growls from where he leans against the wall scowling at me.

"Aw, Isaiah, I didn't know you cared!" I croon, earning a glare of pure poison from him. "Yes, I did find something important. I found the tunnels."

Rob looks up eagerly from where he leans against the wall beside Isaiah, his face lighting up. "You found their exact location?"

"Opened the door and everything. They're pretty amazing and hidden really well. I barely found them," I say, shifting my weight from foot to foot.

"How do you get into them?" Jax asks, looking mildly interested despite the important subject we're speaking about.

"There's a small stone in the wall just past the foot of the bed of the priest in his private quarters. It's just barely lighter than the others and slightly more worn. Pull that out, stick your arm into the hole, and there's a metal latch. Pull the latch, and the whole wall swings out and opens the tunnels."

"Did you go in by yourself?" Alex asks, seeming even more surprised for some reason.

"No, I ran out of time," I explain, pretending to be regretful. To be honest, I didn't want to go in. After my stint in solitary confinement, locked up in the dark for two days straight, going into a pitch-black tunnel isn't very appealing. I'll just have to suck it up when the time comes to leave. Or maybe I can smuggle a torch.

"But now we know for sure that they exist and we can get to them relatively easily. I can try to go in and explore them tomorrow while the priest is out," Rob says excitedly, practically bouncing up and down.

"Good, our escape route is secure," Jax says, cutting right to the chase. "But we have other problems. Number one: how do we know whom we can trust? Watching seers is getting us nowhere; everyone is too distrustful."

"What if we've been going about this the wrong way?" Aiden cuts in, taking a step forward. All eyes turn to him.

"What do you mean?" Jax asks, frowning. "We've been trying to-"

"Watch for trustworthy seers, I know. But what if we're going about it the wrong way? I mean, think about it. I can tell you the name of almost every brainwashed seer in this facility, and that's just me. If we all work on the list together, we might be able to name all of them. Then all of the seers remaining will be the ones that most likely want to escape."

"Narrowing it down to the trustworthy," I say slowly, a smile spreading across my face. "That's brilliant!"

"But how do we keep the brainwashed away or incapacitated while we escape?" Rob asks, rubbing his face and looking tired.

"It's a simple matter of numbers. After we raid the barracks and go to the classrooms to get the others, we can overpower the weak and tie them up," Aiden explains.

"You would be the one that knows the most about tying up seers." Tristan scoffs. Aiden flinches slightly, small enough that I think I'm the only one that notices, but I notice. I see the grief in his eyes, and it's enough to set me on fire.

"Shut your mouth!" I spit, angry beyond reason. "For once, just keep your insults to yourself. We are trying to plan an escape for thousands of people, and if you let your pettiness get in the way, you won't be a part of it."

Tristan stares at me for several seconds. His blue eyes are shadowed, before he nods once and turns away, his hands clenched into fists at his sides. I do my best to ignore the rigid silence in the room and turn back to Aiden, who is watching me with bemusement in his eyes. At least he's no longer angry.

"I think that will work. Let's get started on the list now," I say quietly. Aiden nods, smiling slightly.

"Let's do it."

Twenty minutes later, we have what we think is the complete list, though we agree to keep an eye out for seers that aren't on the list. The total number of who we've begun to call traitor seers is eighty-seven. A sad number, especially when you know some of them. I personally know twelve of them, their names, ages, and more. And it hurts to know we'll have to leave them behind. But the needs of the many outweigh the few, and the amount of seers we will be saving is definitely many. Two thousand, four hundred, and thirteen seers. And we hope to save them all.

"Is that all of them?" Addie asks, bending over the list and reading it once more.

"I think so. If we think of more, we can always update it," Rob says, tucking away the list and his charcoal pencil into his pocket.

"When will we do this? I mean, really do this?" Tristan asks, looking resignedly interested.

"I think we should do it sooner rather than later, but we still have more we need to plan." I cut in, frowning. "What about next end of week? Seach?"

"That's soon, but I think we can do it. We just need to arrange teams, times, weapons, supplies, and where we go after we escape," Jax says dryly, ticking each item off on a finger.

"We can do it," I say firmly. "We don't have a choice if we want to get out before any more seers are taken. Rob can explore the tunnels tomorrow to determine where they lead, and he can also work on getting supplies into the tunnel for us to get on our way out. We can meet again on Trie to come up with final plans." I finish, looking around at everybody. One by one, everybody nods slowly.

"Well, there's no disguising who's in charge of this operation," Jax says good-naturedly, looking at Aiden and I with a smile. I grin at Aiden and he returns it, lifting his hand like he would to his fellow soldier. I clasp his hand, feeling light with elation and excitement. We are actually doing it. We're getting out.

But then Aiden's smile disappears and his grip on my hand tightens, bordering painful. He turns my wrist slowly, his eyes burning pools of anger, and my stomach turns. Everyone stares at my now visible tattoo, even Addie and Jax. I tremble slightly, my breath stuttering. The inked numbers on top of my scalsen seem to burn under everyone's attention, darker and more vibrant than ever before.

"What. Is. This?" Aiden growls, his voice shaking with barely contained rage. My breathing speeds up and I look from Addie, who looks afraid, to Jax, desperate for help. Jax meets my gaze, his orange eyes sorrowful. Alex is staring at my arm in bewilderment and disgust, Tristan is looking at me in horror, and basically everyone else is simply staring.

I force myself to look back at Aiden but immediately regret it when his eyes pin me to my spot, overflowing with rage.

"How long have you been hiding this?" he asks in a voice that is dangerously soft.

"Since solitary confinement," I whisper, hating how my hand is starting to shake. But he's so angry…

"I told you about Jax's tattoo just after that. You could have told us then. You could have told us! Instead you chose to hide it. Why is hiding always your go-to solution?" Aiden asks, his voice trembling with restraint.

"Oh, you mean like how lying is yours?" I shoot back, yanking my arm out of his grip and pulling my sleeve down over my tattoo. "I hid my tattoo from you, but at least I didn't lie about my identity."

"That's a weak deflection and you know it!" Aiden snarls, clenching his hands into fists. "Twice today, we've discovered a way you've been lying or keeping secrets. Why are you so scared to let someone in?"

"I don't need to, because I'm fine!" I snap, hating how everyone is staring at me. My eyes burn with tears and I dig my fingernails into my palms, refusing to cry in front of Isaiah.

"Look what they did to you! How can you possibly be fine with that?" Aiden shouts, his eyes burning and appearing slightly damp. Everyone stares; his words, my grief, they all combine together, and suddenly, I snap.

"I'm not fine! I hate it! But I can't get rid of it!" I scream back, hating the warm tears that start to stream down my face. "I didn't ask for it; I didn't ask to be branded like cattle!"

I can't take it, the way they're all staring at me like a broken dish that suddenly has no use.

I spin around and stalk out of the cell, keeping my face down when I pass the guards to hide my tears. Not that it matters; many seers here spend half of their time crying.

I stalk all the way to my cell and lie down on my cot, wrapping my hand around the tattoo over my sleeve and wishing I could just wash it away. But like everything that's happened in the past moons, I can't simply wash it away. That would be too easy.

The punishment for failure to carry out duties as is required will be the same as his responsibilities: his men.

—The Contract of Royal Assassin to King Aldred III

Chapter Sixty-Five

Aiden

My hands tremble with rage as I watch Camari turn and basically run out, pulling on her sleeve fiercely to hide her tattoo. Her tattoo.

I turn to Jax slowly, forcing myself to take slow, controlled breaths. "You knew." My voice comes out as barely more than a whisper as I put the pieces together.

"Everybody else out." Jax orders, holding my gaze with his orange eyes and standing from his cot. They obey and everyone files out, Alex and Rob casting glances at me as they leave. I stand there, staring at Jax, trying to decide if I should punch him. I want to. I *really* want to. Maybe I will.

"Yes I knew. As soon as she yelled at her doctor and spoke her mind I knew what was going to happen," Jax says, his jaw tight with anger. "They don't give these to everybody that goes to solitary confinement. They save the tattoos for the ones they know are the strongest, because usually that tattoo breaks them. You have no clue what it's like to have your name taken away, to have these damn numbers inked onto your skin for the rest of your miserable life. It is something that you can never live down; never leave behind."

"How could you not tell me when you knew what they'd done to her? I could have helped! I could have-"

"Jax wasn't the only one that knew, so don't take all of your anger out on him!" Addie's voice rings out in the cell, surprising me. I thought she left with the others, but I suppose she's usually so quiet that I just hadn't noticed her staying with us. I turn to her, and she's standing tall with anger gleaming in her brown eyes.

"You knew too?" I ask incredulously, struggling to understand. Was I the only one Camari didn't tell?

"Camari and I are in the same group. At our session right after she returned from solitary confinement, the doctor mentioned something about her memento serving her well, and Camari flinched. Later the same night, you told us about Jax's tattoo and how the man who gave it to him had called it a memento, and I put two and two together. That's why she pulled me out of the cell, that's why we argued. I saw the tattoo and she begged me to hide it from you," Addie explains, folding her arms over her stomach.

"Why specifically from me?" I ask, my voice raw. Does she not trust me at all?

Why should she?

"Gods above, you two are dense as wood!" Jax exclaims, raising his eyes to the heavens in exasperation. "She cares about you, you eejit, and she didn't want you to see that the doctor damaged her. Because while she isn't, she most likely believes that that tattoo damages her, that it makes her foul. And she doesn't want you to believe that as well."

"And the moment you found out-" Addie starts, only for Jax to interrupt her.

"You got angrier than I've ever seen you, yelled at her, and looked at her in disgust. So, whether you meant to or not, you proved all of her fears right. Feckin' eejit!"

I swallow hard, looking down at the ground as my anger fades. They're right. I reacted the opposite of how I should have. My mind flashes back to the moment I looked up from the tattoo and looked at her. The fear and hurt on her face makes my stomach turn.

"Shit." I breathe, rubbing my face with my hands and sighing. "I messed up."

"No shite." Jax snaps. "Go fix it now, or you won't get a second chance."

I nod curtly, turning and walking out of the cell as urgency fills me. I seem to have a knack for ruining things between the two of us just as they get good again. I won't do it again.

4567. Permanently engraved on her skin. I'm going to kill the doctor that sent her to solitary confinement, as well as the doctor that thought it was okay to ink her number onto her skin against her will. I'm going to kill them both. Slowly.

That thought comforts me as I walk towards my cell, figuring there aren't many places Camari can be. It is the facility after all, a glorified prison.

Sure enough, I see her red hair in our cell as I near, bright against her gray blanket as she lies curled up on her cot. I slow down as I near, taking a few steps into the cell before I stop in the doorway.

"Are you awake?" I ask lamely, searching for the right thing to say.

"Saying no will just defeat the purpose," she mumbles in reply, making me smile. She always has to get the last word, even to a fault.

I go and sit on the foot of her cot, wincing as it creaks under my added weight. She doesn't sit up, only moving to pull her legs up to her chest. I sit there in silence for several seconds and stare at her, unsure of how to apologize the right way. What if I just make it worse?

I take a deep breath and rake my fingers through my hair before gathering my guts and opening my mouth.

"So, despite the fact that every time I talk, I make things worse, I'm going to try and apologize to you without driving you so far away that you start bunking with Tristan. Though that would be a nightmare for both of us if we're being completely honest." I start, bouncing my knee restlessly. No response.

"I was already pissed at you for sneaking off and being reckless without telling me. And in the face of complete honesty, that had more to do with me than you, so I apologize for that. But, after we kind of fixed things as we were planning in Jax's bunk, I got so excited. I thought, 'I am actually going to get them out of here before they're all irreparably scarred.' I was so excited. After everything I've done, I will be able to right my wrongs finally and free everybody.

"But then I saw the tattoo on your wrist, and I just snapped, Camari. It seems that no matter what I do to prevent it, I cause you pain everywhere you go, and it *kills* me. So I saw what they did to you, realized just what it was, and I just snapped. Because what kind of a person can I be if every time I try to help, I just end up making things worse? I'm finally starting to come to peace with my past, and then something new happens that just makes me hate myself all over again. Don't get me wrong, I fully intend to kill both doctors that made this happen to you; they share a large part of the blame. But, it would be a lie to say I don't share some of it either. And that just kills me, because the last thing I want in the world is to hurt you. Yet I'm really damn good at it." I finish lamely, resting my face in my hands and sighing heavily. Another thing to add to the list of failures: apologizing. At this rate I'll be lucky if she's still even talking to me by next weekend.

I don't expect it when Camari pulls my hand away from my face and laces our fingers together, squeezing tightly.

"It's not your fault, and I'm pretty damn sick of you claiming everything that happens to me is. My life is not yours to live or protect, it's mine. I won't tell you this again so you better listen. What happens to me is not your fault, you hold none of the blame, and you need to forgive yourself, because everyone else worth having in your life already has," Camari says roughly, looking down at the floor as she speaks. "I will give you crap about it for the rest of our lives, and I'm still trying to move on from a few things, but even I've begun to forgive you. Let. It. Go."

I smile, chuckling at her commanding tone. "I'm trying. Are you okay?"

Her brave face falters and she shrugs, tugging one of her strands of hair. "No, but I will be once we get out of here. Once we leave this part of our lives behind."

I squeeze her hand, running my thumb back and forth against her skin. "We will get out, Camari. We will make it."

She falls silent for a moment, but I know something is coming, knowing her expressions, so I wait.

"I need to know," she says finally, still looking at the floor.

"Know what?" I ask slowly. She looks up at me, her dark eyes wide and so open, it hurts me. She hasn't been this open with me since...since Krakent. When she threw herself in my arms, and I fell and never stopped falling.

"I need to know why you did what you did," she whispers, still holding my hand. I swallow, looking away, but her voice brings my eyes back to hers. "I can't leave it behind, not until I know why."

I untangle my fingers from her and stare at the stone floor beneath my feet, leaning my elbows against my knees. She wants the truth. And that's all that I have left to give her.

"Everything I told you in Onaydo was true." I begin, clearing my throat as my voice comes out raspy. "It was just vague. You've filled in most of the holes by now. But…the event I told you about. The thing that made me vow to never be helpless again…"

I sigh, running my hand through my hair, and I feel her small hand come to rest on my back. "I was fourteen and in the army. My fa-King Aldred II, he was growing…delusional, in his old age. I stopped going back up to Sutoran for holidays and celebrations and began to stay with the army. I couldn't explain it but I knew I wasn't welcome there. Come to find out, my father's declining mental state led him to insanity, and he firmly believed that I was going to take the throne from Aldred. he believed that I would try to claim it as my birthright, despite every inclination I gave to the opposite. So, he sent his royal assassin to take care of me."

I hear Camari's small intake of breath, feel her lean closer to me, but continue to stare at the floor. It's easier that way. "I woke up just in time. I survived purely by fate; he tripped over the baldrick I had on the ground of the tent I never cleaned. I used that to my advantage, swept his legs out from beneath him, and killed him. He was the first man that I ever killed. And after that…after that I promised that I would never be taken by surprise again. I would never have to prove myself again. Never again would someone think I am an easy kill. Flash forward six years, and Aldred offered me the position as Royal

Assassin. I was so eager to prove myself to everyone, I didn't think twice before I signed the papers. I should have known; Aldred was our father's son after all. It wasn't until days later, after my men had signed similar but not identical contracts, signing on as my squad, that I received my first order. It was for a seer village up in the northern province of Clodagh. We were to destroy it. I was shocked; I didn't care for seers but the royal assassin had never been used for tasks such as that before. But then I reread my contract, and I understood just how naive and foolish I had been."

I force myself to turn and look at Camari as I finish, as I reveal the last of my secrets. "Aldred had made the royal assassin the new seer hunter, it was my job. But he also made me responsible for any and all negative actions of my men. Any rebellious actions of theirs would be blamed on me and I would be punished. But any rebellious actions of my own would result in their deaths. In all of their deaths."

"No," she whispers, horror and understanding dawning in her eyes.

"Morris doesn't know. He doesn't understand and he defends Aldred to me, but I know the truth, I know what a monster he is. Because if I decided against killing all of those seers, he would kill our brother." I pause, and then decide to spill all of it. "There is something that my men are unaware of and that Miller and I never speak of. He was the only one of my men to rebel once he learned what he had signed on to do, he tried to get out of it. So we were brought to Aldred's siting room for a meeting. Miller was forced to stand and watch as I was punished for his actions."

I pull up my uniform and reveal my left rib to her, raising my arm so that she can see the skin usually concealed by my bicep. The raised scar, the obvious burn. She gasps, her eyes filling, and one of her hands hovers between us as if she wants to touch it, as if she believes she can heal it. "He branded me with the rising sun of Zorda, his crest. So I suppose we both have been branded by evil men."

I drop my shirt and lean forward once more with my elbows on my knees. "Miller never said a word about it again, and neither did I. And so I followed all of my orders. Until I met you and things became unfathomably complicated, to the point that Aldred desired my suffering more than holding up his deal. So he hurt you instead."

I look away from her once more, leaning away from her touch as nausea flows through me at the memories of her being whipped. "I will never forgive myself, Cam. I should have read that contract. I should have found a way to avoid taking you, to avoid killing all of those people. But I couldn't. I didn't." I pause as my voice cracks, swallowing several times as my eyes burn, the voices in my head jeering at me.

"Not a day goes by that I don't know everyone's life would be easier if I…if I wasn't here. Before I met you, I was so close to giving up. I was so close to ending it, and I still think at times that I should. It would be so much easier-"

"Don't you ever say that to me again," Camari says in a voice so harsh it startles me. She rests her palm on my face, turning my head so that I have to meet her gaze, and her eyes are almost black with rage and emotion. "Do you understand me? I never want to hear those disgusting words come out of your mouth unless you are asking me for help to get them out of your head. You are a beautiful, compassionate human. You are imperfect. And I am confident that if I had been put in your shoes, I would have done the same."

I shake my head, smiling bitterly. "No, love, you wouldn't have. It takes someone that is already a monster to kill an innocent woman as she kneels in front of him and begs for her life. I was born with that monster inside of me, and you weren't. You could never be like me."

Camari forces me to look at her once more, her expression more tender. "You killed innocent people because if you didn't, everyone that you cared about would die. I tried to kill a man to save myself. I hate to say it, Aiden, but we are both imperfect. We are both capable of killing. But we are not monsters—you are not a monster. You would never kill just to kill. You would never threaten the life of someone you care about."

"Camari, your life would be so much better if I had never been in it," I whisper, finally voicing the thought that plagues me night and day, the thought I am unable to outrun. She smiles and shakes her head ruefully.

"Aiden, I realize that since I met you I have experienced more danger than I've ever imagined. But I left Krakent. I learned who and what I truly am. I have a family, friends, I have you. My life is so much fuller, all because I found you in the woods and allowed myself to be charmed by your pretty face. Please believe me when I say this: My life would be so much worse without you in it. Think of all of the people here that were here before you. You are about to set them all free. Do you honestly think that they would be better off without you?"

I burn with shame at the tear that makes its way down my face, but she simply wipes it away and takes my hand in hers one more time. "We are both very obviously broken, Lorian. But we can be broken together."

She pulls my head gently onto her shoulder and her words combine with her tender actions, showing me she means everything she says, and a sob tears out of me. Because I want the demons to stop. I do not want to die, and I want to stop living in terror and guilt. I want to live. And maybe I am beginning to believe that I deserve to live.

On the morning of Ayone, I wake already filled with adrenaline. Five days until we escape the facility. It is incredibly hard to believe that just like that, we're almost out of here. It feels like we've been in the facility for years, when in fact it's only been just under a moon. And the day we escape, it will be exactly a moon. Perfect.

Sitting up in my cot, I look out the barred window above my cot, blinking as my eyes adjust to the rising sun. It snowed while I was sleeping I realize, smiling as I look out. The entire world is coated in a layer of white frost that reflects the sunlight and makes everything look brighter. Though maybe that's just my positive mood from last night continuing. I feel light, lighter than I have in two years.

Then I realize just how annoying the snow will make everything. When we escape we'll have to take extra precautions to have supplies to stave off the wet and cold. People can be wet and cold, cold and hungry, or wet and hungry, but all three, and people will just be dead.

"You look like you just smelled something rancid." Tristan's voice carries from his cell, making me scowl.

"I remembered your existence and felt suddenly depressed," I reply without looking over at him. That would just satisfy him. Instead, I rise from my bunk and look closer at the outside world, mostly the trees surrounding the facility. I know this land like I know the back of my hand, maybe even better, and while this is my first time in the facility, I still know where almost everything is. The woods stretch for miles, going well past Sutoran and spanning a good percentage of this corner of the continent. Around three days travel from the edge of Sutoran are some old ruins, and several weeks past that is an abandoned quarry. Both could be incredible shelters for the seers.

"I didn't see you and Camari talking when I got to my cell. Did she finally realize how worthless you are?" Tristan asks, trying once more to get a reaction.

"That would please you wouldn't it?" I ask, looking over at him with raised eyebrows. He smiles and shrugs.

"It would be a lie to say no."

"I appreciate your candor," I say dryly, tugging my shirt back on.

"Why is it so cold?" Camari asks as she sits up and stretches, tugging at her sleeves and wrapping her arms around herself.

"It snowed last night. It's the end of Sealga; it always starts snowing here in Sutoran around this time. It's colder here than on the other side of Spás Folamh," I explain, glancing out at the snow again before looking back at her. She rises from her cot and steps up beside me, peering out the window. For some reason, it seems almost as if she pales a bit. She looks away, returning to her cot and wrapping her blanket around herself.

"Well that complicates things," she says, slouching into the blanket.

"We will adapt our plan to include any possible scenario," I reassure her, rubbing the last of my sleep from my eyes.

"We can't plan for everything." Tristan adds from his cell.

"Well, we will do our best then." I grind out, pinching the bridge of my nose. Gods, can Tristan get on my nerves like no one else.

"I had an idea," Camari says quickly, probably sensing my lack of patience. "Would we be able to contact Miller, Grant, and Morris? If so, we could get them to help us."

"I don't have any way of getting in touch with them. And involving them might endanger them," I reply, swallowing against a pang of grief. After never being separated from my team for more than a week, we've now been separated for a moon and a half. And gods, do I miss my brothers.

"We'll see them soon." Camari says with a smile. I nod, looking away. I appreciate her optimism, but the truth is that we are about to attempt the largest prison break in the history of Zorda. No one has ever escaped the facility; you leave the way you came in, dragged away by guards to the gods know where, or you leave in a wagon full of corpses. I pray we will be the first to break that pattern.

R.C. Huye

For some, love is a rush of adrenaline and a weapon on the thickest battlefield. For others it is a tornado. They evade it for fear of what they might lose to it.

The Religious Texts: The Book of Wisdom

Chapter Sixty-Six

Camari

Over the next two days I notice four more seers that I doubt can be trusted. At this rate, we're going to need a lot of rope. I mention them on Dhá and Jax adds them to the list as we all watch.

"This list is depressingly long," he says as he folds it up again.

"At least we're well prepared!" Addie adds positively.

"Yeah, and by that you mean we're completely unprepared." Isaiah scoffs, rolling his eyes. Addie's smile fades and Alex shoots a venomous look at Isaiah's direction, squeezing Addie's hand.

"What do you mean, unprepared? We move this Beis!" I wring my hands, anxiety making my lungs feel tight.

"Well, I've seen the tunnel and gone down it. It does indeed lead to an exit, and there's a hole in the wall big enough for us to squeeze through. After that, run into the forest and keep moving and you're home free," Rob says, rubbing his eyes and looking tired. "The issue, as always, will be getting everyone into and out of the tunnel, and with the required supplies. I've been hoarding supplies since we started this plan over a year ago and we have more than enough; I've transported all of it into the tunnel as well. We just need to come up with a legitimate game plan, giving everyone an assigned job down to the second. That's where we're unprepared."

"Then let's remedy that," Aiden says, taking the parchment from Jax and flipping it over to the clean side. "Okay, we need to get weapons, disable the guards, gather seers, and get to the tunnels. We'll also need to send people to the other classrooms to get the other seers. All of this is possible if we arrange the proper teams to split up at the proper times."

I smile as I watch him plan, talking to each person with a respectful authority that he must have developed after years in the army. He is in his element and he doesn't even know it.

I glance over around the room and find everyone listening intensely, even Isaiah. Everyone except for Tristan. He's looking at me with a pained expression on his face that makes me worry.

"Are you okay?" I ask him quietly, shifting to stand next to him.

"I'm fine, just listening to the plans," he replies simply. I'm not convinced, but I nod once and look back at Aiden, listening to his planning and joining in where I can. Because gods help me; we are getting out of here on Beis.

An hour later, we've come up with plans, issued orders to Rob, and gone over said plans three times until I could recite everyone's jobs as well as my own. Giving Jax the paper to hide, we take turns leaving his cell one or two at a time to avoid raising suspicions. Aiden and I leave last, Aiden talking about the plans with Jax until I physically pull him out of the cell.

"I forgot to ask Rob exactly how many canteens he has stowed away so far," he says as we walk, frowning in concentration.

"He said he has everything we'll need. Twice."

"But what if we have more seers than planned, what then?"

"We ration and scavenge. I know edible plants and roots, and I'm sure many of them can hunt," I reply calmly as we turn a corner, resisting the urge to laugh as he does exactly what he tells me not to do; overthinks.

"But what if-"

"Aiden, we can't possibly cover every single scenario that might occur," I say, fighting against the memory of a vision on a snowy field. That's one scenario I pray will never occur.

"I can still try," he grumbles, raking his hair back from his face. I reach out and grab his hand, pulling him to a stop.

"Aiden, you're going to drive yourself crazy overthinking everything. Trust me, I am the master of overthinking. You need to relax and have faith that no matter what happens, we've done the best we can. That's all we can do really, is prepare for the unknown!" I tell him gently, trying to ease some of his stress. Aiden nods, clenching his jaw as he sighs heavily. I squeeze his hand, drawing his attention back to me.

"It will be fine," I say softly. Aiden's eyes meet mine and my mouth goes suddenly dry. I swallow, hating the way his eyes are like beacons that I can't turn away from.

"Camari," he says softly, his voice rumbling in his chest. No, I can't do this now. I rip my hand away and turn.

"Let's get back to the cell, we don't-" I start hastily, walking away. His arm catches me gently around the elbow and stops me, turning me to face him.

"No. I need to talk to you now."

"Aiden, please. Can we just-"

"No. I need to tell you this now. I can't keep putting it off, not anymore," he says firmly. I swallow again, looking down at my feet. I don't want to talk about this now. Because I don't know what I want. Or maybe I do, and I'm just scared of it. Either way, I don't want to talk about this now.

Aiden gently tilts my chin up so that my eyes meet his. He looks at me so gently that my knees feel weak. Gods above, his eyes are beautiful.

"Camari, my feelings aren't changing or going away anytime soon, and frankly, I don't want them to. I care about you, and I know everything sucks right now and I've ruined everything several times, but I need to tell you so that I can at least know that where we stand isn't because of me. I need to tell you how I feel so that I don't have to worry about you being mistaken. Half the time I think you consider me as just an acquaintance, but the rest of the time I could swear you return my feelings."

"It's not that simple, Aiden." I sigh, looking away from his eyes and shifting from foot to foot.

"Then explain why it isn't. Don't just say that, *talk to me!*" he begs, dodging in front of my gaze again.

"I'm confused, okay? I don't know what I want! Yes, a good amount of the time I can't help but feel…deeply for you. But that doesn't change many factors that I can't stop coming back to! You lied to me so many times, and I've forgiven you for taking me, there is nothing to forgive, but after you started helping me, you lied again! You lied completely about who you were!"

"I didn't know who I was until I met you," Aiden says, and the complete honesty in his tone threatens to break my self-control. "And yes, I lied to you. I'm sorry about that, but if that's the one reason you're pushing me away, it's not a good one. I promise to never lie to you again. Camari, I'm not going any-where. No matter how hard the world tries, how hard Aldred tries, I will not be separated from you."

I inhale raggedly, a tear slowly making its way down my cheek. "I just don't know if I'm willing to let myself trust you again," I whisper. Aiden looks down at me and I track the movement of his throat as he swallows.

"That's something only you can decide," he says finally. "But if fear is the only thing holding you back, then that's not like the Camari I know."

I watch his back as he turns and walks away, wip-ing the tear from my cheek. I can't shake his words from my head.

I'm not going anywhere.

The days seem to pass slower than ever before, despite the fact that the sun sets far sooner than be-fore. Every waking moment that we can, we spend agonizing over details for Beis. We meet almost every evening, saying what we've learned, and learn-ing how we're doing with supplies. I can't help but feel that most of the work is being done by Aiden and Rob. Aiden is planning almost everything so that our time is used efficiently, remembering every guard's name and station as well as their strengths and weak-nesses, just from observing them. Rob is planning for after the escape, ensuring we have enough supplies to survive, that the barracks will be left 'accidentally' unlocked, and that the priest will be absent all day so that the tunnel is open for the seers. Everyone else simply has to go with their plans. The problem with that, obviously, is Tristan. He's almost mutinous with the fact that Aiden has taken control of the escape, and is even more livid with the fact that we all let him. I'm honestly surprised he hasn't exploded yet. At the same time, I'm concerned for him. He's been acting strange lately, more quiet and distant than usual. I catch him staring at me often, and whenever he sees me looking, he looks away with a frustrated expression. I don't have time to worry about that though, because I have so many other things to worry about. One of those things, the most important actually, is all of the children that might get hurt during the escape. After telling Aiden of my fears, he came up with the idea of assigning each younger child a seer to watch over them during the escape, sort of like a guardian. It's a good idea, but I'm still worried. Addie has already asked to be Molly's guardian, which is a relief at least. She won't be alone during the escape.

Another thing occupying my mind, admittedly selfishly, is Aiden's confession. Or, should I say his promise.

I'm not going anywhere.

It both warms me and fills me with fear. And he's right as well; fear is holding me back. But sometimes fear can be smart, and I'm just not sure if I'm hesitant because of fear, or because of logic. And thinking about it gives me a headache.

Despite the fact that the days are going by at a snail's pace, before I know it, it's the night of Súvig, the night before we escape. I lie on my cot as the guards lock our cell, my hands trembling under my covers. There's no way I'll be able to sleep tonight; I'm too filled with adrenaline. I glance over at Tristan where he is asleep on his cot, his back to me. I wish I knew what is going on with him. But he is grieving, and it's not my place to pry.

"Go to sleep, Camari. Lying awake all night won't help," Aiden mumbles from his cot, making me jump. How does he know I'm awake?

"I can't; I'm too anxious," I reply quietly, wringing my hands. I hear him sigh, followed by the sound of his blanket swishing as he rolls over.

"About anything in particular?"

"No."

"Then push it out of your mind and try to sleep."

"Yes sir," I say sarcastically, rolling onto my side so that I'm more comfortable. I can almost hear his smile across the room.

R.C. Huye

There is rumor that there was a traitor amongst King Declan's court, but no evidence as such has been found.

—Retractions from the Royal Historical Documents

Chapter Sixty-Seven

Tristan

It's Súvig, and I'm completely lost. I'm sick to my stomach as well, but that's not important.

We will escape tomorrow morning, and all I can think about is what should I do? Skies above, I miss Tina. She was the only one keeping me sane. Now I'm stuck with Camari, and she definitely doesn't keep me sane. She makes me wild, so that every time Aiden looks at her with that sappy look, I want to rip his face off. But that's not enough for me. I held out hope that she might return my feelings, and for a while I thought she did. But I should have known better. I heard her conversation with Aiden on Dhá; I heard his confession to her about his feelings. And I heard her admit that she cares for him as well.

Maybe I don't have anything with these seers. But I used to have something, someone. And the assassin took almost everyone away. Tina was the one

612

person that stayed. But then she got taken as well, and now I am alone. But maybe I don't have to be alone anymore. It just means sacrificing something that I've come to love. Not everybody, I couldn't do that. Just one person; the person holding everything together. One sort of love for another. And I don't know what to choose.

The morning of Beis, I'm awake and waiting for the guards to let us out, jiggling my knees impatiently. Aiden and Camari are conferring quietly, Camari appearing anxious. I smile as she begins to pull on a strand of shoulder-length hair, a nervous habit I've come to think cute. But my smile fades as Aiden reaches over and takes her hand, squeezing it silently. She looks up at him and smiles. Her dark eyes soften and my heart hardens.

The guard comes and lets me out, and my stomach churns with nerves. I jump when Camari speaks through the bars, my heart shooting up to my throat.

"Remember, we move at breakfast in an hour. Good luck."

"Good luck," I reply, swallowing hard. I've made my decision. Time to live with it.

"I've heard you might have something I want?" Captain Saul asks, leaning back in his chair and smiling coldly at me. I swallow hard, resisting the urge to glance at the guards behind me.

"Yes, but not for free."

"You honestly think you're in the position to bargain?" he asks, raising his eyebrows in surprise and cold calculation.

"You'll find I don't break easily," I reply coolly, crossing my arms. The captain smiles and sits up straighter, leaning forward on his desk.

"What is it you want, 4494?"

"You took a seer away a few weeks ago, 4497. I want her returned, healthy and whole, to me," I say, forcing myself to retain my calm façade while my heart races. The captain ensnares my gaze and holds it, his light brown eyes seeming to read me. I grit my teeth and force myself to inhale while I hold his gaze, raising my chin. After what feels like hours, the captain nods, smiling as he leans back again.

"That can be easily arranged. What is it you have to give me in return for 4497? It must be valuable."

"I have the identity of a seer organizing a revolution in the facility," I say, my voice coming out raspy. The captain's smile disappears and he sits up, his light eyes turning so dark they appear to have no iris.

"Who?" he demands. I raise an eyebrow, amazed that my mask of confidence has lasted so long.

"Do we have a deal?" I ask again, holding out my right hand. The captain's jaw stiffens as he looks at my outstretched hand, but after a moment he takes it and shakes it firmly.

"Yes. Now, who is the revolutionary?" he asks again, eagerness sparking in his eyes even as he hastily scrubs his hand against his trousers. I swallow against the bile in my throat, taking a deep breath and thinking of Tina, alive and whole.

"4567. The seer's number is 4567."

"And what's the seer's name? We have them in the files by their names," the captain explains, opening a drawer in his desk and revealing many pieces of parchment. So the numbers truly are just a mind game.

My hands begin to shake in my lap, and I clench them into fists, steeling my nerves. I look up and meet Captain Saul's gaze, shoving aside all fear and guilt. I'm doing the right thing. I know it.

"Her name is Camari Dorsar."

R.C. Huye

*R–distraction. C, A, J, & A–Barracks. A, T, & I–
lookout.*

–Recovered Artifacts from the Facility

Chapter Sixty-Eight

Camari

I feel like I'm going to be sick. We are all gathered in the classroom. It's almost eight o'clock. We're moving now.

"Remember, you see a guard, don't hesitate. Kill them before they kill you." Jax instructs, his orange eyes glowing with excitement. I swallow down nausea and nod, my hands shaking in my pockets.

"Where's Tristan?" Addie asks, looking around. I don't bother looking around as well; I know I won't see him. He's disappeared.

"I don't know," I whisper, feeling even sicker. "He knows the plan; he'll catch up."

Aiden and Jax exchange a glance but I purposefully ignore it, clenching my hands into fists to prevent them from shaking. He'll come; he promised.

"Remember; the needs of the many outweigh the few. If one of us gets taken and there's no way to save them, we leave them behind," Aiden says firmly, meeting my gaze. I hear the hidden message; if he gets taken, leave him behind.

Not going to happen.

"Go, we'll make sure nothing horrible happens here," Alex says, taking Addie's hand in his. Aiden nods, and the two of them clasp hands. And then we're moving.

As soon as we begin walking my nerves fade almost into nonexistence. Doing it, living it, is so different than simply reviewing it. All the pieces fall into place, and time slows.

We follow Rob's instructions, going down halls and stairs that are conveniently vacant of guards until we reach the barracks, concealed in the recesses of the facility. Rob is currently busy with his job, faking a distraction and luring every guard he can to the opposite side of the facility, buying us plenty of time.

The barracks is a simple set of wooden doors, locked and usually guarded. Aiden breaks it open with three kicks just above the lock. The wood splinters, cracking loudly, and the doors fly inward. And inside is a treasure trove of weapons. Swords, axes, maces, knives; everything needed to subdue thousands of people all locked inside one room. Everyone starts loading upon weapons for us as well as every seer that will join us. Swords strapped around waists, axes on backs, knives tucked into shoes and shirtsleeves. Aiden and Jax both grab rope as well, to tie up the seers that won't be coming.

We spend just under ten minutes collecting weapons, and when all of us are done, the barracks appears empty.

Serves them right.

"We have enough; let's return to the others," Jax says, gesturing with his hand for all of us to turn back. My nerves return and I realize that this is it. We either escape, or we die. I take a deep breath and push my fears away, imagining them disappearing. It's time to act, not to think.

We turn and begin to walk quickly out of the barracks, but Aiden taps my shoulder, asking me to stay back while gesturing at Jax and the others to keep going.

"We should go; we don't have time-" I begin to say, going to follow Jax, but Aiden grabs my elbow and turns me around, pulling me into his arms before I can even wrap my mind around what is happening. And then he's kissing me.

It's nothing like our kiss before the hearing; that kiss was rushed and small and messy. This…this is something else. Aiden kisses me like I'm the only thing that exists in that moment, like we have all of the time in the world. One hand on the small of my back to keep me close and another cupping my face gently, his lips move against mine in a way that ignites a fire in my belly. I utter a squeak of surprise when our lips first meet and he smiles against my mouth, his lips tightening around mine. And then I slowly melt into him, my body moving on its own accord. I grip his wrists, holding onto him as my legs turn to jelly and my blood burns.

He pulls back far too soon with a sharp inhale, his eyes remaining closed for a second before he presses his forehead against mine and opens them, looking at me as if he can see into my soul. I stare back, my mind lagging as I try to comprehend every-thing that is happening.

Gods above, if that's what it's like to be kissed, then it was worth the wait.

"I figure we might die at any point today, so I just want to make sure you know how I feel in case," Aiden says with a half smile, his eyes pained with fear, though it's not for him. His only worries are for me.

And then he says a sentence that makes my eyes burn with tears, my heart surging in my chest.

"I love you," he whispers, still stroking my cheek with his thumb. I stare dumbly at him, completely at a loss for words.

He loves me.

And then he's pulled away and my skin is cold where he was touching me; I fight the urge to wrap his arms around me again so we can go back in time.

He picks up another sword off the ground and grins at me as I stand there frozen, his hazel eyes glowing with mischief and joy. "Let's go!" he says, turning and walking out of the barracks. I stand there numbly for several seconds before following, raising my free hand to my mouth and finding it warm and slightly swollen.

He loves me.

I trot to catch up with the others, avoiding mak-ing eye contact with anyone as I draw a knife and force myself to focus on the task at hand. I know self-defense and how to fight with a knife, but I'm not strong enough to handle a sword and would just exhaust myself trying. I'll stick to my strengths and let others stick to theirs.

We're halfway to the classroom before we run into the first set of guards. There are only two of them and they are unprepared at the sight of six seers armed with an entire barracks worth of weapons. Aiden moves so swiftly that I barely have time to realize what's going on. One second his sword is drawn; two seconds and the first guard is dead, three seconds and the other guard drops beside the first. Aiden pulls his sword out of the man's gut and looks back at us, nodding that it's all clear. I expect to feel fear at what I just saw. Aiden can kill two men in a single breath; I should be afraid. But I'm not.

"Shit," I whisper. Alex turns, raising his brow at me questioningly.

"What is it; is something wrong?"

"I'm in love with that man," I say to myself, staring at Alex as a smile spreads across my face. Alex groans, throwing his head back in exasperation and gripping his hair in his hands.

"You're finally figuring that out *now*? What is wrong with you people? Gods have *mercy*." Alex turns and jogs out of the room and I follow him, still smiling to myself.

We keep going, stepping around the bodies without giving them a second glance. Addie and Isaiah join us briefly only to peel away to meet Rob and hit the other classrooms, where they will then take the seers to meet us at the tunnel. Tristan is supposed to be with them, but I push away my doubts and promise myself he'll show up.

We meet five more guards, and all are killed in a similar fashion. By the time we reach the classroom, almost everyone has killed someone except me.

We walk in and everyone moves just as planned. Aiden dispatches the two guards at the entrance while everyone else moves to take on the others. I draw a second dagger, holding one primed for slashing and the other for stabbing. There are a total of twelve guards in the classroom. In just over a minute they all lie dead, over a half of them at Aiden's hands.

The seers are all shouting, screaming, and staring, some of them cheering us on while others scream for help. Jax raises his hands for everyone's attention and bellows one sentence. "SHUT UP!"

Complete silence falls.

"Here's what's going to happen;" Jax says, twirling his sword in his hand so that drops of blood fly off of it and splatter on the floor, "we're feckin' getting out of here! If you want to come with us, come here, get a weapon, and do as I say. If you want to alert the guards and have us arrested, and trust me, I know everyone of you that does; we will tie you up. If you fight, you die."

No one hesitates before they move, an incredible amount of seers coming forward for weapons, some of them sobbing with joy that they're escaping, some of them afraid. I hand out every weapon I have except for the switchblade that I've had for weeks, tucking it up my sleeve. In the end, our list of seers plus two don't join us. They take one look at Aiden, with blood dripping from his sword and splattering his clothes, the lore and legend that trails in his shadow as real assassin, and don't put up a fight. Eight minutes later, we have them all tied up and gagged in a corner. We give weapons to all of the seers that look strong enough to put up a fight, instructing them to stick to the outsides of the group. We then assign guardians for each of the younger children just as Aiden said, instructing them to protect the children with their lives. Once we have everything settled as quickly as possible, we set out again. Alex and Jax take the lead, making sure to walk a good bit ahead so that they can intercept any guards and dispatch them. Aiden and I take the far back, ready to intercept any threats from behind. We walk in silence and the only sounds are those of my breathing and the beating of my heart in my ears. Aiden is similarly silent, though he keeps twirling his sword in his hand as we walk, probably happy to be holding a weapon again. I glance at him twice, open my mouth to say something, but then change my mind and keep walking.

"What are your plans after we get out? What do you plan to do first?" I finally ask, breaking the silence.

"I don't know, but I do know I won't return to what I was before," he says firmly, sheathing his sword. "What about you, what will you do?" He turns the question on me with a crooked grin.

"I…I don't know. Maybe find Adeline, but I don't just want to return to Krakent. I can't just go back to what I left like that, it's just not me anymore." I explain, fingering my switchblade. I hesitate, my heart in my throat, before I add quietly, "And it all depends on where you go, of course."

Aiden turns to face me, his eyes burning with emotions that make my heart race, and slows to a stop, his hand reaching out partially towards me as if he's unsure. Before he can speak, I reach out and take his hand with my shaking one, holding his gaze.

"Camari," he says in a low voice, lacing our fingers together, "are-"

Then I hear the footsteps behind us.

Aiden and I spin around, Aiden stepping in front of me immediately to shield me from whatever's coming. My breathing speeds up as the footsteps get louder, my fear returning once more. Aiden reaches behind him and finds my hand again, taking it in his and squeezing it. I squeeze back, interlacing our fingers.

The owners of the footsteps come into sight, and my heart plummets. It's a group of five guards, armed to the teeth. But they're not alone.

Tristan is with them.

R.C. Huye

The land that the Royal Clinic, also known as the facility, is built on belongs to the dutchie of the Bidennore bloodline.

–Zorda: Aristocracy, Geography, and History

Chapter Sixty-Nine

Aiden

Five guards come into view, accompanied by Tristan. I immediately feel uneasy. Tristan isn't shackled, and they aren't holding him. He's walking freely, and the guilt on his face as he looks at Camari tells me all I need to know.

"You little shit!" I spit, stepping further in front of Camari. He turns to me, his face contorting in fury.

"Shut up, just shut up!" he snarls. The guards shift behind him and he glances at him before looking back at Camari, grief visible in his eyes.

"Tristan, what are you doing?" Camari asks quietly from behind me, resting her free hand on my shoulder.

"I'm so sorry, Camari. I had to do it," he whispers, his voice trembling.

"Like hell you did!" I snap, fury flowing through my veins. He turned her in. He *fucking* turned her in. I should have killed him the day I met him.

"I had no choice!"

"What did you do, Tristan?" Camari repeats, her voice now cold as ice. Tristan doesn't reply, but rather turns to the guards behind him.

"That's her, that's 4567. You'll have to restrain him though, or he'll fight for her, the ignorant sot."

The guards move at his words, walking towards us. Camari and I back up and I remember my sheathed sword, but it's too late. Two guards grab me and pull me away from her.

"Stay away from her! Stay away you bastards!" I shout, fighting and twisting in failed attempts to escape their grips. Two guards grab Camari as well, though she also tries to fight, snarling and kicking. Tristan just watches as they hold the both of us, looking impatient.

"We have a deal. You have the revolutionary, now give me 4497; give me Tina!" he demands, his blue eyes flashing. The remaining guard grins and I know what he's going to say before he even speaks.

"You should know better than to bargain with the captain. 4497 is dead; has been for a week. Now get out of my sight before I take you in as well." He smirks, nodding at the guards holding Camari. Tristan's face falls and his hands begin to shake.

"No, you promised that-"

"We make no promises to seer filth!" The guard spits. Tristan's face fills with rage, and next thing I

know, he's moved and kicked one of the guards holding me back between the legs. The guard doubles
over and that's all I need to jerk away from the second guard, pull my sword, and run him through. The
other guard stumbles to his feet but I bring my blade
around and slice open his stomach, watching as he
falls to the ground and bleeds out. I spin around for
Camari, but she's not there.

"Aiden! What the hell is-" Jax comes running
back down the hallway but he stops short at the sight
of me with the two bloody bodies.

"They got Camari. I need to go back for her," I
tell him, fear pumping through my veins. What are
they going to do to her?

"You can't, we need to keep going," Jax argues.

"I'm not leaving her here," I snarl, advancing towards him.

"Lad, calm down. We have over two thousand
innocent seers depending on us to get them out, we
cannot just go after one girl and risk all of them. You
said it yourself; the needs of the many outweigh the
needs of the few!"

"I can and will. I-"

"I know; you're in love with her. But we need
you, Aiden. You know that girl; I call her trouble for
a reason. She can defend herself. If she doesn't get
out right after us, we'll come back for her, but for
now, we need to go." Jax orders, pointing his sword
in the direction he came from. I stand there, clenching my jaw. I can't leave her; I just can't, even for all
of the other seers. Not without knowing she'll be
okay.

But I also have two thousand people depending on me. And I know what she'd want me to do.

"Okay, let's go." I force out. "But we come back as soon as they're out."

Jax nods once and turns, leading the way toward the other seers and away from Camari.

Tristan

She's dead. *She's dead, she's dead, she's dead, she's dead, she's dead.* Saying it doesn't make it feel any more real. How is she dead?

I feel numb as I watch Aiden kill the guards as they drag Camari away. Nothing. All of this was for nothing. I ruined everything for nothing. And now I am truly and completely alone.

Unsure of what to do next, I follow Jax and Aiden as they go to protect the seers that I betrayed.

Blood magic is not simple, nor understandable. It is a way the earth binds itself to its owner and its descendants. If land belongs to one man, it belongs to all he spawns, and it will bend to all.

—The Mythical, Magical, and Mundane: Folklore of Zorda

Chapter Seventy

Camari

The guards drag me down the hallway silently, their fingers digging painfully into my arms. I focus on slowly bringing the switchblade in my sleeve down to my hand without dropping it.

If I drop it, I'm done.

It drops into my hand right as the guard tugs me forward, tripping me, and my heart lurches in my chest as I just barely grab it with the tips of my fingers, securing my hold on it. I unfold it slowly, maintaining a good grip on it the entire time as my heart races in my chest.

All right, this is it.

I stick out my leg and hook the guard's ankle. He trips and falls with a curse, losing his grip on my arm. Refusing to lose momentum, I rip my arm free of the other guard's grip and plunge my blade into his throat without giving myself time to think. Blood bubbles up red and warm and I jerk my knife out and jump to my feet, swallowing down the contents of my stomach as the guard lies there, dead. The second guard is on his feet and he takes a swing at me. I go to duck but I'm too late. His fist connects and a thousand lights flash in my eyes as pain shoots through my head. Despite the pain I manage to dodge his next blow and land a kick to his groin, wiping blood from my lip. He doubles over and I immediately slit his throat, my hand shaking as blood spills onto it. He collapses on top of the other guard, their blood pooling on the floor. The smell of it, metallic and salty, reaches my nostrils. Unable to push it down, I bend over and throw up all over their corpses, spitting mucus out before breathing deeply. They're dead; it's okay. It was necessary.

Then I realize I can hear footsteps coming down the hall, coming from both directions. Guards come from both sides, at least ten in each group. At the head of the group in front of me is Duke Bidennore.

My father.

My hands shake as my father stares at me with a feline grin.

"Well, looks like you're a little murderer after all. The king should have had you killed in the first place," he says with a smile, tilting his head to the side.

"But then I wouldn't get to kill you," I say with a similar smile, shifting my grip on the blade. His eyes flicker to it, and his smile broadens.

"With that? Come now, Camari, that's slightly illogical, don't you think? You're outnumbered, twenty-one to one. You would need an army, child."

"Well, if I die trying, I'd say that's a pretty good way to go." I taunt, sliding into a defensive position.

"You take far too much after your mother. A disappointment, really."

"Interesting. A few months ago that would have been an insult. Now it's an accomplishment."

The duke's smile fades along with his patience. "It's time you die, daughter."

I curtsy while never taking my eyes off of him, spitting blood from my split lip onto the stones before him, sending him a challenge. "Come and do it then."

As one, all of the guards pull their swords, as well as the duke. They advance slowly, the duke grinning like a mad man. Then suddenly, there's a rumble, and the entire facility shakes. The guards falter and look up at the shaking ceiling. The duke steps back, as do the other men, when it continues to rumble. I stumble as the ground shakes, and I press my hand against the damp wall beside me to steady myself.

What the hell is going on?

Suddenly, a huge chunk of the ceiling caves in, falling towards me in slow motion. The guards and the duke run back the way they came with shouts and screams, abandoning me in their haste as the rock falls at their heels. I brace myself against the wall as everything shakes, falling to my knees and wrapping my arms around my head.

More ceiling falls; dust and grime fill the air and make me choke. My heart races with panic and terror, and I turn, struggling to keep my balance on the slick and shaking floors and run towards the tunnel, towards Aiden. The rumbling and shaking get worse and I fall over, catching myself as I fall with my arms. A large piece of rock appears in the corner of my vision and strikes my head, bringing with it a sharp pain. Darkness, a familiar foe by now, descends quickly, blocking everything else out, and I remember no more.

Chapter Seventy-One

Aiden

Jax and I lead the seers to the tunnel, following Camari's instructions to open it. Just before we go in, Isaiah and Rob catch up with us, bringing with them a shocking amount of seers. I pull open the stone door while seers begin to file inside, everyone carrying something from the stash of supplies Rob has hidden for us. It takes a ridiculously long time to get all two thousand and something seers going down the tunnel, but I do my best to urge them along, my heart tugging me back the way I came the entire time.

Once everybody is in, I pull the door behind me so that it's only open a crack. We've lit torches, and seers are lighting the way ahead, following Addie and Alex in a surprisingly calm, if not too slow, manner. I take the back, my hand gripping the hilt of my sword tightly. Nothing has gone according to plan. Camari is supposed to be next to me, bouncing with nerves and excitement at rescuing so many people, her eyes glowing with joy and nerves. But she's not.

I release a steady breath, trying to push away my nerves with it. I will go back for her as soon as the seers are out; I will not be separated from her. Everything will be fine.

I trail my hands along the walls as I walk, feeling the cold stone. It's worn and old, and a few rocks crumble under my touch. Not exactly something to promote enthusiasm. The last thing we need is for the tunnel to collapse because of weak structural integrity.

The seers continue in a calm manner, the guardians taking care of their charges and keeping them quiet. I'm surprised when one of the seers with a weapon stops back to walk beside me, especially since he's one of the seers who has grouped up on me on several different occasions. He's a big guy with matted brown hair and a wide jaw that is always clenched when he's in my presence. I glance at him out of the corner of my eye, but he's staring straight ahead, his shoulders stiff.

"How long is this tunnel?"

I'm surprised when the seer speaks, his voice rumbling deeply in his throat. I look over at him, raising my eyebrows.

"Long."

The man snorts and rolls his eyes, looking away quickly before glancing at me again. "I suppose this is all your doing," he says grudgingly.

"Not at all; I just helped with the plans and execution. Jax and Rob did most of the work," I reply, fixing my grip on the hilt of my sword. Soon, I can go back soon.

"Then I won't thank you."

"I didn't expect you to."

"Mmhmm," he says with a roll of his eyes, sounding doubtful.

"I didn't do this for gratitude; I don't need it."

"Then why did you, the royal assassin, just help execute the biggest prison break in history?" he asks, looking over at me skeptically.

"I'm the ex-royal assassin. And because I'm righting my wrongs."

"It will take more than this to right all of your wrongs." He snaps. I sigh, shoving my hair out of my face.

"Don't I know it. But I have to start somewhere, and this seemed like a good place to start."

"Certainly an extravagant place to start." He snorts, shaking his head.

"Shut up," I say sharply, stopping in the tunnel and turning to the side. He comes to a stop beside me and snarls.

"Excuse me?" he asks quietly, but I raise a hand and cut him off.

"Do you hear that?" I whisper, tilting my head. He copies me for a moment, and we just listen. Footsteps. A rock skittering across the floor. The clanking of metal.

Guards.

I turn and run, followed by the seer, and reach the group up ahead, waving Jax back.

"What is it?" He demands immediately, his hand going to the hilt of his sword.

"Guards, and by the sound of it, a lot of them," I say grimly. Jax curses colorfully and with surprising creativity before he turns and walks back to the seers, who are standing and waiting to find out what's going on.

"We're being pursued. I need able-bodied men with weapons to fall back and stay to fight while everyone else picks up the pace and gets the hell out of here." Murmurs and whimpers break out at his announcement, but everybody starts moving at once. About thirty men with weapons fall back to join us while the others stay to protect the group in case the guards get past us. As one we turn and walk back the way we came while the other seers begin to run for the end of the tunnel. Everyone draws their weapon, and we fall into a defensive position, ready to spill blood. The tunnel, already precarious, begins to rumble and shake slightly as the guards approach and the seers run, making me nervous.

"Just how many guards are coming?" Alex mutters, sweating nervously. The tunnel rumbles and shakes even stronger than before, and dust begins to fall from the ceiling. The guards come into view, and any hopes of fighting our way out diminish greatly. There are at least forty guards, and they're all armed to the teeth. They stop in front of us and draw their swords, the metal whining as it leaves the sheath. But then they stop and look around uneasily. The tunnel's shaking has gotten stronger, and rubble is beginning to fall.

It's going to collapse.

"We need to get out now!" I snap, backing up several paces. The guards in front of me begin to back up as well, a few of them turning and running and leaving their brethren behind. And then as the shaking gets so strong that I almost fall over, a huge chunk of the roof falls just a few feet in front of me, and I watch almost in slow-motion as it lands on the guards. I turn away and shield my face quickly as it breaks apart, showering us in dust and stones. The air is filled with curses and coughs as the dust begins to clear. I look up and find the guards crushed by the stone, their blood staining the walls.

"Bleeding hell." Isaiah breathes.

"Run," I order. As one we all turn and run after the seers, the tunnel still shaking and crumbling around us. We jump rocks and wave dust from our eyes as we run, shouting when we see sunlight ahead. Then it hits me.

Oh gods, Camari is still in the facility.

I skid to a halt just outside the tunnel as everyone keeps running, spotting the seers at the wall waiting anxiously for us. I hear Jax shout my name but ignore him as I turn back. I've just reached the ivy when a huge rumble sounds out and a cloud of dust flies out as the entire facility collapses in on itself, the land beneath it no longer able to support its weight.

"*CAMARI*!" I scream, shoving aside the ivy roughly. A part of the tunnel has collapsed in the exit and blocked it, leaving gaps that are far too small for me to fit through and are still filling in as more rocks fall. I begin to try to move rocks away desperately, pulling and clawing until my fingertips begin to bleed, and even then, I don't stop.

"No, no, no, no, no." I pant, my breath catching in my throat as my eyes burn. I have to get back in. I have to get back in!

"Aiden." Jax's voice comes from behind me, unusually gentle. He rests his hand on my shoulder, but I shrug it off, still trying to heave stones out of the way. He grabs me roughly and pulls me away from the rockslide, turning me to face him and holding me there as I struggle against him. His orange eyes are bright with grief and urgency.

"She's gone, Aiden. I'm sorry, but she's gone."

"She's not *gone* dammit!" I shout back, my voice cracking. Jax softens his tone, still holding my shoulders.

"There are two thousand seers here that need your help. She died helping them. Why don't we see that her job is done?" he says gently. I stare at him, my hands clenched into fists at my sides as I force myself to think. The tunnel collapsed. Half of the facility caved in. People were crushed…

He's right. There's really only one more thing I can do now.

"Okay," I say roughly, my voice still shaking. "Let's go."

One thought won't leave my head, even as I come to the conclusion that I have to go. I promised her, not twenty-four hours ago, that I loved her. I promised her we would never be separated.

I lied.

Jax nods, releasing my shoulders and stepping back. He turns to walk towards the seers and I look over my shoulders once more at the crumbled tunnel exit, the dust still settling. And then I turn my back on the facility filled with panicked guards and workers and walk towards the hole in the wall.

I turn my back on Camari.

We slip through the hole in the crumbled wall one by one, some of the larger seers scraping themselves on the rough stone as they squeeze through. I go through last before I straighten up and look around, taking in what lies before us. The stonewall of the facility is behind us, and in front of us, past a small open space, are the woods. They stretch on for as far as the eye can see, pine and maple trees alike coated in frost and snow. The ground beneath my feet is similarly layered in several inches of powder and the cold is already seeping through my flimsy prison clothes and shoes.

Some of the seers have already delved into the smuggled supplies and pulled out blankets, wrapping them around themselves to fend off the flakes falling from the sky. I spot Addie and Alex conferring quietly with serious expressions, but then, the majority of the seers are doing that. They look happy and joy filled, but also, panicked. They have no idea what to do now, and need to be told what to do and calmed down. Camari will-no. I push the thought away, feeling sick to my stomach.

Turning away from the seers, I spot Jax standing next to Rob, and walk over, nodding to Rob before turning to Jax. "We need to find shelter and get as far away from Sutoran and the facility as we can. After that we need to find somewhere to set up camp and deal with whatever comes up first."

"So what you're saying is we should start walking?" Jax sighs, pinching the bridge of his nose.

"It might be a good idea. The movement will get us further away, keep people warm, and help give them something to do to distract them from…to keep them busy." I finish, clearing my throat and glancing at the seers before I look at Jax and Rob again. Jax holds my gaze for a few seconds of silence before he nods, understanding.

"Then let's go."

He and Rob turn and walk towards the whispering seers, leaving me to follow behind them. He stops in front of them and raises his hands to get their attention. They continue talking and ignore him. Jax clenches his teeth impatiently before shouting, "SHUT UP AND LISTEN!"

Everyone falls silent almost immediately and turns to face us. Jax clears his throat, appearing surprisingly unnerved at having two thousand people stare at him for orders.

"As Aiden has thoughtfully pointed out, we need to get moving as far away from Sutoran as possible. Take blankets if you're cold, pick up the supplies and take a second to gather yourselves. After that, we start walking. We stop either when we collapse or reach shelter, whichever comes first."

Finished, Jax turns back to Rob and me, leaving the seers to do as ordered. They stand there whispering for a few seconds before going and moving about, doing as they're told.

"I'm hoping we can reach the woods by nightfall. If not, we keep walking." Jax says, scratching his collar bone directly above his tattoo.

"You don't think that's wishful thinking? These people have been in a glorified prison for who knows how long, they aren't exactly in shape." Rob points out, glancing behind him.

"Well this is a perfect opportunity for them to get in shape," Jax says firmly. There's no arguing with him. Five minutes later, all of the seers are ready. Jax begins to walk to the front of the group, followed by Rob and I. Glancing over his shoulders, he yells, "Move out!" and starts walking. A couple of seconds later, every seer follows. The only noise is that of the snow crunching under our feet and the quiet murmuring of the seers as they have whispered conversations. I walk in silence with Jax on my right and Isaiah on my left, focusing on taking one step at a time. Putting one step between the facility and myself at a time.

Head injuries have ranges. You may experience a headache and a slight bruise, those are relatively minor. If dizziness, vomiting, and hallucinations occur, seeking help is a necessity.

—Excerpt from the Natural Remedies Guidebook

Chapter Seventy-Two

Camari

I can hear fuzzy voices, far too loud for comfort. They make my head hurt and feel sticky in places, which is strange. There are screams and shouts, followed by silence. The darkness looms in the distance, and after a couple minutes, it swallows me up once more.

The ground has stopped vibrating when the darkness next recedes. I hadn't noticed it was moving last time, but now that it's stopped I've noticed the shaking's absence.

I feel sick. My head hurts so badly that I can't open my eyes because the light makes me sick, makes everything hazy.

There's this thought that keeps evading me. I know it's important, but I just can't place my finger on it. Every time I get close, it swims away again.

I can feel a sticky warmth on the skin of my forehead and scalp, but I don't have the energy to reach up and see what it is. I try once, but I can't get my hand off of the ground.

The darkness returns and everything fades into blissful silence.

I was doing something important. I was getting back to someone important. But then…everything shook. Why did it shake?

What shook?

Who called my name?

I don't know, but I like the darkness. It makes everything else feel better. I sink into its embrace and let it sweep me away from the pain and questions.

Aiden.

Oh gods, where is Aiden?

My eyes crack open and sting as dust from the air settles into them. I blink furiously to clear them, coughing as dust catches in my throat. The movement sends pain spiraling through my head and down my neck and I gasp, trying not to vomit. The light hurts my eyes, hurts my head. I grit my teeth and lift my hand from the ground, bringing it to my head. There's something wet on my skin and in my hair. I touch it gingerly before bringing my hand in front of my face where I can see it. Blood.

Then I remember everything. Being cornered as I tried to make my way back to Aiden. The tunnel collapsing. The rock hitting my head.

Taking a deep breath, I force myself to sit up, crying out as my vision swims and my head shrieks in protest. Turning to the side I heave and throw up the contents of my stomach, gasping for air and squeezing my eyes shut. Gods, everything hurts. I force myself to open my eyes and look around slowly, my hands shaking.

There's debris everywhere, stone and dust coating everything. There are gaping holes in the ceiling and on the walls where stones fell, and I spot a stone with blood on it and assume it's the one that hit me. The facility is a wreck. I can hear screams and shouted orders, but they're far away, muted and fuzzy. No guards have come for me. And I need to move now.

Counting down in my head to get ready, I plant my hands on the ground and push myself to my knees, whimpering as pain shoots through my head again and my vision spins. I spend several seconds with my eyes screwed shut, breathing deeply, until I'm sure the dizzy spell has passed. I open my eyes, move my hands to the wall beside me, and lean against it, bringing up one knee and pressing a hand against it. Counting down from three, I push up again and stand, leaning against the wall as the urge to vomit returns. Several minutes of controlled breaths later, I reopen my eyes and stand off of the wall, though I keep my hand on it so that I don't fall over. I'm up, I'm moving. Now I just need to make it to the tunnel and get through it. I need to reach Aiden.

Swallowing hard, I force myself up again and turn slowly, taking my first shuffled step. Followed by another. And another. Painstakingly slowly, I make my way down the hall, stepping around rubble and, disturbingly, crushed bodies here and there. My head swims and my mouth feels like it's full of dust, but I force myself to keep going, ignoring the blood crusting on my head. My arms are dappled with bruises and cuts from falling debris, and a horrible question occurs to me: how long have I been out?

Hallway. Another hallway. I keep going, one after the other. When I reach a flight of stairs, my heart drops, but I force myself to keep going. Standing on the top level, I lower one foot onto the first step while leaning heavily on the wall before bringing my second foot down slowly. And so I do this again and again. But when there are just four steps I stumble, my head swimming again. I lose my footing and fall forwards, down the final stone steps and onto the ground. If I wasn't in pain before, I sure as hell am now. I feel sick again, but my stomach is empty, so I simply dry retch. My head has started bleeding again, and the light now hurts even worse than before, rainbows spiraling in my vision. But I make myself get up.

It takes a lot longer than before, but I get to my feet and keep walking, wiping blood that drips down my cheek away with my tattered and filthy sleeve.

I'm almost to the tunnel when I hear footsteps. A second later someone rounds the corner in front of me, walking quickly. The doctor.

I freeze when I see him and he acts similarly, slowing to a stop and staring at me. Neither of us moves; neither of us speaks. I force my trembling hands to still so that he can't see my fear, even as I know he's about to drag me away to prison.

But then he smiles. I have no idea what that means, and don't move as he chuckles lightly, walking towards me slowly until he's directly in front of me. His eyes trace the blood dripping down my cheek and the undoubted bruises marring my face.

"You look horrible. Head injury? Those are the worst."

I stare at him in bewilderment as he continues to study me. Finally he meets my eyes again. And steps back. He stops in the middle of the hallway.

"You should probably get out of here before someone remembers you," he says with a grin. Then he turns and starts walking away. Whistling. I stand there, frozen, for several minutes, wondering what the hell just happened.

But he's right; I need to move. I continue walking again, fearful that he'll change his mind and rat me out to any remaining guards. I reach the monastery and find it in the same condition as the rest of the facility, dirty and broken. I shuffle past the paintings and statues of the gods, past the altar, and behind the partial wall.

When I step into the priest's chambers, I find the entrance to the tunnel open, revealing dust filled darkness littered with rocks. I pause in front of the entrance, steeling myself for the darkness. There are no torches, no candles, no flames. Just the darkness. And it's my only way out.

I take three deep breaths, close my eyes, and focus. I can do this. I have no choice. I open my eyes, take one more controlled breath, and walk into the darkness.

The tunnel is a mess. There are stones the size of me, bigger than me, almost everywhere. I have to crawl over them, which is difficult with my head injury. The dust hasn't settled and it fills my nose and mouth, making me cough and my eyes water.

I reach a huge section of fallen rocks that takes up the entire width of the tunnel and trip, falling on my hands and knees. My hand brushes against something soft and cold and I freeze, slowly reaching out my fingertips. My hand meets cold flesh and I whimper, withdrawing quickly. So this large rock crushed someone. Or many someones. How many someones?

I begin to carefully climb over the rubble, almost falling over at several points. The darkness is stifling, but as long as I don't think about it, I'm okay. So, I distract myself. I think about what I'll do once I'm out, where Aiden and I will live and what we'll do. I think about how we'll find Adeline together, how we'll start a life together, far away from the facility.

Those thoughts keep me going until I spot sunlight ahead. I pick up my pace, leaning against the wall as I walk, and the light gets closer. A sob tears out of my throat as I see the exit, the tangled wall of ivy blocking it off from the world. There is rubble blocking almost the entire exit, but I manage to push a few small stones out the way, and pull myself through the hole I made, scraping the skin off my hips as I tear them through. I blink against the bright sunlight and the cold of the snow as it hits me, stealing my breath. I stand there unsteadily on my feet, blinking and taking everything in. I'm out. The sun is starting to set, making the snow glow pink and orange. Meaning I was unconscious for almost an entire day.

I inhale a shaky breath and begin to walk towards the small hole in the outer wall, enjoying the noise of the snow as it crunches under my feet. The cold bites at the blood on my skin and the wound in my head, making it burn and ache. I ignore the pain and lift my face to the falling flakes, crying silently as they land on my face. I made it out of the facility. I'm alive.

I am free.

I crawl through the hole in the wall, falling onto my hands and knees when my balance proves to be untrustworthy still. The snow soaks into my pants and makes them stick to my skin when I stand. My head swims from blood loss and lack of sustenance and my fingertips begin to tingle from the cold. I need to keep moving and put distance between the facility and myself. It would be amazing if I could reach the woods by nightfall, though I doubt it.

Wrapping my arms around myself, I begin to walk.

You are going through them too fast. If you can't prolong survival, we will never accomplish what we have set out to do.

—Recovered Anonymous Correspondence

Chapter Seventy-Three

Aiden

The sun slowly snakes across the sky as we walk, changing the color of the snow as it descends. The seers walk all day and long into the night before finally begging Jax to stop. Jax begrudgingly agrees and seers group together with several people to a blanket, huddling against tree trunks and falling asleep despite the cold. We choose not to light fires that first night, deciding it's too much of a risk with our proximity to the facility. Jax assigns several men with weapons as lookouts and creates two shifts, but, despite my request to be given a shift, leaves me out. I stay up anyway, taking my sword and walking a bit away from the group before I sit down and prepare for a long night. I lay my sheathed sword across my lap and stare into the forest, feeling numb inside and out. I gave up checking behind us hours ago, gave up the hope that somehow she was following. She's gone. Camari Dorsar, the woman that I love, is dead.

I blink as my eyes burn, clenching my hands into fists and taking several controlled breaths. I can't afford to fall apart right now; too many people depend on me. I promised her I would help them, and that's exactly what I plan to do.

But when have you ever kept any of your promises?

"I don't remember Jax assigning you to watch." Alex's voice comes from behind me, accompanied by the crunch of his footsteps in the snow. I don't turn around, choosing not to acknowledge him. He grunts as he lowers himself down beside me, sore where a falling rock struck him in the side.

"It's been a long time since I've seen snow," he says softly, looking up at the falling flakes with a faint smile.

"It snows here every year," I say quietly.

"Yes, but I'm from Darragh, near Krakent. It doesn't snow there often. Sometimes not for years actually; the weather is much warmer there."

I don't reply, thinking about how I promised Camari she would get to go back to Krakent one day. How we met there, and the first time I saw her I knew she was going to be trouble.

"But I like the snow. It's beautiful, and did you know that every snowflake is different? You'd think the gods would run out of ideas, but apparently not."

"Alex, no offense, but I don't give a shit about snowflake designs," I say quietly, clenching my jaw. I force myself to take a deep breath and calm down, relaxing slightly.

"I'm sorry, Aiden. You're not the only one who is grieving. But we got out. There's a lot to be grateful for," Alex says, still staring at the falling snowflakes with a childlike sense of wonderment.

"If you try to give me the grass is always greener speech right now, I will rip your tongue out," I growl, turning and glaring at him. He looks at me with sorrow in his eyes.

"I wasn't going to, I just wanted you to show some emotion, even if it's anger at me."

I turn away again, huffing out a breath.

"It wasn't your fault, Aiden."

I clench my hands into fists again and force myself to sit still.

"She did what she thought was best and so did you."

I clench fistfuls of snow in my hands and squeezing the icy chips painfully.

"She died knowing you loved her."

"SHUT UP!" I roar, jumping up and grabbing my sword before it falls. "You don't know what the hell you're talking about."

"Aiden, not talking about her isn't going to help anything," Alex says, standing from the ground and brushing snow off of his pants. I turn and walk away from him, resisting the urge to punch something.

Not your fault.

Did what was best.

She died knowing you loved her.

No. She died alone, crushed by rubble and probably filled with fear. She died thinking I was coming to save her. She died waiting for someone that didn't come.

The next morning we start out while the sky is still gray and barely lit. The snow stopped falling at some point during the night and a clean layer glitters, waiting to be marred by footsteps.

The seers grumble and complain about getting up so early, but not for long. Getting up and moving early is far better than being stuck in the facility, living every day in fear that you might be the next seer taken away.

The landscape changes as we walk, filtering between heavy forests, open land, and sparse trees. The sky is gray well after the sun has risen, concealed by clouds loaded with snowflakes waiting to drop.

I walk in silence with a small distance between the others and myself, carrying a sack of grain or something on my back. Alex tried to walk beside me at one point, but I didn't want to risk blowing up at him again and saying something I might regret, so I chose to continue walking by myself and avoid that possibility. No one else approaches me except for Jax, and that's only to ask my advice on something or update me on how far we've walked. The facility faded out of view late yesterday evening, and now it is just white snow and trees in every direction.

I continue to walk by myself, focusing on putting one foot in front of the other and thinking about no subject for too long.

R.C. Huye

Much like the landscape, the climates of Zorda are equally confusing. The heat in the southern province of Darragh is received from the Spás Folamh. The bitter cold of Clodagh is a mystery, and a deadly one.

–Zorda: Aristocracy, Geography, and History

Chapter Seventy-Four

Camari

It's so cold. I can't feel my hands or feet and the blood on my face has frozen. I keep falling over because of my numb feet and dizziness, but I make myself get back up every time. I walked until dark and reached an area of sparse trees before falling against a tree trunk and passing out. I woke before the sun rose, feeling colder than I've ever been. I'm pretty sure I have a fever, which implies an infection. Both bad things; both out of my control. The fever is making my thoughts and vision hazy, and I'm confused. At several points I find that I've been walking in circles, or I'll see Aiden and run to him only to collapse in pain and exhaustion when I reach him and discover it's not Aiden at all, but a figment of my imagination.

I keep my semi-lucid mind busy as I walk, thinking about anything and everything. Why did Tristan betray me? What happened to him after I was taken? Is my father alive? Are there people following me?

My stomach is empty and my mouth is as dry as dust. I crunch on handfuls of snow occasionally as I walk, thinking it will help keep me hydrated and maybe bring down any temperature I'm running. The downside of that is it makes me even colder. My fingers are tinged blue, and I keep them tucked under my arms in the hope of warming them, but it makes little difference. I know I'm freezing to death. But a small part of me says that if I keep walking, I'll find Aiden and I'll be okay. As long as I reach Aiden, everything will be okay. So I keep walking.

I walk the entire day, falling over a lot and eating snow to stay alive. By the time night falls once more, I can barely see straight. I collapse against the trunk of a tree and curl into a ball, shivering as snow falls and collects in piles on top of me, too weak to push it off. It's so cold; my very bones are frozen. I lean against the tree, wishing for it to lend me nonexistent warmth. My teeth chatter and a cough I developed the previous day rattles in my chest, making my throat burn and ache.

I'm dying.

After everything I've done to survive, the wilderness is killing me off.

I wrap my arms around myself and do my best to take deep breaths, comforting myself by imagining what it will be like when I find Aiden and the seers again. Alex will be there, being sarcastic about something. And Aiden will be safe and whole, looking at me like he always does, like I'm his whole world.

It's a nice dream, and accompanied by the fevered thoughts I'm having, it soon feels very real. I fall asleep with a faint smile on my face.

Aiden

That night we set up an actual camp when we stop, reaching a small clearing and deciding it worth the risk. We build several large fires to keep us warm, set up makeshift shelters out of blankets and sticks, and cook a little bit of food from our supplies. The seers laugh and cheer as they go about their work, every last one of them happy to be free, to be alive.

I fall asleep against a tree, choosing to stay out of the celebrations. I don't have anything to celebrate.

Jax decides to stay in the camp for the next day, giving the seers a day to rest and collect themselves. I don't like the idea of sitting still, but I don't object. They could use a rest after all; they've earned it.

I pass most of the day keeping watch, though I take breaks to gather more firewood occasionally. I don't see anyone, and I seriously doubt we're being pursued. We left the facility in a state of havoc, walls crumbling inward, literally. But, it doesn't hurt to be cautious.

That afternoon I return to the camp to get some food, grateful once again for the supplies Rob smuggled out for us. There's a pot of water boiling over one of the fires but I bypass that and go for the sack of apples, taking one and wiping it on my sleeve before biting into it. And choking on it.

Tristan is sitting by one of the fires by himself, warming his hands and looking comfortable. Tristan is here. Comfortable and alive, while she is dead. Because of him.

I see red as I stare at him, warm and safe while Camari's body is lying under rubble, crushed and abandoned. Before I know what I'm doing, I have my sword out and I'm stalking towards him, my apple forgotten on the ground. He looks up when he hears me coming, his eyes widening, and he scrambles to his feet. I hold my sword out, pointing it at his chest. He backs up, his hands clenched into fists, but I advance with him.

"Aiden!" Jax, Rob, and Alex run towards me, followed by seers that begin to gather, curious about what is going on.

"Put the sword down. Whatever disagreement you two have can be worked out in a better way," Rob says calmly, raising his hands in what's meant to be a soothing gesture.

"No it can't," I growl, pressing the sword against his chest. Tristan glares at me, but I just press the sword harder, enjoying his flinch.

"Aiden, you need to stop and think-"

"Do you know how they knew where Camari would be? Do you know how they knew she was a rebel like us?" I ask without looking away from Tristan, staring into his blue eyes, at the hatred in their depths. The feeling is mutual.

Jax falls silent and I know he's starting to wonder just what happened before he found me in the hallway with the dead guards.

"It's because Tristan here, *sold her out*. He reported her to the guards and watched as they dragged her away. He did all of this for a girl that was already dead. He risked the lives of thousands of seers for one dead girl. And she trusted you!" I spit, my hand shaking with rage. Oh how I long to run him through.

"Is this true?" Isaiah asks quietly from the edge of the gathered crowd, his voice dangerously low. Tristan never takes his eyes from mine, still looking at me with pure hatred that I more than return. I don't think I've ever despised someone more.

"I'm sorry she died, sorrier than you'll ever know. But I don't regret trying to get Tina back!" He snaps.

"Camari is dead!" I roar, advancing several steps towards him. "Because of you! She is gone because of you."

"I know, and I will have to live with that for the rest of my life," Tristan says, taking a few more steps back without breaking eye contact. "But I'm sick of you. I'm sick of you acting like you knew her better than me, like you cared for her more than me. I loved her too!"

"You gave her away! That's not love! You don't know what love is," I snarl, shifting my grip on my sword and imagining driving it into his gut.

"I chose one love over another. You're not even grieved that she's dead, you're just pissed that she didn't love you when-" Tristan cuts off and scrambles back to avoid the swipe of my sword through the air, his eyes widening with panic. Pure bloodlust drives me forward and I take another swipe, this time at his side. He just barely dodges and looks around desperately. His eyes land on a sheathed sword propped up on a sack of grain near him. We both turn and lunge for it at the exact same time, but he's closer. He grabs it before I can and draws it, facing me with a bitter curl of his lip. "I'm ready for you to die now. One moon of knowing you has been more than enough. Killing you will be a treat."

I laugh bitterly, raising my sword. "Good luck."

And then Tristan attacks.

To die is mysteriously a part of living. To actively be aware that you are dying can be a blessing, or a curse.

—The Religious Texts: The Book of Wisdom

Chapter Seventy-Five

Camari

It's late in the day I think. I'm not completely sure. I still can't feel my hands, and my fingers are now blue and painful, but I don't really care anymore. I've been walking since dawn. I don't know where I'm going anymore. I could be walking in circles without realizing, yet again. I fall over more than I walk now, and the trees are the only things keeping me up. My head hurts and is really fuzzy, confusing things. My vision keeps swimming and going blurry, making me fall over even more. I can't escape the knowledge of what is happening to me. I'm dying.

My fantasy may remain just that, a fantasy. I may never hear another of Alex's sarcastic comments, followed up by a grin that takes the sting out of his words. And I may never see Aiden and look at him like he's my whole world, the way he deserves to be looked at. The way I feel about him might never be known.

THE CURSE OF THE BLESSED

I emerge from a tree line into an open clearing, stumbling onto my bruised and torn knees before slowly getting up again, and I begin to climb a large hill, digging my fingernails into the snow to haul myself up. The cold bites into my skin as the snow gets beneath my torn and ragged nails, making my hands burn horribly with a cold sort of heat that is far worse than the heat I was complaining about just three moons ago. My breath catches in my throat, becoming sobs as I climb on my hands and knees, telling myself that after this hill I'll be done, I'll be with Aiden and my family. I know it's a lie, but it's all I have.

It takes a long time and all of my energy, but I make it to the top of the hill and collapse, panting and sobbing. I'm so cold that even my tears aren't warm; my breaths burn and scratch my throat and chest, making me cough again, though that only makes the pain intensify. It's like there are leaves and burrs in my chest, thorns digging in deeper with each breath. And it's so cold.

I crack my eyes open again when I hear voices. I could just be imagining it; it wouldn't be the first time this morning that I hear something that isn't there. But these are different. More…real. Present, flawed, realistic.

I push myself up slowly, my arms and legs trembling like a newborn calf. Blinking fog from my eyes, I stare at the open space below the hill, at the snow glinting and glittering in the sunlight. At the fires burning, the promise of warmth and dryness calling to me like nothing else. And there, at the bottom of the hill, are people. Not just any people.

Seers.

I sob in relief and disbelief, searching the crowd for that one face I long to see more than any other, for the person who makes me feel safe and loved despite all of my flaws. And there he is, standing in the middle of the crowd. Tears of relief stream down my face as I see him, and my legs give out beneath me, dropping me to my knees. But then my relief stills as I really take in what lies before me. A snowy hill, a gathered crowd below, and Aiden in the middle of the crowd. Dueling with someone. My heart stops and I can't breathe, my lungs refusing to expand as horror fills my mind. No. Please no, not now. Oh gods no.

I watch as Aiden fights with another man, his movements quick and determined, bloodthirsty. His sword meets his opponents, the sun glinting off of the joined blades, and they turn so that I can finally see the other man's face. After weeks of wondering and procrastinating over who it could be, reality sinks in, and I feel sick. It's Tristan. Oh gods, it's Tristan. Tristan is going to kill Aiden.

No.

I start forward, trying to stand and run to Aiden, but end up falling down the hill, my legs too weak to carry me down. I land in a heap and gasp, sobbing as fresh blood begins to ooze down my face and as my entire body aches with new injuries. But I get up again.

I stand on legs that threaten to collapse, refusing to give up when I'm so close. I begin to take one slow, shaky step at a time toward the seers, toward Aiden. I fall several times but get up again and again, willing myself to move faster. I'm almost to the gathered seers, to the fight, when I pause and look for a moment. Aiden is incredible at sword fighting, possibly the best there's ever been, but Tristan is surprisingly good, and Aiden seems exhausted. He stumbles, making mistakes he wouldn't usually make, and his strikes appear slow. They turn again and I get a good glimpse of his face, finally close enough to actually see him. Why does he look so…broken?

I keep going, whimpering and gasping with each breath. I reach the crowd and begin to weakly push my way through, leaning heavily on people as I pass. The crowd jostles me back, and my vision swims as my feet threaten to fall away. I finally make it to the front of the crowd and fall past them, landing on one knee and panting as the clanging of steel floods my senses. I scream Aiden's name, though I doubt he can hear me over the noise of both the crowd and the shrieking swords. And then it happens.

Aiden trips as he turns towards where I kneel, revealing an opening in his side. Tristan strikes. Everything seems to freeze and suddenly, I realize something important. I had the vision all wrong. I shouted his name and caused his mistake; I'm the one that caused the vision in the first place. But what if what I saw isn't what I think it was? I saw Tristan go towards Aiden with his sword, ready for the kill, and then I saw blood. But what if that blood wasn't his?

I move without thinking, using strength I didn't know I had. One step, two steps, three steps. The entire world seems to slow as I run forward. My breaths are loud in my ears, drowning everything else out.

Tristan's sword gets closer and closer to Aiden's exposed gut as Aiden tries and fails to bring his sword up to block it. And then I dive in front of the sword.

The blade pierces my side, cutting through fabric and flesh and bringing a blinding pain that drowns out everything else. And then I'm falling.

Death is chosen by the gods, as is life. But one's life is forfeit to the whims of man when they threaten others.

—Excerpt from the Zordan Laws and Commandments

Chapter Seventy-Six

Aiden

Tristan and I begin to fight and I realize right away that he's a better sword fighter than expected. Not as good as me, but good. And I'm weak, under-fed, and exhausted. I fight sloppily, making foolish mistakes as my foggy brain slows down my thoughts. Tristan goes after me with a bloodlust, but I do the same to him. I block or parry all of his blows, my arms burning with exertion after weeks of ill use. He pulls his sword around and swipes at my side but I dodge it and return his blow with a swipe at his leg. The only difference is that I hit my target. It's a shallow cut, but a painful one, and Tristan curses colorfully as blood begins to drip onto the snow beneath him. I'm filled with a cold satisfaction, eager to end him. He's a good swordsman; I'll give him that. But I'm better.

We continue to fight, egged on by the shouts and calls of the gathered seers as they watch us. I see Alex at one point, watching with worry evident on his face, but I vow to give him nothing to worry about. Tristan isn't walking away alive.

But then I see a flash of fiery copper in the corner of my vision. I hear someone shout my name. I hear *her*. My heart thunders, my stupid, treacherous heart that still believes it could possibly be her, just because I so long for it to be.

I reflexively begin to turn towards where I imagined her voice, already knowing she won't be there but being completely unable to resist the chance. Tristan takes my momentary distraction as an advantage. It all happens in the blink of an eye. He lunges towards me, his sword outstretched. I turn too late to recover and watch as his blade approaches my gut, trying and failing to block his sword with mine. I watch it get closer and closer, bracing myself for the pain of death. And then someone dives in front of me and the sword goes into them instead.

Several people scream as blood spatters the snow, bright crimson against blinding white. Time slows and pulls to a halt as I move in slow motion, grabbing the person who's been stabbed before they fall. They scream in pain, a scream I know, a scream that makes me want to hurt and kill whoever has caused it. Tristan pulls back, horror filling his eyes, and drops his sword as the person collapses. And I catch her, unable to believe who I'm seeing. Camari lays in my arms, weak and covered in blood and cuts. She has blood crusted all over her face and bruises everywhere. And she's bleeding out of her right side where Tristan has stabbed her.

"*NO!*" I scream, lowering her to the ground and pressing my hands to her side in an attempt at stopping the bleeding. Blood soaks her torn and muddied uniform, staining it a rust brown, It seeps into the ground beneath her and the snow eats it up, turning a bright crimson that makes my heart pump with fear.

How is she here?

A few people run to get bandages, or someone they say can help, but the majority of seers simply stare in horror, frozen to their spots. I can't take my eyes off of her; unable to comprehend that she's alive. And it might not be for much longer.

Her eyelids flutter weakly as she looks up at me, gasping for air, her chest rising and falling weakly. Too weakly.

"I came back to you," she whispers, smiling. I choke on a laugh that sounds more like a sob, tears dripping down my face and landing on her cheeks.

"Yes, you did, so don't leave yet, don't leave me."

"I won't. I fixed it," she mutters, blinking furiously as if there's something in her eyes. "I stopped your death. I changed my vision. Seers *can* change the future."

"Camari, stay with me. You promised you'd stay with me!" I remind her, pressing my hands harder against her side. She groans, but her eyes open again.

"I tried to talk to you…I hit my head. Couldn't find you. It hurts; everything hurts."

"Don't worry, it won't hurt for much longer. We'll make you better, I promise!" I sob, grabbing a blanket that someone gives me and pressing it against her side, hating how fast it becomes soaked with blood. "We still have work to do, remember?"

"I needed to tell you…" she whispers, her eyes falling shut before flickering open weakly.

"Stay with me dammit! Stay awake, Camari! What did you need to tell me?" I demand, desperate to keep her awake. She doesn't reply and I look up, staring around me desperately. No one moves to help; no one has answers. *Someone do something!*

Camari's eyes flicker open again, even weaker than before, and she looks up at me and smiles. And then her eyes flicker shut as if she's a book that just finished its last chapter. They don't open again.

"Camari. Camari!" I press against her wound as hard as I can, but she doesn't stir again. I look around desperately at the gathered crowd. *"Somebody help us!"*

No one steps forward. And Camari's eyes stay closed.

Camari

I lay in Aiden's arms, struggling to stay awake but failing as my eyes shut and the darkness sweeps me away. The feeling of the warm blood on my skin, the unbearable pain in my side, and Aiden's strong arms around me all fade away, replaced by the void of nothingness that consumes everything.

THE CURSE OF THE BLESSED

I hate the cold. It works in unison with the darkness, strengthening and stealing me away. I fight it, wanting to return to Aiden. But it's so strong, and it works quickly, stealing my thoughts and needs away. It's so strong and comforting.

I let it take me.

Acknowledgments

This feels very similar to starting a book: I know everything I would like to say but have no idea where to start. I honestly never thought I would make it this far, so the fact that I am sitting down to write my acknowledgments is incredibly surreal. Maybe I'll wake up in the real world tomorrow, but for now, I will enjoy this beautiful dream.

First and foremost, thanks be to God for the miracles He worked on my behalf. To Him be all the glory and praise, for I am nothing but dust without Him. *Totus Tuus*.

To my mother, who taught me to read at a young age and made me reread that damn eagle short story until I got it perfect. You have never let me quit anything, and I am eternally grateful for it.

To my father, who patiently listened to my rants about fantasy kingdoms and seer villagers while he washed dishes; you may be the only person who truly understands how I see the world.

To Ephraim, who endured my excited rants, obnoxious procrastinations, questions that he had no way of knowing the answer to, and excessive tears as I wrote and experienced all of the emotions of my characters. A lesser man could not have handled it. Thank you for not having me committed.

To Sarah and Mary, who had absolutely no idea what I was doing but who showered me with support and love for years as I created TCOTB. You two are the sweetest, most incredible girls that I know.

To my godparents who supported me in every way possible; I doubt I would be here if it weren't for you, and I hope you know that.

THE CURSE OF THE BLESSED

To Madalyn, who was the only person I would let read this, and for encouraging my delusions. You gave me the courage I needed to take this leap.

To G.B., who did absolutely nothing whatsoever and had no idea this book even existed until I began the publishing process, but asked me to include him, so why not?

To all of the people who discovered this dream of mine when I began to make it a reality, and who showed me nothing but excitement and intrigue. You all have no idea how much that meant to me and how happy I was beneath my very self-conscious, blushing face. Thank you.

To Ryan for this incredible opportunity and to the entire team: Alan, the project manager extraordinaire Antonio, John, Roy, Steve, Walter, the editing queen Fara, and Zach. Thank you all for helping me accomplish this goal. It means more than you could ever know.

To the authors of all the books I read and fell in love with; my world would not exist if your worlds hadn't inspired me to create my own.

And finally, to Camari and Aiden. To their story that I am fortunate enough to write down. They both own a piece of my soul.

About the Author

R.C. Huye is a Louisiana native from a large Catholic family. She currently lives with her two cats, who enjoy deleting her documents and giving her heart attacks.

There has never been a time when she wasn't creating fantasy worlds or stories in her head, and she has somehow managed to make it through life in a constant state of daydream. Her writing is driven by her love for religion, political orders, and the dualities between those two systems. *The Curse of the Blessed* is her debut novel.